I0778964

ISBN: 978-1-961615-15-1
Imprint: Thornewood Studios

MIDNIGHT AND AMBER

By S.L. Thorne

DEDICATION

For my mother
This one is her fault

This book has been a long, winding, often rocky road. When this book was born, sometime just before the turn of the century, I was dating a man who was pretty much Portholus and Landros all rolled into one. The subsequent stories were originally just episodic adventures that grew into something so much greater than what it began. Everything was looking up, and it was shaping up to become my first completed novel.

And then the other shoe dropped. The man who had shaped one of my principals faded, replaced by some withdrawn, lacklustre copy, and the relationship soured. I couldn't bring myself to work on it after that. Not for a long time.

And so, a few years later, Olivia fleshed out more than the vague idea I had for her, took on a life (or death) of her own, and Love In Ruins became my first published novel.

Fast-forward two decades. Once again, I am reading to my mother (she used to be my old sounding board, but time and distance changed that). I've been going to her house every week to read to her. I've read all the books I've published, some of what I've been working on, and I began to run out of material. So, I dug up this old thing, dusted it off, and began reading it: ten chapters of what was basically a short-handed collection of stories. And only a few chapters short of complete, so of course the muse started poking me again, with all the persistence of a mockingbird's beak. The result is what rests in your hands. Probably some 25 years later, but here at last.

I hope it was worth the wait.

TABLE OF CONTENTS

I

The Rock
of
Mystery

ONE

Lark met him just after the war began. It was a strange night, dark and drizzly, with bursts in the distance that were not necessarily thunder. She walked down the cobbled streets, far from pleased with the evening's take at the Cinnamon Tree. It had been a horrid evening all around. Her singing had gone largely ignored. Dancing had only made things worse, leaving her parrying lewd suggestions and requests for private, more horizontal dances. When that last drunkard had grabbed her ankle and almost made her fall, she had kicked back to free herself, then promptly packed up and left. She decided that this war was no good for business.

She had not gotten very far when the skies opened up, and the rains began in earnest. She paused in the middle of the street and swore to the skies in *Romeri*. As she was beginning to think that perhaps this rain was a good thing, to clean the foul city air and streets, she noticed a sheltered overhang. It was at the construction site of a new shrine, temple, or whatever they were planning to build from all that quarried stone. It seemed a suitable place to wait for the rain to stop. Readjusting the pack on her shoulder, she dashed for it.

Landros was the first to see the girl darting out of the rain. He just stood there in silence with the rest of his friends who had volunteered to guard the temple construction site for the evening. She was a Gypsy, one of the Romer; young, somewhere between seventeen and forty he guessed. He had never been very good at human ages. He did noticed, however, that she was very well put together. One might almost say voluptuous, ...almost. She was small and lightly built, about his height of five-seven, and maybe all of a hundred and ten pounds drenched. Which she was.

The white cotton of her blouse melted against her, revealing light, olive-gold skin, though the tight, red velvet vest protected her obvious assets. Her bright, multi-colored skirt clung enchantingly to her slim, dusky legs. A gold scarf folded into a band and tied behind her neck held her long, dark curls out of her face. And there was a spray of soggy flowers pinned on one side above her jeweled, but very human, ears. Her eyes were black and flashed as she set down her patchwork shoulder bag and stared out into the dark fall of rain, taking a deep breath of the night air.

She sighed then and turned to face the five others who had also taken shelter here, not at all surprised by their presence. Her face, as she turned it into the faint glow of the lantern inside the arched doorway, was definitely handsome, with strong features that did not overpower her natural, exotic beauty. The earthy scent of wild orchids and morning meadows rose from her body, tantalizing, musky, and warm. She smiled, obviously in a fervent hope that these men were friendly but without real fear. It was as if she believed herself fully capable of protecting herself with the curved scimitar tucked into the sash at her right hip.

"*Droshvi*," she said. Her voice was mellow and rich, a practiced singing voice that promised to be very different from any Elven singer he had ever heard, as exotic as the rest of her. The Romeri accent rolled off her tongue like a purr, adding to the image of mystery she presented. He felt his body begin to react in spite of himself.

'She's human,' he reminded himself with a growl.

"*Droshvi*," she repeated when no one answered her, then caught herself. "Hello," she corrected. The accent of her native tongue carried heavily over into her Tembian, seeming to rumble in her throat.

Adrick was the first to react, and began strutting immediately, the pompous cock'rel that he was. He strode up to her, taking up her hand and bowing over it, his eyes never straying far from those gloriously dark, wet breasts as if mesmerized. "Adrick, Brother of the Temple of Three, at your most gracious service, my lady! Allow me to introduce my company."

He gestured broadly to a dagger-bearing elf to his right, "This is Lithgorin in the cloak and Sister Rue." A half-elven woman in a light blue gown and purple cloak nodded to her from behind Lithgorin. "The tree leaning up against the wall over there is Barak Hillvale." Barak waved shyly to her.

She gazed at each of them, coming to rest finally on himself. Tightening his jaw and forcing himself back under impatient control, he turned from that gaze and went into the archway behind him.

"Oh," added Adrick, noting the direction of her attention. "And the sullen one in the back there is Landros. And you are, my dear?" he finished, looking at her expectantly.

"Lark," she answered.

"Lark...?"

She smiled secretively. "Just Lark," she purred. She set her things down by the wall, checking her violin case for damage as she did so. "And why might you be here on such nasty night?"

"Ah," Adrick gestured grandly. "We have been asked by the holiest Temple of Three this evening, to guard this, the site of their newest shrine, for the proud sum of fifty harps. And you?"

Before Adrick could get an answer, Landros appeared back in the doorway, his face livid. He seized the slightly taller man by the shirt and growled in his face, "HOW MUCH?!"

"I did say each. ... Didn't I?"

Lark found the scene amusing. 'Ah, entertainment at last,' she thought, idly sifting through her pack whilst she kept a close eye on the pair.

"Do you mean to tell me that you dragged me out on a cold rainy night to guard this goddess-forsaken pile of rubble for a pittance of fifty pieces of silver!?"

Adrick sputtered. "But it is for the temple. I would have volunteered us for nothing, but I knew you would not have agreed."

The elf seemed on the verge of doing some manner of violence to his half-human friend but brought himself under control, and, just as suddenly as he had seized the man, he thrust him aside in disgust. He turned his back on him and stood at the edge of the overhang.

The priest called after him in righteous self-defense, "You ought to be grateful, Landros. Time may quickly come when those fifty harps will not buy you a loaf of bread!"

Humming softly to herself, Lark began looking Landros over. the elf gazed out at the night as if the rain had been sent as a personal insult. He was not exactly handsome, but he was pleasant enough to look on, with strong lines but delicate elven boning and shape. His hair clung wetly to his tanned neck and shoulders, straight and dark gold. He was slight of stature, no taller than she, but nicely muscled and well-defined. He moved like a lithe wild animal newly penned in a circus cage. His eyes were the most striking thing about him, a deep amber that turned to stare into her soul and seemed uncertain how to react to find her observing him so closely.

Very much disturbed by the Romeri girl's intent gaze, Landros went inside, out of the wind and the rain and the presence of her, to watch the inner courtyard from the back of the guardhouse. Even more infuriating, it seemed, was that she appeared genuinely innocent of the reaction she was causing.

Shrugging his abruptness off to rudeness and anger, Lark put the surly elf from her mind. Her humming changed to singing as a means to pass the time and ease the memory of how this evening had begun.

Inside, Landros heard her. His instinct had been correct. Her voice was rich and velvety in the way no elven voice could be. Her accent added the touch of a purr to it, very sultry.

Sultry, that was the best way to describe her, he thought. That was the *only* way to describe her.

He abruptly realized that he had stopped fuming to listen to her, that his impatience and anger were leaching away like the rain into the earth outside. Then, just as suddenly, she stopped.

Adrick trotted up, hushing her almost rudely. "Please, my dear. This is a temple, holy ground, a place of peace!"

"Sometimes, Adrick....," Landros growled under his breath in Elvish. "Just can't leave things well enough alone, can you?"

She just stared at the priest, stunned. No one had ever asked her to stop singing before. Ignored her, yes. Asked her to stop...? "What..." she began when she found her tongue. "What has your god against music?"

"Goddess, actually," he began, drawing himself up with all the pomp and arrogance and self-righteousness he could muster. "The Maiden is a goddess. And she has nothing against music, per se. Still, her temple is a location of learning and should be kept as a place of peace . Even though it is not yet built."

'Pompous windbag,' Landros thought.

'Arrogant popinjay!' thought Lark.

Disgruntled, she turned away. She stared out into the rain, trying to decide whether it was worth it to get even wetter than she was or to stick it out here. The priest's arrogance was overwhelming. She began to regret, and not for the first time, not leaving this city a week earlier than she had tried to, before the siege and the sealing of the city gates. Just seven days, and she would have been free. Now she was trapped here, in this filthy, reeking prison of stone and cobbles and unwashed bodies. Sometimes she wished she could just fly away, like Nightingale, her familiar.

The woman stepped up to her, put her hand gently on her shoulder, and smiled. "Oh, don't let him get to you. He is a bit overzealous at times."

She raised an eyebrow. "Bit?"

Rue half-laughed. "Something of an understatement, yes. Tell me, you are a Gypsy, no? One of the roamers?"

Lark gave her a long look, but the woman's attitude did not set off any anti-Gypsy warning signals. She seemed friendly and genuinely curious, though she wore the same style and color of robes as Adrick, purple and pale blue. "Am Romeri, yes," she answered.

"Do you, perhaps, read fortunes?"

Lark brightened at the question. Finally, the opportunity for a properly turned coin!

Landros stood watching the inner courtyard. Something caught his eye near the rear of the unfinished wall, just beyond the enclosure of the shrine itself. Something out of place. He turned and passed through the archway, intent on grabbing Adrick or Barak and investigate.

Lark, at that moment, had herself turned. "I get rune stones," she said and bent from the waist to rummage through her pack.

He stopped, staring; his reason for coming out here completely gone from his mind as the hem of her voluminous skirts rode up in the back, giving him an excellent view of lovely calves. The dampness of the skirts only served to further accentuate her other assets. She stood, her hair swinging back out of her face with a toss of her head. A flower fell from her temple. She moved to pick it up, and he almost paused for another view but reined himself in sharply.

"Lark," he said, moving more to the side of her. "Do me a favor, would you?"

"*Sesha?*" she asked, somewhat confused, pausing in the act of reaching for the blossom.

"You... you are a very good-looking young woman," he began, not quite certain how to put this without getting himself slapped. "For a human," he added. "If you were an elf, you'd be damned good-looking. But you are still very good-looking. But you are also a distraction. I am trying to work over here, and I can't do that with you...." he gestured ineffectively, trying to indicate what she had been doing.

She straightened, resting half-made fists on the upper slope of her hips, waiting, amusement clear in her black eyes.

"If you have to get anything out of your bag, do it like this...." He then squatted beside the flower, exaggerating the bending of his knees, and picked it up. "That way, I can work," he placed the soggy blossom in her hand, "and you can get your rune stones. Thank you." He then turned, trying to remember why he had come out here in the first place.

A long, low wolf whistle broke the heavy night air, repeated, louder this time. Lark stiffened and held up her slim hand for silence. Then, a breath later, she slid the scimitar from its place without so much as a hiss of silk. "Trouble," she whispered.

He stepped between the women and the sound, a long sword seeming to materialize into his hand so quickly was it drawn.

"What do you mean, trouble?" Adrick puffed, not even trying to keep his voice down. "It was only someone admiring a pretty lady. Perhaps yourself in your present, rather revealing state...."

She silenced him with her hand across his mouth, black eyes flashing inches from his as she leaned in. "That is my familiar," she hissed tightly. "And sound means trouble."

"Mumiryer?" he mumbled through her hand.

"Familiar," she nodded and let him go.

"Where?" Landros asked quietly.

"That way," she pointed. "About...." she paused, trying to translate the bird's thoughts, "our number of them, I think. Sorry, mockingbirds cannot count."

Landros gestured for Adrick, Lithgorin, and Rue to sneak around the other side of the wall and for Barak to come with him, hoping to pin the trouble between them. There was no question of the girl following. He seriously doubted she would have stayed put if he had tied her to the archway posts.

Silently, or as nearly as possible with so many humans in tow, they slipped out into the rain towards the courtyard grounds of the half-built temple. From behind them, the Romeri whispered softly, "Follow sound of whip-poor-will."

The wolf whistle ceased. A few seconds passed, and the sounds of 'whip-poor-will, whip-poor-will' could be heard a few hundred yards away. The lightning and other magical flashes from the siege mages cast eerie shadows among the half-standing walls and the columns that lay about in pieces waiting to be erected to full glory. Soon, they began to hear talking and crude laughter just beyond the outside wall. In the darkness, Landros made out five figures vaguely man-shaped, possibly human. This he communicated with Barak, knowing the large human was, for all intents and purposes, blind in the darkness.

As he turned to whisper to the girl, he could not find her. He breathed a sigh of relief. 'One less thing to worry about. At least the girl has some sense.' He waited a few more moments until he could see the glimmer of the others just beyond the group of men.

"Hah! She didn't put up much of a fight, did she?" joked one, unaware they were being stalked.

"Nah, too scared. It was almost no fun at all, no challenge."

There was a pause as one of them glared incredulously at the speaker.

"I said almost," came the gravelly reply, and the laughter began anew.

"Come on, Feris said to meet him at the Hog's Blood in half an hour. If we want our pay, anyway, and I don't know about you, but I....."

Lightning flashed in the distance, illuminating a wild-looking figure on the top of the temple wall beside them. Long dark hair fanned out wickedly in the wind, and her arms were upraised in what could have been an arcane gesture as if the storm had come at her bidding alone. An instant later, before the one man who saw this could react and warn his friends, the net hit him, bearing him to the ground and pinning him beneath the weight of the man who had stood next to him.

Chaos erupted. Both halves of the party converged in the middle, taking the remaining three by complete surprise. Less than a minute after the combat began, it was over.

Lark stepped out of the trees next to the wall, near where they were gathering the men. There was a flash of movement beneath her hair, and a mockingbird peeked his head out into the rain at the jumble of prisoners. "Saw place just inside building where can be put for keeping."

With a nod, Landros began helping the others carry, push and kick the villains into the temple grounds. Thankfully, the area Lark had pointed out was relatively dry; the roof had already been partly erected. They interrogated the two who were still conscious. Barak seized one of them and picked him up by his arms. He felt very vulnerable, dangling in the air, his toes easily a foot off the ground. Barak turned him around to face Landros.

"Tell the man what he wants to know, or I make a wish," he said in the man's ear.

He stepped obligingly up. "What were you doing on the temple grounds?" the elf asked as menacingly as he could muster with rainwater running down the narrow locks plastered to his face.

"Nothing. We were just passing by," he insisted, trying to sound indignant.

"No. I saw you just on the other side of the wall by the main building, *inside* the grounds. So don't feign innocent with me, or I'll let him split you like a wishbone."

He thought about it for a moment and glanced up and back at the black giant holding him.

Barak grinned.

"I don't know anything, I tell you!!" he choked

"Who is Feris?" Lithgorin growled, a mere shadow in the corner.

"Uhhhh, a fence. A broker. He... he finds jobs for people."

"And your job was?" Landros smiled tightly. It was not a friendly gesture.

"Nothing, really. Just take the artifact and go! Hells, that rock is already on its way to the client!"

"Rock? Hey, Adrick, wasn't there something about a gemstone or a magical rock around here?" Landros asked.

Adrick trotted up quickly from magically binding the others. "Yes. I believe so. I think they placed a famous or powerful stone in the altar before they sealed it today. It is standard practice to...."

Landros ignored the rest of his speech. He pulled the man's face as close to his as he could stomach. His breath reeked of onions and garlic and other equally foul human foods. "Where is the rock?" he demanded.

"I don't know!!" the man insisted. Landros held his breath, gritting his teeth against the stench. "Truly!! I work for Feris! We do not know who hired him to hire us! Just that it was somebody powerful. He probably has it already!"

"If the rock is so long gone, why are you still hanging about?"

The man kicked to try and free himself in a desperate, weak gesture. Barak spread his arms further, pulling him higher up, and he felt the slow burn in his shoulders. "There was a detail to take care of," he spouted reluctantly.

"What detail? The woman?"

He stopped struggling. "Um, we ran into a priestess," he answered meekly. "She, um, tried to stop us, but um, she couldn't, so, um, we.... she fainted! Yeah, and we...." His mind raced, trying desperately to give the insane elf what he wanted and still be able to keep his arms attached. "We put her into the altar." He braced himself, expecting to get his arms pulled from their sockets and his head to follow shortly. Barak tightened his grip on the man's wrists, but no rending of limbs occurred. After a few short seconds, he ventured a peek.

Landros had merely gathered himself, trying to keep from ripping the guy's head off himself, and settled for landing a hard fist along the man's jaw. The body promptly went slack in Barak's hold, and the man let go. They watched the limp figure crumple onto the stone floor.

"Not bad," Barak mused, impressed by the display of strength from the little man.

"Hmm," Landros mused in response. "Do you think it's too much to hope he cracked his head when he landed?"

"Probably."

Without another word, Landros began walking back into the main chamber of the temple, to where the altar had been set up just that afternoon with great pomp and ceremony. The others followed, leaving the thugs securely bound in the corner.

The main chamber was a grand place, to be filled with archways and mosaics and alcoves. At the end of the large room was a narrow dais on which stood the marble altar. He set to examining the altar cap but could find no way to get a grip on it or to attach the ropes above it. Even with Barak helping him, it would not move.

It begged the question of how they had gotten it open and closed on their own. How they got in and were not heard or caught he could clearly see... and, ironically, hear. There was a section of the wall that was incomplete, and some spell active here that dampened sound. Had it not been raining; they would have been patrolling the grounds and caught the bastards. He growled to himself, cursing the rain for the twentieth time tonight.

He stepped back until he could hear again, directed Adrick towards the breach in the wall. "Get rid of that silence spell, would you?"

Barak leaned against the capstone, making an attempt to move it, but Landros waved him off.

"Hold on a minute," Landros told him and went back for his pack. He donned a pair of stiff leather gauntlets, flexing his fingers to ensure a proper, snug fit. Even Lark could tell there was magic in them. "Now," he said, returning to the problem at hand.

There was a tiny, subtle crack in the air and the faint smell of ozone, and sound rushed back into the area. The elf gestured to the priest as he stood there, wiggling a finger in his ear to relieve pressure. "Adrick, get that long pole over there. We'll use that as a lever. Ladies, if you would step out of the way?"

Rue crossed her arms and huffed, "And what if we want to help?" she snapped.

He stood and gave her a stiff bow. "My lady, if you believe yourself stronger than Adrick or Lith, by all means, please, take their place. For there is only room for four of us here."

She waved him off with a sneer, though her lips curled almost instantly into a smile. He flicked a curt salute to her teasing and turned back to the capstone.

Adrick placed the pole and set himself. Barak stood in the middle, with Lith and Landros on either side of him, and, counting off, they heaved. The stone groaned, shifted, then crashed to the floor, where it broke neatly down the middle.

"Oh, Maid Jeliana is going to be pissed," Adrick muttered, staring forlornly at the broken stone.

Landros ignored him, looking into the surprisingly deep hollow. The altar was at least twelve feet deep, and he could just make out the priestess's body lying at odd angles at the bottom. "I see her," he said. "Somebody get me a rope." As it was being dug out, he gave a quick eye measure of the hole. "This is going to be tight," he muttered.

"I'll go down." They all looked at Lark. "I'm only one will fit down there with her. You most certainly won't," she snapped, lightly pushing Barak out of her way. Without waiting for anyone's agreement, she perched on the edge and swung her legs into the hole, dangling them patiently as she waited for them to rig up a makeshift harness for her. Once the rope was secured, she pulled off her muddy slippers and tossed them aside. Just before descending, she pulled out a small pendant of a songbird from a hidden pocket in her tight vest and slipped it around her throat. At a word, light sprang into the room with the equivalence of full daylight emanating from the pendant.

"Now, can see," she said and allowed them to ease her down below the level of the top before she set her feet on opposite sides of the shaft and deftly 'walked' the rest of the way.

Above, Lithgorin mused aloud. "Nimble little minx. Attractive, too."

Landros only grunted in response.

Lithgorin merely rolled his eyes and muttered something in Elvish about him not knowing a handsome woman if she bit him.

"She's alive!!" Lark's call echoed up the shaft. "Anyone got healing draughts up there? Would rather not risk moving her until had one."

"Hold on a second," Rue called. "We'll lower it by rope."

"Just toss down," she called.

Wary, Rue aimed carefully so that the bottle would not hit the sides and break on the way. The girl caught it deftly and, carefully straddling the priestess in the tight space, slowly poured some into her bloody mouth. Once there were signs of life in her, Lark fed her the rest of the potion. A few moments later, she felt confident enough to slip the harness on her and have her hauled up. The moment she was out of the hole, Adrick and Rue fell to work, leaving Landros and Barak to send the rope back down after Lark.

The priestess opened her eyes, glanced at both of them, and smiled weakly. "Thank the Maiden. You must get me to the main temple. They have stolen the Rock of Mystery, and it cannot be allowed to remain in their hands."

Adrick nodded, gathering her up in his arms carefully, and walked away.

Pulling Lark from the hole and winding up the rope, the others followed, collecting the prisoners from their corner and marching them in front, gathering their gear on the way out of the site.

She shouldered her bag and stared after them, not yet stepping out into the rain again. She looked north to where she had left her caravan and the promise of dry clothes and a warm stove with piping hot tea. She looked after the small group marching determinedly toward the Temple of Three and sighed. By her ear, the mockingbird peeped a confused question.

"Sesha, I know, Nightingale, I know. But.... there might be some adventure in this. I do not know, but ...I may regret this, but... oh, hells!" she muttered and darted out into the rain after them.

TWO

The Temple of Three was a grand building. It stood out in the night like a beacon of light. It was a monstrous edifice of white marble with blue veins, showing proud evidence of having been the target of enemy attacks and stood largely in one piece. The statue of the three goddesses that stood over the doorway had blackened chunks missing from the alcove in which they rest, but itself was wholly undamaged. Adrick barged into the atrium of the House of the Maiden without bothering to wait for the door to be opened for him. He gestured with his head, and Barak grabbed the nearest sleepy-eyed acolyte and presented her in front of Adrick.

"Get me a Healer," he said.

The girl looked at Adrick, then at the priestess in his arms and tore herself from Barak's light grasp, and ran down the long, shadowed hallway.

Lithgorin and Landros found someone to take the prisoners off their hands. A city guard was there for an injury, and agreed to take them into custody. After they were patched up, of course.

A moment later, three lower-level brothers showed up, took the woman from Adrick, and left with her down a hallway to the left. The third priest, only fourth circle from his vestments, turned to them. "If you will come with me, please," he intoned. Without waiting for them to reply or resist, he walked down to a cross corridor about a hundred yards down. He turned to face them at this intersection and gestured down the left-hand passage. "Wait down here, please," and he turned and left them standing in the hallway.

It was clearly a receiving area. There was a narrow blue, purple and black carpet that ran down the center and several chairs lining the walls. Some of the chairs were padded, some plain wood, though they all looked comfortable. There was even a cloak rack with a basin at the bottom to catch dripping water from rain-soaked robes.

Lark thoughtfully stood off the carpet so as not to ruin it with her muddy shoes. Nightingale immediately sought a drier perch on the back of the cloak rack. Landros began pacing almost immediately, wearing a dark trail into the carpet. Glancing over at Adrick, Lark scowled and leaned back against the wall, gathering that if he had not allowed her to sing at the half-built shrine, he surely would not let her sing here. She crossed her arms over her ample chest and sulked. It seems no one was interested in her singing of late, and that irked her to no end.

Gratefully, the wait was not long, and a lower brother clad in darker tones approached them with his purple skullcap twisted in his hands. "Are you... the people who found... rescued Sister Shalia?" he stammered.

"Yes," Landros snapped before the more diplomatic Adrick could puff himself up enough to speak.

"She is well and resting. But her report is most distressing. The Hierophant of the Temple of Three, Derren D'Meysen, wishes to see you in his office. At once." With that, the little man turned and gestured for the group to follow in the opposite direction, down the other hallway. At the end of it, he stopped, opened a wide door and steped aside.

As Lark followed the others into the room and the door was closed behind them, she was taken in by the pure splendor of the room. Books were everywhere in every imaginable language, and the whole place reeked with the faintly acrid scent of magic that made her nose tingle. Even Nightingale gave a single low whistle of awe, earning for himself a glare from Adrick, not that the mocking-bird noticed or cared. Behind an enormous mahogany desk piled high with scrolls and books and loose papers, sat the Hierophant himself. He looked as if he had been summoned from his bed not too long before.

"Greetings," he said. "Please, be seated. I have much I need to discuss with you." He waited only until they had made moves to seat themselves before he began. "It seems that we are in your debt and find ourselves in the position of getting even deeper," he said, cursorily. "It is customary for a new shrine or temple to have a powerful artifact sealed within the altar or cornerstone. This, I am certain you are aware of," he added with a nod to the two priests. "There are many reasons for this, from providing magical protection to containing and protecting a powerful or dangerous artifact. Before the siege began, we had already begun the shrine for the rock, recovered not a year ago by adventurers such as yourselves. As the usual protections and what have you had not yet been put in place (which is what Sister Shalia was working on when she was assaulted) and with the situation we find ourselves in outside the gates, we have had to resort to hiring gentlemen such as yourselves. ... Oh, excuse me, and ladies, to guard it until that time. It has now been stolen, and it must be returned. The longer it remains missing, the greater the consequences garnered, both for this temple and this city.

"Sister Shalia has informed me that the men who assaulted her were working for a certain political mage by the name of Willem Whitewalker, and the article was sent on its way to his secondary private residence in Cove Street near the east wall. He must not be given time to study this artifact and discover its uses."

Landros fumed silently. The men he had interrogated had claimed not to have known who hired them.

"And what might uses be?" Lark asked. Adrick glared fiercely at her. She ignored him. Already she was sick of his posturing and puffing self-importance.

"Let us suffice it to say that it is not called the Rock of Mystery for nothing and get it back. There will be a substantial reward for its return."

Adrick stood, speaking out before the Romer could embarrass him by asking how much. "Whatever you deign to give us will be more than generous."

　　　　　　　　　　　　　　　　　　　

Lark stifled a smile as she heard a low growl from Landros.

"Very good, very good. Your kindness and generosity will no doubt be well rewarded by the Trinity. Go, please. Time is of the essence."

As they were being escorted from the room, Lark thought to herself, 'How kind of him, not to mention if had been guarding properly, rock would never have been taken in first place.'

They were brought to the main doors of the temple and ushered outside. They stood for a moment on the temple steps, checking their gear to make certain they had everything they would need. It was at this moment that the rain stopped. "One could not hope for better sign," Lark piped, pulling a dry shawl from her oiled pack and wrapping it around her shoulders.

Adrick looked over at her. "Is the lady joining us, then?"

Lark could not be sure of his motivations in asking. It was too easy to read suspicion into his face. Few people trusted the Romers, and there were many preconceptions as to a Gypsy's occupation (and none of them flattering,) and she had already had her fill of those tonight. She measured her words carefully. "Might be some use. Am small and climb well, and have built-in alarm," she gestured to the mockingbird, tucking himself into what he hoped would be a dry place. She shrugged. "Besides, Gypsy is good luck."

Landros stifled the comment that rose in his mind and settled for glancing away. "If she wants to come, let her," he snapped and walked down the steps.

Adrick looked to Lithgorin. He only shrugged and followed Landros.

He turned to Barak, who also shrugged. "She caught two all by herself," and went with the others.

Rue smiled before he could ask her. "I believe we might yet have need of her services, and she has already cast her lot with us by helping in the shrine."

Adrick, apparently not pleased with the results of his little poll, grumphed and walked after Barak.

Lark shouldered her bag and stared after him. "Humph, glad am wanted," she said sarcastically.

Rue put her arm around her shoulders. "Oh, don't mind him. He's just too full of himself to realize that others have their value. So tell me, how do you read your stones? Do you toss them, draw them or lay them like the Tarot?"

Lark began warming to the quiet Sister and walked with her companionably down the dark street. "All depends upon time and moment. Sometimes do full reading, casting all and removing face down. Those you interpret by position. But am not so good at this form. Gruma is. Have watched Old Ruby throw stones onto cloth and read them even though she hasn't been able to truly see more than shadows since she was, oh, my age, I guess." She shrugged. "Mostly, I lay them out and do one or three stone read-ings on quiet evenings in taverns. Single silver is popular price, especially in current times," she mused, glancing over her shoulders at the di-rection of the city walls. Even at this late hour, there were faint flashes on the horizon: enemy activity.

"Perhaps, when this excursion is over, I can entreat you to read the stones for me?"

"Certainly."

The rest of the walk was quieter as they passed through the closely shuttered neighborhoods of the middle class. Once or twice they encountered a drunkard or two staggering home in slurred song or half-deranged mutterings or sleeping off the effects of the empty bottle cradled in his arms. Lark listened to the sounds of the city around her. In sleep, it was almost like death. The noises that were about were ominous and suspicious, hollow and artificial. Not at all like the unquiet of the open countryside, which even at its most still was full of chirring life.

Her companions walked with varying degrees of stealth. Barak was not exactly quiet. His big feet made noises with each step of his hard riding boots. His stride was unmistakable. The others were relatively quieter. She barely heard the soft padding of leather boots on the cobbles from Lithgorin or Landros. Even Adrick and Rue made more noise with the soft swishing of robes and cloaks than the two full elves made with their swords and light armor. Lark, wearing only her dancing slippers, was fairly quiet herself.

The tambourine, muffled in her pack by scarves and other stuff, made only slightly more noise than her feet.

The neighborhood thinned out to a quiet residential area. The address resulted in a high, spiked fence surrounding a relatively small house on a grassy lot. There were trees near the front and some low shrubs by the walls. Other than that, it was a barren place. The house itself was less than grand; hardly the house for a great mage or a politician, even as a secondary residence. There did not seem to be any lights on inside.

Lithgorin tried to peer in the ground floor windows but could not see anything. Lark noticed a small second-story widow's walk with picture windows. She set her pack down at the base of the tree and slipped out of her shoes. Kilting up her skirts between her legs, she hopped up to grab the lowest branch of the tree closest to the house; then, quickly, deftly, and gracefully climbed into the upper branches and peered in. She still could not see inside. It was as if the windows were not windows at all but a painting of windows in darkness.

Below, Lithgorin stared appreciatively up at her. "Damn, but she's nimble," he muttered to Landros. "I've seen master second-story men go up ladders with less grace than that."

Lark heard the comment but did not reply. She was staring irately at Adrick, who had used a spell to fly up and was peering in the windows himself. She gained some small measure of satisfaction when he landed and shrugged, unable to see anything either.

Lithgorin grinned up at her when she did not descend immediately. "Are you coming back down? Or do you need rescuing?"

Lark folded her arms on a branch at chest level and peered down at him, "Behave yourself, you elven letch," she taunted.

He spread his arms wide, grinning. "Or what?!" he dared.

She thought for a second. "Or will not dance for you later."

That brought him up short.

Barak nudged him pointedly. "You'd better behave. I want to see her dance."

Lithgorin sheepishly lowered his arms and shrugged playfully up at her. "Sorry. Please, by all means, join us within?" he invited hopefully.

She relented, definitely beginning to like the attention. The evening was not turning out to be the complete disaster it had begun. Carefully, she climbed down to the lowest branch and landed lightly beside her things. She looked at her shoes, all muddy and disgusting. She did not want to put them back on again but did anyway. They were just as cold as they promised to be. "Is last time I walk home in dancing slippers. Now on, I carry spare boots!"

Rue laughed quietly, and the pair of them followed the others onto the porch of the house.

Adrick stood in front, staring at the door, wondering how he should go about this and whether or not to knock.

Finally, Landros snapped. "Look, Adrick, either open the door and go in or knock, but do something!"

Lithgorin reached around Adrick and tried the doorknob. The door swung wide open without so much as a creak. The two of them stared for a second inside the house. Adrick fingered his holy symbol and gazed at the doorway with his eyes tuned for magic but found no mystic portal or teleportation device embedded in the innocent wood.

Lithgorin poked his head in, looked back at the outside of the building, then back inside. "This place," he said, "is definitely enchanted." Politely stepping inside and out of the way, he allowed the others to enter.

The first thing they noticed was that the inside of the house was bigger than the outside. The second thing was the banquet spread out over a trestle table easily the length of the outside of the house and piled high with food. The aromas were tantalizing and, given the growing scarcity, seemed somehow perverse. Golden plates, platinum goblets, and silk napkins elaborately decorated the table with sprays of exotic flowers, and clear, glistening statuettes adorned the fine, embroidered tablecloth. The walls were covered by rich tapestries and colorful, exotic hangings, and from somewhere unseen came the strains of music.

They gaped for a short minute, then began looking about for other signs of life. There was nothing. No musicians, no host, no party-goers, no nothing. Just the table and its ready spread, the roast fowl still steaming on its plate. They searched for the better part of an hour but found nothing that could have been the object they sought. Adrick even scanned for magic, but everything glowed mildly to his eyes. Nothing jumped out at him as significant. He shrugged, "It's all minor-level magic," he reported, confused and at a loss for ideas.

'Maybe this whole place isn't even real?' Landros thought but held his silence. Magic was not his way or his skill, and he would not intrude upon Adrick to tell him his work.

The music, however, was beginning to get on Lark's nerves. "Is too pompous!" she finally snapped. "Too stuffy!" Frustrated and looking for release, she grabbed her fiddle from its case in open defiance: of the war, the siege, the lack of appreciation, everything.

While the others poked and prodded the walls behind the curtains, looking for doors or secret passages, she began tuning up the violin. She frowned. The dampness had done nothing for its tone. Still, she was determined to play out her frustrations. She struck a chord. Adrick glared, but Rue put a hand on his arm and shook her head once. Sullen, he went back to searching.

At first, she echoed what the magical musicians were playing, adding a touch of sass to the sound. The mockingbird perched himself on the arm of a candelabra and happily sang along. Then, once the music started to bend to her tastes, she warped it, going off into a wild, freewheeling reel, forcing the other music to bend or be overwhelmed. The magic could only bend so far and did not follow her completely on her wild bent, but she did not notice when it returned to its slower, stuffy pace. She was absorbed in her playing. And she was not the only one.

There was one thing Lark had never been able to do, and that was stand still while she played. She was a dancer first and foremost and simply could not resist leading the music, flowing with the sound and shaping it with her body, taking it over and carrying it away into her own spinning world. Making the music herself changed nothing. It made no difference to her that she had never met anyone who danced while they fiddled. She danced anyway.

She whirled around the table, pausing only momentarily to taunt Barak with a warning melody when he stopped to pick at the food. He smiled and backed off, watching her while the others searched for the secret door they knew had to be there. Even Adrick, though, paused occasionally to watch when she danced past him. When she passed Landros, he more than paused.

She was oblivious to everything around her but the music, and she danced with complete abandon. He could see that. So it struck him as strange when he noticed she was also in complete control of every tiny movement. Most Elven dances were composed of carefully executed steps, each gesture precise and laden with significance. No two steps followed the same pattern with her. Each bend and twist and reeling of her body seemed to follow no form or structure or mean anything, and yet... that seemed to be the point. It was natural and completely free. He had never seen anyone move like that, human, elven, or fey, and he found he could not take his eyes off her.

'Just imagine what she could do if she were not playing that thing,' he thought. He leaned sideways into what he thought to be a sturdy object and found it to be a very lightweight torch post. He stumbled and caught his balance. The top of the post caught the curtain behind him, sending it clattering down almost around his ears. The post itself hit the wall behind it with a sharp, resounding crash that caused even the phantom musicians to go silent.

Lark stopped, startled. Lithgorin hid a smirk. He had seen the whole thing. Adrick only scowled and looked around nervously, expecting someone or something to come to investigate. Landros looked back at the now bare wall and saw the chink the brass post had made in the smooth stone. Then he saw the line down the middle of that chink. Investigating closer, he quickly determined that it was not just a stone line. It was a doorway.

"Hey, Lith," he called, trying to ignore the other elf's reaction to the accident. "What do you make of this?" he asked pointedly.

"I think you should pay more attention...."

"Not that, feather-brain," he growled, pointing, "That!"

Lithgorin came over and checked out the flaw in the wall. "Well, well, well. It seems our little lark has inspired a serendipitous disaster. Let's get her open, boys!" he chuckled and rubbed his hands to warm them up for the work ahead.

Adrick gestured for people to step back, pushing Lith out of the way. "Allow the professional," he intoned.

Lithgorin snorted indignantly. "What do you think I am?" he snapped.

Adrick ignored him like he ignored everything else. He immediately began uttering a string of what seemed to be senseless syllables to the untrained ear. Even Lark knew they were arcane. She knew a few spells herself and had heard of this one, a spell of opening. A moment later, the door obligingly swung out.

It appeared to be an innocent closet, dimensions unknown. Lithgorin stepped inside and promptly vanished. Even the elves could not see him with their more sensitive eyes. Landros muttered what must have been an Elvish obscenity and pushed in after him, sword in hand. Adrick followed.

Rue looked over at Lark and shrugged, "If one goes, we all go," she sighed and stepped through, with Lark close behind her.

They found themselves in a hot, dark place, filled with fires and spouting volcanoes oozing magma-like sores across the landscape. Before them stood a monstrous creature, well over seven feet in height, with foot-long talons and great leathery wings bathed in flames. Its body was lean and wiry, with a thick, warty hide, and its face was a twisted, elongated version of a dog-like beast. The spittle that dripped from its open jaws sizzled and steamed as it struck the hot ground. It tilted back its head and loosed a soul-shaking howl that caused Lark to cover her ears and cringe away. She half-turned as she took a step back, trying to retreat through the doorway, but there was no doorway, only a blackened, gnarled bush with leaves of tiny flames. The hem of her skirts began to smolder.

Everything happened in a matter of seconds. Adrick reached for his holy symbol. Lithgorin pulled his sword. Barak followed suit. Rue began to call upon her goddess for spells. The mockingbird panicked completely. Lark screamed as the fabric burst into flame.

Landros just stood there and refused to believe. This could not be happening. Illusions could be convincing; he knew this. He had suspected the whole house of being an illusion before; now, he believed it. "This cannot be real," he said calmly. He turned to face them. "Think about it. It cannot be real. Adrick, you yourself checked for magic. Would you not have noticed a teleport trap or a dimensional gateway?"

Adrick gaped at him, his spell fizzling in his hand. "Well, of course, I would have, but... You can't be... Lithgorin! Kill that thing!!" he shouted as the beast reached for Landros's unguarded back. The claw went right through him, and the beast suddenly vanished, as did the images of hell surrounding them. Lith's sword sparked as it hit the metal sconce on the wall a mere two feet in front of him. Rue managed to rein in her own spell before she could waste it on the illusion.

Lark stopped mid-shriek as the flames licking at her skirts were suddenly not there anymore. She stared down in disbelief at the bush-turned-to-rock in the corner in front of her. She looked back at the others, startled, then back at the rock. Putting her fists on her cocked hips, she stared at the offensive stone. "If had been snake, would have bitten me."

Rue breathed a sigh of relief. Barak just sat down. Lithgorin did not put away his sword yet, still not convinced they were only in a closet. Adrick began to physically touch the walls to make sure they were real.

Landros reached over and picked up the small boulder, about the size of a skull, inadvertently brushing against Lark's thigh as he did so. He stole a quick glance up at her. She did not seem to have noticed the brief contact, but he did. The hairs stood up on the back of his neck, and a chill chased its way down his spine. He forced himself back under control and stared at the rock in his hand. It was relatively plain, a shapeless hunk of jasper about ten or fifteen pounds in weight and carved with simple runes on its surface.

"This is it?" he sneered. "Sitting out plain as day in a broom closet, protected only by an illusion?"

"Perhaps is generating illusions?" Lark suggested.

"Humph, possible," Adrick muttered, coming over to take the rock from his friend. He carefully turned it over in his hands. "Hmmm, yes, it is magical in nature. A phantasmic enchantment, I believe. Entirely possible that the girl is right. Well, we had best get going and return this to the temple. They will be able to say for certain if this is what we seek. I do not see any reason for hanging about in this closet any longer."

They quickly re-entered the banquet room, ...which had changed. It was now no bigger than a large shack, filled with cobwebs and broken crates. There was a dim rattling from the corners, like the clicking of sticks together. A dusty hissing noise joined the rattling in the darkness.

Lark activated her pendant, filling the room with light, and saw a monstrous serpent of bone rising in front of her. She started, then calmed. "More illusion," she growled and headed for the door, ignoring the skeletal leviathan beginning to react to her passing.

It struck lightning fast, and sparks flew from the stone floor where its teeth landed. The nose of the beast hit her and sent her sprawling into the crates, which fell on top of her, half crumbling to sawdust on impact. The wind knocked out of her; she did not even scream. There was a burst of light as the first crate struck, then blackness consumed her.

Landros leaped in, twin swords flashing, his reactions slightly faster than Lithgorin or Barak. Nightingale flew at the creature, screeching and beating at it uselessly with his wings, trying to peck out the red eyes glowing in the empty sockets. The beast, not seeing the elf lunging for it, snapped at the bird, catching it in its mouth. Nightingale flew about in the skull, still trying to get at its eyes from the inside, then slipped out through the open bones. It became aware of Landros very suddenly as his long swords connected viciously with its spine. Lith charged in, hacking at the lower sections, while Barak fended off the head with his shield and broadsword.

Rue snapped out of her shock, holding up her holy symbol in one hand and Adrick's hand in the other, fingers braided. He fumbled for his own symbol, holding it up to meet hers, and aimed the joined pair at the great serpent. They began chanting in unison. The snake noticed them and tried to reach them but was prevented by the three fighters and the bird, which kept distracting it, blocking its vision. The combined hands of the priests began to glow, a holy fire that formed a ring from the circle of their arms. The serpent hissing madly and backed away, trying to creep back to its nest in the corner.

Barak reached up as the head arched away and grabbed the ribs just below it. He used all his strength and weight and pulled downward, slamming the skull into the floor but pinning himself inside the rib cage. "NOW!!!" he grunted, straining from trying to hold on to the now writhing bones.

The tail lashed, smashing crates and boxes and windows, losing splinters and bone fragments and whole vertebrae here and there. Landros and Lithgorin stood on opposite sides of the head, swords raised high, and together, with cruel precision, cleaved the skull in two. Smashed, the lights that were its eyes began to dim and fade out until all that remained were a pair of smoldering coals on the floor beneath the fragments of bone. Once certain the animating force had left, the two priests lowered their arms and disconnected their medallions. The glow faded, and once again, the room lay in darkness.

From the pile of fallen crates, there was a faint glimmer of light and movement. Barak struggled out of the serpent, breaking bones as he did. Landros and Lithgorin crossed to the slowly shifting pile and began removing the debris. Nightingale perched on Landros's shoulder and tried to maintain his balance there. It was difficult with the constant movement the elf was making, and he gave up, finding a place on the crates just above their heads from which to observe and direct their work.

Landros found her hand, grabbed it, and pulled. Nightingale shrieked in pain as his mistress was unable to. He stopped pulling. Lithgorin continued hauling the fragments of crating aside, uncovering more and more of the pendant's light. Adrick and Rue crossed over, careful of the stuff on the floor that was being tossed willy-nilly, ready to help should there be a need for their services.

Lark's hand closed weakly on Landros's wrist, just strong enough to tell him she was relatively all right. He could tell that she was trying to help from below by the minute pulling and shifting. Following her arm down with his other hand, he tried to dig her out that way, but she dug her nails into his wrist suddenly as the bird shrieked again. He stopped, puzzled, and settled for helping Lithgorin move larger pieces, bolts of rotting cloth which were the contents of the crates, ...just pushing things out of the way. He found it hard to work with only one hand, but she refused to let go ...or simply could not.

As Barak finally freed himself and went to help, a large section of it was kicked out at knee level, narrowly missing his shins. Her nails dug into Landros's arm again, this time followed by an audible but stifled shrill of pain. Barak began pulling at the debris around her legs, tossing aside whole pieces as if they were nothing. There was a great deal of sawdust and shredded wood, and beetles remaining, coating her from head to toe as she sat gingerly up, coughing.

She had yet to let go.

Lark cleared her vision, brushing hair and sawdust out of her face with her other hand. "That... not illusion," she choked. Carefully, she felt at the back of her head the knot that was growing there. "He had hard head," she added with a dry chuckle.

Landros laughed. He did not know why he laughed. He just did. Here she was, covered head to toe in sawdust and rotted cloth, having just been knocked out and buried by an undead leviathan, and she was making jokes.

Nightingale felt a subtle shifting below him and heard the faint pop and tearing of wood beginning to consider giving way. He shrilled a warning and flew from his perch. Lark glanced up, confused, unable to make any sense out of his tangled thoughts and her still-clouded head. Landros looked up and saw the tall column of crates tipping. He threw his weight backward, pulling her towards him by the hand still clutching his arm, and fell with her, screaming, on top of him. The crates tumbled down, a mass of moldy old straw and broken pottery and damp, rotting wood.

Lark rolled off of him, clutching desperately at her arm, unable to let go. Her fingers would not obey. Bolts of pain shot up and down the limb like sailor's lightning. She stared at him, her dark eyes wide, suddenly realizing who it was she had been clinging so desperately to in those dark moments she had lain buried. She had lost feeling in her hand and had not realized that she still had hold of him until he had pulled her out of danger and woke it up again.

And she was puzzled by the fact that she could not seem to let go, and now, with the pain, she was afraid to try or move at all.

Rue squatted beside them and gingerly pulled back her sleeve. Lark looked expectantly up at her.

"It is broken," Rue said. "It is but a small matter to fix. Give me a moment."

Landros watched Lark as she watched Rue work the holy fire again. The priestess gently rubbed it into the arm over the break, seeping into the skin and around the bone, making it visible to the naked eye. Lark still had not let go of him. Her grip was like that of the dead, stiff and unyielding, and her nails were beginning to leave their mark.

The bone was clearly visible now, enveloped as it was in the blue light, and the break was cruelly obvious. "Landros, I need you to pull, gently but firmly. She will not feel anything while I hold her arm, and I need the bone straight to heal it straight."

Hesitantly, Landros pulled lightly, afraid to tug too hard lest he hurt her. "Mister," Rue snapped. "I know for a fact you can pull harder than that. I promise you she will not feel it. Just give it a quick tug, and..."

Goaded, Landros yanked back, still not using his full strength, knowing that would certainly be too much. Lark never so much as gasped, though her eyes widened as she watched the bones fall back into place. Rue began praying in a near whisper, tracing symbols across the break, knitting them neatly back together. The fire still burning on her fingertips, she reached around and touched the back of Lark's head, where the growing knot was. Lark winced, but her headache eased.

"Thank you," she smiled, testing the sore spot with her other hand.

"You... can let go now."

She looked up at Landros, at the faint, pained smile on his face, then down at her hand, still latched onto his wrist. It looked strange, as if it did not belong to her. The fingers were still stiff, but the muscles were relaxing quickly as the light faded from her arm. She released him, pulling the limb close and rubbing it before drawing her sleeve back over it. "Thank you for saving," she said quietly, not looking him in the eye. She was still a bit in shock from the whole encounter.

"It was nothing," he mumbled, feeling something strange inside that he could not explain. He was too close to her suddenly.

As he peeled back the cuff of his glove, he observed several deep red marks on his wrist.

She peered at them and gasped an apology. "Did I...?"

He looked up at her with a grin. "Through leather!"

"Did not intend..."

He gave a snort of laughter. "Gods help me, woman, if you ever intend!" He got up and offered her his hand to help her up. She hesitated, then laughed at herself and allowed him to pull her to her feet.

"No more snake bones?" she asked as the others gathered near.

"I do not believe so," Adrick said. "Still, I would think it wise to move quickly, as magical alarms have no doubt been set off, and the master of this house may be here soon."

In full agreement, they quickly found the door rusting on its hinges and headed out. Stepping onto the porch, expecting at any minute to be greeted by ten armed men and a highly peeved mage, they were greeted instead by the rising sun.

"Is it really that late?" Rue exclaimed.

Lark squinted at the growing light. "Try 'that early.' And yes, most certainly is." She headed down the short path to the front gate. "Shall we return item quickly, my friends? Would like to find my caravan sometime today. And think shall sleep for week!"

Rue chorused her with an emphatic, "Here! Here!"

The six of them headed off down the streets for the temple district, Nightingale chirruping his sprightly little heart out from Lark's shoulder. There were few people out and about yet. Most folks were either sleeping, just getting up, eating their morning meal, or nursing the hangovers from the night before. Leaning against a lamppost in one of the lower middle sections of town, they passed by one of the drunks from their journey to the 'politician's house,' still snoring away and hugging the lamppost dearly.

"Maybe we can get this done in time to maybe grab some breakfast somewhere," Landros suggested. "And maybe a hot bath and clean, dry clothes," he added to himself, pulling at his rain-stiffened tunic.

They reached the temple quicker than they had expected to and were met on the front steps by an acolyte who waited impatiently, playing at bones. He jumped up when they arrived. "You have it?" he asked.

Adrick nodded. The young man hesitated, wondering whether or not to take his word for it, then gestured for them to follow him. "Quickly, quickly, the master waits!"

They obeyed, but Rue thought for a moment. This was very odd. She was not originally from the local temple, but a small country-side church fifty or more miles away, but she had never heard a high priest referred to as 'master,' not even by secular servants. She shrugged it off. She was on holy ground and safe now. Paranoia was very unbecoming of a priestess of the Maiden.

They were led through a back gate into a small but elaborate courtyard garden. The boy closed the gate behind them and dropped the bolt in place. Rue saw this and turned to ask Adrick if this was standard practice here, when they were confronted by six well-armed men and a seventh in simple robes.

Before anyone else had a chance to react, Landros spat out some Elvish phrase that caused Rue to blush with widened eyes and the other elves to look up in shock. Landros pushed his way to the front of the small group.

"Now, look," he began, quite civilly; but there was something very dangerous that was heavily restrained in his voice. He began ticking off points on his slim fingers. "I have been up all night. I am tired, I am wet, and I am hungry. I am frustrated, and I am in a bad mood. I am trying to make a date for breakfast, and she doesn't even know it yet."

"What don't I know?" Lark piped, only having caught the tail end of his little speech. She had been paying too much attention to fishing for a bit of colored sand without being noticed.

"See what I mean?" he snapped, gesturing in her direction. "Now. You have two choices. You can walk away right now in one piece. I will not stop you. Or you can die. Your choice."

The seven men looked at each other for a moment, obviously not impressed or just plain stupid, one of the two. They attacked.

With a gesture and a word and a spray of multicolored sand, a fan of bright-colored lights sprang from Lark's outstretched fingers, hitting the two forward fighters and the mage full in the face. The spell brewing in the mage's hand fizzled as he staggered back, trying to clear his vision. One fighter immediately passed out, while his companion just reeled in confusion.

Landros drew both swords and leaped at the nearest man. "Why do they never listen?" he asked of no one in particular as he cleaved into his target. Adrick popped off an arc of flames at the three closing in from the side, narrowly missing the third, who dodged into Rue. She clobbered him soundly on the top of his head with a small mace she had hidden in her robes. Lithgorin turned to deal with the 'acolyte' who was suddenly far more than a small boy, but a stunted, though well-armed man. Barak just waded in swinging, and what he hit usually went flying. Lark pulled the scimitar from her sash and began whaling on anyone unfortunate enough to get too close, kicking them into a pile in the flowerbeds.

The fight did not last more than a minute or two. Injuries were minimal, and none of the thugs were going to be moving anytime soon. Adrick marched to the cottage door, throwing it open, frantically looking for some sign that they were indeed in the Temple of Three.

Inside the room was a table, a few chairs, and a single man who was most certainly not Derren D'Meysen, Hierophant of the Temple of Three. He stood.

"Ah, I see you have come to return my property. Please," he said, holding out his hand most genially, as if this were no more than a social call, "just hand it over, and there will be no trouble at all."

Adrick huffed himself up to his full height, trying to sound and look imposing. "How is it that you have insinuated yourself into the high Temple of Three?"

The man laughed. "Look about you, mage-priest. You are not in your precious temple. You were led to believe that was how you were walking, but you came here instead. You saw what you wanted to see. You are in my house, on my property. Now hand me the stone!"

"Rot in Hell," he snarled, hurling a small pellet of iron at the man and invoking two words in an arcane tongue that Lark had never heard before. Lightning ripped through the roof and struck the man where he stood.

He let loose a scream of rage and pain and turned a ring on his hand as the fighters leaped for him. Barak fell over a chair as the man vanished and hit the floor with a loud crash.

"He'll be back," Rue groaned. "We know what he looks like now, provided that was his real face. Did anyone think to check?" she asked, looking straight at Adrick. He merely shook his head.

Landros suddenly began ushering everyone outside. "Go on; it is obvious there is nothing more here." He was a little rougher and more insistent with the men than he was with the two ladies. Once everyone was outside in the garden, he closed the door behind them. Confused and dazed, they stepped out into the yard.

Not so strangely, it was an unkempt place, with more rocks and weeds than the gloriously blooming flowers that had been there moments before. And the 'temple' was no more than a cottage. Suddenly, from within, came a loud crashing noise, followed by a clattering and banging. It sounded oddly like a large table being thrown against a wall. Nightingale gave a low, two-note whistle and shrank a little deeper into Lark's hair. A few moments later, Landros walked out, a bit lighter in step than when he went in.

Lark gave him a cocked smile. "Feel better now?" she asked.

"Much, thank you," he said with a deep, calm breath. "Now, shall we go to the *real* temple before he decides to show his ugly mug again?"

Curious, Barak peeked back inside the house. The table lay in pieces against the back wall, and there was not a single upright or whole chair in the room. Giving a low, appreciative whistle, Barak quietly closed the door and followed the others out of the yard. He kept his eye on the little elf most of the way back, wondering how such a small man could be as strong as he was. The elf certainly did not look that strong. Maybe elves just did not get big bulging muscles as humans did, he reasoned.

Arriving back at the true Temple of Three, they were not made to wait this time but were welcomed and bid to follow immediately.

Rue paused just inside the doorway to place a coin into the basin below a small statue of the Maiden. Breathing her prayer, she watched carefully as the coin glowed blue and vanished appropriately. Satisfied she was truly in the temple, she allowed the acolyte to lead them to the Hierophant's study.

He stood upon their arrival, "Ah, welcome, welcome back," he began. Then he took in their condition, the stone now in Adrick's hands, and sat back down again. "I see you have been successful."

Adrick held out the stone with great ceremony, presenting it to the Hierophant with a flourish. D'Meysen absently took it as if only then remembering that there was a rock to be dealt with. He turned in his chair and, tilting back a crooked stack of books, set it into place to hold them upright. Adrick's jaw hit the floor in shock.

"Whoa, whoa, whoa, hold it!" Landros snapped. "If that thing is such a powerful magic item, shouldn't it be placed in a vault somewhere or a magically protected place? You just used it for a bookend!"

"Oh, that," he admitted with a shrug. "That is relatively unimportant."

"Unimportant?!"

Rue started at the outburst. She had been expecting Landros to be the one to blow up, not the quiet Romeri girl beside her.

"We just risk our lives breaking into house of politician-mage for thing, and you say is unimportant?!" she cried. In her fury, her accent became thicker. The outburst was followed by a short stream of Romeri, which no one understood. Even the mockingbird was upset.

The man sighed. "Look at it again."

Stubbornly, Lark obeyed. All she saw where he had placed the stone was a statue of a small man pushing against the books to hold them up. It winked at her.

"You see," he continued, "it protects itself mostly. Half of what you no doubt encountered last night and this morning was generated by the stone. It... has an ego, you see, and likes pleasant surroundings and beautiful things. It has other powers, which we will use to protect the city, but, for now, until the shrine is built and truly protected, I will keep it here, where it will be quite safe. We will compensate you for your evening's work. And I apologize again for any trouble it may have caused you."

He gestured to the corner of the room, and an acolyte stepped forward, handing him a small bag that clinked when it shifted. D'Meysen took it and waved him away, setting the bag in front of them on the desk. "Please, by all means, take this and divide it as a gesture of our good faith."

There was something in his eyes as he met those of each of them which discouraged further questioning.

Rue picked up the bag and slipped it beneath her robes with a small bow to the priest. "You would best be warned, then," she said, "that the thief will be searching actively for it and us."

"I am certain he will. But why would he seek you? He does not know you," he asked, puzzled.

"Because we met him. Face to vicious face," Lark snapped.

The priest grew quiet. "You saw him? And he saw you?" They nodded. "Describe him."

Adrick obeyed, painting as vivid a description of the man as he could. Lark, mischievous as ever, did him one better, calling up a smoky image of the man outlined in the air. She gave it a touch of color and form. The vision faded to nothing, and there was a long silence in the room.

"He will be taken care of. Consider this a report, and if we have a need, we may call upon you to testify at some point in the future. For now, go. You have earned your rest."

THREE

No one said a word until they were standing in the street outside the temple. They stood there for a moment or more, still half in shock but quickly coming out of it to breathe deeply of relief.

Rue peered into the bag of money. "We need to go somewhere to divide this," she said.

"Fine, whatever," Landros snapped. "I just want a fireplace."

"You said something about breakfast," Barak muttered. "Breakfast would have a fireplace."

Lark turned. "Is wish table for counting," she said, gesturing to Rue. "Is wish place for fire," she aimed at Landros. "Think all want for breakfast and wine. Fine, so you follow *me* now. Make all happy."

Lithgorin brightened visibly. "You'll dance for us?" he asked, but she did not hear him, as she had already started walking down the street. He grabbed Barak by the sleeve. "Hey, I behaved. She said she'd dance for us. Come on!"

That and the promise of food was motivation enough for the big man.

Lark led them to an inn called the Cinnamon Tree, about five blocks from where they had met her running out of the rain. The tap room was clean and empty and smelled heavily of bread baking in the back. A man with a healthy beer gut was behind the bar, putting away clean mugs that a young blonde woman had brought in from the kitchen. At the moment, they were the only people in the room. The woman looked up as they entered and acted surprised to see them.

"Lark, what are you doing up so early?!" she asked, confused.

"Late, Lily," she grinned. "Am up late. Very very late."

The woman's eyes widened, "You haven't been to bed?"

Lark shrugged. "Never made back to caravan."

Landros ignored the exchange and headed for the fireplace. It had been swept clean recently, but there was no trace of a fire at the moment. He looked up at Lily. "Mind if I light this, Miss?" he asked.

"Yeah, sure, go ahead," she answered absently, crossing over to where Lark had set her things down. "What happened? Don't tell me that varmint, Coolie, followed you to cause more trouble!"

She shook her head, leaning against the table to pull her shoes off. "Rain happen. Then they happen," she jerked her head toward her companions, who were making themselves comfortable at a table. "Then more happen. Think shall need bed for few hours as well as bath. Do not think will make it home," she chuckled. She held out her shoes by the back of the heels with two fingers. "Here, see what can do with those, se'vah? If not salvageable, toss."

Lily gingerly took the mud-caked slippers from her. "I am not sure Heleda will allow these anywhere near her wash tub, much less try to clean them." She turned, heading into the back. "I'll get your bath started."

"Oh, wait bit, se'vah? Think want breakfast first. Is breakfast ready?"

"Oh, it will be," she said. "Just because you don't come in before late morning does not mean that breakfast is not ready any earlier. You'll just have to wait a little on the bread, though."

"Whatever," she chuckled, "just bring lots. Have feeling these boys have big appetite."

Lark sat down next to Rue, who was emptying the contents of a bag onto the table. Lark picked up a plain gold ring. "What this," she asked, "and where come from?"

"Not sure yet," Rue answered, setting another ring and a medallion on the table beside it. "I found those on the thugs at the fake temple. And these in all that debris you so conveniently crashed into."

Adrick sat down, a mug of ale in hand. "Well, that," he said, pointing to the medallion, "looks a lot like a talisman of Lethmordath. A friend of mine has one. It is supposed to increase one's capacity for channeling magic. As for the rings..." He picked up a ring of simple red jasper, slipping it onto his finger. He sat up straight suddenly. "Hey!" he exclaimed with a smile. "There is a warmth spell on this!" He pulled the ring off and set it down, holding out his hand to Lark. "Let me see that one."

She handed it over. "His beer is better," she said, pointing to his mug of ale.

"Huh?" he asked, looking up confusedly from the ring. "Oh. I'll try it next." He played with it for a few minutes and found an inscription. "I'll be right back," he said, getting up. "Probably safer to try this outside."

While he was gone, Rue divided the coins into even stacks and arranged them in six bunches.

There was a shout from the fireplace from Barak as Landros finally got a fire going. It cracked and sizzled nicely. The warmth from the newly lit fire crept into their cold bones as they stood in front of it.

"That feels nice," Barak said, turning his back to the fire to warm his other side.

Adrick re-entered the taproom, grinning, just as Lily returned with a very heavy tray full of sweet bread, ham, bacon, and a half-dozen boiled eggs. She set it on the table next to them so as not to disturb the counting. "Sorry about there being only six eggs. With all the noise and the attacks, the hens are laying somewhat thin. You're the first here, so... you get what I don't need for cooking."

Landros and Barak came over to the table with the food on it, helping themselves.

"So, what is the ring?" Rue asked as she peeled her own egg.

"Vanishing," Adrick answered and set it on the table. He reached rudely in front of Lark to grab an egg and a sticky bun.

"Have you ever seen a wand like that one before?" he asked with his mouth full, pointing over at an ivory stick with a piece of quartz fastened to the end with gold wire.

Rue shook her head. "That's the trouble with wands and rings; no two are ever alike, not even the same kind of wand. I'll have to identify it later. Wands are a little riskier for waving around to find out what they do," she added, eyeing Adrick warningly. She ate her egg, staring at the items and the piles of gold on the table. "We do have a problem, though."

"Such as?" Lithgorin asked, leaning back in his chair and taking a mug of beer from a tray being held out to him by a young boy who stared straight ahead.

"Such as there is gold enough to even things out, but there are four items and six of us," Adrick pointed out.

"So," Landros began, propping his foot up on a nearby chair and taking a mug. "Thank you, boy," he said. "Who can use the medallion? The talisman, or whatever you called it?" He looked back at the child as he walked around him to Barak and Lark, never watching where he was walking but never missing a step.

Lark caught his attention. She held two fingers over her eyes, indicating that he was blind. Landros raised his eyebrows, impressed, especially when the boy smiled up at her when she traded a mug of mulled wine for a piece of silver with a marble-sized bit of rock sugar on top of it.

Adrick grunted, crossing his arms over his chest. "Any one of us, except you, Lith, Barak, and the Gypsy."

Lark chose to take offense. "Is for mage-types, *sesket*?" Adrick nodded. "Well, in case did not notice, 'Gypsy' threw spell or two herself this morning!"

He held up his hands in surrender. "I stand corrected. I know I want the talisman, and I am sure Rue... and you would like it as well. It would be useful to most of us."

"That's only half of us." Barak laughed at the man's exaggeration. "Why don't we dice for the stuff?"

Lark looked up at him, thoroughly confused. He pulled a pair of bone dice out of his pocket and put them on the table. "You know, like playing knucklebones. Gambling. But we play for the items. We each roll both dice, but whoever rolls highest gets the first pick, and so on.”

“Don’t know about that,” Lark began, leery of the whole business.

“I’ve done it lots of times with other groups,” he offered helpfully. He held up his broadsword. “I got this that way. It works real nice against dead things that don’t behave dead.”

Even Landros did not seem to like the idea very much. “Well, is there anything on the table that anyone wants that no one else does?” It did not take very long to discover this was not the case. He shook his head. “As long as no one chooses an item they cannot use, then I suppose we do not really have a choice.” With that, he picked up the dice and handed them to Lark. “Ladies first,” he said, catching her dark eyes with his. He tore his gaze away quickly, reaching for a slice of ham with his knife.

Lark reluctantly shook the dice in her hand and then tossed them onto the table. They came up snake-eyes. She got up, wandering over to the bar with her glass.

“Rue,” Landros prompted, watching Lark as the priestess reached for them.

“Hey,” Adrick called after her, teasing. “I thought you said that Gypsies were good luck!”

Refusing to be baited, she called back. “Gypsy good luck to others! Gypsy no good luck for Gypsy!” She set her mug on the bar. “Neneis, put some more wine in this, will you?! Is little weak this morning.”

He obliged her, “Maybe you are a little tart this morning?” he suggested with a grin.

“Not for you,” she smiled back. “Never for you.”

By the time she sauntered back to the table, the items had been divided. Adrick got the talisman, Rue the warmth ring. Lithgorin was already wearing the vanishing ring, and Landros was packing the wand away as carefully as he could. Barak grinned at her as he pocketed his dice, showing her his otherwise empty hands with a sympathetic shrug. She just smiled back at him, helping herself to breakfast.

Rue handed her a stack of gold coins. "There's about a thirty or so there," she said. Lark nodded and dropped the coins carelessly into her bag.

Landros reached purposefully over the table to get a piece of fresh bread to eat with his ham and whispered, his head close to Lark's. "How long has he been blind?" he asked, nodding in his direction.

"Since birth, I think. Lily does very well with him. He has unerring sense of placement." She glanced over to where the child sat in a chair beside the fire, just staring blankly off into the room, listening but not apparently paying any attention. "May look like zombie when works, but boy has passion. And quick mind. Been teaching how to play fiddle. Is getting good."

Rue was speaking with Adrick. "I know I'm from a small temple, but... don't you find it odd that a man is the high priest of a temple to a triple *goddess*? I mean, even a wee burg like Dramkis has at least a Mother in charge."

Adrick shook his head, swallowing, "We've got a Maiden, a Mother, and a Crone," he bragged. "You met our Maid when you arrived. But we're such a big temple ...there is so much to keep track of between what is basically three temples in one... so we have a 'hierophant.' He's more of a... an administrator."

Lark frowned and was about to ask what an administrator was when Rue exclaimed, "Oh! So he handles the resources, coordinates between the branches as well as between temple and town," she nodded, getting it.

It struck her then what purpose D'Meysen must serve. "Is captain!" she grinned, understanding completely. "Is no wonder so pompous," she added.

Before anyone could ask for clarification, Lithgorin called her name. She looked over.

"Are you going to dance for us?" he asked boldly.

"Depends on how much wine have had," she called back, intending that to be an end to it.

Landros stood there about a second, thinking, then reached purposefully into his pack and produced a small jug and a tiny bone cup. He unstopped the jug with a distinct *thung!* and poured a perfectly clear liquid. He held it out.

She took it, looked at it, smelled it. "What is?" she asked, unable to identify it.

"Trust me," he said. "Just drink it." He watched her, his own expression unreadable.

She shrugged and tossed it down. It did not bother her at first. There was hardly any taste to it at all. Then she felt a slow burn develop down the back of her throat and all the way into her stomach. "...punch," she said, her voice somewhat raspy as she handed the cup back to him.

Adrick stared in disbelief. He knew what was in that jug, had had some of it himself once. "Did she say 'punch'?" he asked Rue.

"No," Lark coughed and cleared her throat. "Said 'packs punch'."

"Humph," Adrick muttered, crossing his arms and leaning back in his chair. "More like getting kicked by a mule."

Barak chuckled. "Just cause you were pukin' your guts out...." Adrick rewarded him with an elbow in the stomach.

Lithgorin pressed his own point, trying his best to look charming. "So, is that enough wine? Will you dance? You sort of promised."

Lark sighed. She was feeling warm now, very mellow. The exercise would do her good and get her muscles loosened up. "Fine, fine. But, afterward, I get bath, agreed?!"

He laughed in triumph. "Agreed."

Lily, who was behind the bar at that point, looked up at Lark and nodded. She slipped upstairs to get the bath ready. Her son, Dane, appeared immediately to Lark's left as she pulled out her fiddle case.

"May I play for you? Please?" he asked.

She looked down at him, then touched his cheek tenderly. "How can I say no to that handsome face?"

The boy beamed as if she had just bestowed on him a great and rare honor. She opened the case and tested the tuning before laying it carefully in the boy's outstretched hands.

Without missing a step, he bowed to her and wound his way back to his corner. Putting his hand on the seat first, he sat down and caressed the instrument before laying it under his chin. "Sing for me," he crooned to the dark, satiny wood and began to play.

Lark looked around for a moment, seeking a clear enough area. The others seated themselves and watched, some eagerly, some with a sneer of disdain. Satisfied, she listened to the music with her eyes closed for a few minutes.

"Dane, are choking her," she said. He loosened his grip on the neck of the violin, and the notes flowed sweeter. He was not a poor player, not as good as what had she displayed in the illusionary feast hall, but good enough to dance by. She slowly leaned into the melody to feel it, steal it, and remold it with her body.

As she danced, she began to unwind, to unravel herself piece by piece. Everything that had happened to her that night ran through her mind and out of her body, completely on display for any who could read it. The incident with Coolie and his drunken cohorts resulted in stiffness and oddness to her movement as if her heart were somehow not in what she was doing. Then came the rain and her meeting with those amber eyes shining in the darkness.

She was in front of Landros and suddenly realized it, turning away from what was suddenly being awakened within her. In her mind, she could not escape him or the music. Her soul would not let her flee the images of those eyes turning to her, half-shadowed in darkness and highlighted by lightning. The fight in the rain, the capture, the rescue, the frustrations of being misled and tricked by magic and illusions, all of this flowed through her, controlling her movements, her inspiration. She had never danced like this before, not even in the evenings around her family's bonfire.

Even Adrick was impressed to silence. He had not intended to watch but had made the mistake of looking up at her as she whirled past him. There was such an expression of emotion in that swirl of red and black fabric. He found it something of a release as if she were opening him up and letting all the stress and dis-comforting thoughts and the frustrations spill out. It lightened his mood considerably. He was almost starting to like the girl, heathen though she was.

Barak just found her fascinating. She seemed to fly as she went from floor to chair to table without breaking her stride. He watched in amazement, wondering how her body could twist and bend like that without breaking anything.

Lithgorin was very pleased with himself. It was everything he had expected it to be and more. The way her skirts fanned out when she turned displayed long, shapely legs and firm, smooth calves. "Incredible," he mumbled. "Absolutely incredible."

Rue was happily tapping out an appropriate rhythm on the table, letting herself be carried to faraway places by the music.

Landros just stood watching, thoroughly engrossed and oblivious to everything but the movements of her lithe body. He had been right and wished seriously that he had not been. She was a beautiful dancer while she played the violin. She was almost something ethereal when she danced alone. It did not matter that the music was not as good or as moving. How much of this was Lark and how much the moonshine he had given her did not seem to matter. She had been swallowed whole by the movement and had become the dance.

He was going to regret this; he just knew it. This whole night and agreeing to help Adrick on his 'little mission for the church'. And especially this, watching this human girl dancing. Darker of tone though she was, with her softer, wider features so far from the pale, angular, sylvan beauties he was used to admiring, she was beautiful almost beyond mortality. There was life in her small body, bursting out of her like the radiance of a star, and that passion was infectious. It was a feeling he had almost forgotten.

Lark stopped suddenly. It was over. The music crescendoed and ended, and she felt a sudden weakness that she was unaccustomed to, as if whatever had driven her, or possessed her, had suddenly slipped away and taken all her energy with it. She wavered. She stared down at Landros, who was, mysteriously, right at her feet. The gaze trapped them both, and neither could look away. Suddenly, her knees buckled, and she tumbled.

He reacted quickly, not really certain himself what had happened. One minute she was standing above him, breathing heavily and glistening with her exertion. The next, she was in his arms, clinging to his neck in momentary panic.

Standing there, holding her slight weight, wondering what was to happen next, he did the only thing he could think of. He kissed her. It was like someone had touched a torch to a keg of black powder. There was a sudden sizzling as the flames took their effect, and then the world exploded.

Lark just stared deeply into his amber eyes, too affected to move. She had been kissed before, but nothing like that had ever happened in her life. She had never reacted with her complete body before, from the lips he had touched down to her dirty, bare toes.

His own body reacted suddenly and unexpectedly. He set her to her feet, uncertain of her reaction. She was barely breathing, and she had gone hot and cold all at once. She did not remove her arms from his neck but held on still, afraid to fall if she should let go.

Nothing, and no one moved. Lithgorin just sat there with his mouth gaping, slowly turning green with envy.

Lark wrestled herself back under control, softening. Her breathing became something closer to normal, but there was still a spark burning, smoldering deep inside. She assumed it was a reaction to his proximity and decided, all at once, to explore it. Noting Lily standing at the foot of the stairs, towels in hand, she smiled weakly at Landros and decided to trust her body to get her up the stairs on her own.

"I think bath is ready," she murmured huskily. She stepped away and came back when he did not move. "I think," she said, taking a deep breath, "that you could use one, too." With that, she kissed him again, deeply, waking him up completely, and then slowly walked towards the stairs.

It took Landros a few seconds to snap out of his surprise at her returned kiss and realize what she had said and what she had meant. Without a word, he turned and followed, taking the towels from Lily as he hit the staircase. There might as well have been no one else in the room for all the note he took of his other company. All his attention was locked on the slowly swaying hips of the girl ahead of him on the stairs.

At the bottom, Lily smiled, though a little surprised, and crossed over to the table where the lovers had left their belongings. Humming quietly to herself, she began gathering up Lark's things first. "Dane, sweetheart, will you bring me the fiddle?"

Sadly, the boy left off caressing the instrument and carried it to his mother.

The mockingbird paused in his stealing of the sugared currants from the sticky buns to look up towards the second floor with a chirp of abandonment.

"Will you... I've never seen him act like that before," stammered Adrick. "Have you?" he asked Lithgorin.

Lith only shook his head, not quite willing to believe yet that she just went upstairs with Landros the Pathfinder: a brusque, acid-witted Elven ranger who had commented earlier that she was only 'very good looking' because she wasn't an elf; who had already made it quite known that he was not interested in her.

Rue smiled and patted Lith on the shoulder. "It happens," she said, trying to soothe his hurt ego. "Come, gentlemen. Are we ready to go?"

"Go? Hells!" Lithgorin exclaimed, snapping out of it. "I'm going to stay right here until they come back down!"

"Here, here!" Barak crowed.

Adrick just shook his head and drank his ale.

Lily snorted from behind the bar, where she was stashing Lark's bag. "You folks are gonna be here a while."

"What makes you say that, good lady?" Adrick asked.

"Oh, I'd say the look on her face," she said with a hint of sarcasm laced with a healthy portion of amusement. "I've seen it before. And I tell you, they're going to be a while."

"She's done this before?" Lithgorin choked, suddenly upset that she might be treading carelessly with his friend's heart. He had not taken her for a tawdry.

"Who, Lark?" she asked, with a tone of shock. "Lark's never done anything like this to my knowledge. She's usually very straightforward about what liberties are not permitted by the patrons. She's never gone upstairs with anyone before."

"But you said..."

"I said I have seen that look before. I did not say where." With that, she collected the bag the elf had brought with him and put it beneath the bar with Lark's things.

"Hey, what are you doing with Landros's stuff!?" Barak exclaimed.

"I am putting it behind the bar where it will be safe," she calmly explained. "I do have other customers coming in and out of here, and quite a few showing up soon. I cannot have your things spread out all over the taproom, and I cannot be responsible for stuff left lying about. When he's ready for it, he can ask for it. 'Til then...." She disappeared promptly into the kitchen.

Lithgorin propped his elbows on the table and planted his chin on his fists. "Barak," he said after a few minutes.

"Yes?"

"Tell me you brought cards."

FOUR

Lark led him down the upstairs hallway to a door that stood ajar. She glanced back at him briefly before disappearing inside. Landros felt that glance deep down inside. The image of a sylph-like creature leading him into a trap to devour him at her leisure suddenly sprang to mind, but he followed anyway, vaguely amused by the unlikely thought.

The room was fair-sized, nicely lit by the fire in the grate and the light streaming in from the cracks in the shuttered window. A pair of lamps rested on either side of a large bed on small tables. A tall screen blocked off the middle of the room, behind which he could see the outline of a huge tub and Lark unlacing the front of her vest, nicely silhouetted by the fire. Her voice came from the other side of the screen. "Leave clothes in basket and put outside... if want them washed."

He looked around, confused for a minute, until he saw a wide, open basket just inside the doorway. Lark's gold scarf already lay inside it. He tossed the towels and his sword belt onto the bed and began to shrug out of his shirt. Pulling his head out of the cloth, he looked up to see the vest draped over the top of the screen like a discarded corset and watched, unable to move, as she gracefully slipped her blouse over her head and onto the top of the screen only to slither to the floor. She did not seem to notice. Her skirt was unfastened and fell obediently over her hips to her ankles. Standing over the tub, she paused to stretch languidly before stepping in and disappearing. Landros found himself deeply aroused by the sight.

She snapped him out of his self-induced paralysis by asking him a question. One he did not hear. She repeated herself. "Said, would be dear and throw my things into basket?" She laughed when he still did not move. "If not outside, Lily will come inside to look. Have bad habit of forgetting."

Landros certainly did not want that. He obliged, reaching around the screen to snatch up the skirt, gathering the other articles, and tossing them all into the basket. Sawdust and rotted wood fibers scattered onto the floor and hung like dust motes in the air. He finished undressing, dropping his own clothes in, and scooting the basket just outside the door. Then he dropped the latch. There was a sudden gasp and splash from behind him. He crossed on silent, bare feet to the screen and peered around it.

The tub was huge, large enough for a man like Barak to be comfortable, easily big enough for two elf-sized individuals. There was a three-legged table beside it with a bar of soap, a glass bottle of some thick, milky liquid, and a large sponge. Lark was brushing her wet hair back out of her face with both hands, having just come up out of the water. She reached over for the glass bottle, removed the stopper, and started to pour some of it into her hands, but Landros reached out and took it from her.

She jumped, glanced up at him, unconsciously curling up. Her position and the water distorted his view, but he could be patient. He just smiled, pouring the thick liquid into his own hands, and began to work it into her long black curls. As he worked, massaging her scalp gently with his fingers, he smelled honey. He took a deep breath of it. "What is this?" he asked. "And why does it smell like honey?"

She smiled, making herself relax. "Because is honey. Is one of Lily's specialities. Is mix of soap with milk and honey. Is getting expensive, so only get maybe once, twice month. Must have realized is needed." She gave a soft moan of pleasure. "Is very good to me. Do not charge so much for bath and laundry, but then, am tipping better than most."

She leaned back in the water to rinse and glanced up at him. All she could see was from the chest up, but she was keenly aware that there was no cloth on his body; and that he suddenly had a full, unobscured view of her own nakedness. She closed her eyes, swallowing her nervousness, and sank underneath the water.

She was every bit as beautiful uncovered as she was when tantalizingly dressed. Lying beneath the surface, her hair fanning out as she worked the soap out of it, she looked very much like a dark-skinned sea nymph taunting him just out of his reach. It struck him then as entirely possible that she was not real at all. After all, the night had been fraught with illusions, and he was not exactly the most charming or handsome man in the group. Lith he knew to be a ladies' man, but she had blown him off without even thinking. Her eyes had been on himself entirely. Why? She was Romeri, which placed her deep in mystery, and she was a woman, which placed her deeper into confusing.

'Landros,' he told himself. 'What does it matter her motives? She is interested. Just stop thinking and enjoy the morning.'

She came up for air, pushing her hair back from her face and twisting it to wring it out, then dropping it over her left shoulder. The strands that hit the water fanned out, trying to hide her moderate, bell-shaped breasts. She was beginning to feel a little self-conscious, uncertain what to expect or how to proceed when she felt his hands on her shoulders. They slid slowly down her back, causing her to straighten slightly, arching into them, then gently pushed her forward. Without warning, he was in the water behind her. Her breath caught in her chest, and she wondered if she would regret the decision to invite him up, to explore these strange feelings that had welled up inside her when she had danced.

Just when she was beginning to think that perhaps it had been the clear wine he had given her, it happened again. His hands began stroking her back tenderly, moving stealthily around to her not-quite flat stomach, awakening the butterflies she had not known lived inside it. She felt his breath gently on her shoulder as he pressed a kiss there.

It felt very different from when Arturi had tried that several years ago. This kiss did not leave her cold and wanting to push him away. This kiss left her very warm and mellow. And did not stop there but moved to her throat, long and slow. She could feel his entire body behind her and, curiously, the state it was in. It confused her, made her tense, a bit more than nervous, but a bit less than frightened. She had never known a man before and knew, without a doubt, that she would soon. The thought both excited and frightened her.

The hands had moved. The left upward to sample the shape and softness of her breast, the right to explore the soft firmness of her thighs. They seemed to be everywhere, weakening her. And everywhere they touched, the butterflies rose in a ticklish cloud, moved unerringly back to the pit of her stomach and lower, where they melted into a warm, liquid mass slowly coming to a boil. She leaned back against his chest and surrendered completely to the soft but insistent kisses against her throat.

Her behavior confused him. She was reacting very well to his touch, opening up like a flower to the sun, but... there was a touch of fear to her as her fingers nimbly caressed his thighs in the water. She traced the lower contours of his muscles, as if afraid to go higher, as if she had never done this before. If that were true, he was even more confounded. He decided to find out.

She leaned back against him, trusting him to keep her above the water, her head turned to the side to permit the gentle explorations of his lips. He touched his cheek to hers, tilted her face towards his while his left hand moved to her inner thigh. As she yielded, he caught her mouth with his in a deep, passionate kiss, one she fully returned.

She tasted like she smelled, wild and fresh, like sunny meadows and fragrant orchids. There was a hunger building in her, responding eagerly to every touch, however light. He steeled himself as his other hand began its explorations, fingers deft and slow, prepared for any reaction. If she were as innocent as he suspected, she would be quite startled by the touch. But she could not be. He had seen the way she danced, the way she had used her body to her advantage. She was too free, too in tune with her own sexuality to be the innocent... that she was!

She took a deep, startled breath, her whole body tensing. Her eyes opened, gazed fiercely into his. He deepened the kiss, both as an apology and as a means to keep her from crying out. She did not know what had been sparked, but the fire did not slacken because his hands moved elsewhere, which they had, and swiftly. She realized what he had just discovered and what he was trying to do, but she would have none of it. No gallant backing out. She half-turned, reaching up and holding him to the kiss, telling him that she would not let go, not let him walk away without finishing what he had begun just because she had never done this before.

Even for someone of his intelligence, it was very obvious what the girl wanted. She wanted to be a woman; wanted him to make her one. He was confused now, thrown off by every preconception his mind had formed about the Romeri, Romer women and women in general. He took her by the arms and held her back, staring deeply into her eyes to be certain this was what she wanted. There was hurt confusion in those midnight depths. Deciding, he stood and got out of the tub.

She sat up, looking at him with her luscious mouth slightly parted, mystified. She looked like she might, at any moment, gather her senses enough to fly into a rage of wounded rejection.

He held out his hand to her, his face unreadable. Her eyes never left his, but she took the hand and allowed him to stand her up. He pulled her suddenly towards him, sweeping her wet body into his arms, to her complete surprise, and carried her to the bed.

He lay her gently in the center of the vast feather mattress, ignoring the fact that they were both drenched and dripping. He crawled in after her. Her mood improved rather suddenly, becoming playful. Her confidence had definitely returned. She reached for the towels he had thrown on the foot of the bed earlier, but he stopped her, pulling her back and pressing her into the pillows for a kiss. "But am wet," she complained with an insistent smile.

"So am I. So what?" he answered with a very intense gaze that told her he would not be put off for that.

She just lay there, gazing up at him, breathing heavily from his nearness ...his intoxicating nearness. For the first time, she looked at his body. It was scarred but young by her standards, though she knew he had to be more than twice her grandmother's age. Elves usually were. His chest was smooth and soft and strong, like silk. Very unlike the men she knew. She had seen many shirtless men around camp, but none but the youngest boys were hairless. What little hair he had was pale gold and soft as a baby's first locks. His skin was not quite tawny, a cream touched by the sun. His muscles flowed smoothly into one another, did not cut sharply across his arms and legs like her brothers' did. She had always been told that girls looked for men much like their fathers. Well, this young elf was as far from her father as an apple was from a rose. They were both red, but beyond that... there was nothing to compare.

Tentatively, she reached up, ran her fingers down his chest, across his thigh, then around back and up again. She knew he was looking at her, gazing at her fully displayed nakedness, and suddenly did not mind. What he found was obviously pleasing. He kissed her again, this time not limiting himself to her face and throat. That kisses could go other places had never occurred to her, but she liked it. His hands took up their previous occupation almost absently, and before he was through, she was more than ready for him. She took everything he had to give and ran with it, taking it up and reciprocating.

She was very imaginative and proved good at improvising. Every move was an exploration, both of him and of herself, as if this were simply a new dance. She had the brass of a more experienced woman, with none of the jaded qualities, and all of the innocent delights of a maiden.

And her passion was infectious. He had noticed that before. She proved it now. She aroused feelings in him he could neither explain, describe, nor name, but he welcomed them, completely unaware of what was being awakened. She was delicious and alive. So very much alive. He had met no one with such an abundance of life and passion and so willing to give so freely. He suddenly believed it possible to fall hopelessly in love with someone you had just met, someone you did not truly know. As he stared deep into her eyes, he realized that they were not black as he had first assumed. They were actually blue, a deep, dark blue bordering on midnight, and the more aroused she was, the more blue they became.

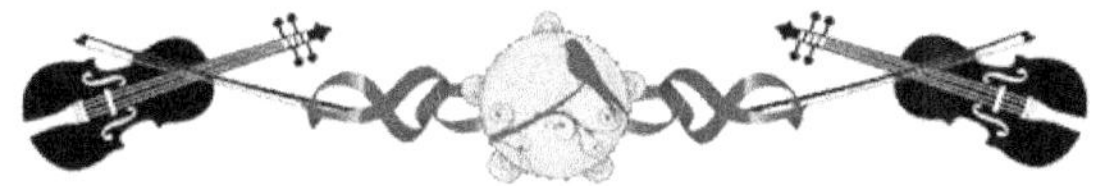

Lark did not know what had drawn her to this moment, lying here, exhausted, beside this golden creature wrapped in damp linen. She rolled onto her side, propping her head on her fist to watch him stretched out on his stomach. His breath was regular and even in sleep. She touched his back, tracing his spine and muscles, rubbing lightly wherever her fingers took a fancy to roam. She only knew that from the moment she had connected with those golden-brown eyes in the rain, she would eventually have come to this. *Sagavis* her grandmother called it: kismet. An irrevocable drawing of one person to another, undeniable to men or gods.

Lark did not worship gods. She believed they only had power over you if you believed, and they were certainly not worth the trouble. They were fickle and deceitful, and petty. She took care not to offend them, but worship them? Never. Yet she believed in Fate with all her heart. Fate had brought her to this moment. It had to have. Fate could be cruel, she knew. And cold. Who knew if tomorrow would see this man still alive, much less in her arms another night? Perhaps that, too, was for the best. She could never have him, anyway. Her father would not allow it. That he was wonderful and gentle and kind and strong and passionate would not matter. All Father would see would be that he was Gegenta, Not Romeri, The Outsider, and therefore not for his daughter, Illyana Petrovna Rushavska.

She suddenly realized that he had been watching her, observing the brooding look on her face. She smiled for him, bent and kissed his forehead, then rolled away and attempted to leave the bed, but found the movement arrested. He pulled her onto his chest, brushed tendrils of black hair from her eyes, tucked them behind her ears, and ran his fingers along her cheek. She leaned lightly into the caress, half-closing her eyes.

"What bothers you, *Ellinoia*?" he asked.

"*Ellinoia*?" she questioned.

He smiled. "Songbird. It is Elvish for songbird."

"Ellinoia," she purred. "Beautiful word."

"But what ails thee?" he insisted.

She sighed, "Oh, everything." A frown creased his face. She smiled. "Oh, not that. NEVER that. Everything outside this room. War, family, work, ...life in general. All that waits outside that door."

He kissed her fingertips. "Ah, but that door can wait a few more hours." He gestured with his head towards the line of light on the floor from the window. "The sun is still up." With that, he rolled her over, pinning her, squealing, underneath him and started all over again, successfully driving all thoughts of trouble from her mind.

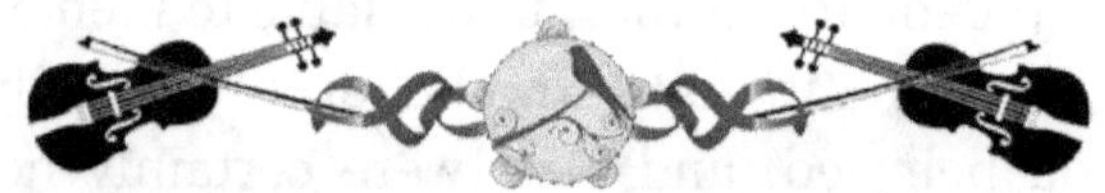

It was well after sundown when she finally wrapped herself in a towel and opened the door. She pulled the basket inside and laid out their clothes.

Landros sat up, watching her as the large toweling sheet kept slipping. He laughed when she finally gave up and let it fall. He watched her dress.

She adjusted herself carefully: tightened every loop of lacing so that it lay flat, pulled and puffed at her blouse so that it displayed just enough cleavage to tantalize but not enough to mistake her profession. She pulled a brush from her patchwork bag and raked it through her hair. Her curls took on a life of their own and refused to obey the bristles. He chuckled as tiny blue sparks began popping from her stokes.

She glared at him. "Will you quit?!" This only made him laugh harder. Finally, she snatched up his pants and threw them at him. "Oh, put clothes on!" she snapped and turned away, but she was smiling.

She crossed to the tub, still full of bath water, and dipped the brush into it. Her hair stopped sparking and did as she told it. She folded up the gold scarf and tied it around her head, knotting it neatly at her temple, leaving the ends to dangle at her ear. As he finally got out of the bed and began to dress, she collected her jewelry and put it on. There was not much. Only four bangles and her earrings, and a single emerald ring on her right forefinger.

He had seen Romeri women with far more, to the point of being gaudy. But then, they had also been much older and too heavily made up to be attractive. She began humming quietly to herself as she wrapped a tasseled shawl around her hips.

She paused in front of him, bent to kiss him. "Some of us do have to work for living," she smiled. "Lily should have supper ready, but are welcome to join." She headed for the door, opened it, and paused. She looked back at him, smiling dreamily, casting a longing gaze around the room, finally coming to rest on the tub. "Never look at THAT in quite same way again," she smiled and quietly closed the door behind her, leaving Landros completely lost in thought.

He did not waste much time trying to sort his thoughts, realizing very quickly that it was impossible. He dressed, slinging his sword belt casually over his shoulder. He glanced back at the room. Nothing was out of place but the bed and the dead flowers on the dressing table. He felt genuinely happy for the first time in a long time. With a deep sigh of satisfaction, he went downstairs.

In the taproom, he was startled to see, amid the score of patrons, his friends still seated at the same table, setting aside cards for plates of steaming food. Adrick caught sight of him trotting down the stairs and, instead of waving him over, elbowed Lithgorin with a grin. Lith looked up and gave a very obvious 'ye gods!' roll of his eyes. Barak turned and lifted his mug with a wide grin.

"Our man of the hour!" Adrick called.

"Yeah," snorted Lithgorin, leaning back in his chair, "but how much of that was sleep?"

"Oh," Rue said, sipping at her wine, "I'd say only about a fourth of it." She smiled at him as well, but more kindly, raising her glass to him and not in the crude way the others had.

Landros crossed the taproom, planted his fists and leaned over the table. "You mean..." he began. He caught himself as his fist slipped. He looked down and saw a scattered hand of cards with a black deuce sticking to his knuckles. Pulling it off, he tossed it down.

"Barak!" Lithgorin shouted as his chair hit the floor. "You mean you held me off with a pair of two's!?" Barak grinned and shrugged. Lith buried his head in his hands. "Goddess, what a day this has been!!!" he groaned.

"You mean to tell me that you waited for us to come down-stairs?!" Landros exclaimed, but not as genuinely angry as he might have been. He was in too good a mood. He looked over at the priestess. "Rue? You, too? I expected..."

"Hey, it was their idea," she pointed. "I just stayed for the cards."

"Yeah, she's a little too good at cards for a lady," Barak grumbled.

"Oh, that's just dandy," Landros groaned. "Just don't tell me you made bets on how long it would take."

There was a long silence at the table. He looked at each of their faces, then turned and left without getting an answer. He did not really need one. Their expressions said it all. They broke out laughing as he walked away.

He saw Lark sitting at a small table in the corner, chatting quietly with the innkeeper as she brought her supper. Her familiar hopped directly onto Lily's hand, then to the plate, and began picking off the choice parts. The woman looked up as Landros seated himself next to Lark.

"Be right back," she smiled and slipped through the nearby kitchen door.

Landros said nothing, just leaned back in his chair, and observed the room. Lily returned very shortly with a steaming plate of meat and vegetables and a full mug of beer. "Oh," she said, ignoring calls for her attention at another table, "your things are under the bar, sir. Just ask Neneis for them when you are ready to go. Unless, of course, you are keeping the room for the night?"

"Lily!" Lark exclaimed, obviously embarrassed. "I think is someone bellow for you."

"Don't they always?" she sighed. "Oh, you better watch it, though. Coolie's back," she warned as she weaved out onto the floor again.

"Coolie?" Landros asked, digging into his food. It was simple, leaner on the meat and heavier on filler than in recent weeks, but better than at his own residence. Glancing over, he noticed that Lark's plate held barely a third of what his held. He frowned. "You work for her, and that's all she feeds you? I know supplies are short, but..."

She smiled. "Eat much bigger lunch than supper. Am only eating this much because sort of skipped that meal," she said with an arched brow. "I try not to eat too heavy when work."

"I see. And Coolie?"

She sighed and slumped back in her chair, only picking at her food. "See burly pig over by fireplace? Third table."

"The one with the freshly broken nose?"

"That's him. And my fault."

He looked over at her in surprise.

She shrugged. "He grabbed ankle while was dancing last night and almost broke my neck. Kicked him in face and left. Is why was walking home so early last night when ran into you. If had worked as late as usual, would have stayed here and never met you, so is better he tripped me, *sesket*?" She brushed the back of her hand against his cheek affectionately. "Besides, looks better with broken nose, yes?"

Landros just grunted. "He will be no trouble tonight. Rest assured."

She smiled. "Just try not to kill him, please? Is bad for business. And believe me, business is bad enough."

She finished her supper, making little in the way of small talk, shooing the bird from Landros's plate when he came looking for tasty bits. Landros just chuckled and offered him the seeded crust of his bread. Popping the last bit of cheese in her mouth with a long swig of the wine in her mug, she got up and headed for the bar.

She suddenly reversed her direction and returned, stopping in front of him. She dipped her finger into her cup and quickly traced a tiny symbol on his forehead. Wyn, the rune for joy. She then covered it with a kiss and headed back for the bar.

He grabbed her wrist, though gently. "What was that?" he asked.

"Wish," she smiled. "In case do not meet again." Without another word, she slipped from his grasp and over to the bar, taking her instruments from a very irate Neneis. She gave him a swift apology and hurried to her stool on the hearth.

She first took out a painted and be-ribboned tambourine and laid it skin down on the hearth at her feet, next to Dane, who had curled up expectantly beside her. Nightingale flew to her stool and perched there. She started to pull her violin from her bag but changed her mind. "Lily!" she called as the woman passed by her. "May borrow father's mandolin? Left mine in caravan."

"Sure! Dane, go get Papa's." But the boy had already darted off to fetch it.

"Thank you, sweetling," Lark purred, taking the instrument from the boy upon his return. She tuned it up and began singing. For some reason, she did not feel like dancing just yet.

Landros realized she was singing the same song she had tried to sing last night, the one that Adrick had interrupted. He listened, forgetting about his food. He noticed a certain mellowness to her voice that had not been there last night. But then, it had been raining. That might have had something to do with it.

"...don't you think?"

Landros started. He stared blankly at Adrick as if he had never seen him before in his life. "Huh?!"

Adrick shook his head and pushed a tall glass of red wine at him. "She has you bad," he smirked, dropping into a chair next to him.

"What are you talking about?" he growled, suddenly in a foul mood. He took the glass of wine and drank deeply. Seconds later, he began choking. His mouth was burning. He fumbled for his own mug, tipped it back to find it empty, and grabbed Lark's. There was just enough left. "What in the abyss is this stuff!?" he demanded as soon as he could breathe again.

"Fire wine? You like it?" Adrick asked innocently.

He looked into the glass, noticed something floating obscurely at the bottom. He fished it out. It looked vaguely like a pickled pepper. "Peppers? You put pepper in your wine?"

"It's good that way," he frowned, insulted. "Gives it a nice kick. Lots of fire."

"That's what I get for drinking with a fire mage," he groaned, dropping the pepper back into the glass and pushing it back at him. "Surprised you aren't drinking lamp oil," he growled.

Adrick looked offended. "I have a refined palate, thank you."

Landros raised his mug and caught Lily's attention. She nodded. "Now, what was it you came over here to bother me about?"

Adrick sighed, drank the wine, and started over. "We are leaving. Moving on. Wondered if you were coming, but somehow..." he drifted off, sipping thoughtfully at his wine as he glanced over at Lark, singing in the corner. "Somehow, I don't think so."

Landros shook his head. "It has nothing to do with that girl."

"That human girl," Adrick added.

"You know, you can be such an ass sometimes, Adrick."

He just grinned. "Yeah, I know. But are you coming?"

"Not this time. I think I have had my fill of late, wet nights doing piss-ant jobs for little more than cherry stones. I intend to do something a little more with myself."

"Like getting starry-eyed over some bit of Gypsy fluff? Be careful there, Landros. She's a wanderer. As soon as the siege is lifted, she's gone. Just like all of her kind. Flirt with the locals, rake them for what you can get, and leave them before they've counted the livestock."

"You are a friend, Adrick," he said calmly, though he felt far from it. "So, I am going to give you this warning. You had better watch your footing."

"All I am saying, Landros, is be careful." With that, he got up and left.

Landros was no longer in a good mood.

The crowd was much better tonight. There were more people, and they seemed in need of forgetfulness however they could find it. Lark traded the mandolin for her violin eventually, and played it, for once without dancing, ...much. It was a mournful melody; one the Romeri were famous for. It was the kind of song that could bring even the hardest man to tears.

She cast a small spell and controlled it with the music to allow it to tell the song's tale. A pair of lovers rose from the instrument, ghostly and pale, mere wisps of smoke. A second man grabbed the girl away: the jealous father. The lover was left to fight for her, to fight an enormous monster the father had summoned. He won but died of his wounds on the field. The girl wept over him, throwing herself upon the funeral pyre as they burned him. Then the song ended, and the misty figures faded.

She felt it was high time to lighten the mood and changed the spell, summoning up a cloak from the rack, a pair of gloves, and someone's feathered cap. They came up behind her, looking as if they were being worn by some invisible person as she began to play something more of a danceable tune. She ignored the crowd as they reacted, tried to warn her. It tapped her obediently on the shoulder. She turned with a feigned start and stopped playing. The figure doffed its cap and bowed with a flourish, holding out its hand to her. She smiled, curtseyed deeply, and handed the fiddle to the blind boy, who happily played a waltzy melody. She danced with her make-believe ghost, much to everyone's amusement. And when someone tried to cut in, the 'ghost' pushed him back into his seat to the roar of the crowd.

She danced around the room, winking at Landros when she passed the table where he still sat, watching. His mood started to pick up again.

Several hours later, she returned to the table, counting the money in her tambourine. "Not bad," she mused. "Much better than last night." She looked up at him. "Still here?" she teased. "Friends left hours ago."

He shrugged, setting a glass of cool water in front of her. "So?"

She stacked her money in three neat piles. "Fourteen silver and three pieces of gold," she announced. She pulled four of the silver and one of the gold aside and dropped them into the pocket of Lily's apron as she passed with her arms loaded with dirty tankards. "Thank you!" she called after the disappearing figure. Lily only grunted in response.

Landros looked down at the meager amount on the table and was confused by her apparent pride. "Bad night," he commented.

She shook her head. "Last night was bad night. Four coppers and tin slug."

"But so little..."

"This," she said, holding the coins up in one hand. "This little bit means more to me than all gold your friend gave last night. Because THIS is confirmation of art. Means have done what set out to do, and that is chase away people's troubles for little while. To bring joy to otherwise bleak hearts. I do for myself, but that brings joy to others brings joy to me. Have had people drop gems into tambourine street-side. Have had bag with two hundred pieces of gold dropped at feet for street-side busking. But none meant as much as wildflower put there by ragged beggar girl who had nothing else to give, but wanted to thank me for giving hope in beauty. Wove that flower into my vas, so that would never forget why I dance, why I play."

He was moved deeply. Let Adrick say what he may; the girl had an honest heart. No money-grubbing, anything-for-a-coin woman, this. "Vas?" he asked.

"Is braided belt every Romer child is given when born. Is never finished until person dies. Few Romeri actually wear theirs, is too precious. Is summation of lives. But every one of us has one. Bits and pieces, beads, knots, ribbons, dried flowers, are all woven into belt to mark significant events in life."

"Ah, interesting," he mused. "They must be very colorful."

"Can be," she shrugged, putting her money away and leaning wearily on her fist, drinking her water.

"Tell me about these two hundred gold pieces?" he asked, sensing an amusing story there. The sudden glint in her eyes confirmed his theory.

She laughed. "Alright. Was freelance job to recover stolen objects: box of letters and wedding ring. Somehow ended up on job with these clowns. One was holy knight of ...Annur, Anhr, someone strange like this, one of Northern gods. Even wore this ridiculous short skirt and leather and bronze armor that did not look like protected much. He and I had falling out over box of letters we try to recover what was supposed to have been sold to pawn broker. I buy box with jewel I had and discover two more rings in box than supposed to have. So, I read first bit on paper to see if were right letters. Were actually some nonsense about sheep shearing! Was bilked and not happy. Made stink with shop keeper and got jewel back, but knight was very upset had read letters, so just decided not to deal with him."

"Why was he upset about you reading the letters?"

"Because had promised not to. Well, he had promised. I did nothing of sort and only read first line to confirm was right prize, but... anyway, is neither here nor other place. Went to different jeweler, and I decide to stay outside. Two of them go in, knight and this farmer went 'round back in case thief was still there and try to go out that way. Left outside all by self, I take out timbrel and begin busking. Just singing for hell of it, really, to calm self.

"Well, few people drop stuff in as pass, few silvers from man with cows, copper or two from passers-by and gold piece from some cock-a-doodle strutting down street with lady. Then, carriage pull up. Inside were two young noble types, whispering back and forth with each other and trying to get other to ask something." He watched as her eyes lit up with mischief. "Finally, they call over and I ask if gentles had request. Well, they asked if was alone, which was at moment. They were having party and wanted me to come. At first, think they need dancer and wish for me to entertain. But no, they want I entertain all right, but not way I thought. Said had money, and held bag out of window."

She had to take a moment to stop laughing. "First of all, to deal with them, had to stop singing. Farmer out back heard not singing and thought, 'Girl stop singing. Must be in trouble. I go see,' and comes around corner like bulldog looking for fox in chicken coop! Two dandies see and hit roof of carriage, shouting at driver to "Go! GO!" and take off full tilt; drop bag at feet!

"I pick up and look in as farmer came over, ask if was problem. Just said, 'Oh, no. No problem. Here, here is commission,' and hand him fist-full of gold from bag. Guess they thought was angry father or jealous husband or something!"

Lark was laughing so hard there were tears running from her eyes. Landros was getting a bellyache himself. He was laughing so much he could not take a drink from his mug, though he desperately needed one. Every time he picked up the glass, he started again.

"When stopped to count money, was nearly two hundred gold! *Lunasa*! Went out, bought caravan and pair of horses to pull!"

Lily materialized beside the table, picking up the empties. "Lark, I know you are enjoying yourself immensely, but I need to close the taproom. Now, you two either run on home or upstairs one."

"Oh, have to go home tonight," Lark grinned, getting up, still trying to bring herself under control. "Have to feed horses. Considering did not get to today. No doubt damned piebald has cribbed way through another wagon wheel!"

Landros got up and drained his own mug before handing it to Lily with money for his meal and drinks. "Eats wood, huh?" he asked, shouldering his pack.

Lark nodded. "Good-night, Lily," she called.

"Good-night. Oh, and see if that nice Elven gentleman with you will walk you home tonight? Maybe you'll actually make it this time! And Coolie...."

"Will not be a problem, ma'am," Landros finished for her, putting his arm around Lark's shoulders.

"You just see to that, you hear?" she answered. "She's the best thing that ever happened to the Cinnamon Tree, and Dane'll be heartbroken if his fiddle teacher gets hurt."

They stepped out into the chill night together. The moon was just beginning to break over the dingy buildings. "So, where do you live, my lady?" he asked.

"Tent Town," she answered.

He stopped. "Tent Town? What are you doing out in that rat's nest?!" he exclaimed.

She shrugged. "Was only place could find inside city to park wagon."

"Surely there are safer places," he began.

"Yes, but city watch does not appreciate Romer caravan in them." She shrugged and stepped out into the still-muddy street. "Am safe enough," she insisted, untying her shawl from her hips and wrapping it around her arms. Nightingale shifted his position on her shoulder, nestling underneath her hair for warmth.

Landros suddenly noticed she was barefoot. "Where are your shoes?"

"Probably on midden heap. Heleda could not save them." She began walking backwards, holding up a warning finger to him. "Do not try what am thinking you are thinking. You cannot and will not carry me all way to Tent Town. Have been walking barefoots since could walk, is no hardship for me." She looked down. "Is much better on grass, though," she laughed.

Despite the heavy, damp chill and the constant, impending threat of attack, it was a pleasant night. Landros did notice a figure following at a distance, not doing a very good job of sneaking about. He stopped, drew a sword, and just stood there. After a few minutes, the footsteps faded in the opposite direction. Lark kept walking but looked quizzically at him as he caught up. "What was that?" she asked.

He shrugged, "Nothing. Probably Coolie. But as I said before, there will be no trouble tonight." He smiled mysteriously as he slipped his arm around her waist. "I have plans for tonight. ...The Lady willing, of course," he added, glancing down for confirmation.

She scowled, "Like had plans for this morning? And this afternoon? *Lunasa*, man, when is girl supposed to sleep?" she mocked but leaned into his embrace. "Will warn you, bed is narrow."

"Oh, I think we'll manage."

Tent Town was simply a small gathering of tents and lean-tos that had sprouted up on the edge of the old fairgrounds. Adventurers, pilgrims, and other travelers, unwilling or unable to pay the inn prices, had been setting up their camps here for years until it became a permanent part of the town, enclosed by its own short fragment of the city wall. It was relatively quiet at this hour, with only a handful of people skulking about here and there. Lark's caravan was parked off to the side of the 'town' near an ancient oak, and was probably the only real roofed building in the area.

It was a typical wooden vardo, brightly painted from the look of it. Lark took a lantern off the hook and lit it. She opened the door but did not go up the fold-away steps. She unslung her bag and set it just inside. Nightingale flew immediately into a small hanging house just off the eaves and chirruped a sleepy goodnight. "Can toss belongings inside. Have check horses."

Landros set his bag next to hers and followed her around the side of the wagon, narrowly missing a long string about a foot off the ground, weighted down with bits of bright metal, dented pots, and old cowbells. There were two cart horses in the stringed-in enclosure. They were eagerly nuzzling her, looking for their food. She hung the lantern up on a hook on the side of the wagon and lifted the driver's seat to rummage in the box beneath it.

He took a moment to look the horses over. The mare was a sturdy brown animal, solidly built and placid. She did not seem likely to panic at much and was very affectionate. The piebald, however, was a very showy animal by contrast. He was an unusual black and white pinto of no particular breeding. He was younger than the mare and about as spirited as his mistress. The mare, he noticed, was loose in the enclosure. The pied, on the other hand, was staked out on a rope that ended just out of reach of the wagon. Even so, there were telltale signs on one wheel and on the red overhang of the roof of a viscous cribbing habit.

Lark returned with two buckets of rough grain and set them down in front of the beasts. They both dove eagerly into them. She noticed where Landros's gaze had gone and patted the gelding affectionately. "Nasty habit. Have no idea why does that. Has ever since I bought. Kassie doesn't, but sometimes just want to strangle Dolal." She slapped his rear end out of her way as she went to check on their water supply. With the recent rain, it was full enough. She took the lamp off its hook and gestured for him to follow her back to the rear of the wagon. She hung the lamp up again and seated herself on the short platform on the back, and cleaned her feet in a small pot of water set out for that purpose.

"They are nice animals. That gelding looks like trouble, though."

"He can be handful. You know horses?" she asked, snatching a towel from just inside to dry her feet.

"Animals in general," he shrugged. "I am a pathfinder by trade."

"Oh," she smiled, standing. "Not guardsman of construction site?"

"Poor joke, my dear," he growled, giving her rump a firm smack as he picked up the lantern and followed her inside.

"Heathen," she growled back.

The caravan was very tight. There was limited cabinet space, most of it being underneath the narrow bed. There was a shelf just over the bed where a mandolin lay in its case. She put her violin next to it and hung her bag on a hook beside the small metal stove. She bent and opened the tiny door and started a fire with a scrap of wool and a long, bent rod, like a pair of tongs, whose ends she snapped together. Sparks fell, lighting the wool. She quickly had a nice little fire going, added what she assumed would be enough wood 'til morning, and closed the door. She turned to him as he looked around, rubbing her arms to warm them.

"Is small, as said, but is home."

He sat down on the edge of the bed. "Oh, it makes all the difference in the world when it's yours. What, what is this bed stuffed with?" he asked with a bit of surprise. It did not crackle like straw, but, though soft, it did not feel like feathers.

"Wool. Cannot sleep on hay or straw. Keeps awake itching, no matter how thick blankets. Sleep on ground first. Though grass is nice, too. When is cold, I sleep inside, and wool keeps me nice and warm. On warm summer nights, I like to sleep outside under stars or under wagon."

She shivered. The heat was only just beginning to pervade the room. Moving to the head of the bed, she turned her back to him. She stuck her little finger into a very tiny knothole and pulled, opening a small, secret compartment into which she stored her rings and other jewelry. Removing her earrings, she dropped them in beside a glistening opal pair. She paused, touching the opals gently, remembering the last time she had seen her mother wearing the milky stones. She brushed back the tears that threatened to overwhelm her at her mother's memory and closed the compartment.

Landros leaned back against the wall and watched her put her precious things into her little hideaway. On the whole, the wagon did not seem like a very secure place. "How do you protect yourself against thieves?" he asked.

She smiled, turning. "Oh, easily enough. Have little to protect. If get past magic warding door, have things inside to distract. Look behind you." He turned and saw what had to be the most conspicuous secret compartment he had ever seen. "Obvious, *sesket*? First place they look. Keep only rube stuff there. Junk. Few silvers. If detect for magic, have surprise for this too. Is find these." She pulled the small drawer out and dumped into his hand three hunks of various colored jasper that glowed faintly. "Little spell. Magic aura. Thieves see glow and snatch like prizes. Look no further. Have to identify before realize stones are worthless. If learn then. See, Gypsies have little tricks to protect self. Do not always need locks to turn homes into prisons or strapping young men to protect more valued treasures. Though young men are nice," she purred, pausing to brush a kiss to his lips. "And if all this is not enough, this is nice deterrent too," she said, unsheathing her scimitar. She hung the scabbard next to her bag and placed the bare blade on a pair of display hooks about two feet above her pillow.

"Is that to make certain that I behave myself?" he asked, pulling her closer to him.

"Oh, no. Is to make certain that you do not," she teased, pulling him down with her with a firm, undeniable kiss.

Landros woke to the sound of a bird singing just outside, splashing and carrying on in the shallow water pan on the doorstep. He groaned. "What'd he do, bring a girlfriend home?" He rolled over, into the warm body of Lark next to him. She gave a soft little moan and snuggled back against his chest. He wrapped his arms around her, kissing her shoulder softly before falling back asleep for a few more hours.

The sun was well up by the time he woke again. This time Lark was not in the wagon. He sat up, wondering what time of day it was. There was the rapid sound of hoof-beats outside. He reached to the floor for his pants and found them lying neatly across the foot of the bed over his ankles. He snatched them on and darted outside to see Lark sliding from the piebald's bare back and putting him back on his short line. She smiled to see him, holding up a small sack. "Lunch."

She dragged him back inside. "Sorry, did not mean to startle. But needs riding once in while or get frisky." She folded down a shelf across from the bed, making a very neat table that could be reached while sitting on the bed, and spread out the contents of her bag. There was a bit of cold mutton, a hunk of cheese and warm rolls, and winter apples for each of them.

He discovered quickly that she had a hearty appetite in the middle of the day, very different from her meal of the previous evening. Nightingale flew in through the open window and began scrounging for his share. As they ate, Landros reached into his pack and pulled out the wand he had so carefully packed away ...was it really only two nights ago? He stared at it, thinking as he had been most of the night. Finally, he handed it to her.

"What is?" she asked, trying not to talk with her mouth full.

"A wand," he answered, biting into his apple. He screwed up his face. The apple was tart.

She looked at it, turning it. "This is wand were dicing for other night, *sesket*?" she asked suspiciously.

He shrugged, figuring if he played it right, she might actually accept the gift and not bite his head off and kick him out the door. "Yes, it is. But I do not really use wands all that much. Never get the chance. That is why I am not a spell-caster. I am mostly a front-line fighter, though I'm no slouch as an archer. Adrick said it has the command word 'wherefore' on it. Probably some kind of detection wand, he thought. Might be worth it to get it identified. I figure you could use it more than I could, whatever it turns out to be."

"Should not one of others get this?" she asked.

"I won it. I can give it where I please," he snapped. He softened. "I am sorry. Please, just take it. To remember me by."

She gave him a shocked smile, "Like am going to forget last two days!"

"Ah, you never know," he quipped, sliding out from under the table. He grabbed the apple firmly in his mouth and pulled on his shirt. He bit down and caught the fruit as it fell, setting it on the table while he tucked himself in and pulled on his boots.

Lark lounged back against the wall, thinking, turning the wand in her hands. This was an incredible gift he had given her. She had been given many things by admirers, but never magic things. Though, she had also never slept with any of them. ...She sensed that there was some other reason he had made the gift, one that he was not going to share with her. Suddenly, she did not wish to become but a single night's memory to him. 'Ah, well,' she thought, 'if is truly *Sagavis*, then will not regret this. If is not.... well, shall play that hand when is dealt.'

"Also have gift for you," she said, closing the table and sitting him down beside her. "You are wanderer, like me. Can tell this about you. Is in blood. If ever need camp and Romer one stands near, tell them this: that are friend to Illyana Petrovna Rushavska, and will be given place to sleep and food for belly for single night. Help, if is not too dear, will also be yours. If they question this, tell them I owe favor. Give no one else this name, and never give 'Lark' with same. The name Petrov Rushavska carries great weight amid clans, so neither forget nor abuse privilege. Now go, before decide to keep here another day and night. And may fortune ever smile upon you." She gave him one last kiss before letting him go, and then went out to tend the horses.

Her sudden disappearance puzzled him, as did her parting words. Perhaps, he thought, she is simply not one for goodbyes. He was not very fond of them himself, finding them awkward at best, final at worst. So, he slung his pack over his shoulder and, grabbing the remains of his apple, walked back into the main of town to his own apartment. Though, for the first time in a long time, with a light heart.

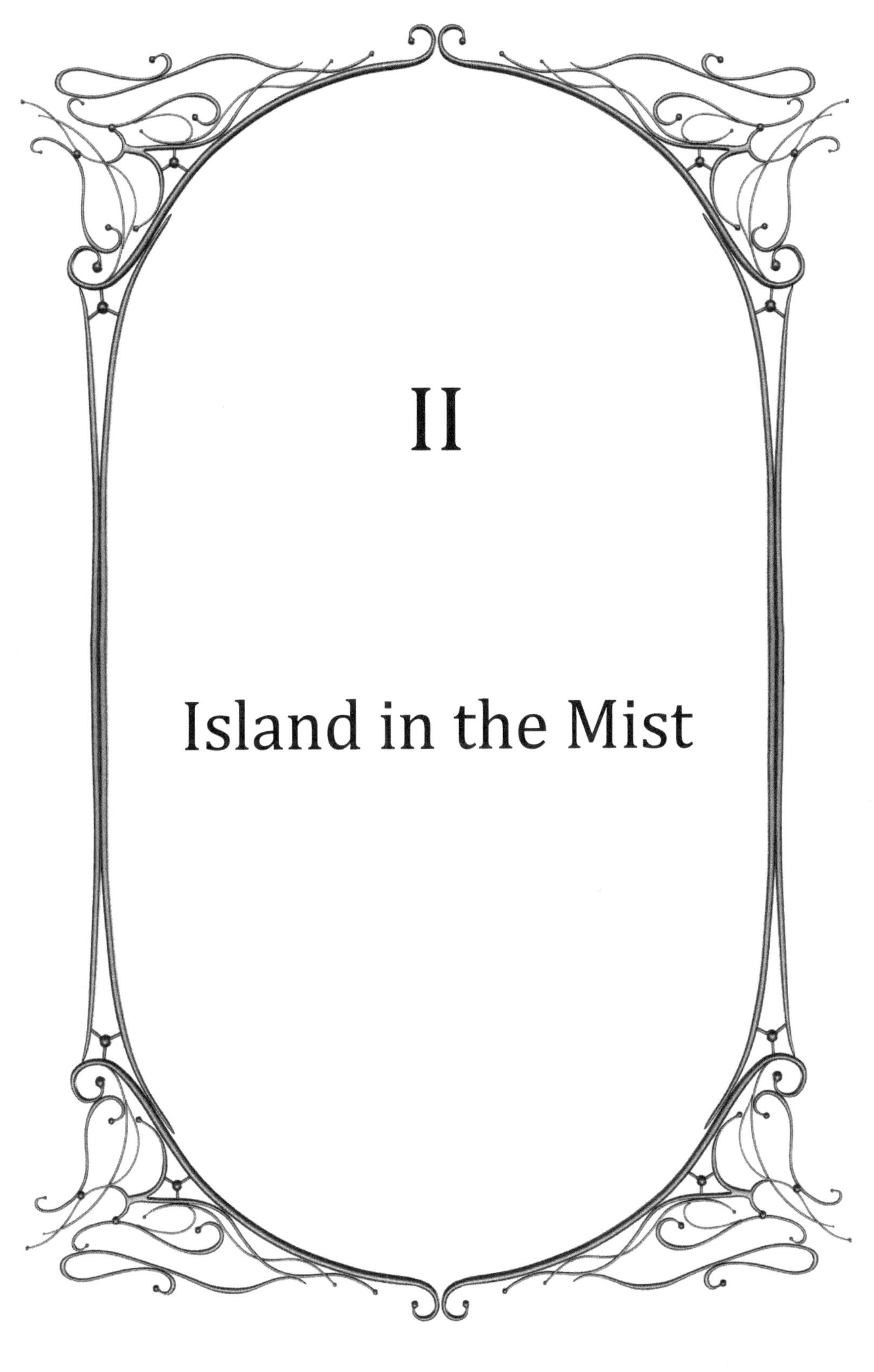

II

Island in the Mist

ONE

Lark was feeling imprisoned by the siege. She had been caged within the city walls for close to a month now, not counting the two she had spent here before the siege had begun. It had been different then. The city had not felt so much the prison when she could have left whenever she chose. Her days were beginning to melt into one another, become a routine of: work, eat, sleep, dance. She was becoming like the gegenta around her, sedentary and ordinary, and it sickened her soul.

She looked at the grass growing up beneath the wheels of her wagon with disgust. Her father would be very unhappy to see that. But ingrained in her, too, was the reluctance to leave her home behind. She had worked hard on the wagon. It was a symbol of her freedom, of her good fortune, considering how she had gotten the money for it. Oh, she would leave it behind quickly enough if forced to flee; but she had not yet come to that point. Or so she kept telling herself.

With a sigh, she filled a bucket with feed and set it out for the two horses. The pied jostled the mare for his share, and it was then that Lark noticed he was favoring a foot. Running her hands with practiced ease down his hip, she pinched the hock in just the right place, allowing her to bend and lift the hoof. Not only was there a small stone lodged there, but a narrow split beginning to form. She let him go and fetched her tools, tucking them into the sash at her waist. Bracing his hind leg between her knees, she drew the pick, and worked the stone loose.

Dolal began to fidget, and the stone went flying.

She checked the frog with her thumb, pressing lightly, discovering a small bruise. A black and white tail hit her in the face. She elbowed him lightly, hissing something under her breath in Romeri.

She traded the pick for the knife and cut off the cracked part of the hoof little by little. Satisfied she had gotten all of the damage, she put away the knife. Dolal, watching her, saw her reach back for the file and chose that moment to resist. He set his foot down. Lark barely kept herself from sprawling into the dirt. She turned and glared at him. He glared back.

Behind them, someone started laughing.

She spun, her eyes flashing blackly. She knew that laugh. Stomping over to the tree under which shade the laugher lounged, she slapped him in the stomach with the file, passing it off. "Fine, Ox. You think so funny, *you* file!" She cocked her fists on her hips and glared up at her brother. He had not changed one bit.

Ivan was a big man, well-named. Ox just fit him, even when he was a child. He was already in his late twenties and had the body of a blacksmith, though he rarely did any real metal working, having no access to a forge. Mostly, he was an animal handler. His thick, black hair was long, kept back in a ponytail, and his mustache was always smartly curled. He had the same dark eyes as his sister, large and deceptively blue. He was a very handsome man, and he knew it. His large, dark muscles rippled bare in the afternoon sun as he wore only a red felt vest and no shirt. His blue trousers were sashed in gold, and a bag and a blade hung from it.

Still chuckling, he took the file and crossed to the horse. He spoke softly, trying to calm the beast.

Dolal was very calm. He just did not want his hoof filed. As Ivan picked up the foot, the horse was surprisingly passive. Then, as he went to place the hoof between his thighs, he found himself lying face-first in the dirt with the horse and his sister both laughing at him.

Growling, he got up, grabbed the hoof, and planted himself, holding it firmly with his thumb on the nerve just under the hock, effectively disabling it. After a few seconds, the horse gave up, and Ivan went to work.

"*Keep telling you,*" he said in Romeri, fingering the newly pared edge. "*Have to shoe them if want to keep them in city.*"

"*Never intended to keep spotted nightmare in city,*" she sulked, pulling a bit of hard bread out of her pocket and chewing on it. Nightingale perched on her shoulder immediately, and she began feeding him little bits of it without thinking.

"*Need to move wagon,*" he added as he filed, half-eyeing the knee-high grass on the far side and the ragged clumps on the horses' side. "*Even if only few sites away.*"

She spread her arms wide, gesturing broadly to the whole of the tight, disordered encampments, dislodging the bird with a start. "*And where to, sesket?*" she demanded. "*Where in broad stink-hole called Portswain am to find place to put wagon? Since siege, has been complaints of how much room have been taking! Now is want I move?*"

He began to gesture at the wheels, letting Dolal go. The horse quickly sidled away.

She threw up her hands again in a helpless, frustrated gesture, "*I know, Ivan, I know! Believe me. I hate it! Hells, even have regular job!*"

He looked at her in disgusted surprise. He crossed to her. "*That's it, Yani. Is time to go, to leave wagon, even horses...*" He watched as her eyes darkened. He shook off her protests. "*You can trade them for sizeable sum to city now for portable wealth that will easily trade elsewhere for another wagon and pair. Maybe even for gold, if are not too picky. Siege has made animals very precious here. Surprised have not been stolen!*

"*We are north-west now, near Alsteadt. There are festivals and food in plenty.*" He reached for the crust of her bread. "*You won't have to eat stale heels of black bread there. Fresh meat and new cheeses....*"

She struck his hand away, "*NO!*" she hissed. "*I left caravan for reason. I am not Ranie. Gruma is. Cannot live my life as transition. Father will never be able to take orders from me. He is too used to giving them. Cannot live this way, is true, but neither can go back to stay. No, Ivan Petrovich, matter is settled. I stay. Even with grass growing under wagon. When I leave, will be on my terms.*"

Ivan stared at his sister, knowing from experience that she was not going to give, not even an inch on this. He sighed and made a generic yielding gesture. "Ah, women!" he growled, shifting back to Tembian. "You are still as stubborn as day you came out backwards! Will you at least cook food I brought for us?" he asked, holding out a small sack.

Lark knew when to surrender. She snatched the bag and growled at him in a low voice, not willing to give in even when giving in, "Only if keep fool mouth shut. Or will have neighbors banging on door for share!" she hissed.

She went inside the wagon, gesturing for him to follow. Just before going in, Ivan searched for and caught sight of a scruffy, shadowed figure watching from behind the nearby tree. He made a gesture with his hand, and the figure moved to obey, slinking past the horses and underneath the wagon. He shut the door behind him. His sister was closing the shutters tightly to keep most of the smells of cooking food from drifting too far. She opened the sack and found a narrow haunch of smoked venison and a loaf of fresh, sweet, unleavened Romeri bread. She sighed with contentment. "*Ah, brother. One thing your wife does well is make bread!*"

"*Is not only thing,*" he grinned. "*I do have three sons. But bread-making... cooking in general, was one skill you did not get from mamma.*"

"*Sesket,*" she replied, shaking her head in agreement. "*But I get by.*" She began stoking up the small iron stove.

She put the meat in a covered pot to heat and set the bread beside it. At the bottom of the bag, she found a pair of Alphasian oranges, with the leaves still green, clinging to the stem. She brought them out, setting them on a shelf, and pulled the table down. "*Are trying to spoil me, Ivan. Are trying to show me bounty is good if I come home, but will not work. I know your conniving ways. Am not some animal for you to charm into traveling with you. But I will feed you, brother. Then, after, I think will take to meet Lily. For drinks.*"

Ivan made himself comfortable on the bed. "*And who is this Lily? Am beyond my days of chasing skirts, Illyana.*"

She smiled as she set a pair of plates and mugs on the table. "*Jena keeping tight leash on you these days?*"

He sighed happily, "*Usually does when she is pregnant,*" he boasted.

"*What, again? So, what wish for this time? Another strapping young son?*"

He shook his head as she slid in beside him. "*No. Actually, think would like little girl. Someone to keep Jena happy and who'll not be running off to join bride's caravan.*"

"*I think meat is done,*" she said, going to check it. It was not, but she needed an excuse to ignore the obvious barb her brother had just dealt. He had not taken well to the idea of her leaving the caravan. Romeri women did not leave their families. They brought their husbands into them. Ivan had not left his father's caravan because his wife had been one of the very few survivors of hers.

Jena had been found eighteen years ago, along with five other children, hiding in the woods not far from the burnt-out shells of their family's wagons. Jena, Rosita, Julan, Ferran, and Victor, victims of a rabid anti-Romer purge to the far west, had grown up as part of the Rushavska clan. The two women had both found love within the clan: Jena with Ivan, and Rosita, the oldest of the five at nineteen, had taken up with their father a few years after their mother had died. Of the boys, only two were left. Julan had been apprenticed to another clan to learn black-smithing, a tricky trade for perpetual travelers; Victor had married a handsome young woman from the Kesenata clan and now rode with them, as was the custom. Ferran had died not many years after they had been found in the same wave of plague that had taken Danine, Ivan and Illyana's mother.

None of these thoughts or memories did anything to help Lark's mood. She pulled the meat from the stove, setting it on the table. They ate in relative silence, sharing the meat and bread and a small bottle of weak wine she pulled from a cabinet. Ivan picked the bottle up and examined it. It was a cheap wine, no label, probably no more than some farmer's home brew.

"Never were much of drinker, Petrovna," he mused, setting the bottle down. *"But when did, had better tastes."*

She sighed. *"The water here is questionable at best. Have small cistern on roof. But even that is sometimes contaminated by smoke and ash from siege. Here we are too close to gates, and water is precious. Wine... wine is cheap and mostly safe to drink. I water it down when I have fair water, to last me for when I do not. There is well nearby, but..."*

"Yet still you persist, sister? Still, you remain determined to stay here, in this city between two levels of hell?"

"Is not quite that bad," she said. *"Some moments, I must admit, were quite... pleasant,"* she mused, her mind drifting back to two nights but a month past and the scent of a certain elf which still clung faintly to her pillow. *"But yes, will not go. If can get wagon out, then will go, but until then, please, stop asking me."*

The truth was, even *she* could not understand her reluctance to leave. She had never been opposed to leaving a place when the atmosphere became hostile. Almost all of her people did. And, she thought, that might be part of why they were never trusted anywhere because they would always leave the moment there was trouble.

She got up, picked up the few dishes, and wiped them carefully clean with a damp cloth before putting them away. There was a bit of the meat left, which she put back into the sack and gave to her brother. He took it reluctantly. Lark went outside. He got up to follow, stopping to put the bag on a hook where he could later claim to have casually forgotten it.

When he stepped out into the late-afternoon sun, she was staring at something under the wagon. He covered the smile that threatened. "What is problem, sister?" he asked, putting on a stern face.

She held up her hand, shaking her head, then bent down. She made soft coaxing noises, holding out her hand with tiny gestures.

Her body language was subtle, but Ivan recognized what she was doing. He smiled. He had taught her that trick. She used her knowledge of body language in everything she did, but it showed best in her dancing and her handling of men. But it still worked with common beasts. He seated himself on the back of the wagon and watched as she managed to convince the tall, lanky, scruffy-looking dog out from under the wagon to lick her palm.

The animal was obviously a wolfhound, at least three feet at the shoulder with curly, scraggly hair of a soft fawn. Or at least it would have been if he had been remotely clean. He was filthy, but friendly. Before she had finished checking him out fully, he was licking her face. "Is huge," she whispered, awed.

"Wolfhounds usually are," Ivan muttered, filling a pipe as he watched the pair.

She narrowed her eyes at him. "He friend of yours?" she asked.

He shrugged. "Not really. Chased off some kids were tormenting in Bayside." It was not exactly a lie. Some kids *were* tormenting him when he left him outside the inn long enough to inquire after his sister. She had not been easy to find. He very carefully neglected to tell her about the four good knives he had traded for the beast in Keristan or the past four months he had spent training him. "He would not hurt them no matter what they did to him, though I have seen him kill rats. He can be vicious when need arises."

'Exactly kind of dog she needs to protect her in this pit,' he thought. Never mind the fact that the leggy pup had grown a bit bigger than he had expected him to. He laughed as the dog, in his fervor of greeting her, knocked her over.

Lark rolled over in a fit of giggles, begging the slobbery, wet, tickling kisses to stop. Finally, she got up enough breath to shout, "Off! Sit!! Down, boy!"

To her surprise, he backed off and sat. She sat up, looking up into his liquid brown eyes as he cocked his head rather intelligently at her. Standing, she dusted herself off as best she could and stared down at the dog, her fists on her hips. His head came almost to her shoulder, even seated. "All right, can stay. But two things: first, have to have name." She thought for a minute. "Ivaska. Is good name. Second.... get bath." And she began casting.

She wove a mini-spell, taking its components from the surroundings; water from a nearby puddle filled with undrinkable water, a scrub brush from the horse box, and a bit of wind to work the bath. The magic sifted the mud from the water, making it bathable, if still not drinkable. It carried the brush in windy hands and scrubbed the huge animal even as it began raining on him. The poor thing tried to get out of the rain but found himself held by the same winds and just stood there, shaking. When she was satisfied that he was suitably clean, she dropped her hands and allowed him to shake himself.

Tired, she perched on the back of the wagon next to her brother and watched the animal as he comically looked about for the invisible bathers, sniffed suspiciously at the still brush, test pounced.

"Nice trick," Ivan mused.

"Tiring. Takes lot out of me, for effects like that," she answered, resting her chin in her hand.

Ivaska shook himself dry and grabbed the brush, playing with it, shaking it as if trying to kill it.

"Is not illusion then?"

"Not that spell, no. Is minor capriccio. Has limitations, but within those can do just about anything. Little things. Like washing dog. Or horse," she grinned, glancing over at him. "Or making rain on irritating brothers." He glared over at her, not much amused and only half daring her to try it. He continued to puff away. "I use mostly when dance, to make invisible partner from cloak rack, make will-o-wispies come and go. Is really very minor magic. Not more than poltergeist, though poltergeist can do more moving of things."

She got up suddenly, took the brush from the dog, and put it away. "Let us go. If go now, might actually be able to drink with you before have to work. And have lesson to give do not wish to be late for."

She refused to say more, going into the wagon and grabbing her gear and violin. She took a moment to put on a few bracelets and other jewelry and to add garlands of multicolored ribbon to the shoulders of her vest with small brass pins. Tying a belled sash around her waist, she shouldered her bag, slipped into a pair of soft boots, and joined her brother on the doorstep. She faced the door for a moment, mumbling quietly, and traced a glowing rune onto the surface: ken reversed, the sign of the closed door. Nightingale perched himself on her shoulder and stared questioningly at the dog. Ivaska was sitting at attention, head held high, and chest puffed up, looking smart and ready to go, if a little shaggy. One ear went up in question.

Lark put her fist on her hip as she looked at the dog. "Now, where he learn this trick, am wonder?" She glared at her brother, who immediately found emptying his pipe to be an intense operation, taking all of his concentration. All of her brother's dogs eventually learned that trick. She sighed. Not quite willing to fight over this, and she did kind of like the scruffy monster. "What else he know?" she asked. "Can guard? Will stay quiet on command? Does he sing like your other hounds?"

Ivan popped his head up immediately. "No," he said, holding up his finger pointedly. "This one does *not* sing. He does not even open mouth unless is food in front of it, or when something not right."

"Good. Ivaska, come. We go to work." She hopped off the wagon and began walking down the narrow path between the cramped tents and ramshackle lean-tos. Ivaska trotted obediently at her side, looking about him as if they were on holiday through the countryside and not tromping through the worst section of town next to Bayside. Ivan caught up quickly and strolled possessively beside her, glaring at anyone who looked too hard at her as they passed.

She pointed out things of interest to him as they crossed town. Telling him which corners were generally good for busking and which were apt to gain solicitations other than music or dance. Showing him places where the City Watchmen did not like minstrels or bards to hang about, or other 'loiterers' for that matter. She pointed out the street which headed down into Bayside, a place one did not travel alone at night, nor unarmed. Bayside was a place even the Night Watch would not go.

Finally, they came to the Cinnamon Tree, where Nightingale swiftly flew to his usual perch on the mantle.

Lily was carrying a tray loaded with clean mugs and set them down on the bar for Neneis to put away. She sauntered over as she saw Lark come in, weaving past the handful of customers.

"You're early!" she smiled. "And who, pray tell, is tall, dark, and handsome here?"

"Tall, dark, and handsome is brother," she replied with a wry grin. "Ox, meet Lily, owner of Cinnamon Tree. Lily, this is brother, best known as Ox, for obvious reasons."

Ivan bent over her hand, caressing it tenderly as he did so. "Is pleasure," he said. "Such rare flower, hidden amidst this midden heap."

Lark pulled Lily away. "Oh, never mind his ranting, is good and married," she said, glaring over her shoulder at him.

Lily laughed, "Doesn't mean he can't look, darlin'."

"Hah, you don't know his wife!"

"Hah, you don't know my wife!" they said simultaneously.

Lily laughed, looking from one to the other of them. "Oh, I can tell the two of you are related! Holy hand bells!" she cried, catching sight of Ivaska peeking up at her from behind Ivan. "It's a hell-hound!" She raised the tray between her and the dog.

"Oh, this is Ivaska. Is... gift from brother," she added, yeeing him sideways. "Thought perhaps would serve good deterrent for thiefs and Coolies."

"Oh, that he certainly would be..." she breathed, beginning to relax bit by bit as the dog just looked at her curiously. "But he's so big!"

"Will stay out of way, promise." Lark gestured to the fireplace and told Ivaska to go. He looked up at her for a moment, then slinked across the taproom and plopped himself down on the hearth, resting his head on his paws with a sigh.

"Well, I suppose it will be all right...."

Dane entered the room from the kitchen, reaching for the wall with one hand, the other filled with a roll stuffed with sliced meat and toasted cheese. He felt his way carefully to the seat beside the hearth, eating as he went. He stopped mid-bite, smelling something out of place. Mother and Romeri watched as the boy became aware of the animal, and the animal became aware of the approaching sandwich.

Dane found the stool and set his supper on it, then walked carefully towards the fireplace and the strange smell. He stopped at the hearth's edge and bent down, feeling for what was there. Hands met fur. Ivaska looked up at the boy, sniffed him, then stood up. Dane, hand still on the dog's side, felt the back of the dog rise to his own height and scrambled back, startled. He backed into a chair someone had left out and fell onto his rump. He held his breath as he felt the beast stand over him. Ivaska sniffed him again, snuffling around his ears and tow-colored hair, and began licking him.

Lark saw Lily visibly relax as she heard her son giggling on the floor. "All right," she sighed, "he can stay if he stays out of trouble."

Ivan burst out laughing when, from the floor across the room, they heard Dane inquire, "Can he have the soup bones, mama?"

"No!" she called. "Maybe! ...After there is soup from them!" She threw up her hands, tucked her tray under her arm, and went to see if the men in the corner needed anything else.

Ivan sat drinking a mug of Neneis's good beer, watching his sister teaching the blind boy to play the violin. People filtered in as the evening wore on, and Lark turned from teaching to playing. She set her tambourine down in front of Ivaska and told him to guard it. The first time someone tried to toss his pennies into it, he growled, but she was quick to correct that behavior.

Many of the customers seemed to have come solely to watch his sister work her magic of forgetfulness. She had a way of dismissing everything but the movements of her body. Their mother had had that way. He understood more of Lark's movement than anyone because he could read the body language. His sister, it seemed, had no end of admirers among the crowd. Always had and always will. But they were gegenta, no one she would give a second glance or thought to, so he did not worry. He watched as she deftly, swiftly, and sharply put down each and every admirer's suggestion, but in such a way as to keep them coming back, begging for more abuse, and to keep the money flowing into her timbrel. He smiled. She played them like a well-strung fiddle, getting from them what she desired without giving a wink more than she wished.

After a while of watching and listening, he asked the boy for the fiddle and played for his sister. He sawed a wild Romeri tune the child was not yet able to play. Lark threw herself into the music, and Dane listened, wholly entranced. When the instrument was finally laid back in the his hands, it was almost hot to the touch.

Ivan ruffled his hair fondly. "You have potential, boy," he said. Dane fairly glowed.

Lark, glistening with sweat, turned to her brother, herself beaming. The look on his face caused the smile to fade. She brought them over to a side table and drank deeply of the mug of water waiting there. "What is, brother?" she asked.

"Is time for me to go. Jena...."

"I remember," she nodded. "Is impossible pregnant. Go, keep her happy."

They embraced and kissed each other's cheeks. He paused to say a few Romeri words to Ivaska, which Lark did not hear, and left. She watched him go with a heavier heart than she expected, wishing she could go with him, but at the same time, glad she was not. Hate it here though she may, there was something holding her back, something other than the wagon and her stubborn pride. Something she could not place. She made a small gesture that left everything in the hands of fate and went back to work.

TWO

It was well after midnight when she finally strolled homeward, Ivaska tagging sleepily along beside her. Her pocket was heavy for once. There had been several adventurers freshly returned from questing with heavier pouches and thirsty palates, and they spread their money freely. There was even a gemstone or two there. They would make nice earrings, she thought, fingering them through the cloth. She smiled. She was tired but in a very good way. It had been a long time since she had a real Romeri violin played where she could go all out. She could not dance the same when she played for herself.

Ivaska growled. He froze, staring down a side street. She stopped and tried to get him to come on, to ignore whatever it was, but a scream punctuated the night, and the dog took off towards the sound. Growling herself, she activated the light pendant at her throat and ran after him, drawing her scimitar. Nightingale took flight, being careful to stay within her light as she ran.

She did not have to go far. Two large men were pursuing a young woman down the street. Another man, following her closely, stopped and turned, holding a rather ineffective short sword to try and cover her retreat. Lark dropped her bag beside her and reached into the pouch at her hip. Pulling out a bit of blue sand, she cast it toward combat, chanting the spell as she did so. The smaller of the two staggered back, blind and stunned, as the sudden arch of flashing lights pierced into his brain like a migraine. The other shrugged it off, changing his direction towards Lark and the very obvious area of light. Ivaska leaped at the staggering man, reaching for his throat ferociously. The young man, also staggered back, unable to see anything but flashing lights.

As the pursuers neared Lark's field of clear vision, she noted quickly that these were no ordinary men. They were easily eight or nine feet tall and had but a single eye in the middle of their hairy, fanged faces. Lark hesitated only a second, spinning under the descending club and bringing her scimitar up across his midriff as she slipped under his guard. The foul leather armor split at the seams, oozing fouler, purplish blood. As it turned to swing again, she cut into the back of its thigh and danced out of the way.

The third swing barely missed her as she ducked in, swinging wildly, making contact, but only just. Slashing upward, she finally connected with a vital, unprotected area and neatly severed the artery. She danced aside, narrowly avoiding the spray of hot, black blood as the beast crumbled and fell. She turned to the other monster, desperately trying to get a hold of the dog attacking it or at least ward it off. A huge fist connected with Ivaska's side, but not with any real force. He took the chance to seize the throat and clung there, kicking and growling, trying to rip out a hunk of meat. Lark managed to hit the arm reaching for the dog, rendering it useless even as the blood running from its throat brought it to its knees. She brought her sword across the back of its neck, severing the spine. Ivaska hung on until the blood stopped flowing, and he could no longer feel the heartbeat through his jaws.

The young man continued to swing wildly, unable to see anything at all. She looked over at him and realized that she must have caught him in the backlash of the spell. She called out to him in as soothing a voice as she could. "Is over. Can stop fighting..."

He did not react but kept swinging, turning about protectively. Lark mustered herself up to her most commanding. "Put down blade, man!" she snapped. "Is dead!"

This time, he heard her. He paused, aiming the blade in the direction of her voice. "Who are you? Where are you? Why can I not see?"

"Put down sword, friend, before hit me. Monsters are dead." Hesitantly, he obeyed. She introduced herself.

"I cast spell on beasts. Caught you, too. Will wear off soon. Never lasts long, only long enough. So sit, relax. Will stay with until is clear."

He felt for the ground, satisfied that he was not standing in a puddle, and knelt. She walked up to him, tilted his head back, and looked into his eyes. She saw the bright spots of light still dancing there. "Am sorry," she said. "Did not think would be hit, standing with back to me. Never happened before."

"Who are you?" he asked.

"Am... Lark, as said. Am Romeri dancer."

"Thank you," he sighed. "You saved our lives."

"Our?" she asked.

"Yes. Miranda..." he stopped and looked blindly about, beginning to panic. "Miranda!!" he yelled. He grabbed Lark's arm, "She does not know this city! She could get lost, get hurt, attacked...."

She disentangled herself. "Ivaska, go get girl. But be nice!" she added. The dog trotted off, following the faint scent of frightened woman. "Will bring her back. Will wait long enough for eyes to see again, then must go. Have worked all night and need to get back to wagon."

There was a deep barking from just up the street. Then Ivaska returned, running, slowed just short of them, and trotted over to sit at Lark's side.

"What is going on?" he asked, confused. "I can see a very large something next to you, and you not more than colored shadow...."

The girl was not far behind the dog, accompanied by four of the Night Watch. She pointed in shock at the dead figures, then at Lark and her companion.

Lark looked up. "You Miranda, *sesket*?"

She dumbly nodded.

"Good, then is yours. Will be able to see soon. Sorry again." She waved at the night watch. "All yours, boys," and darted off down the street with the dog at her heels.

Behind her, she heard the Night Watch start to pursue her, but the young man called them back. "No, she helped! She saved our lives! Let her be!"

Lark smiled, feeling quite satisfied with herself in spite of her tiredness. Ivaska would need another bath, though. He was covered in blood.

She took a shortcut to Tent Town.

As soon as home was in sight, Nightingale disappeared into his house. Lighting the lantern hanging from the other eave, she doused her pendant and turned to face the dog. Casting one last small cantrip, she called forth another rain shower over the beast, rinsing away the blood still clinging to him.

He looked up at her with large, pathetic eyes, asking what he had done to deserve this, but did not try to escape. She kindly redirected a nearby breeze to swiftly dry him, then opened the door to the wagon. Stowing her stuff, she called him in and made him lie down on the floor by the bed. He flopped over, stretching out as best he could, making her step over him as she undressed and sank gratefully into the mattress. She was asleep almost immediately.

THREE

There was a sudden pounding on the wagon door. Lark jumped awake, snatching the scimitar from over her head. Ivaska began barking immediately, his deep, booming voice painfully filling the small room. With a mental nudge, she woke Nightingale, who peeked out of his house sleepily and stared down at the three men banging on her door. He gave a small chirp and crawled back into his nest. "'Same clothes'?" she replied, thoroughly confused. "What you mean 'same clothes'?"

She saw a mental flash of uniformed men and understood. The Watch. She groaned.

They renewed their banging, "Gypsy Lark! This is the City Watch! You are needed!"

"Damn it!" she swore. "Just got to sleep!"

Purely out of spite, she focused on the outside of the door, gestured with two fingers, and uttered a single word. Tiny blue sparks of light flew from her hands, through the door and began swarming the watchmen. She smiled with satisfaction at their resultant exclamations and shouts of, "Get it off, get it off!!"

She got up, threw on a skirt and a blouse, grabbed her scimitar again, and opened the door, ready for battle. The men were dancing about, swatting at the lights as if they were a swarm of bees. She gave an exaggerated sigh and, with a wave of her hand, banished the lights, canceling the spell. "So sorry," she said. "Thought were disreputes."

The corporal straightened himself and his uniform and huffed, "We *said* we were the City Watch, madam!"

"Yeeeess, and if believed everyone who said that...." she answered, rolling her eyes. "What is want?" she snapped.

He made himself look his most officious. "We are sent to collect you. There is a matter of great import, and it is believed you have the necessary skills." His tone of voice and the angle of his beaky nose gave her the distinct impression that he thought no such thing.

She cocked a fist on her hip. "And if do not?" she asked.

He sputtered a half-second. "That... that is for the magistrate to decide. For now, you must come with us."

She disappeared inside without a word, leaving him face-to-face with a very unhappy wolfhound. Inside, Lark pulled on her boots, threw on a vest, and grabbed her pack from its hook. "Have got to move," she growled, taking down her violin. She opened her secret drawer, sliding on three gold bangles and only one or two rings. Her grandmother's emerald went straight to its place on the first finger of her right hand. She pulled her hair back with a comb and headed out the door, pausing only to grab her shawl from behind it. Ivaska moved out of her way, never taking his eyes off the watchmen, nor stopped showing his teeth.

"Ivaska, out." He obediently got down from the wagon, seating himself between the men and her. The corporal backed up.

She tossed her pack to the man, who reacted just quickly enough to catch it. "Make useful," she said. "And careful, have delicate instrument inside." Growling, he handed the pack to the private behind him, who slung it over his shoulder.

Lark's hands now empty, she shook her bracelets up her arm and began weaving her locking spell. The rune lit up on the surface of the door and faded. Tossing her hair out of her face, she reached up and knocked on the bottom of the brightly painted birdhouse. There was an irate and sleepy chittering from within.

She put her fists on her hips and glared at the swinging box. "And if send by magic? How you 'catch up' then, *sesket*?" Silence. A grudging peep. "*Lunasa*! But you are lazy!!" She lifted the roof flap, reached in and pulled the complaining bird out of the box, and stuffed him into a pocket.

She hopped off the wagon, folding up the steps, and began to follow the watchmen. Ivaska started to trot alongside, but she stopped him. "Ivaska, no. You stay." He looked up at her suddenly, cocking his head sideways, flopping one ear into the air. "No, cannot come. You stay. These puffas have made too much of leaving. If take you, will have no wagon when come home. Stay. Guard horses."

The two privates glanced from each other to the neighborhood and the subtle stirrings taking place around them and had the decency to look a bit sheepish. The corporal showed no remorse whatsoever; he just stood there, tapping his foot impatiently, with his arms crossed over his chest.

Sulking, Ivaska turned around and crawled under the wagon, groaning and growling to himself as he lay down.

Lacing up her vest, Lark once again followed them. "This," she warned the corporal as they walked, "had best be urgent."

By the time they had reached their destination, the mockingbird had woken himself up enough to climb out of her skirt pocket and up onto her shoulder, riding there in stubborn silence. "You think I like more than you?" she asked him as he gave a sulking chirp.

Lark was taken into the private house of the Magistrate. She casually observed the opulence of it as she was led into a sitting room. The place was virtually untouched by the ravages of the war outside. The private politely returned her pack before bowing out of the room and leaving her there.

Lark was apparently not the only soul dragged out at this ungodly hour. Rue was there, dozing in a chair. A dwarf was leaning against the wall, grumbling about disturbed sleep. And there was a tall, handsome human in flashy clothes, who did not seem any the worse for the late hour. She leaned towards him and nodded towards the door. "Don't see why they no send *them* out on missions in middle of night. 'Stead of wasting them waking honest folk to do their jobs."

"Ah," he sighed, "but perhaps it is their job to wake honest folk? Though surely you were not asleep at this early hour?" he inquired.

"Most certainly, though only just. Been dancing and playing since afternoon and need beauty sleep."

He made a very flamboyant bow, "Keltree Danhaven at your humble service, my lady," he kissed her hand. "But allow me the liberty to say you most certainly have no need of beauty sleep."

She smiled, almost purred. "Bold young cock'rel, aren't you? I am called Lark."

"I take it Lark is a bard?" he asked.

"I dance," she smiled, shrugging off the question. 'Dashing,' she thought, openly admiring his flashing blue eyes and ready smile and handsome face. 'Real charmer. Little too much so.'

Rue woke at the sound of voices and sat up. "Oh!" she exclaimed, sighting Lark. "My dear girl! How have you been?"

"Well enough, Sister, well enough. Could certainly have used more sleep, though."

"Couldn't we all," she drawled, rising. She extended her hand to Keltree. "I am Sister Rue. And you are?"

Keltree bowed to her, introducing himself as charmingly as he had been with Lark. 'Ladies' man,' she thought. 'As suspected.'

Lark looked around. "Who is sullen one in corner?" she asked.

"That is Rog Thrathrog," Keltree answered. "He's just upset that they pulled him out of a deep slumber over his ale in the tavern where I was entertaining."

"Entertaining?" she asked, confused. "Is most odd."

"How so?"

"That would call for two bards."

He gave a self-deprecating laugh. "Oh, I am no minstrel by any means or stretch of the imagination. I am a thrill-seeker and storyteller and would-be dragon-slayer. This is not my first summoning of this nature. Often I have been sent upon dangerous expeditions that the City Watch have neither the heart nor the men to spare for. I, unlike their useless rumps, am expendable but very tough to kill."

"Still," she mused. "Is rather odd...."

Lark's train of thought was interrupted by the opening of the door and the sudden addition of another human. He glared over his shoulder at the departing watchmen. He turned to the group, tried to smile, and tipped his hat to the two ladies, gazing long and admiringly at Lark's blouse line. She put her hands on her hips. "And you are?" she asked.

"Ebastion Shadowfalk," he replied.

"No, you are? What is do?"

He looked confused. "Strong arm," he answered. "Sort of a mercenary. Why?"

He never got his answer as a servant came into the room. "His eminence will see you in his study. Follow me, please."

The dwarf peeled himself away from the wall, "Bout flamin' time," he snarled with a deep drawl.

The servant led them down a hallway to another equally elaborate room. There was a large desk and some shelves containing only a handful of books and interesting odds and ends. There were no other chairs in the room. The desk chair was occupied by an imposing man whom Lark did not recognize but took, by the gold medallion of office, to be the Magistrate himself. Standing to the left of him were two young people, a man and a woman whom Lark instantly recognized.

Astonished, she stepped forward. "You? But?!"

The young man bowed to her. "Forgive me, my lady, for having you summoned, but after what you did with those monsters... I asked for you specifically."

Keltree and Rog raised their eyebrows at that and glanced in surprise at Lark, reassessing her. Ebastion had not been paying attention but was looking about the room in suspicion.

The Magistrate cleared his throat rudely. "Why don't I allow Merrick and his sister Miranda to explain why you are here," he said sarcastically.

Merrick gave a half bow in the Magistrate's direction, not catching the sarcasm. "Thank you, your excellency." He turned back to Lark immediately. "I did not have time to ask you to further aid us before you flitted off this evening. I fully understood your desire not to involve yourself in the long questioning and clean-up regarding the monsters which attacked my sister and me. It has been a long night for everyone, and again, I apologize most sincerely for repaying your kindness by waking you at such an hour."

Lark smiled. "Are even then. Now, why for you drag me out of bed?"

He leaned back against the desk. "My sister and I are from Evandair, the small fishing town on the island across the bay. We escaped just a few days ago."

"Escaped?" asked Rue. "Aren't you inside the blockade?"

"Ah, yes..." Merrick began, but it was Miranda who explained.

When she spoke, her voice was breathy and uncertain. "Yes, escaped. We thought it was a sickness. ...We were wrong."

"We are a small village, really," her brother continued. "Nothing like Portswain. When people began to behave strangely, we noticed quickly, but we thought little of it. We thought, as my sister said, that it was an illness. No sooner an individual began behaving oddly: they would retire, lock themselves up in their homes and not come out for a long while. When they did, if they did, they were changed somehow."

"They looked weak, sickly, as if they had long been ill," Miranda injected. "And they spoke little. But then, no one tried to engage them in conversations for fear they were not yet well enough not to spread their illness."

"First, it was only the odd bachelor, or old maid, or widow, people who lived alone. When whole families began to fall ill, we rightly feared we had a plague on our hands." He shook his head. "It was not until a few days ago that we discovered what nature of plague. I fear it is too late, even now."

"What kind of plague?" Keltree asked.

"An undead one," Miranda whispered. She was trembling, staring off into the air as if she could see every speck, and feared what she saw moving within. Lark had seen such stares on seers but knew this was not such a trance. Her voice was dry and brittle as she spoke, still whispering as if afraid to be heard.

"I saw them, saw *him*. Up in the mountains. He was... Eridinne brought it down with her. His taint. She stays there now, near him, and visits the village to bring him fresh victims. I saw her and Julian on the bluff." She shuddered.

"Julian was waiting for me. I was late. I guess Eridinne saw him as alone and easy prey. It was like a bird caught by a snake's gaze. He let her... touch him... kiss him.... then followed her up the mountain to the caves. *He* was waiting there for them. ...I... I saw him.... kiss Julian, here," she shivered as she touched herself where the neck arcs into the shoulder.

"He did something to him... I fled and returned home. I was too afraid to sleep. I saw Julian the next morning and... he had changed. He was different. He... he had the plague." She drifted off, still whispering, but under her breath, unintelligible. Her brother wrapped his arms around her and set her down in a chair back in the shadows.

Merrick turned back to them. "You can see that we have a serious problem. I did not believe her when she told me.... then Julian tried to get her alone, never saying much, as if I was not even there. She refused to see him, and it did not bother him as it should have. He is under that man's spell somehow. That Eridinne is involved in this does not surprise me. She has dabbled in the darker aspects of spell-craft for years, but this... this seems beyond her. The town is full of half-zombies. And I am certain there is something worse somewhere. We cannot take on this mysterious man, but perhaps you can." His eyes came to rest on Lark, shining with admiration, "You with your light and magic and that flashing sword. Please! There is no telling how far this will spread."

"Or even if it will reach Portswain itself," the Magistrate interrupted, retaking control of the meeting. "If this is not a plot by the enemy to steal into our very port! And so, you were sent for. Each of you has some reputation for this sort of ... freelancing," he added with some obvious distaste. "Sister Rue was sent by the Temple of Three to aid in the question of undead things. The rest of you are… well, what you are. I want this menace stopped on those shores. You will be compensated for your troubles."

"You speak as if have no choice," Lark snapped.

"You would refuse to help the city out in its hour of need?" he asked, his eyes narrowing suspiciously. Lark felt him begging her for some excuse not to trust her, to accuse her of spying, or worse.

She turned her back on him and faced the brother. "Will do this for *you*, Merrick. Because is *you* asking. Not for this fat man in his palatial jail," she snapped, defiant. Lark knew not to push too far, but she felt she had to get some of her own back. She did not like being bullied into things.

"I will go with you," Merrick injected quickly, not giving the Magistrate time to react. "To show you the caves where Miranda thinks the source lives, this mysterious man of hers, which I am not convinced is not a conjuration of Eridinne's."

He turned to his sister, and took her hands in his. "Miranda. You will stay here in Portswain. I want you to go to the temple and stay there. They have already said they will take care of you. I will be back in a few days, and maybe by then this will be all over."

She stared into his eyes. "Promise?" she whispered.

He kissed her fingertips. "I promise."

Realizing this could mean more than a day gone and, not trusting her neighbors with her animals, Lark quickly dug a scrap of paper from her bag. Tearing off just enough, she used a wrapped coal stick to write a quick note, asking Lily to send someone for her animals and that she might be a couple of days. She gave it to Nightingale and sent him off out a window, the opening of which earned her another glare from the Magistrate.

"How will we get to Evandair?" Keltree asked him, pulling the attention away from her. "We *are* under siege."

"There is a ship waiting for you at the docks. It will sneak you back to Evandair and return you here when the job has been completed."

"Ship? Ferget it," snapped Rog and headed for the door. "Ain't goin' on no ship!"

Ebastion planted himself in the way. Rog tried to move him physically.

"What's wrong with a ship?" Ebastion asked.

"Ground don't stay still. Rog don't go where ground ain't still. Rog sinks like stone."

Lark pulled out a bit of quartz from her pack, discreetly made it glow, and held it out to the dwarf. "Here."

He paused for a moment and looked at the rock suspiciously. "What is it?"

"Take. As long as have this in pocket, and believe will not sink, then will not sink."

He stared at the rock glowing in her hand. He looked up at her pretty, sincere face and believed her, sort of. She placed it on his open hand. "In my pocket," he repeated, making sure he had his instructions right.

"In pocket," she nodded.

He shouldered a mean-looking war hammer. "Come on, let's get this over with," he growled, pushing Ebastion out of the way and marching out the door.

"Masterfully done," Keltree whispered.

Lark smiled. "Use number twenty-three for simple magic aura," she replied.

A member of the Night Watch was assigned to escort them to the ship. They traveled swiftly as if trying to get there before the dwarf could change his mind. The ship was waiting at the dock, a single sailor at the rail watching for them. He called out as he saw their bobbing lights approach. **"Ho, there! You the island folk?"**

"Aye," called the watchman. **"And five adventurers to aid!"**

"Come aboard! We're ready to get underway!!"

The watchman stepped aside and gestured for them to proceed on board. "Farewell, and good winds," he said, bowing in their direction. He gazed after them until the gangplank had been drawn up behind them as if wishing all the while that it had been his lot to join them. Finally, he turned and wandered back to his regular beat.

They found themselves face-to-face with the ship's captain. "Head on down below, folks, ladies. The bosun'll show ye's yer bunks. Keep down and keep lights to a minimum. There're pirates lurkin' in the bay from the blockades, an' I don't want ta run th' risk." He gestured at the fiddle hanging from Lark's backpack. "And you, young lady, none of that playin', ye' hear? Sound travels farther'n light n' twice as clear. **Bosun***!*"

A small, withered man appeared at the summons, separating himself from the other sailors that had begun moving like ghosts across the surface of the ship, setting the sails. He nodded and gestured for the group to follow him down. The passage below was very narrow, with steep stairs, and opened into an equally narrow hallway. He gestured to a series of bunks at the rear of the ship and two hammocks that stretched across the passage. "You can use these," he said, his voice low and coarse from years of salt air. "If there is an attack, the ladies stay here. You," he pointed at the men, then at the staircase they had just come down, "go up the stairs here and help with the fight. We take on water, go that way," he pointed at the steps opposite. "There are small boats on the starboard side. Would suggest sleeping now. Ain't gonna be much time fer it later." With that, he pressed forward and disappeared up the back steps.

A half second after he left, Nightingale flew down, complaining about having to fly at night and how lucky she was that someone was already up in the kitchen.

Lark ignored him, tested the stuffing of the nearest bunk, and turned her nose up at the musty straw and rushes. She stowed her belongings out of the way and climbed into one of the hammocks. Nightingale found himself a niche in the rafters and tucked himself in.

"My lady," Keltree began, "would you not be more comfortable in one of the bunks?"

"No," she replied shortly. "But thank you. Hammock is nice for sea travel. Do not feel motion of boat so badly."

Rog changed direction the instant he heard that and hauled himself into the other hammock. He glared over at her as it swayed violently for a moment. Once the initial rocking slowed and it settled into a steadier counter-motion to the waves, he relaxed a little. He was still uncertain about this whole boat business, but he checked to make sure the rock was still in his pocket and slowly went to sleep, certainly not willing to show his unease in front of the others.

FOUR

Lark woke well before anyone else. She yawned and stretched. Climbing out of the hammock, she silently tip-toed her way past the filled bunks and down to a hatch she remembered passing when they had come on board. Slipping down the ladder, she found herself in the tiny kitchen/mess hall. The cook was just finishing clean-up after the crew's meal and getting ready his own.

Lark sauntered over and leaned on the narrow counter that separated the kitchen from the small eating area. "Good morning!" she chirped.

"Mornin'?" he laughed. "Try noon, sweets."

"Noon?" she asked, distraught. "Is later than ever sleep! Must be late nights at Magistrate's." She rubbed her eyes, her temples, then dragged her nails through her hair to pull it back.

"Must be," he muttered.

"Have coffee any-ways?"

"Sure. Allus have coffee." He began rummaging through his stores, looking for a cup. When he found one, he checked it against the lamp to see if it was clean, wiped it just to be sure, then filled it with the steaming brew. "'Ere ye go." He smiled at her.

She took a long draught from the mug and made a face. "Awugh! Nothing like foul coffee to wake body, *sesket*?" She managed a smile.

"You don't like me coffee?" he asked.

"Don't like coffee. But tell you something, it wakes body!" she chuckled. "Mmm, but something else smells good."

He moved over to the stove, turning over something she could not see in a pan. "M'lunch. Allus save out a bit fer meself. 'F'n I didn't, I'd never get nuthin'!" He thought a moment, glancing over his shoulder at her. "Care fer sum?"

"Mmm, is tempting. What is?"

He shrugged, "Jus' sum salt fish an' journey-cake. Nuthin' fancy."

"Maybe little." He brought the pan over and gestured for her to take what she wanted. She looked at it for a minute. She was starved, but she was aware that this was the man's meal he was offering her. She took a very small piece of each, about her usual supper portions.

"'Ey, that all yer gunna eat? Or ye jus' not partial to fish?"

She gave him her most disarming smile. "Have to watch figure," she said.

"Humph, sure lotsa men do 'nuffa that fer ya. Side's," he shrugged, leaning on the counter and stuffing his mouth with the journey-cake, "wimmins need more meat on 'um."

She laughed, "Maybe big belly good for babies, not good for dancing. Dancing make for flat, tight tummy," she said, giving hers a good thump.

She spent a few amiable minutes with the cook, chatting about nothing in particular. It was quickly clear that the man did not get much in the way of company. He spent the crew's eating time feeding them and survived himself on what he picked at while cooking or scrounged up after everyone had left. She got up after he had finished eating and gone back to the clean-up. "Should be getting back," she mused. "Thank you for breakfast. And company."

"Hold up," he said, reaching into a tin under the counter. He pulled out a biscuit and closed it back. "Jus' don't tell Captain," he grinned and went back to work, whistling.

When Keltree woke, Lark was lying in her hammock, sharing the last of her biscuit with her familiar. He sat up, careful not to hit his head on the upper bunk.

"Good morning," he crowed, stretching.

"Morning!" she answered. "Sleep well?"

"Well enough," he smiled. "You?"

"Sesha. So, what do you think are getting selves into?"

"Not certain, really," he mused, absently rubbing the back of his neck. "Could be any manner of things magical. It could be an artifact this Eridinne has uncovered which has begun to corrupt the populace. It could be a necromancer creating his own version of undead. Hells, it could even be a vampire, for all I know of such things. All I can be certain of is that this certainly sounds like a charm in effect."

The others began to stir, awakened by the conversation. There was a sharp thunk and an "OWW!" from behind Lark as Ebastion cracked his head against the upper bunk.

"Low bridge there, lanky," Rog chuckled.

"And how did you sleep, Rog?" Lark asked.

"Enough," he grumbled, not willing to admit he had slept better than he had expected to. Lark noticed that he did not get out of his hammock though.

At that moment, the ship lurched. Keltree grabbed hold of the overhead beam to keep his balance. Merrick and Ebastion were thrown back into the bunks, and Rue fell to the floor. Rog seized the edges of the hammock in a white-knuckled grip, all the color leached from his face.

The bosun appeared halfway down the stairs. "Yo, folks, we's in port and comin' about! Be plankin' up in half hour! Git'cher gear and git up here, but stay outta the way!"

Rog was the first one on deck. He fought his way out of the hammock, snatched up his stuff, and charged after the bosun. Of course, on reaching the upper deck and seeing all the rolling water surrounding the ship, he instantly regretted his decision. He seated himself on a huge coil of rope and locked his eyes on the approaching dock, blocking everything else out.

Below decks, Lark and the others gathered their things at a more leisurely pace before coming up on board just as they reached the dock. There was only one other ship in the small port, a small fishing vessel.

"Where did all the ships go?" Merrick asked. "There used to be quite a fishing fleet here."

"We'll find out shortly," Keltree told him.

Nightingale perched himself cheerily on Lark's shoulder as they disembarked. Rog was the first one on the dock and did not stop walking until he reached the dry land just beyond that. He pulled the rock out of his pocket and held it out to Lark. "Thanks," he said.

She shook her head. "No, you keep. I do not need."

He shrugged, "Whatever," and stuffed it back into his pocket. Lark caught a glimpse of Keltree smiling knowingly at her. She returned the grin.

Ebastion frowned at the foggy sky and the hazy position the sun held in it. "Did it take us all day to get here?" He turned to look back across the water, trying to see Portswain on the far shore. "Why the hells did it take so long?"

"Because the wind was not in our favor," Keltree explained. "And neither the tides." Ebastion frowned. "Ships are powered by the wind. If they need to sail into the wind they have to do it sideways, to tack. They go back and forth across the bay. It takes twice as long."

Ebastion nodded thoughtfully, accepting the explanation.

They turned to looked about the deserted wharf, at the empty fisheries and barreling piers and warehouses. Beyond the docks, the town rose haphazardly through a series of steppes, some clusters of houses and other buildings situated higher up the mountain than others, half-disappearing in the mist and haze that enveloped the peak.

"So where to?" Rue asked.

Merrick pointed westward to the mountain rising visibly above the stepped town. "That way is the bluff and the caves."

Ebastion held up a finger. "All well and good, my friends, but... I would like to stop and get some information first. It would behoove us to gather the local gossip. At such a place as...." he glanced around. "Ah! This conveniently located tavern!" he gestured to a building just to the left with a dingy sign swinging in the breeze that read 'The Dirty Griffin'.

They looked at each other.

Keltree shrugged. "Sounds like a good idea to me. And none of us have eaten yet."

Lark held her silence. Nightingale chirruped an energetic note at the mention of food. "Oh, you always hungry!" she laughed as they turned towards the tavern.

It was early yet. They did not expect to find a horde of people inside, but none of them expected what they did find: nobody. There were no customers at all. The place was as deserted as the wharf.

Merrick looked around in shock and touched a sticky place on the bar with disbelief. "Things are worse," he breathed. "Jinga would never let anything dry on his bar. He spent hours a day polishing it. He must have fallen to the 'illness'. I tell you, even sick, that man... This is not normal."

Rue set her bag on a table and reached into it, handing each person a bottle.

"What is this?" Ebastion asked, holding it up to the light.

"Holy water," she answered. "I was given a small supply before they ushered me off with the Night Watch. I can make more if I have to, but it takes time we may not have. So, use this sparingly and only when you think it will do any good."

She shouldered her pack and headed outside again.

The afternoon was heavily overcast, but with no rain or threat of rain, just the heavy, oppressive, gray mass of clouds. The streets were deserted: not even a single watchman on patrol. They walked across the town unchallenged.

"Do not undead have problem with daylight?" Lark asked as they passed into what was obviously the road to the higher steppes.

Keltree looked up at the sky. "Usually," he mused. "But with this overcast, my lady, I do not know."

"Just as well," she sighed. "Place is dead. Where search first?"

"Eridinne's may be a good start," Merrick suggested. "I will take you there. Perhaps there will be notes or a journal if we are lucky. Letters... an explanation..."

He led them upward towards the high steppes and the mountain.

The way grew misty, and the fog drifted downward to fill the town. Visibility was low, casting an eerie glow on everything. The higher they went up the streets, the heavier the blanket became. The buildings they passed grew fewer, set further back from the road as the size of the house and wealth of the occupant grew.

"We must be getting close," Keltree commented. "Most assuredly, there is something up this way he does not wish us to see. Be careful and stay close."

They walked closer together, blades at the ready. Figures and images spun through the cold fog just out of clear view or reach, tricks of light and shadow amid the swirling mist. More than once, one of the men swung at something they thought they saw, and more than once it turned out to be a tree or a lamppost or nothing at all. The road sloped steadily upwards. Even Nightingale had begun to feel the oppression and clung tightly to Lark's shoulder.

At last, the yellowed corner of a house loomed in the fog to their right. "I think this is it," Merrick whispered. "I'm pretty sure this is Eridinne's."

Keltree sized up what he could see of the house. "Mighty big for a woman alone," he mused.

"She inherited it a couple of years ago. How she keeps it up, I don't know."

They cautiously spread out, examining the outside of the residence, looking for signs of life within.

"Now remember, we want answers from her," Rue warned, looking pointedly at Ebastion and Rog. "So don't attack her out of hand, and for the Maiden's sake, don't kill her!"

"Can we at least beat 'er senseless?" Rog grumbled.

Rue sighed, "Only if she attacks you!"

Lark leaned up against a rear wall, peering into the window. It looked into a sitting room, with papers and books and scrolls covering every available surface. Inside were two people, a pale, russet woman and a man who sat in a large, comfortable chair. All she could see of him was that he had long, dark brown hair and very long fingers. They were speaking to each other, and Lark focused on the woman's lips to read what she was saying.

"And then I shall be Queen here, yes?"

There was a moment as she listened to his reply.

"Oh, no," she continued. "I would not want more. I shall be content with my little island ...so long as you are not too far away." She held out her hands to him, drawing him from the chair into her embrace. Lark thought it odd that she did not kiss him but, instead, tilted her head to nestle it against his shoulder. He turned her into the light of the pale lamp, and Lark stared in fascination as he bared her long white neck and sank a kiss there.

Just as she was going to turn and whisper to the others, his eyes flicked up to meet hers, and she was unable to look away. Indeed, they were incredibly handsome eyes set in the most compellingly expressive face. He had to be the most attractive man she had ever seen, and she found she could not resist the minute gesture of invitation he made to her as he lifted his head and smiled with his red lips.

Without another thought, Lark dropped her patchwork bag and walked around to the nearest door. Nightingale, confused by her behavior, refused to follow and settled on the windowsill watching inside.

Rue saw the bird and the abandoned bag and picked it up. Looking around for Lark, she peered in the window. Everyone heard the door open and close.

The front door was separated from the sitting room by a very short hallway. Lark paused at the open door, hesitating. Once again, the man was seated in the chair, waiting for her, his long brown hair curling over one shoulder. The woman stood behind him, leaning on the back with her arms folded, but Lark did not acknowledge her. The man consumed her thoughts and attention.

He beckoned. "Come, come, my dear. We must wait for your friends."

She came readily, gliding across the floor to sit at his feet.

He reached out, caressing her hair, tracing one delicate eyebrow with a long ivory finger. The smell of him was intoxicating. "Quite the exotic, isn't she?" he asked the woman behind him.

She purred. "Mmmm, yes. Would you like to keep her, my lord? As a pet? Or a bride, perhaps?"

"Perhaps," he mused thoughtfully, considering it. "But her friends are here. Perhaps we should deal with them first?"

Keltree filled the doorway and took in the occupants of the room and the patiently smiling man waiting with steepled fingers. Finally, he stepped aside, allowing the others entry.

The man's smile broadened. "I was wondering when you would come. Where is your lovely sister, young man? Julian has been asking for her."

Merrick snarled something unintelligible and tried to lunge for him, but Keltree held him back.

"We have come from the mainland," he intoned. "And I am afraid we are going to have to ask you to leave."

"Why should I? I was invited, after all."

"The witch does not speak for the whole town!" Merrick shouted, straining against Keltree's arm. Rue pulled him back.

"Be that as it may," Keltree continued, "I am afraid we are going to have to ask you to release the unnatural hold you have on this town."

"And I am equally afraid that I cannot do that. I need them, you see." He reached up and patted Eridinne's hand fondly. "And I have a promise to keep."

"Then we will have to use force. I was hoping to avoid...."

"Oh really?" the man laughed. "I am so sorry, but I believe the army of Portswain is... otherwise occupied at the moment," he said with a knowing gleam in his dark eyes.

"And what might you know a' that?" Rog growled.

"Plenty. Enough," he shrugged. "But none of that matters, does it, my dear?" he purred, stroking Lark's hair tenderly with a taloned hand. "My exotic flower."

"Lark, come over here, please," Keltree said firmly.

She glanced over her shoulder at him, her eyes slightly glassy and dreamy. She laid her head on the man's knee, watching Keltree and the others suspiciously.

Rue put two and two together with what little she knew of vampires and the undead. She sidled further out of his view, behind the men, and closed her eyes. She prayed silently, making minute motions with her hands, begging her goddess to uncloud Lark's mind and remove the spell that had obviously been placed on her.

"You hear that, my beautiful? He wants to take you away from me. You do not want that, now, do you?"

He reached out to touch her cheek tenderly.

Rue's prayer began to take effect.

For a moment, Lark felt a driving need for that approaching caress, that loving reassurance. The next second, it felt as if someone had hit her in the stomach with a battering ram. She felt something cold and evil nearing her face and focused suddenly on the pale, twisted talon coming towards her and threw herself backward. She scrambled quickly to her feet and darted behind Keltree.

The man sat there, startled for a moment by her unexpected reaction. Then he leaned back in the chair, laughing ironically. "Ah," he sighed, "that is one. But she will be mine again soon enough. You, too, priestess," he purred. "As for the rest of you, I think I shall give you to Eridinne once you are docile enough. For cattle."

Rog snorted rudely at the suggestion.

Hiding behind the tall human, with Rue checking her over briefly, Lark began piecing things together on her own. Namely, the embrace she had witnessed through the window. That, coupled with the thin line of blood on Eridinne's throat, his red lips, the fog, the strange plague-like affliction, and the faint reek of death that now filled the room, all spoke of a creature her Gruma once told of around the family campfire: the vampire.

"I think you will find us more than up to the task of removing you, Mister....?" Keltree questioned, trying to buy a moment's time to think how best to make a successful attack. The man was obviously powerful.

"My lord will do nicely," he responded.

"Eat pig poop, pasty face," Rog snarled, tightening his grip on his weapon as he noticed Lark reaching into Keltree's backpack for something. He quickly figured out what she was reaching for and waited.

Keltree felt the hands in his pack and just kept talking, trusting Rue to do whatever it was priests did against the unholy. "And just what vested interest have *you* in this, Miss?" he asked Eridinne.

"A crown," she purred, giving him a hungry, appraising look even as she reached down to rest her hand on the vampire's shoulder. "I still have no consort. Care to volunteer, handsome?"

"No, thank you. I prefer more even relationships...."

A bottle sailed over Keltree's head. He had just enough time to register it as one of the holy waters before it exploded against Eridinne's temple, showering both of them with a spray of fluid. Steam rose from the man's clothes and face where the water struck. He screamed with rage and pain, Eridinne more from sudden fright.

Everything happened at once. The men leaped for the vampire, weapons sailing violently downward. Rue began chanting, channeling energy into her body and focusing it through her medallion of faith. The vampire seized Eridinne's hand, and the pair of them vanished into thin air. The weapons struck the leather upholstery uselessly.

Lark spun, pulling her scimitar, fully expecting the pair to materialize behind them, but no one was there. No one appeared. After a few minutes, it was confirmed that they were indeed gone, perhaps to his cavern retreat, and they relaxed a fraction.

Rue passed Lark her belongings, and they began to sift through the mountains of papers in the room, looking for anything incriminating.

Rog plopped himself into the recently vacated chair and began cleaning his fingernails with a knife.

"Aren't you going to help?" Ebastion asked him.

"Nope," he replied without looking up.

"Why not?" Merrick asked.

"Cain't read," he replied. "Not what *you* call writin', anyhow." He saw a book on the arm-table he was using for a footstool and grabbed it. "*This,*" he said, holding it up. "*This* is writin'." He grabbed a piece of paper that lay half under it, glanced over it, and held it up, too. "This *ain't*. This is chicken scratch!" He folded the paper neatly and sailed it into Ebastion's face. He then settled back and flipped through the book.

Ebastion snatched the paper out of the air and started to throw it aside, intending some violence to the dwarf, but stopped to pull a feather out of his mouth. He looked down at the parchment in his fist. There were hundreds of little folds and other fragments of down, telltale signs of delivery via a messenger bird. He unwadded it and read it aloud.

"To our dearest ally and faithful friend, E.R."

Everyone, even Rog, stopped to listen.

"Go on," Rue prompted when he failed to continue immediately.

"We are in wholehearted agreement on the matter of the City of Portswain and feel that it could be put to far better use in our expert hands. Your aid and that of your island ally will indeed go far towards our eventual conquest of the port city, and we agree to grant you total dominance over that small province in exchange for freeing our ships for more important things than blockade duty. To this end, we will be sending you four catapults by the end of the week to be mounted on the east-west edges of the island to prevent the entrance or exit of ships from the Portswain harbor, effectively cutting them off from the sea. Again, you have our heartfelt congratulations on your little coup, as most such are rarely as complete and total as yours. Looking forward to crowning you myself at the completion of this minor inconvenience. Sincerely, R.N."

"Oh, my Goddess!" Rue gasped, covering her gaping mouth in horror and crossing her fingers.

"Jackpot!" Rog grunted.

"I'll say," Keltree said, coming around to collect the letter from Ebastion and tucking it safely into his shirt.

"No, no, no, no, not that stupid thing," Rog growled. "This here!" he waved the book. "It's about summonin' things... undead things... and the control thereof."

"I thought you could not read," Merrick asked, glancing at the gold-lettered spine of the book. "I most certainly can't read that."

"That's because it's in an ancient script that we dwarves still use as a common tongue, you ninny!" He snatched the book back. "Some of the more magical texts were written in Runic, and this here's one of 'em. It says here all we need to know about our charmin' undead friend."

"How can be sure?" Lark asked.

He smiled at her. "Because dear Lady," he held the book up so she could see the pages inside, pointing to a section, "she was so kind as to dog-ear and underline."

She leaned on the arm of the chair behind him, reading over his shoulder. She could not read it as well as he could, but she recognized some of the characters as the runes from which her true magic sprang. He skimmed through it quickly, then tucked the long leather strip back into place on the page and popped it into his pack. He scrambled out of the chair.

"Well, aren't you going to tell us what it says?" Ebastion snapped.

Rog sighed and turned. "It says that a priest, which would be you, darlin'," he said, giving Rue a gentle poke in the ribs, eliciting a startled giggle from her, "can hold him to his place with the power of faith and a single word: His name. Which, conveniently, is contained herein," he added, patting his pack, "as the witch needed his name to summon him. Enablin' us to destroy him. But we gotta find him first. Shall we go?" he asked with a sweeping, bowed gesture towards the door.

They filed out, still clinging tightly to weapons and ready now for anything.

The fog had gotten heavier since they had been inside, and if it had not been for the mystic link between Lark and the mockingbird, Nightingale would never have made it back to her shoulder. As it was, he scrambled in under the shelter of her hair and tucked himself up to keep out the growing chill.

FIVE

Merrick guided them steadily upward, and no one argued that the most likely place of catching the vampire was up in the caves where he originally resided.

The fog spun in and around them, making it hard to see one another, even from only a few feet away. Lark heard a whisper echoing out of the mist. It was very faint, so faint she did not notice it at first, but it grew steadily as the fog thickened. The voices reminded her of the feathers of barn swallows in the rafters or owls winging through the night. She heard a definite direction to one of them, as if it were right behind her. The instant she turned to look, she lost sight of the others.

She stilled the sudden rise of panic and concentrated, trusting her innate sense of direction to tell her which way they had been going. It did not occur to her to call out. She was still on the road, she was convinced of that, and it was only a matter of finding its edges to tell her which way it ran. She walked forward in the direction she was suddenly certain was correct.

Within moments, a large structure loomed ahead of her, a barn with a wide-open door. She saw a flicker of movement within, a flash of dull purple which might have been Rue's robes. The voices grew louder as she approached.

She entered the barn, calling softly, "Rue? Keltree? ...Rog?" There was no answer. None of the others were there. The barn was empty save for a pale, flickering light at the back of a stall near the rear of the building.

She cautiously approached, hearing the voices clearly now in her head, whispering seductive phrases and meaningless endearments. Stopping fifteen feet from the stall door, she stared into the well-shadowed light and tried desperately to see who it was or what. She made out a man's figure and slowly realized that the light was not a light, but his eyes, glowing softly in the darkness, beckoning to her. She felt the draw like a physical chain, trying to pull her into the stall, into the deathly embrace, and balked.

Nightingale shrilled a warning, seconds too late, flying up into the rafters as hands grabbed Lark from behind. One thick, callused palm covered her nose and mouth, preventing her from screaming or breathing. The other came around her waist and lifted her off the ground, physically carrying her closer towards the stall and the man that awaited her within. She dropped her bag and sword and fought back, kicking and struggling desperately, but the man was incredibly strong, and his grip was beyond her ability to break. As he neared the stall door, she kicked against the framework, forcing her captor to stagger back to regain his balance, which was not easily maintained while holding on to her writhing body.

Nightingale shrieked at the top of his tiny lungs, mangling the wolf whistle signal until it was barely recognizable, and deliberately set the roosting pigeons flying out of the barn in a panic.

Lark began to suffocate. Her lungs were burning even as she tried to catch the hand with her teeth to make him let go, but he expected that and pressed harder against her face, partially cupping her chin to keep her jaw tightly closed. Her head began to spin as the glowing eyes came closer and closer.

Suddenly, he let go of her, and she fell, reeling forward into the stall at the vampire's feet. She looked up at him, grinning through the burn scars on his face that were slowly fading even as she watched. She scrambled back, seized a nearby pitchfork, and hurled it at him. It struck the back of the stall, shattering a dimly lit lamp hanging there, but he was already gone. The straw ignited where the lamp fell and blazed up, spreading quickly. Laughter filled the air, cold and deep, coming from nowhere and everywhere at once.

She turned and saw the man who had grabbed her lying unconscious on the floor at Keltree's feet. Ebastion and Merrick were right behind him, with Rog and Rue just coming through the door. She could only stare, gasping for breath.

Suddenly, Keltree's eyes widened, and he lunged for her. She flinched just as his body impacted with hers, throwing both of them into a nearby haystack just as a jet of flame spewed out of the stall where Lark had just been standing. The clothes of the man lying on the floor caught fire, and he was quickly crisped to a cinder as a wall of flame separated the pair from the others, blocking off the door. The laughing continued, fading out slowly.

"*Lark! Keltree!*" shouted Ebastion and Rog over the flames.

Rue screamed as a beam fell, collapsing the hayloft over the stalls.

"We're all right! Get out!! We'll make a back door!!" Keltree shouted, pulling Lark to her feet and hauling her toward the back of the barn, praying fervently for a second exit.

Rog hesitated, unwilling to leave them at the mercy of the flames. Ebastion snatched up the bright, patchwork bag lying on the floor near the fire but not burning yet, and grabbed Rog's sleeve, trying to keep him from doing something heroically stupid like charging through. "He'll get them out!!" he yelled over the roar of the fire and the screaming of the wood.

Rog hesitated another moment, then reached into the edge of the firewall and snatched out the scimitar she had dropped. It was hot, but he maintained his grip on it as he followed the human out of the barn.

Keltree and Lark found themselves against a solid wall under the overhang of the loft. There was no other obvious exit, and part of the upper floor collapsed behind them, trapping them there as if by design. He glanced up at the flames dancing across the wood above their heads, eating its way through, then looked down at her. "I am sorry, girl. Truly."

In her mind, she heard the whispering beginning again. 'Come to me, and I will save you. Give in to me, and the fire will not touch you..."

"NO!" she snarled, turned to the wall, desperate and determined enough to try something she had never tried before. Summoning up the magic within her and chanting softly to herself, she drew the rune of opening on the face of the wall. She had always used it to lock things, to seal her door to prevent theft. She had never reversed it before, not to open something where there was no opening. It flared to life on the ancient surface, shrinking the boards, causing them to groan and pop.

The whispering became louder, unintelligible, fierce, and angry. The fire burned madly at the loft supports, behaving like a living thing trying to stop them before they could escape. He saw the change in the wall's integrity and threw his weight against it, battering it with his shoulder. She concentrated, despite the whispering attempt to disrupt her thoughts. She pulled at the wood, willing the boards to separate and collapse. With a final, desperate kick, the wall caved in, and he grabbed her, pulling her through just as the rest of the loft fell and forced a wave of heat and flames out through the narrow opening.

Her skirt caught fire, and he quickly helped her to beat it out with his gloved hands. He then pulled her further away from the barn as it groaned and moaned. She turned, watched in horror as it sank, still ablaze, into itself.

"Nightingale!" she choked, trying desperately to sense her familiar.

A voice came out of the fog nearby. "See, I told you they got out all right!" Rue called over her shoulder as she appeared within view. Nightingale flew from her shoulder to Lark's, chattering his frantic concern.

She stroked the dull gray and white breast to calm him, slowly succeeding. The others materialized quickly out of the smoke and mist like rising ghosts. Keltree got to his feet and pulled Lark to hers.

"Are you both physically sound?" Rue asked, giving them a quick appraisal.

"Yes." He looked at Lark to confirm his statement even as he made it. "Other than a little too much smoke in the lungs, and a bit of singeing, I think we are well enough."

"Good."

Ebastion handed Lark her bag. She took it with a sigh. "Is becoming habit." She checked its contents briefly, satisfied herself that the violin had not suffered too much damage. She looked up as Rog cleared his throat. He held her scimitar out to her by its hilt, his hand wrapped in a strip of linen and smelled oddly of herbal ointments. "Thank you," she said, taking the weapon. "What... you do?" she asked, pointing hesitantly at the bandage.

Rog shrugged. "Weapon was hotter'n I expected. 't's all right," he drawled and turned away, uncomfortable. "Shall we stay closer together now?"

Lark rose, made sure her pack was secure on her back, and hefted the scimitar. "Am ready to end this."

Wordlessly, they filed towards the mountain top, each one making certain to keep at least one other person within arm's reach at all times. Noises came to them out of the fog as they left the town's cobbled streets for what seemed little more than a goat's path. Noises that came near and darted away, teasing, taunting. Shadows loomed on all sides, but no one turned to chase them. The way grew steadily steeper.

It came as quite a surprise when one of those shadows suddenly attacked. It was a villager, a man in a dirty sheepskin vest and trousers, who lunged at Rue. Ebastion, closest to the priestess, punched the man and sent him sprawling. He scrambled to his feet, lurching for another attack, but Merrick grabbed a fist full of vest and hurled him back down the path. The sound of his rapid and unchecked descent drifted up to them through the fog, muffled. They pressed on.

Nothing else attacked.

The ground leveled off suddenly, turning to soft grass instead of rough gravel and dirt. The fog cleared partly, swirling around them to form a ring about twenty feet wide. It was a mossy area, with only the shadows of a few trees just at the edge of their view and the ground obscured by a low roll of fog ankle-deep. From somewhere very nearby came the sound of crashing waves far below.

"The bluff," Merrick whispered to Keltree. "A lover's place."

"Perfect meeting grounds, would you not say?" The vampire seemed to materialize out of the edge of the fog on the far side of the clearing. He smiled and took a deep breath. "A bit singed, are we, my dear?" He laughed, rumbling the noise deep in his throat, a feral sound.

A chill ran up the back of Lark's neck. Reaching into her pouch, she pulled a bit of sand out, flinging it in a broad arch towards him, casting as she did. The lights sprang from her hand but were somehow dimmed by the muted light, their colors weak. He stood there, completely unaffected. She quickly stepped out of his view, behind the safety of the three larger men. The vampire laughed again.

"Afraid, my dear? And well you should be. But they will not protect you, not for long. Then we shall see what can be done with you and your lovely friend."

Keltree stepped forward, sword in hand.

"Ah-ah!" the vampire chided suddenly. "Beware, my young friend. There is a cliff... around here somewhere...." his laughter faded in, surrounding them in the small area.

Rog grabbed Rue's sleeve and pulled her down to his level, whispering a single word into her ear. "Azeyzath."

Rue nodded minutely, straightening up. She strode to the front of the small group, and, confused, the men let her by but closed in behind her, forming a tight semi-ring. Confident, she held her medallion of faith tightly in her left hand, an iron circle with the symbol of a right hand with crossed fingers. Meeting the man, eye for eye, she raised her own right hand, slim fingers crossed, the others folded down, and began to chant. A blue glow sprang to life in her left hand, flowing from the medallion to her hand to her arm, suffusing itself through her body, culminating in a nimbus around her upraised fingers.

The vampire laughed. "And what shall you do with that? Have your goddess strike me dead? I am already dead, and that will do you noOO!!" he bellowed suddenly, as the word 'Azeyzath' was embedded in the prayer.

The fighters closed. Keltree swung his sword in a mighty arch with a blow that might have cleaved the arm off a mortal man, but this was not a mortal man, and the blow came nowhere near him. Instead, the vampire seemed to move faster than Keltree and, seizing his wrist in one hand, broke it and rammed his other into his stomach. Keltree folded, his blood covering the vampire's stiff, taloned fingers. Ebastion lunged for his back, but his blow rolled off, and he fell through the ring of the mist and disappeared without a sound.

The vampire turned to face Merrick, but knowing he was not the best of fighters, he had wisely taken a step back. Rog circled him like a hungry wolf, waiting for an opening or a mistake. Rue's prayer magic may be preventing the vampire from using his powers, but he was far from helpless.

Lark remembered the holy water and the burn marks that had been on his face in the barn. They were not there now, but perhaps... She set her pack on the grass beside her and opened it up, rummaging desperately for the bottle. It was tangled in the webbing of her silk net, giving her a suddenly brilliant idea. She pulled it all out, wadding the net tightly up in one hand, and, pulling the cork with her teeth, poured the water onto it with her other. Once it was good and soaked, she stood, spreading it open, preparing it to throw. She passed the chanting priestess and approached the combat. Ebastion had found his way back into the ring, badly cut up but circling with the other two.

"Move," she hissed.

Merrick looked down, saw the net in her hand and the concentration in her eye, and obliged.

The vampire pointed with bloody talons. "You think to conquer me with a bit of silk webbing?" he scoffed. "It will not help you now, but it might prove an interesting diversion for us later," he suggested, baiting her, fending off the others at the same time. "Come on, come close enough to dance properly," he purred, making a feint for her, then lunged for Rue.

Lark threw the net.

He screamed. The net began to sizzle and burn, sending up steam and smoke from his body. He fought to get it off, tangling himself further. As Rog and the others leapt in to finish him, an arch of light leaped from Rue's crossed fingers into his twisted body.

Writhing, screaming with rage and pain, he looked into Lark's eyes, reached towards her with one hand that had slipped through the holes of the net, hatred glowing in his eyes. Rog's hammer came up, smashing into his jaw just as Ebastion struck the back of his neck with his sword. The head would have gone flying but for the net. In a moment, there was nothing but an outline of him in damp ashes amid his clothes. Lark just stared at the inert form, shaking. Nightingale gently butted his head against her cheek, nudging her, and gave a small, hopeless chirp. Rog touched her hand with as much tenderness and gentleness as he knew how.

A scream filled the air as the fog slowly thinned. Rue lowered her arms, coming out of the prayer trance, only now becoming aware that the crisis was over and the enemy was dead. She never saw Eridinne streak out of the mist, a dagger raised, reaching for her unprotected back.

Ebastion spun, swinging his sword in an arch that barely missed Rue and cleaved the woman's head clean from her body. It flew back down the pathway she had just come, rolling and bouncing until the hair became entangled in the brush and bramble alongside. The body collapsed onto Rue, snapping her out of her stupor completely. She jumped back, now covered in the spray of blood.

Lark looked down at Rog, still not really seeing him. Just beyond him, she saw a secondary form lying still on the grass. She moved past the dwarf to the figure, falling to her knees beside it. She touched his neck, felt the faintly throbbing pulse of life there, and took up his cold hand. "Rue," she managed. "Rue...!"

The priestess hurried over, kneeling on the other side of Keltree, began to check him over to assess the damage. "I... I do not know if I can help him," she whispered.

Lark looked fiercely across at her. "You healed arm in warehouse, and knot on head. Can heal this!"

"No," Rue protested, shaking her head. "Not this. There is too much blood... I ...I do not have the strength left in me."

Lark grabbed her hand, forcing the woman to look her in the eye. "Thought you called upon your goddess for power? What, has she abandoned you now Keltree need her most?! Or is life not precious to her?!"

Rue tried to snatch her hand away but could not break Lark's grip. "I still have to channel the power, and my body... is too weak to focus it!"

Lark sighed. "Is like magic that way. I understand. But *have* to try!" she insisted. "Will die unless you close wound."

"I... I will try. But no promises."

Lark let go of her hand. "Is not you who have promises to keep."

Rue took out a small knife and cut his shirt away from the wound. Blood still flowed freely from the five deep holes in his belly. She sat back on her heels and concentrated, holding her medallion in one hand so tightly that it left an imprint on her palm. Her other hand, she placed upon the wound, a finger to each. The blue fire was long in coming and thin, weak.

Lark stared down at his still form, at the shallow breathing and the still bubbling fountains of blood. She gripped his hand, willing the pale fire illuminating Rue's hand to fill him and heal the wound. Suddenly, she saw a tracing of blue glowing on his stomach, a blazing rune tracing itself above the wound and on the back of Rue's hand. It was the same rune she used to lock her doors, the rune of closing.

On Keltree's forehead, another rune appeared, the mark of peace and healing and life. As she stared wide-eyed at this mysterious occurrence, the light faded and dissolved into him. But the marks remained, traced there in blood. She noticed with surprise that her own hand was covered in it, the glow just now fading from her fingers; that it had been her hand that had made those marks and invoked the power that helped Rue seal the wound and stop the flow of life. As she sat in shock, Rue collapsed into a dead faint.

Ebastion bent, laid a hand against Rue's cheek. "She's all right," he whispered.

"Exhausted, prob'ly," Rog muttered.

"You're hurting me," Keltree rasped in a very hoarse voice.

Lark looked down, touched his face gently. "All is right now. Will live," she smiled.

"Yes, but my hand. You are hurting me."

"OH!" she exclaimed, letting go. He winced as his hand struck the ground. "Sorry!" He tried to smile at her, but it was just too much effort.

Rue moaned and sat up with a little help from Ebastion. "What?" she muttered, holding her head. Keltree turned slowly to look at her and closed his eyes again. "He's...!??"

"He'll live," Rog snapped. "Thanks to the two of ya, whatever ya did. But I think that arm is broken," he pointed.

Rue held out her hand. "Let me see it."

Lark gently lifted the limb, passing it across his body to Rue, trying not to jostle it too much. Rue unlaced his bracer and probed the wrist and forearm tenderly. She nodded. "Wrist. There is no way that I can set or heal it, not now. Lark, hold his hand out as straight as you can," she instructed, passing it back to her. She gave instructions to Rog on splinting the wrist and immobilizing it across his chest. She shakily got to her feet. "We need to find some way to carry him back to the ship."

Ebastion caught her as she started to collapse again. "Easy there. Don't want to have to carry you back as well." He sat her down with her back to a tree, insisting she rest until they were ready to leave. He handed her a small pouch. "Here," he said. "Look after these for now. We can look at them and divide them later."

"What is this?" she asked.

He shrugged, "Loot."

She just shook her head and smiled at him, opening the bag and fingering the contents.

The fog had begun to lift, rolling back up the mountain from the village below. Not far to the left of them, the fading mist exposed the cliff, and they watched a glorious sunset out over the open sea. The vampire's few remains were gathered in a pouch, which Lark then opened and cast to the wind from the cliffs' edge.

She stood for a long time watching as the ashes drifted and scattered in the drafts.

She activated her light pendant, giving them enough to see by in the encroaching night. They had collected Eridinne's head and set it beside her body, covering that with the remains of the vampire's clothes. It was not long before someone appeared at the head of the path, having seen the light and followed it.

"Merrick," called the voice.

Merrick looked up to see the man in the sheepskin vest staggering into the light. "Julian!" he shouted but remained wary, not rushing up to meet him.

The man had numerous cuts and bruises but otherwise looked all right. "Not... exactly fair of you to push me down the hill like that," he chuckled, leaning back against a nearby rock. "That hurt!"

"You are yourself?!" he exclaimed, not yet ready to believe it.

"I'm talkin' to ya, aren't I?"

"The spell is more than likely broken," Rue called from her resting place. "Ebastion, check his eyes."

Julian spread his hands in surrender as Ebastion, still holding tight to his sword, cautiously tilted his head and peered into his eyes. "What am I looking for?"

"Are they glassy?"

"Bloodshot, but no, not glassy."

"Then he is well again. Put your weapon away."

Ebastion stepped back, giving him room, but still did not put down his sword.

"What happened here?" Julian asked, crossing to his friend.

"We killed the vampire," Merrick snarled sarcastically. He took a playful punch at the man's arm. "And you deserved a rolling down the hill for attacking a holy woman!"

"Holy woman? Vampire? What in the deep are you talking about?"

Merrick merely gestured to the covered body. "Listen," he added. "See if you can get us something to carry our injured on. One of these brave souls was nearly killed in the fight, and we need to get him back to Portswain soon."

"I'll be right back," he said and quickly disappeared down a side path.

"Where's he goin'?" Rog grunted, still wrapping Keltree's arm with the bandages Rue had given him.

"He is the local goatherd. He lives but a little ways off."

"And was not first to fall 'ill'?" Lark asked.

He shook his head. "This mountain is bigger than it looks, miss. He was probably off tending his goats, and when he is, he is a hard man to find. Probably did not even know there was an illness in town."

Lark and Rog had finished binding Keltree's wrist and secured it across his chest to prevent any jostling by the time Julian returned. He carried on his back a narrow birch frame with a pair of hides lashed to it to form a rough cot. "It don't look like much, I know," he apologized when Lark gave a disparaging look at it. "But it has served me well for the last ten years. I think it will just do the trick."

Between Ebastion and Julian, they lifted Keltree onto the cot. He only groaned twice as they shifted him into place, trying to make him as comfortable as they could. His feet hung off the end considerably.

"Long fella, ain't he?" Julian muttered. "Oh well, don't matter none. This'll get him down to the docks."

Lark went to gather up her pack, but Rog took it from her, slinging it on his own back next to his. "I'll get this. You get her," he grunted, gesturing to Rue, and began leading the way down the path without another word.

"Wait," she called. "If are going first, at least carry light," she said, taking her pendant from her neck and placing it around his.

He smirked up at her before flipping the chain to hang the pendant down his back to give them light enough to follow and started walking.

Keltree's pack was placed at the foot of the stretcher, on his legs, and Julian and Ebastion carried the cot. Merrick shouldered the remaining packs and followed. Lark, with Rue leaning on her for support, brought up the rear, with Nightingale fussing nearly continuously about the rough ride.

SIX

By the time they had arrived in the village, most of the inhabitants were up and about, milling in the doorways of their houses in confusion. When the small parade came down from the mountain, a hail of questions assailed them. A crowd quickly gathered, blocking their way to the docks.

Merrick tried to calm the people and answer the questions the best he could. He was rescued by the appearance of the village headman, or what passed for public authority on the small island. He took a moment to explain everything that had taken place or been discovered that night. When he finished, the man stood silent. The crowd gathered tightly about, waiting to hear what he would have to say, whether or not the wild story would be believed.

He merely nodded, then turned to address the crowd. "Go home, go back to bed. The crisis is over. The plague is over. Go home. We will figure things out in the morning." He turned to the group, extending his hand to each of them in turn. "My gratitude to you knows no depths, and our freedom knows no price. I will send a letter myself to Portswain proclaiming all you have done for us tonight and for your selfless sacrifice. Merrick, go get your sister or tend her as needed. Your property will be looked after in your absence."

Merrick nodded. "Eridinne...." he began.

The man cut him off. "We will take care of the witch's body. Worry not. Go, take care of your wounded." With that, he physically ushered off the lingering onlookers, allowing the party to finally make their slow way down to the docks where the ship waited at anchor.

Julian helped them to carry Keltree down to the sleeping quarters and move him onto a bunk. He gathered his cot up and paused long enough to say his goodbyes. "Tell your sister I'm sorry," he told Merrick. "I'll be waiting for her on the bluff like I promised. Every night 'til she comes."

"You could be waiting a while," he warned, uncertain if his sister would be well enough, mentally, to come home too soon.

He shrugged, grinning broadly. "I'm stubborn that way," he said and left.

Lark stowed her belongings in the sling above her hammock and went back up on the deck. She shifted the shawl from her hips to her shoulders and stood well out of the sailors' way at the bow. She gazed at the host of stars that seemed to touch the very water and, far off in the distance, the pinprick lights of Portswain. The small vessel lurched as the wind took the sails.

She remained on deck for at least an hour, leaning on the rail, watching the tiny flashes in the dark that might have been fish jumping in the water. It was very calming, soothing. She loved it, but she did not believe she could live her life at sea. It was too confining. The moon had already risen by the time she went back down to the bunks.

There were few sailors asleep here. Most of them she had passed on the decks, up in the rigging, tending to the business of sailing at night against the wind. Her pendant lay in the folds of her pack, light leaking out of it. She smiled. Rog had given it back but had not known how to turn it off. She noticed in passing that his hammock was empty. In fact, none of them were there but for Rue, sound asleep in her upper bunk, and Keltree.

She reached into her pack to turn off the pendant.

"Lark?" Keltree whispered, his voice rougher than she was used to it being. She knelt quickly beside him, forgetting her pendant altogether. He took her hand in his good one, though his grip was weak. "The others are below, in the galley. Where have you been?" he asked.

"Watching sea," she whispered. She brushed damp locks of hair back from his face. "How feel?"

"Weak. Hot. But alive, thanks to you, my dark angel."

"Was Rue what healed you..." she protested.

"No. The others told me what you did. You did something... gave her the strength to push herself beyond her endurance. But that is not what I wished to speak with you about."

"Should not be speaking at all," she chided. "Should rest." Up in the corner beam, Nightingale peeped a quiet agreement, re-tucking his head under his wing. "See, he agrees... for once."

"Nevertheless, I will say my piece. We found some things. While you were on deck, we divided them. Yes, there will be a reward upon our return, perhaps of monetary significance, but... this is over and above that. Here." He put a ring in her hand. Where he had produced it from, she could only guess. One moment she was holding his empty hand and the next, the ring was in hers. She turned it in her palm, leaning back to look at it in the faint gleam of her light. It seemed to be a plain gold band set with a black cabochon opal. "It matches your eyes," he whispered. "I thought you should get it."

"Thank you," she whispered. "Have weakness for opals," she admitted, beginning to feel kind of warm inside as she slipped the ring on an empty finger and admired it in the faint light. It seemed to gleam with a life of its own.

"This, however, is from me," he continued, holding a silver-hilted dagger by its plain leather scabbard.

"No. Is no reason for gift," she protested.

"Yes, there is. I owe you my life, twice. I cannot repay that. But at least I can help you protect yours. It is a Knife of Edges. I picked it up in the far North, up in the desert lands a few years ago...."

"Magic?! No! Cannot!" she said.

"You'll wake Rue," he hissed, wincing in pain. He took a deep breath. "Listen. This dagger... was given to me by a young desert man whose life I saved. He paid that debt. I owe you doubly, and I insist you take it. My lady, please," he softened, trying reason. "It is the tradition of the piece. When my debt to you is paid, you may pass it on when you owe a life debt. It would aid me in my recovery to know that you are better protected. Keep it... in your boot," he smiled, "...so that when you drop your scimitar, you will not be without a weapon."

She sighed, accepted it, turning it over in her hand. It was surprisingly lighter than she had expected it to be. "Am often barefoot," she whispered.

He laid back on the bed, staring straight above him, trying to suppress a painful laugh. "Then, my dark, exotic flower, strap it to your thigh."

She smiled, gave a soft chuckle. "Very well, then. Accept gift. Now lie back and sleep."

She got up and tucked the dagger into her pack. Deactivating the pendant's light, she tucked it into her rune bag with her other jewelry and climbed into her hammock.

She was standing on the deck of the ship, that much she was certain. It was pitch dark, but she knew there was a fog, thick and heavy, pressing in on her. She could feel it, like a living thing, smothering her in the cool damp. She heard the hissing of the waves against the hull, the creak of the rigging, and the soft snapping of the sails, but her sense of direction had no point of reference. Putting her hand to her throat, she touched her pendant and whispered the word that would bring her light, but nothing happened. That was when she heard it, the laughter.

Her heart skipped. Panic rose, choking her. She could feel him out there, in the darkness, unblind. He was cold and evil and hungry for revenge, and he was hunting her.

She ran, not caring that there was nowhere to run to, nothing in the fog but the wind and the ocean and the ship. It was not long before she found the rail. She grabbed the nearby rigging in time to keep from falling overboard. Turning, she looked blindly behind her. He was there, somewhere, getting closer, taking his time.

Why should he hurry? Where was she going to go?

Lark grabbed the rigging in one hand, pulled herself up onto the rail, and threw herself over the side. The wind snapped through her clothes as she fell endlessly through the fog, and then there was pain as her body struck the floor.

Floor? Slowly, she opened her eyes. Her cheek hurt, like her forehead, shoulder, hip, and everything else. She touched the floor with her hand to convince herself that it *was* the floor.

Nearby, someone stirred and mumbled, "Whowhatsit?" followed by a renewed snore.

Someone whispered her name in the darkness.

She looked around, but it was still dark in the belly of the small ship. The voice came again, nearby. Rog.

"I said, are you all right, girl?" he whispered.

"Yes," she hissed. "Just... fell out of bed."

"I saw that," he grumbled.

"*Sesha*, am fine. Hurt bit, startled, but unhurt."

"What threw you out the bed?" he asked after a moment.

She slowly sat up and put a hand to her forehead to rub a sore spot. "Don't... don't remember. Was dreaming, but do not remember what." It confused her that she could not remember. It had been so vivid!

"Hmmm, probably something from th' island. It was a rough evenin'. It'll pass in a few days."

She reached up, blindly feeling for the edge of the hammock.

"Higher," he directed. "And a little more left."

She looked in the direction his voice had come from. "You can see?" she whispered, incredulous.

He smirked. "When you live underground, you learn to see in the dark."

Lark did not respond. She dragged herself to her feet, fumbled for and found her hammock, and climbed back in. She lay there a few moments. "Good night, Rog," she whispered.

"Good night," he grunted.

It was a long time before Lark fell asleep again.

III

Babes in the Woods

ONE

Lark sat bolt upright, gasping for breath. Ivaska, startled, lifted his large head from the floor, lifting one floppy ear as he looked at her over his shoulder. Listening intently, she threw open the window over the bed to see a thin fog drifting amid the tents and shacks. She strained every sense she had, certain that he was out there, the man from her dreams. She never saw him, but she knew he was there, coming ever closer. The sheer terror she felt convinced her of it.

Ivaska got up onto the bed, crowding her, but otherwise unconcerned with invisible bogeymen. She told herself that if he were really out there, Ivaska would have let her know. She closed the window and lay back down, curling up next to him, taking advantage of his heat. She took a little comfort from his deep, steady breathing and sheer solidness. Not for the first time in the past three weeks, she silently thanked her brother for giving the dog to her. Even still, it was a while before she dared to close her eyes and fall asleep again. This time, thankfully, she did not dream.

It had been a bad night. The worst in months. A single penny was the whole of the evening's earnings. If she kept this up, how was she going to eat? Especially with the price of food these days. Of course, if she kept this up, money would be the least of her worries.

The chair across from her scraped back. She looked up as Lily sat down, setting a mug of steaming wine in front of each of them. Neither woman said anything for a moment, just stared at the bit of dented copper on the table between them. Finally, "Lark, that has to be the worst performance you have ever given."

Lark pushed the wine away and stood, "Perhaps should start circulating again, try elsewhere."

Lily stopped her with a hand on her arm, made her sit back down. "Going elsewhere isn't going to help and you know it. Your heart isn't in it anymore. You've been going steadily downhill since you got back from Evandair, and you look awful."

Lark buried her head in her arms. "So I feel."

"Are you ill? I heard there was a plague or something over that way."

"No," Lark answered. "Not sick. Not... not sleeping."

"Why not?" she asked gently, waving idly to the last few customers as they bade her goodnight and left. "Is it that handsome rake you said nearly got killed over there? What was his name? Delfy? Fell-trin...."

"Keltree," Lark supplied. "And no, is well Rue says. Is breaking hearts all over town."

She hesitated. "Yours?"

Lark thought a moment. No, she decided, that was not the case. She shook her head.

"Then what?" Lily insisted.

Lark sighed, toyed with her mug without really drinking. "Is nightmares," she confessed. "Have had since island. Can't sleep for dreaming. Even jumping at shadows, I am now. Poor 'Gale, he has my bad dreams, so he sleeps when I do not. He has no more chipper," she muttered, tenderly ruffling his chest feathers as he dozed in her empty tambourine. She sighed again, stifled a yawn, and sat back, drinking deeply from the wine. "If only there is sleep dreams cannot reach, maybe could rest," she mumbled wishfully.

Lily got up suddenly and disappeared into the back without a word. Confused, Lark waited. When Lily did not return after a few minutes, she began to pack her meager belongings. She looked up as she came back, something small tucked into her hand.

She took Lark's arm, pulling her to her feet. "Come on," she said, picking up Lark's mug with practiced ease without dropping what was in her palm. "Grab featherbrain," she added, waiting just long enough for the Romer to scoop up the small bird and grab her tambourine before ushering her up the stairs. Ivaska lifted his head at the sound of the timbrel and, seeing his mistress leaving him, bounded after them.

Lily took her to a small upstairs room and lit the single lamp inside. It was not the room with the bathtub. This one was very narrow, smaller than her caravan, with a steeply sloped roof. It held only a small bed, no wider than Lark's own, a night table, and a low chest. She put the mug and the object on the table and, opened the chest, pulled out a heavy quilt. She glanced over her shoulder at Lark, who was staring dumbly at her. "Don't just stand there; get ready for bed."

Too tired to argue and genuinely curious, Lark set her things down and obeyed. Nightingale, realizing that they were here for the duration, found himself a cozy corner in the rafters, used before him by numerous other feathered transients. She unlaced her vest and laid it on the chest lid, adding her skirt to the pile. Her slippers she put underneath the table and set her jewels on top of it, next to the mug of wine. She stood there, wearing only her low-tied peasant blouse, and waited.

Lily returned to the chest to get one more blanket, which she lay on the bed and folded back. "There," she said. "That ought to be thick enough."

"Thick enough for what?" Lark asked, staring oddly at the heavy quilt now padding the mattress.

"The mattress is straw. Not fresh, but clean. And I know how you hate straw beds. Now get in it," she finished, pointing to it.

"Yes, mama," Lark grinned tiredly and climbed between the quilts. She allowed Lily to fold it up over her lap. "Now what?"

Lily picked up a small brown bottle she had set on the table and measured out a few careful drops into the wine. She closed it and set it back on the table, picked up the mug, and held it out. "Drink," she ordered.

"What is?" Lark asked, accepting it but stopping to smell it before sipping. There was a distinct bite to it now.

"Laudanum," Lily answered.

"What is for?" she asked, drinking.

"It will help you sleep. My sister gave it to me when Dane's father died two years ago. I promise you: no dreams will reach you where this will take you. Use it sparingly, though. All you need is but a little."

She took the mug when it was empty and set it down to draw the covers over her. Lark curled up against the pillow, feeling the warm, spicy wine carry the sweet heaviness of the drug throughout her body. Her feet felt leaden, her hands completely clumsy. She looked up at Lily slowly, trying to fight it. She brushed her cheek tenderly, a gesture that reminded Lark of her mother with a pang. "No, don't fight it," she whispered. "Go with it. It will bring you peace. At least for a little while."

The sensations were bittersweet as her body grew heavier and numb. She was only dimly aware of Lily taking the mug, blowing out the lamp, and closing the door quietly behind her. No sooner she was out of the room, Ivaska was on the bed, making himself comfortable, keeping her warm. Then she knew nothing else.

Lark was unable to tell what time it was when she finally woke. The room was very dim, but she could hear life outside her door, in the taproom below. She yawned, stretched, sitting up. Ivaska was not in the room, which she found curious. She was certain he had climbed up onto the bed with her. Or had she dreamed that?

No. She had slept completely without dreams, blissfully. With a sigh, she climbed out of the still-warm bed, and reached for her skirt. She left her vest behind and stepped out into the hallway barefoot. The smell of breakfast hit her in a wave as she came near the stairs.

The taproom was moderately crowded, with late breakfasters wolfing down their meager meals. Lark wove through them to the end of the bar, as her usual table was occupied. She filched a hot roll from the tray as a young brunette, one of Lily's few help, carried it out of the kitchen over her short head. Lark tossed the roll from one hand to the other, trying to cool it off enough to be able to eat it.

"Serves you right," Lily grunted, coming out of the back with a plate of breakfast ham and eggs destined for the very rich, very fat man sitting at Lark's usual table.

Lark bit into the roll, heedless of the heat now, imagining the taste of those eggs. She guessed the meal on that man's plate had cost easily fifteen laurels. Ten for the eggs alone.

Lily drifted back by her, leaning over the bar to take the tray of dirty mugs and dishes Neneis handed her. "About time you got up," she teased, gesturing for Lark to follow her into the kitchen.

She laughed. "Is no later than usual."

Once the kitchen door swung closed behind them, the noise level dropped off instantly. The kitchen was a soft bustle of activity, but it was quiet and warm compared to the busy taproom. The dog was stretched out in front of the stove, chewing on a small bone. "I see Ivaska has had breakfast. Really did not need do so much."

Lily set the tray down on the side of the washtub and turned to face Lark with her hands on her hips. "What choice did I have? The beast had to be fed, or he would have stolen the food off my customer's knives!"

Lark looked at her, confused. "Was fed yesterday," she protested.

"Yeah," she laughed, tapping her chest. "Because I fed him. You were still asleep."

"Asleep?"

"Yes, asleep. You slept all night, all day, and all night again. Next time, only put one drop, all right?" She hesitated a second. "And maybe don't use wine," she added.

Still stunned by the revelation of her long slumber, Lark's head reeled. "Next time?"

"Yes, next time. The nightmares probably will not go away just because you had one good night's rest." She began to load up her tray with her customers' needs.

"Is right, more likely." Lark leaned back against the frame of the door, head spinning from facts. "Where can I get some of this... ladnum?"

"Lau*dan*um," she corrected, "and keep that bottle."

"But is yours...."

Lily shrugged, "I don't need it anymore." She disappeared into the larder for a moment, locking it behind her as she came out with a gold key that made Lark's nose twitch. She carved a cheese up, putting it on a plate on the tray. She handed Lark a slice and dropped a small green apple in her pocket.

"You give me apples?" Lark questioned, overwhelmed by the generosity the woman was exhibiting. "Have not seen apples in city for weeks! Cannot give me apple!"

"Why not?" she shrugged, setting fresh, hot bread on the plate.

"Because you could sell for... twelve harps, this apple, is why!"

Lily waved her hand dismissively before gathering up the remainder of the wheel and unlocking the pantry again.

Lark followed her into the small chamber, lit by a ring of glowing metal hanging from the ceiling and stocked floor to ceiling with food and cooking supplies, a good bit of it already cut into. She suppressed a sneeze.

"Lily, wait. I must know. Why are so good to me?"

"Why must you know?" Lily's pale blue eyes met Lark's dark ones as she turned from setting the cheese next to a whole wheel. "Why? Is it not enough that I am?"

"Have worked for other taverns, none of them so good to workers. Why you? Why me?"

Lily sighed. "Because I like you. Because the Tree likes you. My customers come to see *you* as much as for my cooking and soaps and washing. ...When you are yourself," she added with a twinkle in her eye. "You are a friend. I care what happens to you. And you have stolen my son's heart. And my gratitude for teaching him a viable trade. There, is that reason enough? Go on, go get yourself some fresh air. Maybe a walk will help clear your head. I have work to do. I'll see you tonight. If you're up to it."

Lark was stunned. She followed her out of the pantry, nibbling mindlessly at the slice of cheese while she thought about what she had said.

Lily interrupted her introspection as she picked up the tray and nodded towards the hearth. "Oh, and when you go, take that monster over there with you. He's getting in the way back here and making Heleda nervous."

She laughed, heading up the back stairs to her room. She finished getting dressed, lacing her vest tightly and adding her belled sash to her hips. Carefully tucking the little brown bottle in her pack, she took note of how little was left. Maybe a few days at most.

She paused to freshen up the room a bit, putting the quilts away in the chest before shouldering her bag and heading back down into the kitchen.

Nightingale met her immediately, chirping his happy concerns. She chuckled and brushed a bit of sugar from his beak. He had been stealing sugared currants again. She called Ivaska to her and slipped out the back door.

She roamed the city aimlessly for a while, letting her mind wander freely. She decided suddenly that Lily had been more than generous of late and wanted to do something for her. Taking quick stock of her location, she turned immediately in the opposite direction, towards the marketplace.

The market was bustling, in spite of the siege, although few frivolous objects were for sale anymore. The prices of useful items were outrageous. She did notice that the merchants seemed far more desperate for even the most basic sale. She saw a bright copper kettle and thought it would make a nice addition to Lily's kitchen, but then thought of the polishing it would need and decided against it.

She wandered down towards the silk merchant, who, surprisingly enough, was still in business and having a devil of a time interesting anyone in his wares. He was more than happy to show her everything he had in stock, piece by piece. She considered buying Lily a silk dress only for a moment. The widow was not the kind of person to remain idle for very long, and silk was simply not for working in. Seeing some brightly colored ribbons hanging just under the stall's eaves, she decided one of those would do for now. She was settling on the right shade of blue to compliment Lily's eyes and fine golden hair when she heard a familiar voice out of the crowd.

"Will you do something about those bells? You are making entirely too much damn noise!"

She spun, scanning the masses for the source of the voice. A peep from Nightingale made her look left, and she caught a glimpse of green and brown just across the way. "*You!*" she cried, pointing. "Stay right where are!" She left the startled silk merchant hanging and wove her way quickly through the traffic.

Landros watched as she darted in and out amid the crowd. He had heard the bells and taken a chance. As Luck, or Fate, or whatever would have it, it paid off. He did not know why the sight of the dusky, black-haired Romeri girl rushing across the street to meet him made his heart jump. Maybe it had something to do with the blue and white scarves making up her skirt that displayed more than obscured her gorgeous legs. Maybe, yeah. That had to be it.

She threw herself into his arms with a squeal of delight.

He spun her, trying to catch his balance, and set her down, laughing. "Well, hello to you too, darlin'. Haven't seen you in a while. What are you up to?"

"Looking for gift for Lily."

"Find anything?"

She shook her head. "Not really. Nothing that is right. So, what have been into?"

Nightingale flew over, settling on Landros' shoulder, peeping his own greeting.

"And hello to you too, feathered one. Still stealing currents?" Nightingale glanced away with a chagrined chirp. Landros chuckled. "I thought so." He turned back to Lark. "Oh, not much. Been keeping myself busy here and there. So have you, or so Rue tells me."

Their conversation was interrupted by the appearance of Adrick. He barged right up, only peripherally acknowledging that Landros had been speaking with someone. "Landros, there you are!" He took the elf by the arm. "Come, we have to hurry. There is a job for us, and this time I promise it is important."

Landros pulled his arm away. "Good morning, Adrick," he said, refusing to let his sudden good mood be spoiled. "Thank you, but I have other plans. Lark, I believe we were discussing a picnic?" he asked her.

They hadn't. "Would love to," she laughed.

"You can flirt with the tart later, Landros. This is important," he insisted, again trying to usher him off.

Landros stiffened. Adrick felt the difference in his arm and turned to look fully at him.

"Adrick, you remember Lark, don't you?" he said tightly. "And I believe we had this discussion already."

Adrick looked over at her, really seeing her for the first time. "Oh, I am terribly sorry. I had no idea it was you," he said, trying to recover the situation quickly. "Forgive me for canceling the picnic, but... it is about the children."

His manner changed instantly. "What about the children?"

"Some of them are... well... missing. The Lord Mayor himself is gathering a small force to go and rescue them. If we do not hurry, we will be late..."

Landros did not wait to hear the rest of his speech. He turned to Lark and gave her a quick kiss. "I am sorry, but I promise you, we'll have that picnic as soon as I get back."

"Wait. Come with you!" she replied.

"Miss, this will be no place for..." Adrick began.

Lark rounded on him, giving him an intense, 'I dare you to stop me' glare, her eyes blackening.

He threw up his hands, surrendering. "Fine, but can we please go?"

"Ivaska!" Lark called, falling into pace with the two men. Ivaska stopped sniffing at gutter trash and trotted up obediently, falling into step at her side.

Landros glanced over at the animal. "Funny," he said. "I don't remember the dog."

Lark just laughed.

TWO

The City Hall was a huge place, though small compared to the tri-winged temple a few scant blocks away from it. It was sparsely furnished, but the Spartan decor was a mere mask of the opulence it actually contained. It was designed to give one the feeling of stability and the blind inevitability of justice, but Lark saw through it all. She quickly noted the richness of the threads used in the few tapestries that hung, glorifying the city and its inhabitants; the exotic and rare woods used in the desks of even moderately important people.

But, unlike the temple, this building had taken damage from the siege. Some large rock or spell had caved in a whole quarter of the structure near the front, and even now, there were dwarves and other strong backs trying to clear the mess. Lark shook her head at the waste. She knew of other places that needed repairing more desperately than this, places people lived...

Adrick showed a piece of paper to a sergeant on duty, and they were escorted immediately to a guarded office in a back hallway, clearly marked MAGISTRATE.

The guard nodded to the sergeant and opened the door for them. As Lark started to follow, the guard put his hand on her chest, stopping her.

"I would remove that hand if you want to keep it," Landros warned. The guard obeyed but still refused to allow her to pass.

"Only those who will be sent on the mission are permitted inside. And I do not remember the Magistrate mentioning any women," he glared.

Lark put her fists on her hips. She could feel her rising anger as a physical heat, boiling to the surface.

"*I* brought her," Landros said through clenched teeth. Lark noted that Adrick had gone inside and left the scene of the discussion completely. "I have found her to be an admirable fighter when given the chance. Though her usefulness is not primarily in active combat."

"I know very well what a woman is good for, sir." Lark flushed instantly; her eyes narrowed. There was no trace of blue in them at all. "But that does not change the fact that she is not going in. I have my orders, and they do not include...."

"What is going on out here, Corporal?!" a large man roared, stepping out of the room.

The corporal came to instant attention. Even Landros gave a small bow in the man's direction.

"Your Lordship!" the corporal answered stiffly. "Sir! I was instructed to allow only the adventurers to be sent on the mission, sir! This woman is trying to enter, sir!"

The man sized Lark up, even as she looked him over unabashedly. He was most certainly not what she had expected for the Lord Mayor of Portswain. He was heavy-set, which she had expected, though not really fat. He was built like her father but taller. And he was not at all unhandsome. His dark beard was well-trimmed, and his clothes were simple, if of good cloth. He wore no satins, no furs, no velvets. Only his shirt was silk, and that was obviously well-worn. There was no gold chain of office around his neck as she had expected, and he had a very commanding air about him. He was obviously a man of the people and not a politician. He raised an eyebrow at her indifference to his rank.

"A Gypsy girl," he mused. "Have you any skills other than music and dancing?" he asked. There was no hostility in his deep, bear-like voice.

Lark grabbed the hilt of her scimitar in her left hand, and pulled it sideways, half out of the scabbard, angled away from her. "Is not for decoration, this. *Do* know how to use."

"Spunky," he mused. "I like that, but... if you encounter the enemy, girl, can you handle yourself then?"

A pair of hands settled on Lark's shoulders from behind. She almost finished pulling the blade at that touch, but Nightingale's indifference and the voice that spoke changed her mind. "I will vouch for her usefulness, my lord."

"Ah, Danhaven," the Mayor sighed, pleased. "If you are certain?"

"She saved my life more than once. If you care to make further inquiries, you may ask the Magistrate about her involvement in the Evandair affair a few weeks ago. Besides, my lord," he added with his characteristic roguish grin, "if we are going after children, would it not be better to have a woman along?"

The mayor laughed, scratching his beard. "True, true. But... I have this feeling this little 'woman' might actually take offense to that statement."

"And would be right," she smiled, rocking back ever so purposefully on Keltree's foot. He pulled back with a sudden yelp.

The Mayor chuckled, stepping aside with a sweeping bow. "Won't you join us, my lady?" he asked.

Lark gave him a pretty little curtsy, never taking her eyes off him. "Why, thank you. Don' mind if do," she grinned, slipping into the dark, close room.

The magistrate's office was very crowded. The official himself was standing behind the desk, pouring over a map and arguing with a familiar dwarven figure. The Magistrate looked up, and his face darkened when he saw her, but he said nothing when the Mayor appeared just behind her. Adrick was there, nodding occasionally and discounting half of what Rog was suggesting. When Landros, Keltree, herself, and the Mayor entered, there was barely room to move. It was hot and close with so many male bodies.

Landros pulled a chair over for Lark just as Adrick was reaching blindly behind himself for it. Adrick managed to glance in time to not end up on the floor. He scowled in their direction as she sat down, and Landros stood directly behind her with his arms folded across his chest. The Mayor was very quick to get things started.

He cleared his throat. "All right. Most of you know why you were sent for. For those who do not, about a dozen children from various parts of town, mostly from the lower class, poorer, unprotected neighborhoods, were found missing from their beds this morning."

Lark paled and began paying very close attention. Landros stiffened. For once, he was glad Adrick had come looking for him.

"There were no witnesses, no signs of break-in or running away," he sighed, soul weary, perching on the edge of the desk. The Magistrate quickly snatched something before he could sit on it, glaring coldly at the man's back. "The priesthood of the Temple of Three noticed mystic disturbances at what they thought to be random locations throughout town. Since these disturbances were of similar nature to those discovered at the locations of our recent 'random monster attacks', they sent some of their people to investigate and found a child missing at each and every location. They found residues of teleportation magic and are right now preparing a spell to teleport you to the recipient location in hopes of you finding traces of the children and tracking down both them and their kidnappers. The *problem* with this whole escapade is the slight fact that the area of destination is right smack in enemy territory."

He got off the desk and opened the map, pointed to a small, squared-off section about two miles or so outside the city walls in the forested mountains. "This is where the temple will be sending you. We have reports of patrols up this way, not all of which are completely human. There are rumors of goblinoids." He folded the map and handed it to Rog, who tucked it away on his person.

"You were chosen because none of you have direct ties to either military or politics. Should you be captured, you cannot be forced to give vital information to the enemy, as none of you have any." He looked long and hard at Lark. "I do not think I need to impress upon you the dangers present for *you* specifically, should you be taken prisoner. No one here would think ill of you if you were to back down."

Lark smiled softly. "Concern is noted and appreciated. However, risk is mine to take."

He nodded, not pleased but satisfied. "Very well then, if you head to the Temple, I believe they should be ready for you. I am afraid I do not have much to offer you in the way of provisions, but with a forester among you," he gestured in Landros's direction, "food should not really be much of a problem. However," he turned to Lark, "if the lady would like, I believe I could find some leather armor about that might fit?" he asked.

"Thank you again, but no. Am best protected when can move freely. Have to be able to hit to hurt," she grinned. With that, she shouldered her bag, threw the Magistrate a saucy wink just to annoy him, and headed out the door.

Once they were out on the steps, Landros leaned over to her. "What did you do to tick off the Magistrate?" he asked quietly.

She scratched Ivaska's head fondly. "Oh, nothing, really."

"She wouldn't let him talk," Rog smirked as they stepped out into the busy street.

"And she was a woman," Keltree added. "Ah, and what a woman!" he sighed happily. "Young Merrick, the lad we were summoned to aid a few weeks back, asked for her specifically and would not take no for an answer, I am told. And you know the good Magistrate's opinions of women?" Landros nodded. "Well, he took it personally when he had to tender both herself and gentle Rue his gratitude for their aid in solving the problem."

"You seem to have a knack for getting yourself into trouble, young lady," Landros grinned.

"OH!" Lark exclaimed, stopping dead in her tracks. "Lily!! If don't tell am leaving, will worry!" She looked around, saw a young boy running out of an alley nearby, chasing another laughing child. "**Boy**!" she called, trotting over. "Come! Have errand!"

He stopped, looked as though he was about to bolt, then crossed the street to meet her. "Yeah, lady?"

"Know you where Cinnamon Tree is?"

"It's a Inn, i'n'it?" he asked, scratching his thin leg.

"*Sesha.*"

"Yeah, I know where it is. Ya want directions?"

"No, want message run."

The boy grinned and held out his hand. "That'll cost ya."

Lark reached into her pocket and pulled out the apple Lily had given her that morning. "Is all have right now. Play cards right and might get lunch out of, too." His eyes widened, and he grabbed for the fruit. She pulled it out of his reach. "Will run message?"

"Yeah, lady! Anything you want!"

She gave him the fruit, which he promptly tucked into his shirt. "Ask for Lily. Tell her Romeri sent you. Tell her had to go on ...." she fished for the word.

"A mission," Landros supplied. "Tell her she's with her elven friend and that I'll bring her back as soon as I can. Though it may be a few days. Got it?"

"Yes, sir!!" he exclaimed and repeated the message. "Find Lily at the Cinnomom Tree. Tell her the Romer went on a mission with her elf friend and will be back as soon as they can. Few days. Right!" and he bolted off down the street, cutting through an alley.

Lark and Landros had to run to catch up with the others.

At the Temple, they were ushered into a small inner courtyard where a large circle had been drawn on the flagstones with colored chalks. Lark took her belled belt off and folded it carefully up, and put it in her bag, trading it for a warmer shawl which she tied at her hips. She made certain that her instruments were secured and would not be able to give away their position should stealth be required. She removed her dancing shoes, not wishing to ruin them wandering through the wilderness.

They were each given a small pack of dry provisions with an apology that there could not be more. One of the priests took note of Lark's bare feet.

"Have you no shoes, miss?" he asked politely.

She smiled. "Am fine, really. I like bare foots."

"If we are ready?" called a tall, lean priest in dark blue robes and a long bluish-gray beard. "Yes then, gather into the circle, but step carefully. Mind the dog. Good boy. Now, I am not sending you to the exact location of the original destination as I have been asked. I cannot, and I simply do not think it wise. I can tell you that you will be within a mile of it, so bear that in mind. Also, intelligence and scrys tell us that the enemy is in the region and is actively blocking such attempts to find the children. The mere fact that I have found a hole through which I can teleport you, surprises me, but oh well," he said, finally taking a breath. "Here we go. And may the Matron keep you safe in this most holy of endeavors," he said, making the sign of a closed fist circled over his heart.

No sooner he raised his arms and began to gesture than a sudden vertigo struck them. Ivaska spread his legs to try to get his balance, whimpering. Lark stumbled against Landros, who was in no better position himself, and fell against Rog, who, surprisingly, managed to keep his equilibrium. She fell forward, catching the ground with her hands. To her amazement, she felt grass growing up between her fingers and watched, stunned, as a clump of wildflowers grew and bloomed virtually under her nose. The vertigo ceased, and they found themselves in a wooded area halfway up a long slope.

Ivaska continued to cower, not trusting his surroundings at all. Lark got to her feet shakily, trying to center herself again, and went to him. She stroked the large shaggy head tenderly and spoke low, steady words to him, slowly calming the animal. Rog and Landros watched, fascinated as she charmed the dog out of his fear.

Keltree leaned over to Adrick and commented, "She certainly has a way with dumb animals, doesn't she?"

Adrick grumbled, staring hard at his friend. "Yes, she does. Of all varieties." With that, he turned and began to climb to the top of the rise. Keltree watched him go, a look of concerned confusion on his face.

"Is he ready to travel?" Keltree asked Lark.

"Think so," she answered and bent to the dog again, whispering in Romeri. He licked her ear and got up, began sniffing around.

They stayed loosely together, no one person more than fifteen feet from another, hunting for tracks, trails, or signs of magic. Lark sent Nightingale up to search from the sky.

They hunted for nearly an hour with no sign of either enemy or the missing children. "You would think," Landros complained, getting up from inspecting the ground, "that two dozen kids and prospective guards would have left some sort of trail."

"Perhaps we ain't looking in th' right place?" Rog suggested.

A low, urgent wolf whistle came from a nearby tree. Lark put her hand on her scimitar. "Enemy patrol," she whispered. "Up left."

Keltree and Rog both put their bodies physically between her and the incoming enemy. Landros began backing up closer to her.

Eight men stepped into view, mostly, but not entirely, human. Seeing the five men, they set hands on their own weapons, save for the one who had been using his as a machete. The tallest of the eight stepped forward, drew himself up to his most imposing, and demanded. "What's the password?!"

Lark noted the faint protrusion of tusks in his mouth when he spoke. That and his cliff-like forehead spoke of goblin blood.

Keltree looked calmly from him to the others of his own party, then back at him. "You mean you don't know?"

"Don't know what?" he demanded.

"The password."

"Of course I know the bloody password!" he roared.

"Then what is the password!?" Keltree asked firmly.

"I asked *you* the password!"

Keltree sighed, looked down at Rog, and shook his head sadly. "They don't know the password, boys. I suppose we'll have to detain them."

"Now, hold on just a bloody minute!! Just who are you, and what are you doin' out here!?" the leader demanded.

One of his men whispered to another, "Are they the relief, Sarge?"

Keltree burst out laughing. "Hah ha!! Relief! You hear that, lads? He thinks we're his relief!"

Lark stifled a giggle as the others laughed heartily.

"No, we are not your relief."

"Aw, peckernuts!" the sergeant grumbled. "Come on, when is headquarters gonna send us some relief? We been out here almost a month now! At least... at least share us some a'yore provisions?" he asked, taking a hopeful step forward. "Not much left about but squirrels."

Keltree held out his sword, pointing it at him. "Not until you give us the password."

"Cockatrice! It's cockatrice!" he shouted, backing away from the rapier's sharp point.

"Wrong answer, bud," Rog chuckled, fondling the head of his war hammer.

"Like hell, it is!" the sergeant exclaimed.

Adrick cocked his head thoughtfully. "Actually, I think the man is right, commander. The last password we had *was* cockatrice. But they changed that a few weeks ago. Just before you were given command, actually, sir."

"Ah, I see," Keltree mused thoughtfully. "And you say you have been out here for five weeks with no relief?"

"Yes, sir!" the motley group chorused.

"Six!" one offered up, out of sync with his compatriots.

"Well, I shall have to report this when I get back to base camp. ...In a couple of weeks."

Their faces fell. Suddenly, one of the men began tugging on his sergeant's sleeve. "Sarge," he whispered loudly. "Look, look! They gots a woman!"

"A woman!?" The sergeant straightened up, peeking around Keltree to get a glimpse or two of Lark. "And what, do tell, is you doing out here with a woman?!" he demanded suspiciously.

Adrick stepped forward and leaned in conspiratorially. "She's a present."

"A present?" he grunted skeptically.

"You know, a slave girl, for 'you know who'? We caught her early this morning. She's a notoriously good dancer."

The Sergeant licked his lips as he leered at her.

Landros adjusted his position, more effectively blocking their view of her, aided by Keltree and Rog. Lark slowly set down her pack and blade, motioned Ivaska to stay put, and began to slip off into the woods.

"Say," the sergeant was saying. "If you ain't got any food to spare us, perhaps you might see your way to... maybe... loaning her to us for an hour or so? It *has* been five weeks...." He grinned hopefully.

Adrick mused thoughtfully, rubbing his chin. "I don't know. Commander?"

Keltree noticed the direction of the dog's attention and made a guess at what the girl was doing. He rubbed the back of his neck as if nursing some fond injury. He shook his head. "She is a feisty one, that Gypsy. I think she would fight too much."

One of the sergeant's men grinned. "An' where is the 'arm in that, sir?"

"Because it would visibly damage the merchandise, and we want her to at least 'look' pure enough when we hand her over, you ninny," Adrick snapped, slapping the man upside the back of his head.

"Speakin' a' feisty," another man added, "she done bolted."

Keltree turned and looked angry, "What?! Damn you!" he growled at his nearest target, which happened to be Rog. "You stunted toad! You were supposed to be keeping an eye on her!"

"Sorry! The little minx bit me onct already! I wasn't gonna git *too* close!" he growled back, dodging the poorly aimed blow.

"I'll get her," Landros snarled and bolted into the woods.

"And try not to bruise her, you green-eared pike!" Keltree shouted after him.

Landros ran through the woods, not too fast, but trying to cool his temper. He understood that it was all a smoke screen and that they were in serious danger unless the cards were played very carefully. But it still bothered him.

He paused and began looking about for signs of her. They were quite blatant... for a little while. Then they suddenly disappeared. He doubled back, thinking perhaps he had overrun the trail in his preoccupation. No, there was no trail. It just ended. But he could smell her, faintly, somewhere very close by.

An acorn struck his shoulder. He looked up in the branches. She was sitting on a limb about fifteen feet up, peering down at him. Catching his eye, she smiled.

"Come to capture, eh?" she laughed softly.

"Shhh, quietly," he hissed, looking back over his shoulder. "I think we are still close enough to be heard if you scream loud enough." He gestured for her to climb down to him.

She began to work her way down. "I know," she whispered. "Is why stopped here. That and, if pursued, would not think would stop so close. From here, could send illusion or poltergeist for them to chase."

She landed lightly beside him and picked a leaf out of her hair.

"You ready to go back?" he asked. His heart was pounding in his chest, and he did not know why.

"How we do this?" she whispered, her inexplicable delight dancing in her eyes.

He was almost mesmerized. 'Damn the girl,' he thought. Here they were in very real danger of more than their lives, and she was enjoying herself! And damned it all if he was not practically giddy himself. The whole scenario was almost comical if he could forgive Adrick's ready, almost eager solution to the problem. He sighed. "How do we do this?" he repeated, looking the situation over for a moment. He shrugged, "Like this." He bent down, snatched her wrist, grabbed her waist, and tossed her neatly over his shoulder.

The wind was knocked out of her with a very loud "Ooof!"

"Sorry," he whispered. "You all right?"

"All right?!" she growled. "Is no way to treat Romeri Princess!" she hissed, not really angry but feeling an instinctive need to protest the indignity. She swatted her open hand on his backside as hard as she could and struck something hard under the cloak instead, which might have been a blade hilt. She rubbed her hand in pain.

His blood went cold suddenly. He stopped and twisted his head to look back at her. She was trying to get her hair out of her face enough to glare at him. "You wouldn't lie to me about a thing like that, would you?" he asked.

She gave an indignant grunt, forgetting her hand for a moment. "Would lie 'bout thing like that?!" she mocked. "Of *course*, would lie 'bout thing like that!" she hissed. "Have been lying since left father's caravan, lying by not admitting! When Gruma thinks am ready, will be queen, but am not willing yet to be Rushavska queen."

Landros took a moment to allow this news to sink in. He, an elven wanderer born of non-noble wanderer parents, had bedded a princess. Hell, had been gifted with her virginity. And here he was with her slung over his shoulder like a sack of flour, pretending she was a slave girl destined for the enemy leader. He shrugged. 'Ain't life funny that way', he thought.

"You're a princess. I'm an elf. I guess that makes us both about four steps above everyone else."

She gaped. "You arrogant...!" she began.

He began walking back to camp. He gave her rump a sound swat, "Now scream like a good little captive," he grinned, walking back towards the others, enjoying this way more than he should.

He almost lost his grip when she suddenly began to kick and yell at the top of her lungs in Romeri. Landros began uttering a few profanities of his own, complaining less than quietly in Elvish about her being a little too into her role. He nearly dropped her when a flailing heel caught him soundly in the face. She stopped, trying to see how badly she had hurt him. "Sorry," she whispered.

He put his hand to his nose and looked at the blood on his fingers. "Why don't we play dead?" he suggested.

She suddenly screamed, loud and shrill, then cut herself off mid-shriek and went limp across his back. "Not bad," he frowned. He put on his best scowl, which was not all that hard considering his face was throbbing, and stalked back to where the others waited. He had to admit, she was a lot easier to carry when she was playing dead weight.

He almost dropped her again and began backpedaling when Ivaska came charging through the woods towards them and skidded to a halt a few steps away, growling.

"Uh, Lark.... do something about your friend here," he said slowly.

"Well, turn me to see him!" she snapped. Landros hesitated but turned just enough so that Ivaska could see her face. "SIT!" she hissed. She spoke to him in Romeri, convincing him to behave, that no harm was coming to her. He cocked his head and gave her a very confused stare but sat and behaved himself and followed them quietly.

Keltree was pacing the small area, furious, stopped now and again to 'have words' with Rog or Adrick. Adrick was playing the calming advisor, continuously going back and forth between the players, dropping hints to the enemy men that the commander was 'a bit mad, you know' and subject to 'complete and total blind rages'. "No one's safe then, no one," he mused, shaking his head sadly, bustling back to Keltree to whisper soothingly to him.

"Ah, sir, see?" he said, gesturing broadly as Landros re-entered the tiny glade with Lark's limp body over his shoulder and the dog trotting close behind. "I told you he was a most excellent tracker. If anyone could find her, it was he."

Keltree glared. "I thought I told you no bruises, Private?" he snarled coldly. "What did you do to her?"

"She fell out of a tree, sir," Landros snapped and wiped his nose on the back of his sleeve. He glanced down at the dog, who cocked his head at him, looking strangely at Lark's limp body. "Can we go now, sir, before she wakes up and tries to take a bite out of *me*?" he asked, cocking a sideways glance at the enemy patrol, who were openly admiring the exposed calves and round, well-displayed hips. He turned his back to them, changing their view to something less rewarding.

"Yes, before she tries to get away again," Keltree grumbled, "and you have to do some real damage to her. If she can't dance, then she's no good to me. Come on then, pick up these things, and let's get moving!"

He turned to the patrol. "I'll speak to the duty sergeant when I return about your relief. 'Til then, buck up. You're doing a bang-up job out here. Really." He started to move off through the woods. "Oh," he added as an afterthought. "By the way. The new password is Basilisk."

"Thank you, sir! No more trouble now. Come on, men, let's go," he grumbled, shuffling his small band into a rough sort of order and moving them through the woods. A couple of them continued to watch the retreating figure of the unconscious woman longingly until the sergeant gave them a good rap upside the heads to get them to fall back in line.

Keltree led the way through the woods, with Adrick close behind him and Rog trotting between him and Landros, who brought up the rear with Lark and the dog. Thankfully, Ivaska had fallen into line beside him with no trouble.

After a few minutes, Lark ventured to lift her head and peeked through her hair to see if they were safely away. Seeing nothing and confirming this with the songbird following at a distance, she allowed herself to relax. She opened her eyes again and saw something odd flash past her narrow field of vision just below the brush level. She tried to push herself upright but could not get the leverage for some reason. She grabbed the tail of Landros's tunic and tugged. "Stop, stop," she rasped. The blood rushing to her head made her voice hoarse.

He turned around, "What?"

"Put down," she breathed.

He stopped and set her on her feet. She took a moment to catch her breath and her balance, trying to rub some of the soreness out of her stomach where it had been folded over his shoulder.

Ivaska began nosing her, showing concern with the strangeness that he had just witnessed and wanting praise for doing as he had been told. She gave him an idle scratch and pushed him away. "Saw something."

She backtracked a short way, bending to look under several bushes before she found what she had seen. She stood, a dirty rag doll dressed as a soldier in her hands.

Landros came up behind her and looked over her shoulder. "What is it?" he asked.

She sniffed it, taking a deep breath. There was the faint, spicy-musty smell of magic embedded in the doll. "Think know how children stolen. Adrick!" she called, stepping around Landros to try and catch up to the priest.

Landros grabbed her by the waist, "Hey, shhh!" he warned. "Keep your voice down. We may not be far enough away yet."

"Nightingale says they know nothing but get away. Is well out of earshot." She slipped out of his grasp and trotted to catch up with the others. "Adrick!"

The others stopped, suddenly realizing that the two had fallen behind. "Yes?" he asked disdainfully. "What is it?"

"Is found this." She handed him the doll. "Think was magic, what used to get children out here."

Skeptical, he took it from her and gave it a cursory inspection. He was about to pass it back to her as insignificant when his eyes suddenly widened, and he gave it a more thorough look over.

"Well, what you see?" she asked eagerly.

"It was magic, of that I am certain. A one-charge, spent teleportation enchantment. What puzzles me, good lady, is how in the nine hells you knew? I barely saw the flash." He looked her over, reassessing his opinion of her.

"Smelled magic," she shrugged. "Don't you?"

He took a deep sniff of the doll and choked. "No, all I can smell is sticky fingers and dirt, I'm afraid. But you can *smell* magic?" he asked incredulously.

"Only spent magic. Or if place is loaded. Is unmistakable. Thought all who use could smell. But is good. Now have something for Ivaska to follow. Found back there," she pointed and led them to the place where she had found it.

She showed the toy to Ivaska, whispered to him, and stood. He began snuffling through the under-brush and moved steadily forward through the woods, away from the path, at an angle from where they had been headed. Lark took a deep breath herself. "Magic here, too. Use to cover trail, maybe?"

"Very likely, young lady. *Very* likely," Adrick mused.

They followed Ivaska through the woods.

Keltree cleared his throat, "Now that we are out of their hearing, I wish to, first of all, apologize for my behavior back there. The things I said were unforgivably crass, and I can only apologize. It is by no means or stretch of the imagination a reflection of my feelings toward any of you. Second," he said, holding up his hand as voices rose to protest. "Second, I wish to congratulate you all on your quick thinking, ready wit, and intuitive acting. Good show, men, one and all!"

He turned to Lark and bent over her hand. "As for you, my dear. Superlative. Absolutely superlative! By the time you were brought back, they were so much in terror of my temper they were wishing for any excuse to be quit of us!" he grinned. "But," he sighed, "you did not have to abuse the poor private so. After all, he was only doing his duty."

She put her hands on her hips and glared over at Landros, fully enjoying the fun. "Was enjoying duty far too much."

Landros looked up, saw the stern, unyielding expression on her face, and feared deep in his heart that he had indeed gone too far. Then she was laughing at him. She walked over, cleaning the remains of dried blood from his face with a bit of damp cloth. "Are supposed to laugh, ninny," she chuckled. "Or did hurt you too much, *sesket*?"

"*Sesket*?" he asked, confused. "What is this word, *sesket*?" She used it a lot, now that he thought about it.

She stepped back, thought for a second, trying to translate the word. "Too many meanings. Is, you use when... Means, 'tell me that', or 'did it not', or 'is this not so', or 'understand'?"

He shook his head. "No, I don't."

She laughed. "Use it when want someone to agree with what said or dare them to prove wrong... Has too many translation," she sighed.

"No kidding," he chuckled. He put his arm around her shoulders and followed after the dog. He rubbed his still sore nose. "I'll tell you one thing, goddesses help anyone who tries to take you alive!"

She slipped her arm around his waist as they walked. She looked back over her shoulder at Keltree. He stood watching them, a broad smile on his handsome face.

THREE

Night fell and found them no nearer to their goal. Rog sat down on the woody hillside and opened the map, reading it by the growing starlight. He began grumbling to himself.

Lark sat down beside him. "What is?" she asked.

"Ah," he growled. "Nothin'. We're a good ways from Portswain, but I cain't figure out a place they could be takin' the youngun's."

She laid a hand on Rog's shoulder. "Will find them, Rog. No worry."

"Yeah, but... will we find them in time?" he asked her, his eyes blazing as he met hers. He got up and wandered a little ways away.

"We'd best make a camp," Keltree suggested. "But after that last enemy patrol we encountered, I do not think it wise that we have a fire. If we sleep close together, we should be warm enough."

Adrick snapped his blanket open. "Give me a few minutes, and I might be able to do something about that."

Landros noticed Lark staring off after the dwarf, chewing thoughtfully on her lower lip. He sat down next to her. "Hey, what's the matter?"

She did not answer him. Instead, she reached into her pack and pulled out a small bag of red velvet. She untied it and opened it wide, spreading it out on the ground like a cloth. She mumbled a few words as she passed her hand over it, and a soft, faint glow began, tiny witch-lights floating above her fingers. She tossed them up, setting them to float just above her eye level, and then gathered the small, marked agates in both hands and, shook them, dropped them back onto the cloth.

Keltree noticed the light and came over, started to say something, then noticed what she was doing. He squatted across from her. Adrick started to say something about the light as well, but Keltree motioned him to silence and gestured him over. Adrick stood behind Lark and watched.

She mumbled to herself, a chant her Gruma had taught her long ago, as she passed her hands over the spread runes. One by one, she turned seven stones on the cloth and read their symbols and positions by the were-lights. "Are at sea," she whispered. "Or will be. ...Is unclear." She pointed to a pair of stones off to the side, an arrow pointing away from the rest of them, towards her, and a straight line lying askew of it. "Are going south. But... will not go south. Will stop in east, not far. Island."

"Southeast?" Adrick whispered.

Rog, having heard this, whipped out his map again and compared it to the pattern on the cloth. He tugged Keltree's sleeve and pointed out an indentation of the coastline not far away. "There is a cove here," he whispered, keeping his voice low so as not to disturb her. "A smuggler-pirate's paradise, a good place to hide a waitin' ship. We might be able to catch them if we press on now."

"No," Lark said, not looking up. "No. Cannot catch them. No, *should* not catch them. Are too many now. Will be less when land. Is town near and is boat waiting. Go there, and sail after."

Landros laid an urgent hand on her arm. "Where is this island?"

She looked blankly at him. "I... I don't know." She looked down at the stones on the ground in front of her and pointed to one lying off from the others with but two stones beside it. "Somewhere here. Are not exact or clear." She folded up her cloth, retying the stones safely inside. "Am cold," she shivered, rubbing her arms.

Keltree stood to remove his cloak. Adrick waved him off. "But a moment, my dear," he said with more gentleness than he had previously.

Landros pulled her close to him, wrapping his own cloak around her, sharing its warmth. She leaned back against his chest as Adrick searched for and found a large stone which he set near the center of the scattered bedrolls. He knelt before it and began praying until a soft, reddish glow began around him. Then, he reached out and touched the rock with his crossed fingers, and it glowed brightly, then faded. A few seconds later, the air around them became distinctly warmer.

"Oh, is nice," she moaned, stretching the soles of her feet towards the hot rock. "Now, if only had bit of supper, would be wonderful."

"That," Landros began, "I think *I* can do something about." He slipped out of his cloak, draping the rest of it around her, and reached into his pack. He pulled out a small plaid blanket and unfolded it on the ground before them. With a word, it was suddenly spread with a large, honeyed ham on a steaming platter, mounds of biscuits, and a pot of dark honey. There was a large bowl of spiced vegetables and a steaming pie of possible apple origins from the aroma. "Not bad," he muttered. He picked up the pitcher and, filling his cup with the contents, sampled it. "Mmmmm, cider," he said, then began filling people's mugs.

"Still hot!" Rog gasped, trying to cool his burnt tongue.

"Where did you get this wonderful cloth?" Adrick asked, sampling the vegetable bowl. "And why haven't you shown it to me before?" he muttered, savoring the taste as it melted in his mouth. "This is exquisite!"

Lark took a biscuit and dipped it in the honey pot, enjoying the rich, hot, sticky sweetness. Keltree carved slices off the ham, which Rog helped himself to. Ivaska's head came up, along with his ears, any time the meat came near him. His tail thumped the ground hopefully, but no one seemed to notice.

"I don't flaunt this little item," Landros said, staring at the soft green and brown plaid cloth. "Besides, I've never had the opportunity to use it when you were around."

"All those evenings we've spent eating in greasy taverns and paying those unbelievable prices, and you have the audacity to say that?" he pouted, his mouth full.

"It can only be used once a day and... I've been using it for other...." He let his voice trail off, not quite willing to come out and say exactly what he had been doing with the food in present company.

Adrick, surprisingly, understood exactly what he had been doing with it and did not press.

Landros's heart was soft enough to pain him to see the orphans and poor of the city go hungry or cold, to make him not just wish but to actually do something, but it did not make him any more comfortable talking about it. And bragging was just not to his taste. Far better a good deed often done and not known than a single deed done and crowed from tower to gutter.

Lark chuckled and threw Ivaska a piece of ham, leaning back in the cloak against Landros's chest. "So, where you get?"

"My father, actually. I do not know where he found it or when he acquired it, but it has served me as well as it served him."

"Heirloom," Lark nodded. She held up her hand, showing him the emerald ring on her forefinger. "This Gruma gave me. Is very old. Maybe old as you?" she grinned. "Older, maybe. Keeps safe from ghosts and other wandering spirit. Let me speak to them sometimes and learn."

Rog grunted, "Didn't help much on Evandair. Or were you wearin' it then?" he drawled.

She fingered the stone thoughtfully, suddenly more sober. She wished he had not brought the island up. She had actually managed to forget about it for a little while. "Is not good against... physicals," she finally answered.

"No kiddin'," he grinned.

Landros could tell the topic was bothering her, had felt her sink into herself, shivering at the mention of the island. He put it in the back of his mind to ask her about it later. Now was obviously not the time. Something happened over there, something that disturbed her, like the talk about his father and the blanket disturbed him.

"Say," Keltree cut in, sensing Lark's discomfort, "that was most impressive what you did with the deer earlier."

"Yes," Adrick piped. "Most ingenious, girl. Most. I would not have thought to call up the illusion of a deer to lure away an enemy patrol."

"First patrol complained no game. Made sense. Would have been for naught if you had not given Keltree tree seeming," she replied.

He shook off the credit, "It was only the illusion of a tree."

Rog snorted, "Ain't too tough to make that one look like a tree!"

Landros refilled Rog's flask with cider. "Oh, he's nothing! You should meet our friend Barak Hillvale."

"Thank ya. Big man?" Rog asked.

"Let's just say that you could sit on your own shoulders and still not see him eye to eye," he grinned.

Rog looked over at Keltree, sizing him up quickly, then at Lark with an eyebrow raised. Lark nodded, giggling. Rog drank deeply from his mug. "Humans!" he growled. "As if they ain't big enough!"

They laughed. "What can I say?" Keltree spread his hands mournfully, "but that I must duck my head most doorways I pass?"

Lark smiled, offering Ivaska a piece of biscuit. He ignored it, more interested in the ham in her other hand. He scooted forward, stretching to reach it, begging for it with his large brown eyes. She laughed.

"I think you are feeding the wrong animal the wrong meal, darlin'," Landros laughed as Nightingale landed on her hand and began to help himself to what the dog had turned down.

After a few minutes, Keltree set down his mug, and helped himself to the pie. It did not last more than a few minutes after cutting.

"Well," he began, cleaning his mouth with a corner of his kerchief, "I say that we get some sleep, set short watches, and get going at dawn. Rog, I'll need you and Landros to find this town that Lark mentioned and get us there as quickly as possible, encountering as few patrols as possible."

"That part shouldn't be too hard," he answered. "We're mostly out of what is assumed to be enemy territory. But then, we do not really know for certain how far out they're goin'. My best tactical guess would be no more'n five or ten miles out the city, and we're close to past that. As for finding this town... don't sweat it. If you want, I'll take the first watch."

"That is acceptable. Just wake someone up when you grow tired," Keltree nodded.

The men began to move away from the feast towards bedrolls that were spread in a circle around the rock, keeping them warm. Ivaska looked from one to the other as they walked away. When he was certain no one was looking, he began wolfing down the remains of the ham. Lark reached for a biscuit to put in her pocket for tomorrow and caught him. "Ivaska!" she hissed.

He ducked but did not let go of the ham and began backing off slowly.

Landros held her back as she reached to take it from him. "Oh, let him have it. A big dog like that needs to eat big anyway. He is too thin as it is, and I think we are done with it."

She sighed but gave in, jerking her hand upward in his direction, swearing under her breath.

"Just get him off the blanket," Landros laughed.

She gave him a curt hand signal, and he trotted over to a corner to devour his prize. Landros pulled out the honey and the rest of the biscuits, setting them aside for breakfast. He said the command word again, and everything on the blanket disappeared. He stood and snapped it clean.

"Now, that's the way to wash the dishes!" Rog laughed heartily as he wrapped himself up in his cloak and settled down to his watch.

Lark set Landros's cloak beside him and placed her bag as close to the rock as she could find room. She took her shawl from around her hips, wrapped herself up in it, and laid down on the cold, bare earth with only her bag for a pillow.

Landros looked down from folding the blanket and saw the way she was planning to sleep. 'Doesn't the girl have a blanket?' he asked himself.

She reached secretively into the side pocket of her bag, feeling about for the tiny, carefully stored bottle.

"Lark, what do you think you are doing?" Landros growled from above her.

She jumped. "I..."

"Don't you have a bedroll?" he asked.

She breathed, suddenly realizing that she had been holding it. "No," she answered, relaxing. "Was not planning on going where would need one. Only thing in bag is slippers and musicals."

"You're using your instrument for a pillow?" Keltree asked from across the camp.

She shrugged. "Is in hard leather case. My head will not hurt. Has suffered worse and still in tune. Dog would make better pillow, but he's busy," she grinned. She stifled a shriek, startled by the sudden weight of the picnic blanket descending on her. "What are..."

"Put half of it under you and cover yourself with the other half," Landros said. "The earth will steal your body heat faster than the wind."

"And what will you use?" she protested.

"*I* remembered a bedroll," he grinned.

She sighed and stretched out on the blanket, folding it over her. As she settled down, she took the opportunity to pull out her bottle and take the tiniest sip of it. She tucked it back away and tried to get comfortable on her pack. Soon enough, it did not matter.

Landros spread his bedroll next to hers, bundling himself up in his cloak. He lay there for a long time, very conscious of the woman curled up behind him. Her breathing became deep and regular swiftly. At least she was not having trouble sleeping. But then, she did not have herself occupying her mind. She had leaned back against him so naturally, had fit so well... He drifted to sleep to thoughts of her warm, sinuous body curled up against his, nestled deep in a feather mattress beside a warm fire.

Breakfast was dry biscuits moistened with generous amounts of honey. Rog spent nearly half an hour before sunrise pouring over the map and assessing the nearest possible location for a town as none was marked on the paper, not for miles. Finally, as the sun began creeping over the horizon's edge, he called Keltree over. He knelt beside the dwarf and peered at the map over his shoulder. Rog pointed to a small inlet about a day's walk from their current position. "This is the only place I can figure that would have the capacity to dock a ship. I am still bettin' that this cove right here," he pointed to an indention much closer, "is where they left from. If they'd gone to the town, we'd catch them before they got there, what with so many little ones in tow. But also, less likely for the same reasons."

Keltree sighed, visibly worried. "I just hope we can find this island she mentioned. Before what is going to happen to them happens. I have a very bad feeling about all of this."

He looked over in Lark's direction. Everyone was up and about, packing and stretching the cold and kinks out of their bones. She was still sound asleep, curled up in a tight little ball with one bare foot pressed against the surface of the rock, which was quickly losing its heat as the sun rose. She did not even stir.

He gave Rog a pat on the shoulder. "Good work. We'll head for that inlet and pray for the best just as soon as we can get moving."

He got up, crossed to her, shook her gently, and softly called her name. "Wake up, my lady. We need to get moving."

She did not respond. Fearfully, he pulled back a corner of the blanket, moving it away from her face. Her hair was damp, as was her forehead, though she was cold to the touch. She sighed heavily as he pulled a few damp strands from her face. "Come on, girl. We need you conscious here," he whispered.

Landros came out of the trees not far away. He had been on the last watch and, as soon as the others had begun to stir, he had headed off to do some scouting, found evidence of a patrol. He started running when he saw Keltree bending over the still form of Lark with a strange look on his face. He dropped to his knees beside her. "What is it?!" he exclaimed.

Keltree sat back on his heels to give Landros room and studied him curiously. "I am not sure. I cannot seem to wake her up, and we need to get moving."

"No kidding," he snapped, "there is a patrol fairly close, and I have this feeling they are headed this way. We have maybe ten minutes at the most. We need to move quickly, and we need to move quietly and leave as few tracks as possible."

Keltree got up immediately, going to each and every person, repeating Landros's observation. The news was better than coffee for waking people up and getting them moving.

Landros pulled Lark onto his lap and began tapping her jawbone, shaking her, trying everything he could think of to wake her. "Come on, darlin'," he muttered. "Ellinoia. Lark. Damn it, Illyana," he hissed. "Now, come on, we haven't time for this!" He shook her again. She began to stir, to fight the drug's effects. "That's it, come on." He reached over and pulled a skin of water from his pack, splashing a little on her face.

Rog grabbed Keltree as he passed by him, pulled him down to his level, "What's wrong with Lark?"

Keltree shrugged. "I do not know. She seems to be in a heavy sleep. We are having trouble waking her."

"Maybe the priest ought to look at her?" he growled. He let go of Keltree and strode to where Adrick was tucking the last of his equipment into his pack and finishing off his breakfast. "Priest," he snapped. "Something's wrong with th' girl. Go find out what."

Adrick looked up at the small man, a sneer on his face at his commanding attitude. Before he could say something rude, it dawned on him what the dwarf had said. He looked over where Landros was trying to bring her around. Leaving his pack where it sat, he crossed over and squatted beside them. "What is the problem?" he asked, opening one of her eyes and peering in.

Landros slapped his hand away.

"Believe it or not, Pathfinder, I am trying to help," he snapped. He opened her eye again. This time, Lark slapped his hand away, weakly. "Does she always sleep like a rock?" he asked Landros.

Landros glared. "How the hells am I supposed to know?" Adrick just looked at him. Landros frowned. "Not to my experience, no."

Adrick began turning her face this way and that, opening her eyes, in general, making a pest of himself. Lark began to fidget, sluggishly batting him away until she finally came to, sitting up on her own.

"Cease your devilment, priest," she snapped drowsily.

Ivaska's head came up, staring off in the direction of the woods. Nightingale peeped a low warning.

Before Lark could rouse herself further or complain, both men grabbed an arm and pulled her to her feet. Landros grabbed the blanket and stuffed it into his bag. Adrick snatched up her pack and set it on her shoulder, then grabbed his own. Everyone snagged their things, and Landros began ushering her down the slope after the others.

"What is hurry?!" she hissed.

Landros covered her mouth quickly and jerked his head towards the wood. "Ask your familiar, my dear," he whispered. "Just keep moving."

Nightingale landed on her shoulder and told her about the group of very large, armed men just on the other side of those trees. She stopped in spite of Landros's attempt to keep her moving. "They'll see camp and follow," she hissed.

"There is nothing we can do about that now," he growled, pulling her along.

They did not get far before they heard the patrol behind them. They were not crashing through the under-brush in full chase, but they were there. Keltree silently drew his sword and began to fall behind the others. Rog drew his own weapon and kept pace with him. Landros stepped behind Lark, pulling one of his swords. They kept going but prepared for the attack they were certain was eminent.

After a quarter of a mile, the sounds of the patrol stopped. Keltree paused, listened.

"Did we lose them?" Adrick whispered.

"I am not sure."

Lark sent Nightingale to check. They waited, the sunlight speckling redly through the thinning leaves. Nothing seemed to move in the early morning.

The bird came back, landed on her hand, and peeped confusedly at her.

"Says are lying down. Why are lying down?" He flicked his wings in an avian shrug. "Doesn't know, are just lying down like sleeping," she whispered. "Full of sticks," she added.

"I don't like it," Rog grumbled. "It stinks."

"Nobody move," Landros whispered.

They froze.

An arrow whizzed into their midst, catching the tail of Lark's scarf as it flew passed her ear and pinned it to a tree. Lark whipped out of it and fell into a crouch in the middle of the small group as they stepped back to form a small triad around her and Adrick.

Just as suddenly, twelve dirty, greenish faces peered out of the brush all around them, bows drawn and nocked. She was reaching for her sand, preparing to cast, when Landros took a step towards them, his hands held up in a gesture of peace.

He remembered something from his childhood, something his mother used to tell him and his brother and sisters around the fireplace on late winter nights. It was a story about wild elves who shunned all company but their own and who guarded their forest ranges with deadly jealousy from the predations and intrusions of others. But they were not unapproachable if, like the wild bear, you approached them right. The mere fact that they were face to face with these elves and not pincushions on the forest floor attested to that. He held out his empty hands in a broad gesture of peace and was careful not to smile lest a show of teeth be considered a hostile act. He spoke to them in Elvish, calling them brother in a low, soothing voice. He locked eyes with the nearest of them and held out his hand to him. The bowstring relaxed just a hair.

One of the elves to the left stepped out of the protection of the trees into the ring of bows where they were standing. He echoed Landros's gesture to him, calling him something that might have been brother, and asked him a question. It took Landros a moment to realize what he had said; the dialect was so pronounced and the speech so fast. He covered his mouth to hide the smile, glancing at the ground for a moment. He looked back up at the elf. "*Speak more slowly, brother,*" he requested, slowing his own speech. "*That we may understand one another.*"

The elf suddenly smiled, laughing. He slowed his question, gesturing for the bows to be lowered. "*Friend,*" he said. "*The others,*" he asked, gesturing in the direction of the enemy patrol now feeding the mushrooms a few hundred yards away. "*What they to you?*"

"*Enemy.*"

Seeing Landros speaking calmly with him, the others began to relax. Lark stood, put a hand on Ivaska's head to silence his growling, and moved to stand close at Landros's elbow. The other elf looked her over rather harshly but did not acknowledge her beyond that.

"*Enemy all men hunt here?*"

"*Big city, that way,*" Landros said, pointing back towards Portswain.

"*In big wall?*"

He nodded. "*Enemy all around the city. Keep city in walls, want to destroy. Steal our children.*"

One of the other elves chattered something to his chief so quickly he had no hope of understanding it. The chief looked back at him. "*Large group came here, many little ones. These your children?*"

Landros animated instantly, putting his friends on guard without realizing it. "*You've seen them? And you did not stop them?!*"

"*Calm, friend. No, we did not see. We saw tracks, signs of children.*" He pointed to the rag doll peeking out of Lark's bag. "*Signs.*"

Landros calmed. *"Do you know where there is a human village? Nearby, place for getting big boat?"*

They conferred with each other for a moment. One of the elves stepped forward. "I know this village, friend. I can take you there."

They stared at him.

"You speak the local Human tongue?" Keltree asked him.

He nodded. "I was not always a wild one. They gave me shelter and a life when I had none left. I owe them much." He turned to his chief and held a lengthy, fast-paced conversation which ended with his stepping to Landros's side and the chief placing his hands on Landros's shoulders.

"Friend," he said. *"Snowleaf will go, show you what you need to find. These enemies yours - enemies ours, burning our homes and trees when find. We lost much, will lose more if they stay. Game all but gone, and winter coming. Take care of Snowleaf. He is our brother. Helping you with enemy is helping us with enemy. Need anything, ask. We will provide. Go, and may the forest always walk with you."*

Landros placed his arm on the chief's and thanked him. *"If you need anything. Ask. I will be there,"* he said. *"I swear this by the forest way."*

The chief nodded, then walked past him, stroked the dog's head once, and he and the rest of his men vanished into the forest as if they had melted into it.

"So," Keltree began, holding out his hand to Snowleaf, "what exactly is it we have just agreed to?"

"You have agreed to nothing, actually," he answered, taking it. "It was he made all the promises," he said, pointing to Landros. "My woodling brethren named me Snowleaf, but my mother called me Savaren."

Lark took this opportunity to retrieve her scarf from the tree, inspecting it before tying it to hold her hair out of her face.

"I am Keltree Danhaven. Your friend there is Landros. This is Brother Adrick and Rog Thrathrog." He stepped back, gesturing to Lark as she stood up, flipped her hair back out of her face, and pushed the bright silk band into place. "And the lady there goes by Lark."

Savaren took up her hand, bowed over it, gazing longingly at her, from her wild black curls to the tops of her breast. "Ah, *ellinoia*," he practically purred.

"**Simara** *ellinoia*," Landros said tightly.

Savaren looked up, blinked, and smiled as he looked from girl to elf and back. "*Tell me, brother. Does she know it yet?*"

"Ah, shall we be going then?" Keltree asked, hoping to diffuse any trouble that might be brewing here. He knew from experience that a woman was the cause of many a conflict.

Landros silently fumed. 'Why did I say that?' he demanded of himself. He had called her *his* songbird, but what claim had he to that? What indication had she ever given him in that regard? She was obviously familiar with Keltree, a well-known ladies' man and carouser. But how familiar? Just because she gave him her virginity did not mean he had not been a one-night-stand. It suddenly bothered him very much to think he might have been. Perhaps on this picnic he had promised her... perhaps then he would find out one way or another how she felt. How serious she had been, or how loose.

FOUR

Evening was closing in when they arrived on the slope above the town. It was little more than a village, really, but it was large enough to have a small dock for its shallow harbor.

"This is Hallowell. There," Savaren pointed at the tall mast rising above the town in the harbor, "there is your ship. Gaining passage may be difficult, but gold will buy your way anywhere here. I only hope that you have some with you."

As they stood there, they watched the sails rise and fill. "I think they intend to leave without us," Keltree mused. They hurried down the slope into the village. Savaren pulled his hood up to shadow his face, and Landros followed his example.

The group garnered a few glances as they hurried down the street toward the small dock, but no one stopped them or questioned their hurry. No longer able to see the masts, they began to run.

When they reached the dock, the ship was already riding the tide in the harbor.

"Welp, looks like we missed it!" Rog announced, rocking on his heels in relief.

Lark leaned towards him, "Yes, but if miss boat, cannot rescue little ones."

Rog stopped rocking. After a moment of thinking, he began to curse under his breath in Dwarven.

Looking around, Lark noticed a small boat not far from them, with a man just climbing out of it. She ran over. "Escuse," she said breathlessly. "Favor for me, se'vah?" she pleaded, giving the man her best look of innocent desperation.

"What can I help you with?" he asked.

She pointed out into the harbor. "That boat. Have to get on it."

He shook his head. "Sorry, miss. Can't be done. She's a cargo ship, not a passenger ship, and the Cap'n's a little weird on having women on board."

Lark reached into her pocket and pulled out three pieces of silver, her last harps, and handed them to him. "Take us anyway?"

He grumbled but climbed back down into his boat. "Come on, then."

Ivaska bounded over, looked down at the boat, some feet below him, and whimpered as his mistress began climbing down. The others were quick to follow, though Rog hesitated. He reached into his pack and pulled out Lark's glowing stone and put it in his pocket. Gritting his teeth, he climbed down into the boat.

She looked up and saw Ivaska still on the pier. She grumbled and summoned up a poltergeist to lift him off the dock and down into the boat. He struggled, whimpering. Once his feet were soundly on wood, he promptly crawled between Lark's feet and laid down, tail between his legs and his whole massive body shaking.

"Humph, some guard dog," the boatman muttered as he began to row them out to the ship.

"I understand completely, shaggy," Rog grunted, holding onto the side of the boat with a white-knuckled grip. "I understand completely."

Ten minutes later, they were within shouting distance of the vessel, and the boatman bellowed. **"Hail, Andromeda!"**

A face appeared over the side, a lantern held up to aid his eyes in the approaching dusk. **"Walren! What do you want now?! All crew's been accounted for!"**

"Get the captain! I got passengers!"

"He ain't gonna take passengers, an' you know it!"

"Well," he shouted back, **"these folk ain't gonna take no for an answer!"**

The man shipboard grumbled and disappeared. By the time they reached the side, another man leaned over the rail. His hair was thick and wild in the wind, and one eye was covered by a black patch, but he squinted down at the little boat. **"I don't take no passengers!"** he bellowed.

Lark stood up in the bow, her hands planted firmly on her hips. **"Throw down rope, me bucko! Am not conducting business shouting!** Would ruin voice," she added lower.

Keltree leaned back on his elbows. "Going to negotiate for us?" he asked as they waited. "Do you think it wise, considering it has been stated that he is 'a little weird about women on board'?"

The rope landed practically on top of her, to snickering from above. She grabbed hold. "Precisely why should," she said, testing its security. "Oh, have money to offer him?" she asked. "Used last coin to get this far."

Keltree pulled a small pouch from his belt. "This is part of what I was given by the Lord Mayor to finance us. You can offer all of that if you need to."

She caught the bag neatly, tucked it down the front of her blouse, and began climbing. From above, it appeared as though she were effortlessly walking up the side of the vessel as she used her feet to help. She swung one leg over the rail in short order and balanced there. Pullin the bag from her cleavage, she tossed it to the captain.

He barely caught it, peeked into it, and saw a good number of gold coins with a few small gemstones winking back at him. He tucked it in his fist and glared hard at her.

"That," she said, "is passage for friends and self to small island southeast here. Is not out of way."

"I said before, this ain't no passenger ship. I'm fully loaded and headed South," he growled.

"Should pick up very valuable cargo on island. Stolen cargo will make heroes if get to Portswain safe."

"Portswain?" he exclaimed. He threw the money back at her. "Forget it, lady. No cargo is worth that risk!"

She dangled the bag by its strings. "If take us, wait for return and take back into Portswain, there will be this and more from Lord Mayor himself reward."

His eyes narrowed. "What kind of cargo?"

"Children. Stolen from their beds two nights past. You do nothing but take and wait. Is us do all fighting and hard work getting back. Have priest among us, and I no small hand with magic. Will earn keep or stay out of way."

He looked over the rail at the little boat below, conscious of his men slowly gathering and watching, waiting for his reaction. "Kids, huh? Twice that?" he asked, eyeing the swinging bag of gold. "I don't know. I have a thing about women on my ship."

"She's not a woman; she's a Gypsy!!" Adrick bellowed. **"Gypsy good luck**!" he called in his best imitation of her accent.

She laughed, leaning back dangerously. She hopped up, landed, standing, on the rail, and turned a neat little pirouette. A shower of tiny blue sparks rained down on them, touching each sailor who had gathered. "Luck you need? What is better luck than Romeri Princess?" With that, she called up a series of poltergeists, seeming to summon up the winds to fill the sails. She stopped, and the sails fell completely flat. "What say, Captain?"

"I say get off a'there before you end up in the drink an' I lose out on the rest o' this!" he snarled, snatching the bag. "Move it, you laggards! You, get a ladder and toss it down. I want to be on the Ride before sunrise!"

Lark hopped to the deck, shifted the poltergeist, which she had not fully banished, and used it to haul poor Ivaska up the side and deposit him beside her. The others clambered up quickly enough, and she sent the poltergeist to carry their things. She giggled as she watched Ivaska try to get his sea legs.As a sailor began hauling the ladder back aboard and Walren shifted his oars and rowed for shore again, the captain came over with a young boy in tow.

"Villis," he introduced. "He's the cabin boy. He'll take you down where you can get out of the way. Any of you know sailin'?"

"I know a bit, sir," Keltree admitted, "But probably not enough to be much help and just enough to be in the way."

"Fine, stay out of it then. As for bunking, I've no room for any of you. So, if the lady is not objectionable, you'll all get my cabin, an' I'll bunk with the mate. There should be hammocks enough in the ship's stores. Ma'am, I trust the animal there will keep you out of trouble in that manner?"

She smiled, fondling Ivaska's ears. "Haven't had any trouble yet, sir. Not with these fine gentlemen."

"Right," he grunted. "Now, you want to call up that wind again, miss?"

"Certainly." She swung her arm in a wide arc as if to throw a handful of wind into the sail. The witch-lights flew from her palm to settle like stars in the rigging. The poltergeists called up a nice headwind, and the ship eagerly leapt forward in the water.

"Thank you. Now, which of you knows where you're havin' me take you, and would you care to show me?"

Rog elbowed his way forward. "If you'll just show me to a chartin' table I might be able to do just that. If the fortune teller will join us?" he added pointedly. "After all, Lark, yer the one who told us where it is."

"Will try," she sighed. "But no promises."

The cabin boy led them down below to a comfortable room at the rear of the vessel under the quarter-deck. It was about twice the size of Lark's caravan and contained a sturdy table nailed to the floor and three chairs. There was even a trio of leather-bound books neatly stacked amid the slew of rolled charts. The captain joined them shortly as they were finding places to stow their gear. The cabin boy vanished.

Rog unrolled his map. "Here is where we think it might be," he said. "We were about here when she said that they were goin' Southeast. So, I figured…"

Lark tuned them out completely, gazing with interest at a large, detailed map that consisted mostly of water, with ports and landfalls clearly marked on its edges. She noticed what looked to be a river amidst complex markings, flowing from far north to far south, and off the map on both ends, though it curved a bit here and there. She thought about the children and the ship that must have taken them away, but nothing flared on the wall. No gut feelings or sudden insights. Her eyes kept coming back to the stream in the middle of the ocean. She reached up, ran her fingers along the smooth surface of the paper, feeling the unevenness of the wall behind it. Still nothing.

"What is river in middle of water?" she asked.

The men at the table looked up. "River?" Rog asked. "What's she talkin' about?"

"Here," she pointed. "Looks like rivers on Rog's map, but is ocean here, is not?"

The captain, suddenly realizing what she was talking about, laughed. "Ah, yes, that's the Ride. Yes, it's very like a river in the ocean. It's a strong current that runs south along the coastlines. It's a very common trade route that cuts days off travel time. That's where I was headed before I took you aboard. It's where I'll return when I leave you at Portswain."

"I cain't seem to find any islands that might be it," Rog complained. "Lark, maybe you...?"

She turned back to the map on the wall. "Won't," she said. "Is not on map."

"How are you...." he sputtered.

"Because cannot find it, is why. This map better than yours and is not here."

"So, what's the headin', Miss?" the captain mocked.

"Take Ride."

"But the island...." Rog started.

"Fate will take us, Rog. Just as got us here will get us there."

As the cabin boy returned with his arms full of hammocks, the strains of pipes and a small drum drifted into the room. Savaren looked around, confused.

"'S just the crew piper," the captain explained. "We should be well under way by now, thanks to your ghost wind."

A devilish gleam entered Lark's eyes.

"Lark, resist it," Landros warned, making a fairly accurate guess as to what that look meant.

"Resist?" she grinned, turning her brilliant blue eyes on him. "Is no resist! Is *sagavis, sesket*?"

"Lark, what are you up to?" Keltree asked, suddenly concerned.

"No *sesket*," Landros insisted, still trying to talk her out of it.

"What is sagaveees?" Rog asked.

"Sahgavees," she corrected. "Is ... how you say? ...in blood. Once there... cannot resist, can only surrender! Is drive you for always." There was an excitement in her that was very contagious, uncontainable.

'I'm doomed', Landros thought suddenly. That one word summed her up completely as far as he was concerned. *Sagavis.*

Lark whirled out of the room and up onto the deck, letting loose a swirl of witch-lights as she went. Adrick watched her go and looked over at the scowl on Landros's face. "Is she going to do what I think she's going to?" he asked, trying to hide his smile.

"Yes," his friend growled.

He put his arm around Landros's shoulder and sighed with compassion. "I do not know why you even try, Landros. Honestly, that woman is a force of nature, and you can't resist nature! May as well tell the wind not to blow."

"What, exactly, is that girl going to do?" the captain asked suspiciously.

There was a twinkle of delight in Adrick's eye as he looked over his shoulder. "Dance, what else?"

"I'm in," Keltree exclaimed, dropping the hammock he was trying to untangle and headed for the deck.

"Dance?" Savaren asked.

"Ever seen a Romeri dance?" Keltree asked. Savaren shook his head. "Come on. This is one experience the wild wood has nothing on! Rog! You coming?" he asked the dwarf.

Rog concentrated on tying his hammock off. "Nah, I'll stay here. Guard our things. Getting' tired, ya know. Long walk today for my short little legs."

"Suit yourself," Adrick shrugged and escorted Landros with a comradely arm up onto the deck.

The captain waved the others out of the room ahead of him and stopped to fetch something from a small carved chest in a cubbyhole. He pulled out a bit of reddish-orange root and handed it wordlessly to the dwarf.

Rog stared at the strange, strongly smelling cube and wrinkled his nose. "What's this?"

"Eat it," the captain said. "My friend Froi grayslung swears by the stuff for puttin' your stomach more in tune with the sea."

"grayslung?" he muttered. "A grayslung a sailor?"

"No," the captain laughed. "But he travels with me sometimes, ...when he has to. I know dwarven ways, my friend. Well, enough, anyway. It's yours either way." He put the cube in his hand and left the room.

On deck, the small band found perches on barrels and rope coils and any free space they could in a circle around three figures dancing in the middle. Even Ivaska had found a place to lay down and watch. Lark was learning the hornpipe from the two sailors on either side of her and still dancing circles around them. She made up steps when they did not come fast enough or did not suit her.

Landros watched her intently as she laughed and hopped about. She was breathing easily in spite of her exertion, but she was flushed with elation. She told no story tonight, at least not so far. Her movements were expressions of sheer joy, and it seemed her bare feet hardly touched the deck. The sailors around them clapped the beat, swapping out with the pair dancing with her when they became too tired to continue. Music filled the night, filled the sails, and echoed across the water joyously.

The music ended, and the sailors collapsed tiredly to the deck. Lark stopped, turning from one to another of the ring of men, laughing, out of breath. She caught Landros's eye from his perch halfway up the quarter-deck steps. She smiled, sultry as if sharing a secret, then closed her eyes, concentrating.

One by one, the lanterns went out. One by one, the tiny were-lights she had set in the rigging descended to her, surrounding her with an unearthly glow. She conjured a large, sheer scarf out of the air and spread it between her hands. She began to turn slowly, gazing at every man in turn through the cloth laced with tiny star-lights. Music began somewhere over the water, a slow, haunting violin. The sailors at first looked about them in fear. One even made the warding against the evil eye but was knocked harshly by his neighbor for it.

She smiled and saw the captain leaning warily against the wall of the quarter-deck, not sure yet what to make of her or her effect on his crew. From the depths of the stairwell to the berths, she caught the glint of Rog's pipe. Adrick sat watching with his chin propped in his hand, with his elbow on a barrel. Savaren gaped in awe at the sinuous and subtle movements of her body. Keltree smiled knowingly and turned his gaze up to the steps behind him, to where Landros watched from his dark perch. His stare was intense, locked on more than merely her movements.

She waited, swaying slowly until she got the feel of the ocean and the waves and wind and the night. When it was right, she moved with it, translating the songs of the wild seas through her body to these men who knew them intimately. They knew the subtle ripple of the seaweed in the currents, the crashing of waves on the prow of a ship, the snap of the sails, and the power of a raw storm. All these things she danced as clearly as if she had sung them. The music she played was an extension of herself, as ghostly as the instrument on which she played it. Her steps were rhythmic and smooth, though unpredictable, like the tides she emulated.

She danced not long, but it seemed she had portrayed a lifetime at sea and taken a lifetime to do it. As quickly as she began, she allowed the real flame lights to pop to life and began to tap another beat, a wild, rollicking sailor's melody, which the piper was glad to join in. She pulled two or three of the sailors to their feet, encouraging all to dance, even Savaren. Then left him to their tender mercies, slipping on nearly silent feet towards the bowsprit. She glanced over her shoulder at Landros, then turned and walked into the darkness. Ivaska looked up, watching her go, but did not follow.

The captain leaned towards Keltree and guided his attention to the now empty steps with a twitch of his head. "The sirens have competition tonight."

Keltree shook his head, paring his nails carefully with a small knife. "I don't think sirens have anything on our Lark, at least not where that one is concerned," he smiled. He nodded his head to where the curls of pipe-smoke were thinning. "Even the dwarf is soft on her, I think," he whispered.

The captain raised an eyebrow. "And yourself?" he smirked.

Keltree cleaned his knife and put it away, shook his head again. "Me? I owe that wonderful girl my life. But I think her heart has made up its mind already."

"That'll be trouble," the captain mused, slipping a finger under his patch to rub the eye.

"No kidding," Keltree chuckled. He peered into the darkness after the vanished pair, "I think that I shall call it a night, folks. Party as you wish. Don't worry about keeping me awake," he grinned. "You won't."

Adrick waved him absently off, sipping at a mug of warmed rum someone had handed him.

Savaren tumbled to the deck beside him and drank deeply from the mug Adrick passed him. He lay back, sighing happily, setting it aside. He rested a second, then sat up, looking about for Lark. "Where...?" he began.

Adrick gestured off towards the front of the ship. Savaren looked, squinting, trying to see her. Against the faint glow of moonlight on the horizon, he barely saw her silhouette at the rail and the figure of someone approaching her. He scrambled to his feet, but Adrick pulled him back to the deck and pressed another mug into his hand. "But...!" he protested, pointing.

Adrick pointed to the steps of the quarter-deck where Landros had been sitting. Savaren sank back down. "OH!"

He took a deep drink.

Lark leaned on the rail, gazing out on the expanse of the water as the moon began to rise. It was not long before she felt Landros join her.

He stood behind her for a full three minutes, watching the wind whipping through her hair and clothes, haloed by the pale sliver of light. He wanted to slip behind her, to wrap his arms around her and hold her to him, to breathe in the intoxicating scent of her, to feel her warm body against his chest, her silken hair against his face, and her soft breasts in his hands.

Snapping his thoughts back in line, he took a deep breath and let it out slowly. He moved to the rail beside her, just upwind so that her hair would not obscure his view of her or sting his face, or her scent continue to drive him insane.

Together, neither saying a word, they watched the moon rise, thin and pale over the horizon's edge. There was nothing around them but rippling waves and tiny glimmers of fish leaping about. Even the sailors and the music seemed miles away, coming to them from a great distance.

"There," she pointed suddenly. "Just coming over edge of sea," she said. "You see? Star just below tip of moon?"

"Yes," he whispered, not sure why he whispered. It just seemed right.

"Just below is four other stars. Make wyn, rune of joy. Is sign was born under. Is what I do. Am joy bringer. Is what Illyana mean. That is rising tonight means good things. Means there will be joy for coming home. Only happen if have children. So, follow wyn's tail, and there will find children."

They waited, watched as the rest of the constellation rose. Not knowing what the rune looked like, Landros could not really see it, but he took pleasure in what it meant to her. She was, really, when he thought about it. Peace-bringer. Joy-bearer. He could have used one of those half a century ago. "You will have to tell me my fortune one evening. When we are alone and in a quiet place," he said, surprising himself as he did so.

"Most certainly. Always pleased to read fortunes of others."

'Why doesn't he kiss me?' she wondered. She was surprised by the thought as she gazed at him, but it was what she wanted. That, too, surprised her.

He looked deep into her eyes, black in the dimness. 'Kiss me' they seemed to say. But no. Surely, he was reading his own wishes into things.

After a minute, she looked away, disappointed.

They gazed out over the water for a long time in silence. After a while, the music died down, and all that remained was the sea, singing the same unchanging melody She had sung from the beginning of time, an eternal aria. Sleep began to invade thoughts.

Landros took her hand and turned towards the stern. "Let's go in," he whispered. "It's late."

She slipped her hand out of his, suddenly terrified of the thought of sleep. "No." She pulled her shawl closer over her shoulders. "You go. Will be fine. Can't... cannot sleep now." She gazed at the hurt expression on his face and wanted so much to go with him, even knowing that they could not be together. She touched his cheek softly. "Too much sleep last night?" she offered with a faint smile. "Too much excitement this one."

He covered her hand with his, resisted the urge to kiss it. "If that is what you want?"

Lark nodded.

He sighed and turned away. He looked back only once, to see her standing sideways, staring out to sea as if mesmerized by it. Stuffing the unidentified feelings that were threatening to overwhelm him deep inside, he went to the cabin, determined not to think about her. He only succeeded until he fell asleep, and then... then she filled his dreams with fragrance and warmth and passion and soft, billowy clouds of silk and lights.

FIVE

Landros woke with the others to the smell of fresh eggs, warm biscuits, and oranges. He sat up in the hammock, balancing easily, and rubbed the sleep from his eyes. The cabin boy was setting a steaming tray of food on the table and skittered out as the captain came in.

"Ah, you're awake!" he boomed. "Of course, the smell of breakfast is enough to wake any man, eh? One way or another," he chuckled, with a pointed glance at the dwarf who was trying to decide whether or not the smell was pleasing or nauseating.

Keltree followed the captain's lead and sat down at the table. "You eat well on this vessel," he commented.

The captain nodded, pouring coffee for himself from the urn on the table. "I try to make sure my men have decent fare, at least on the first day out, especially of perishable goods when we can get them. After that, we ration ourselves intelligently. But I promise you, I eat what my men eat, and they respect me for that. You'll find no mutineers on this vessel."

Something felt wrong to Landros. The ship moved oddly, more smoothly. And the room smelled... of breakfast and men, not of perfumed meadows as he had dreamt. He stared numbly about the room, trying to wake up enough to figure out what was not right.

Adrick waved a biscuit under his nose. "Here, some breakfast ought to wake you up," he offered.

"No," he muttered, taking the biscuit. "Something's... different," he muttered.

The captain burst out laughing. "That's the Ride, my boy! Even your land-bound legs can tell the difference! We hit it some hours ago."

Landros suddenly noticed the empty bed, unrumpled except for the large dog curled up on it. "Where's Lark?"

"The Romeri?" the captain asked. "She's on deck. You might want to make her eat something, though. She turned down my invitation to breakfast earlier. She's too thin for a girl her age. She should be more round, especially in the hips and thighs," he observed, shaking his head.

Landros roused himself from his hammock and grabbed a plate of food and a cup of coffee. He leaned close enough to the captain to growl, "I happen to like a woman fit and lean," and headed for the deck.

"Most elves do," the captain muttered at his back, then turned his rather gregarious attentions on his other, less temperamental guests.

As Landros opened the door at the top of the staircase, he could hear the deep, chanting song of the men in the rigging, mending ropes, and securing sails. He looked about for a glimpse of her bright blue skirts near the prow, where he had left her last night. Amid the low voices of the sailors, there came a wordless counter melody sung in a high voice. He turned and saw her sitting in front of the massive wheel, her arms wrapped around her knees, singing with her eyes closed. Silently, he climbed the steps to the quarter deck and stood nearby, watching, listening. When the last round of the song faded, and the sailors were beginning a new shanty for a different task, he slid in beside her and offered her the plate.

Lark looked down at it, startled by its sudden appearance. Her stomach wrenched at the thought of eating anything. She looked over at Landros, at the concern in his amber eyes, and did not push the food away as she had first intended to. She took it but just stared at the contents.

"You did not eat anything yesterday at all. Now you have to eat something."

She shook her head. "Can't think of food. Am hungry, yes, but... is make sick."

"Seasick?" he asked, brushing a handful of hair out of her face when the wind shifted.

"No," she sighed, picked up the biscuit. "Will be start enough," she said, nibbling.

He sat there with her while she ate. She just picked for a bit, but after a few bites, her appetite kicked in, and she actually ate the eggs he had brought.

He began peeling the orange, concentrating on the fruit. "So, you stayed up all night?" he said without looking up. She appeared exhausted.

She did not look at him as she set the plate aside. "Could not sleep," she lied.

He tossed the peels into the empty plate. He could tell she was not telling him everything. He bided his time, as much as it irked him to do so. She would tell him when she was ready to, and until then, he would respect her choice. He handed her half the orange.

They sat there in silence, eating, tossing the seeds onto the plate, watching the sailors at their morning work. Finally, Lark got to her feet. "Think am ready to sleep," she said. "Thank you for breakfast," she smiled tiredly and stepped over him.

He watched as she descended to the main deck, disappearing somewhere beneath his feet. He had to admit he was worried about her.

The cabin was all but deserted when Lark opened the door. Only Villis was there, taking out the remains of the breakfast dishes, and Ivaska curled up on the bed. He sat up as she came in, wagging his tail happily. She ducked under the hammocks hanging every which way and stopped in front of the bed. Ivaska rolled over, groaning to have his belly rubbed. She obliged for a moment, then ran her hands up the length of his body, collapsing on his chest in a tired embrace. He allowed the hug for a few minutes, then began to wiggle, more interested in play.

Tired, she got up, took off her shawl, and laid it on the bed. She stripped off all of her jewelry, dropped them onto the cloth, and then tied them into a neat bundle with the scarf from her hair. Unlacing her vest, she rubbed the tightness from her ribs, and stretched. Slipping it off and rolling it up, she added it to the bundle on the bed and tucked all of it into her bag. She tried dragging a brush through her wind-tangled locks, but eventually gave up and tossed the brush aside. The salt spray had done nothing for her hair.

She was exhausted, but she was still afraid to sleep, afraid of the dreams she was sure would come. Uncorking the little brown bottle, she stared at it, tucked in her palm, uncertain whether or not she should drink. They were not camping out in the woods where they might at any moment be forced to relocate. If something of that nature were to happen here, there was nowhere they could go. She had a flash of the first of her nightmares, of being on deck with nowhere to run. She lifted the bottle to her lips and tilted it back until the sickly-sweet liquid just touched her tongue.

It was not much, but enough, she hoped, to keep the nightmares away. She re-corked it, put it safely in her pack, and crawled between the sheets, forcing Ivaska to relocate. She fell asleep to the gentle, rhythmic motion of the sea.

Not long after Lark had gone down to sleep, Landros found the captain up by the great wheel. "Can we have a conversation?" he asked.

The human sized him up, trying to read the elf's body language to gauge the weight of this conversation. "Do we need privacy?" he finally asked.

Landros shook his head, holding back a swath of his dark golden hair, "Not really, but somewhere out of the wind would be nice."

With a nod, the captain handed the helm over to the sailor hovering nearby and led him down to the nearly empty galley. He acquired coffee for both of them from the cook and sat at a table. "What's on yer mind?"

"All right. Why did you balk when Lark mentioned we needed to be returned to Portswain?"

"Blunt," the captain commented, quietly sipping his coffee.

Landros grinned as he blew on the hot, bitter brew. "I have been told I have no tact."

He chuckled. "The answer is that everyone knows that there is a pirate blockade there right now."

"Pirates, not an enemy navy?"

The captain shifted. "Now why would you ask that?"

Landros sighed, running a hand through his hair. "Do you know that Portswain is currently under siege?"

The news seemed to shock him, but not half as much as it should have. "Do I *know* it? No. Am I surprised? Also no."

"And your response has just been to avoid it?" Landros growled.

"None of my concern. I'm a free captain. I may be Tembian by birth, but more than half my crew hail from elsewhere. I call no land home, and if a port is closed for whatever reason, unless I've a cargo headed there... it's in my best interests to just sail past and not get involved."

Landros grumbled, drank some of the coffee. He really couldn't blame the man. Chances were, if he were in the captain's shoes, his response might have been the same. "Does anyone outside of the city even know our plight?"

The captain shrugged. "Don't really know, son. Word is out on the sea to avoid the area, that, unless yer a pirate looking for action, there is nothing worth the risk. But there really isn't much talk of land-bound matters in a sea-side tavern."

"Surely those who hire you for cargo have gossiped? Made idle comments?"

He shook his head. "I deal with specific agents and all we really discuss is the business at hand. I really wish I had more information for you."

"So do I," he sighed. "Any chance, when all this is over, you could get a letter to the capitol?"

"Ankreve? Maybe. I am supposed to be taking my cargo south. ...But might be as I could pass one on to other ships heading that way."

"That would be very helpful, thank you."

The captain merely nodded and drank his coffee.

Many hours later, Landros opened the cabin door quietly and peered in. The room was dim, but he saw a flash of movement through the webbed jungle of hammocks as Ivaska raised his head. Silently, he worked his way to the bedside. Ivaska began a low growl. "Shhh," he whispered.

The dog sniffed, then licked the outstretched hand, thumping the bed with his tail, begging for attention. Landros ignored him and pulled aside the curtain of dark hair from Lark's sleeping face. She was dead to the world. Uncertain, he laid his hand on her chest, trying not to think about where his palm was. Her breathing was regular, if a little deep for mere sleep. He pulled his hand away, taking note of how hot her skin was. He decided not to wake her for supper. Obviously, she needed sleep more than food at the moment, but he was still worried. It did not seem natural to him.

He pulled the covers over her shoulder and took the dog with him as he crept quietly back across the room. He had a feeling, however, that he could have tromped in here in full field plate, roaring drunk, and she would not have stirred. He resolved to ask Adrick about it over dinner.

Entering the mess hall, he sent the dog to a deserted corner, and went to get some food for the both of them. He was able to procure only a portion of salt pork, some hard bread, a bowl of weak porridge, and a quarter of an apple. He set the bowl down for the dog and cut off a small chunk of the salt pork for him before sitting down with his friends.

Savaren was poking at the porridge, not quite sure what to make of it.

Adrick was soaking his bread in his water to make it soft enough to eat. "The fare seems to become considerably different once you're well out to sea," Adrick was complaining, wrinkling his nose at the rough porridge in front of him.

A nearby sailor nodded. "We eats well first day out, 'til the perishables is gone. After that we's all on tight rations. Less'n we's catch some fish or summat. Then we's feasts 'til all 'at's gone, then it's back to hardtackys 'til we's in port again or catch summat else. Better fare, though, than some vessels I been on. Lucky if they adds a bit o' rat to the porridge there, you are," he grinned widely as he crunched his apple. "'Side's, gots to make the apples last, now don' we? 'Cause when they's gone, it's onions fer us!"

"Still," Adrick grumbled.

The captain sat down at the end of the table with his portion of the pork and bread. "So," he said. "How's the young lady? I noticed she didn't come for supper. Or has she been taken her share?"

Landros shook his head and washed down the dry bread with warm, flat-tasting water. "She is still asleep. I thought it best not to wake her."

"Shouldn' wonder," another sailor added, "Up dancin' and playin' most th' night and still stayin' up to take a whole watch."

"Then pipin' us up to th' riggin' at daybreak!" another injected. "Though it sure was nice havin' a sopraner singing coun'er point," he added, stuffing his mouth. "Ain't been th' same ever since Villis started crackin'...." he laughed.

The captain ignored the jokes and jibes regarding the changing of the cabin boy's voice and turned to his guests/employers. "I do hope she ain't ill. Some don't take well to the salt sea," he asked, eyeing the dwarf.

"I think she is all right," Landros added, tossing the rock-like heel of his bread to Ivaska. "Though, Adrick, I've been meaning to talk to you about it," he began.

"Ever thought that maybe she just sleeps like a rock?" Adrick growled sullenly.

Rog shook his head, wiping his mouth on the back of his sleeve and letting loose a hearty belch. "That she don't," he said. "She might toss an' turn a bit, but she wakes easy enough."

The sailors who heard the statement looked curiously over. Landros glared them down. The captain raised an eyebrow.

"Hey! I traveled with the woman before!" Rog growled in Lark's defense. "I can tell you that Keltree snores like a dwarf, and Adrick there talks in his sleep, and…"

"I do not!" Adrick snapped.

"We get the picture," the captain said, holding up his hand. "No one's disparaging the lady's good name. Far from it." He tossed a glare at his men to back up his words. The hungering, wondering gazes quickly found their porridge intently interesting.

Rog grabbed the table suddenly, all color drained from his face. "Is it my imagination, or is the water gettin' worse?" he gulped.

A sailor suddenly ran into the hall. "Captain, you better get up here! We got a storm comin'!"

The captain jumped to his feet and took the steps three at a time. Landros, Adrick, and Keltree were not far behind him. Savaren remained behind with Rog, neither one of them too keen on going on deck in stormy waters, and both suddenly off their feed.

About half the sailors in the galley followed the captain while the others swiftly secured the abandoned food and returned it to the cook.

Straight ahead in the graying sky was a coal patch of low-hanging clouds flat in the ship's path. The wind was already quite high and snapping hostilely through the canvas.

The pilot yelled in the captain's ear. **"The ride goes straight through it, captain! Ain't no way in any hell we're getting off in time to avoid 'er!"**

"Looks like a hurricane, Koss!" the captain shouted back. **"Get those sails down fast, even if you have to cut the damned ropes!"** he bellowed to the crewmen on deck.

"How long have we got?!" Keltree asked, shielding his face from the wind and spray.

"I'd say about an hour! Maybe less!" Koss answered.

"Tell me what you need, captain," Keltree offered. **"I know I ain't much, but I can haul a rope, and you look like you'll need every hand you've got!"**

"Fine! Koss, put him to work! We've got to get out of the ride if we can!" He then disappeared below to give orders to the rest of the crew still in the mess.

Keltree turned to the others. **"Get below and make sure that Rog is all right! He has a problem with sailing, and this isn't going to help! Make sure that Lark is out of harm's way, and get the dog into the room! Secure our gear while you're at it! If you think you're up to it, get back on deck and help as you can! If not, stay below."**

"Now would be the perfect time for one of her poltergeists," he added to himself and followed the pilot.

Landros and Keltree lent their backs to whatever was needed. Adrick went below to get Rog, Savaren, and the dog situated. He did not come back up.

The storm came on fast, and the rain began within minutes. It started lightly, a stinging shower that turned quickly into a gale-force drencher. From the decks, Keltree and Landros clung desperately to the ropes, trying to secure them and get the sails down. One of the lines securing the center boom snapped, sending the yardarm careening madly. The wind caught the turning canvas, snapped it slack for a second, then jerked it in the opposite direction, pinning it to the mast. Keltree was pulled from the deck by the sudden change, but Landros, aided by another sailor, caught the tail end of the rope and hauled him back to the deck, where he collapsed. The rope was secured, and Landros ran to his side. His eyes were closed, and his teeth clenched tightly in pain as he lay doubled over on the deck.

A wave crashed over the side of the rail, sending both of them sliding. Landros managed to latch on to a loose, flailing rope and grabbed Keltree by the shirt collar with his other, keeping both of them from washing overboard.

The sails finally dropped and were secured as the ship righted, and he was able to get to his feet. One of the sailors jumped to aid him, and between the two of them, they got Keltree to the cabin.

They laid him down on the floor in a corner, and the sailor took his leave again. Adrick bent over him, checking his soaking-wet body for signs of injury. "What happened?"

Keltree could not answer but lay there, stifling the pain, trying to curl up in a ball again, holding his stomach.

"I don't know what happened," Landros answered for him. "One minute he was hauling on the ropes, the next he was up in the air, and when we got him down again he was curled up like this. He couldn't even stand up."

"Did he hit anything? Did anything hit him?" Adrick asked. Keltree cried out when he touched his abdomen. Adrick muttered a low obscenity, continuing with a steady stream of Elvish curses as he began to strip his patient down. Keltree complained in moans and gasps but submitted.

"What? Do you know what is wrong with him?" Landros asked.

"Damn straight I know what is wrong with him," he snarled. "Rue told you...."

His verbal assault of Keltree was cut off when the patient reached up, grabbed the front of his robe, and pulled him close to his face. "You will not tell," he rasped. "Swear me your silence, priest or, so help me, I will crush your tiny windpipe like an overripe fruit."

Adrick untangled himself easily enough and straightened his robe. "Why in the name of the Maiden would it matter?" he huffed.

"Because I don't want it known. Swear it!" he hissed between his teeth, glancing at the still-sleeping form of Lark on the bed.

"All right, all right, I'll swear it. Bloody machismo," he growled.

Keltree lay back and relaxed as much as he could, with the agony twisting his insides.

Landros, confused, went back on deck to help, leaving Savaren and Adrick to get Keltree mended, dry, and warm. His mind was buzzing with all of the secrets around him. Lark keeping things from him, Keltree keeping things from Lark, and himself keeping things from everyone, including his own brother. The storm drove out all of these thoughts as he stepped back out into the wind and rain and lent his back to aiding the vessel through the storm.

It was only a few hours later when the captain sent him below decks, insisting he get some rest. To his body, it felt like it had been days, not hours, since he had been dry and warm. He staggered down into the cabin, debating whether or not he would change into dry clothes or just collapse into the hammock. Stepping inside, he decided to change. The temperature down here was only slightly warmer than up on deck, and his cloak had been appropriated for use on Keltree, who was already beginning to show signs of feverishness, even to his untrained eye.

Rummaging through his pack, he pulled out his only change of clothing: a loose shirt and a pair of green-gray pants. He went out into the companionway to change. Wringing out his wet clothes, he tossed them into a pile and put his clean ones on even though his body was still damp. He sighed. At least he was more comfortable than he had been. He grabbed his things and returned to the cabin, where apparently a disagreement had started in his short absence. He tossed his clothes into a corner next to Keltree's.

Adrick had re-situated his hammock near the injured man and kept an eye on him from his perch. He and Savaren were having a discussion about Lark and her sleeping habits.

"I'll bet you ten silver harps she sleeps through the whole hurricane," Adrick was saying.

Savaren shook his head. "I'll not be taking any bets, I'm afraid. My woodling brethren do not swear by silver or gold. So, gratefully enough, I have none."

"I'll take that bet," Rog growled from under the table. "And make it a whole laurel. No one could sleep through this," he added under his breath.

"A laurel it is, then," Adrick smirked. "I do hope you have the money with you."

Landros looked under the table. The dwarf had wedged himself between his war-hammer and the table legs and sat with his arms locked around two of them. He was white as chalk but did not appear overly ill. He was chewing on something with a very sharp, gingery odor.

"What in the nine hells are you doing under there?" Landros inquired.

"It's the only place I know ain't goin' nowhere!" he snarled. "Nails, you know," he pointed out.

Landros sighed and climbed into his hammock, gazing worriedly over at Lark. The fact that she was apparently sleeping through the storm bothered him.

Lark was not dreaming. She could not be; she had taken the draught to prevent that. So why did it seem that her world was heaving and tossing? Something was digging at her side. She turned, unable to quite rouse herself completely, but no longer comfortable asleep. A sudden lurch nearly catapulted her from the bed. She struggled upright, gazed blurry-eyed around the room. It was dimly lit by a single, wildly swaying hurricane lamp suspended from the cross beam. There was movement from swinging things that seemed to be strung like cobwebs all over the place. Something large and brown came awkwardly towards her. Before she could panic and move away, the bed lurched again, and, with the help of a very large, frightened dog, she ended up on the floor in the brown thing's arms.

Her first truly coherent thought was how comfortable this monster was and how elven it smelled.

"You owe me a laurel, half-breed," Rog snickered.

Lark lifted her head out of the blanket as she realized what it was and found herself almost eye-to-eye with Rog sitting under the table. "Drinking again?" she asked, still a bit druggy.

"I wish," he grunted. He seized a tighter hold on the table leg as the ship tilted sharply. Lark and Landros, still tangled together on the floor, went sliding. Lark shrieked. "See?" Rog taunted as Landros hit the wall with a loud whoof! "What'd I tell ya?! Nails!" he crowed.

The ship hovered at an angle for what seemed like an eternity, then leveled, tilting the other way as she hit a different wave.

"Am awake now," Lark groaned, holding her head. Somehow, she had managed to crack it against the wall. "Now, why is room all tossy-tumbly?"

"We're in the middle of a hurricane," Landros answered and tried getting both of them to their feet. "You might want to get back on the bed."

"Is safer?" she asked, spreading her feet for balance.

"No," he sighed. "But you'll be warmer, and Ivaska would probably appreciate it."

She looked over her shoulder at the huge, shivering lump under the covers on the small bed. "Is small wonder I wake up on floor," she muttered. She let Landros hold on to her as she crossed the tilting deck and crawled in with the whimpering dog.

Reluctantly, he started to go back to his hammock, but she held him back. "Are cold. Come, Ivaska has warmth enough for both. Have hands like ice."

It was an invitation he could not pass up. He settled in with his back against the wall, as far back on the bed as he could get, and pulled her close to him. Between her intense heat and the wolfhound curled up practically on their laps, he began to warm up. He quickly realized there was a price for the heat. Pressed so close to her as he was, all he could smell was her spicy muskiness, flavored with the salt tang of the sea and, of course, dog.

Under the blankets, she took his cold, numb hands and slipped them around her, tucked them up under her breasts. He drew a deep, slow breath, trying to keep his body under control. She nestled back against him, using him as a ballast as the storm tossed them unmercifully.

SIX

It seemed that only moments had passed, but the snores coming from under the table belied that. Landros blinked in the dimness and noticed that the room was no longer lurching violently. The rhythm was slower, thicker, and more sluggish. The others were hanging in their hammocks, sound asleep, completely unaware of the change. Even Lark was asleep against his chest.

He pressed his cheek against her hair, breathing deeply of her. He tightened his arms around her and found her surprisingly cold, even under the blankets and the dog.

She was dreaming. She felt the chill dampness surrounding her, pressing in on her lungs. There was a mist outside the room, a heavy, blinding fog, natural fog, but heavily tainted by the musty, cinnabar scent of magic. Something voluminous was wrapped around her, tightened. She started awake with a small gasp.

Landros lifted his head. "What's the matter?" he whispered soothingly.

She looked up at him as if she had not been expecting to see him there, holding her. And indeed, she had not been. She did not know what she had expected, but it was most certainly not that. She sat up and listened. The storm had stopped, slipped past them. But still remaining was the lingering scent of magic and the heavy press of fog outside. Her heart began to thump heavily in her chest.

Slipping out of his arms, she pushed the dog off of her and climbed out of the bed. She ducked nimbly under hanging bodies and rushed to the door.

Landros grabbed the blanket and followed her, though the dog refused to leave the cabin.

Outside, she tripped over sleeping crewmen in her haste to get up top. As she thrust the door to the deck open, the fog poured in, creeping down the stairs behind her like a living thing. She stopped, staring wild-eyed at the curling wisps around her ankles, and followed them with her eyes to the bottom of the stairs where Landros was tripping over the same sailors.

He stopped and looked up at her. She seemed wildly desperate, an emotion he had never associated with her. She turned her heel and ran out and across the deck without a word. "Lark!" he called and took the stairs two at a time.

She was at the prow when he found her, standing before the captain, arguing. "I say drop anchor!" she insisted. As Landros came up, she grabbed him. "Tell him to drop anchor!"

"What?" he stammered, confused. "Why?"

"That's what I asked her," the captain shrugged. "She wouldn't tell me either."

She threw up her arms in exasperation. "Fine, go get Adrick! Maybe man will listen to man!" she growled and, crossing her arms over her chest, turned her back on both of them.

The two men stared blankly at each other, both thoroughly confused. "Don't look at me," Landros said. "Her instincts are usually right. Would it hurt to drop anchor 'til we find out the reason why?"

The captain scratched his chest under his storm-stiffened tunic. "I suppose. But if'n we're anywhere near the Ride, or as far out as we should be, ain't gonna make no difference." He turned and bellowed to his men, "**Drop anchor**!!"

From somewhere through the fog came the reply of "**Aye aye, Cap'n**!" followed by the creaking of the chain and the resultant splash.

Adrick staggered out of the fog sleepily. "Is it all over?" he asked. "Or is this just the eye?"

"Adrick!" Lark exclaimed as she rounded on him. "Tell him why to drop anchor!"

He shrugged, completely befuddled. "I don't know. Why to drop anchor?" he yawned.

She grabbed him by his sleeve and turned him, made him stare at the fog on the water. "Look, *pashaska*!" she snapped. "Look with other eyes!"

Adrick focused for a moment on the fog, then stood straight up, eyes wide. "Oh, goddess!" he breathed. "By all means, Captain, anchors away, or whatever. You do not want to progress much farther." Without waiting to answer questions, he muttered a few words over his medallion and levitated straight up.

"**Captain**!" came the call from the port side. A sailor came trotting up. "You ain't gonna believe this, sir, but... the anchor's only at six fathoms! It's on somethin' solid, too!"

The captain and Landros both looked over at the Romeri girl standing with her hands on her hips with a miffed 'I told you so' on her face. Landros crossed and wrapped the blanket around her. A moment later, Adrick returned, his face aglow.

"You'll be happy to know, Captain, that the hurricane is well past us and not likely to cross our path again in the near future. Also, there is an island less than a mile from the ship's side. It is of fairly good size, and the fog forms a thick band around it. Judging from the magical nature of it, I think that fog will remain here for a while. It should protect you from island observers, though."

"Which way is out of it?" the captain sighed.

Adrick pointed to the left of the prow. "That way, sir."

"Good. **Hard about**!" he bellowed. "Now, is your friend below well enough to go, or will he be remaining aboard?"

"Well enough?" Lark asked. "What is wrong? Why not well enough?"

"I am quite capable of handling myself, thank you," Keltree said, striding up, looking much like his old self, though a little worn and pale. He draped his arm around Adrick's neck. "Much thanks to this young priest here...."

"You get hurt? How? How badly? Where?" Lark pressed, not heeding Landros's subtle hand pressures to not ask.

Keltree waved it off with a grin. "Oh, nothing. I just took a bit of a bang-up during the storm last night. Nothing for our little nightingale to worry about. Speaking of which, where *is* your little shadow?"

"Tucked away in cabin, hiding with Ivaska, no doubt," she sighed, allowing him to deflect her questions.

"Well," he said, clapping his hands together. "Shall we get our gear and get going then? I have this feeling the longer we wait, the more danger those children are in."

No one argued.

Nightingale flew to Lark's shoulder as soon as she entered the cabin, chirping his eagerness to be out in the open again. As she began to unpack her bag, Ivaska poked his nose into it, trying to find the biscuits that had been in there. She pulled out her red vest and put it on, lacing it, but not quite as tightly as she would have to perform.

"What's goin' on?" Rog demanded as everyone began gathering their belongings. "Where we goin'? Is it over? We gettin' off this tub?"

"Yes," Adrick sighed. "We are getting off this 'tub'."

"**Hot diggety**!" he shouted and proceeded to untangle himself and scramble out from under the table faster than Adrick had ever seen him move before.

Landros picked up his shirt from the corner and held it up. It was still soaked. He looked over to see Keltree glancing down at his own drenched clothing. They met each other's gaze, looked at their clothes, and both of them shook their heads.

"I don't think so," Keltree laughed.

"Maybe if we spread them out, they'll be dry by the time we get back?" Landros suggested.

"Yeah, but where?" he asked, looking around. "Ah, but of course!" Keltree exclaimed and began using his hammock for a clothes line.

Landros followed suit and then turned to make sure that his pack contained everything he thought he might need. He strapped on both of his swords and his quiver of arrows, making sure that his bow had not been damaged by the salt water or air.

Lark put her rings back on but added her other jewelry to the bag with her rune-stones. She did not want to make any noise she did not have to, so she carefully placed her violin and tambourine on one of the shelves in the cabin, along with her belled sash.

Adrick heard the jingle and turned to look. "Brilliant idea," he commented.

She glanced over her shoulder at him and frowned, "Am not complete *pashaska*," she huffed.

Adrick frowned and returned to checking his own belongings.

Lark looked around, trying to locate the doll she had found in the woods, and could not. Nightingale chirped at her. She looked down at Ivaska. He was sitting at complete attention, looking up at her with the doll hanging in his mouth. She held open the bag, and the dog, after a confused moment, dropped the doll into it. She ruffled his ears and tossed the bag over her shoulder.

Keltree held the door open for them, wanting to be under way. "We have everything we might need?" he asked. There were mutters of uncertain agreement as they began to file out. "Lark, my dear, you ARE bringing the dog, yes?"

"*Sesha.*" She clapped her thigh for the dog to follow, and he did …as far as the door. "Ivaska, come on," she coaxed.

He sat down.

Lark did not have time for this. She summoned up a tiny poltergeist and gave him a physical push from the rear, threatening to lift him up again. Startled, he bolted up the stairs onto the deck. Keltree laughed, gestured for Lark to precede him, and followed her.

The fog was still heavy around them, and visibility did not reach from one end of the ship to the other. The dog shivered, looking nervously about. He pressed himself up against Lark as she came up beside him, almost knocking her over. The pilot walked up and handed Keltree a small bag.

"Some light provisions," he said. "Not much, just a bit o' dried meat an' biscuits. 'Nuff fer you an' the kids if'n they ain't feedin' um." He led them over to the port side rail, where a ladder descended to a small longboat that waited for them below. A single sailor sat in the boat, keeping it secured to the vessel for the time being. "We're goin' out o' this unnatural soup, an' we'll wait fer ya out on the North-east side of the fog ring."

Keltree thanked the man. "We do not know how long it will be before we get back," he added.

"Will send Nightingale," Lark interrupted.

"Nightingale?" the man asked, confused.

The bird piped attention to himself with a minute flap of his wings. "*Sesha*. Will send when come. If is in bad shape, are in trouble. If give wolf whistle, trouble is coming for you, *sesket*?"

"Sess ket?" he echoed, even more confused.

Landros touched his arm and whispered a bit of advice. "Just say yes."

"Uh... yes," he said.

Landros clapped him on the shoulder. "Good choice." With that, he climbed over the rail and descended the rope ladder to the waiting boat.

Savaren began tossing him the packs one by one, then followed them down.

Lark used the poltergeist she had not yet dismissed to pick up the dog and lower him into the boat. As soon as his paws touched the wood, he began to struggle. She let him go, but he continued to move about frantically, not liking this at all, until Landros rounded on him and snapped at him to lie down. The dog stopped, cocked an ear at the elf. He pointed to a space just big enough for him near the back, and Ivaska, with head and tail lowered, slinked to it and curled up.

Lark grinned from above, and Landros returned the smile. He spread his arms, gesturing for her to come down. Mischievous as ever, she dropped her bag to him instead. He caught it, glaring back up at her but with a half-smile still on his face.

He helped her from the ladder, and she settled herself on the bench under which Ivaska was sulking.

As Keltree and the others came down, she gave instructions to her familiar. She wanted him to fly up, go to the island and find for them a secluded place to beach the boat, but the bird could not see and was afraid to fly through it. It took some coaxing, but she finally got him to fly straight up, out of the fog, and then over to the island.

As the sailor began to climb back up to the ship and Keltree and Landros bent to the oars, Savaren leaned towards Lark. "Where is your bird friend going?" he whispered.

"To find us landing place," she replied.

"But how will that help us find our way through the fog?"

"He is familiar. Am... in tune with him and his where-'bouts. When is in good place, can guide to follow."

"Oh," he said, not really understanding but realizing that he probably would never be able to anyway.

"Keltree," Adrick began, "I do not think you should be rowing. We would not want to strain yourself before we have to?" he said pointedly.

Keltree glared at him.

Savaren volunteered quickly. "Here, let me. It looks simple enough."

Reluctantly, Keltree allowed the elf to take his place and sat down beside Lark, crossing his arms over his chest. "I am perfectly fine," he muttered.

Lark smiled but did not say anything.

A few minutes went by. The only sound was the splashing of the oars in the water, exaggerated and distorted by the fog. In the prow, Adrick kept an eye out for rocks and other large objects which might pose a danger to the boat. Rog just sat in the bottom, dead center, surrounded by their equipment, and fiddled with the rock through the cloth of his pants, muttering to himself.

Lark touched Landros on the shoulder gently, bent to his ear. "Is that way," she whispered, pointing to the right. "We are moving too much left."

Under Landros's guidance, he and Savaren adjusted the course accordingly.

"Is it a good place?" Keltree asked.

She shrugged. "Is quiet. Trees go to water, he says. Almost make pond, so think is small cove."

"Sounds just about perfect."

After a few minutes, Adrick asked, "Are we still going in the right direction?"

Lark thought a moment, reaching out to sense her familiar's location. "Yes, why?" she asked.

"Because there are now rocks in the way," he replied softly.

"Well then, I guess we go around them," Landros answered and shifted the boat more to the right.

Within seconds the tall rocks were visible in the fog, scant feet from the side of the boat. A few feet passed by, and the rocks moved away, out of sight. "Left," Lark whispered.

It began to get dim around them, growing steadily darker. She activated her light pendant, but it did not help very much. The sounds of the oars and the water splashing against the rocks and the boat hung on their ears like a muffled echo. Ivaska whimpered. The fog began to thin out.

"Slow, slow," Lark hissed. "You pass him."

"If he is at the edge of the water, how could we miss him?" Landros asked, holding up his oar.

"Probably because we've gone under him," Adrick replied, running his hands along a rocky outcropping just beside him. "I think we are in a cave."

"A cave?" Rog said, picking his head up.

The fog slowly cleared, leaving only low-hanging bits skimming the water, and Lark's light spread out across a small underground chamber. The outcropping that Adrick's hand rested on turned out to be a stalactite. He removed his hand quickly.

"I hope its high tide," Landros muttered, eyeing the jagged, rocky daggers only a yard or two above their heads.

"No kidding?" Rog growled sarcastically. He looked over the edge of the boat and examined the water rings on the stalactite. "Hmm, not quite high tide," he said. "But close enough." He gestured to the left, just beyond the reach of the light. "You kin dock us just over there," he said.

"Over where?" Adrick snapped.

"Just row that way," he growled, sitting back down.

Landros and Savaren rowed where he pointed. They were a few yards away before they could see the edge of a natural shelf and a narrow cleft running back from it. Adrick leapt out of the boat onto the ledge as soon as they were close enough. It was rough and uneven but solid. Landros threw him the mooring rope, which he tied to a stalagmite.

The moment the boat ground against the rock, Rog climbed out, followed promptly by the wolfhound.

"Now," began Keltree as he stood up in the boat, "if only there is a way out of this cave to the outside...." He steadied Lark as she stood and reached out for Landros's hand to pull her to the ledge.

Just as they finished emptying the boat, Rog's voice echoed down to them from some distance. "You wanted a way out, fancy pants?" he asked. "Well, you got it!"

They turned and followed the dwarf's voice up into the cleft they had seen from the water. It was just wide enough for them to move through comfortably if they walked at an angle. It was a long, sloping path with many twists and turns, and slowly, the echoing lap of water in the cave gave way to other more land-bound sounds.

"Lark, put that light out," Adrick called softly from up front.

Lark touched the pendant, whispered the command word, and plunged them into darkness. As their eyes adjusted, they began to see the glimmer of daylight ahead.

In a few minutes, they stepped out onto a rocky, lightly forested hill rising above the ring of fog that surrounded the island. They were at least a quarter of a mile from the visible edges. They turned to look behind them at the passage. Even though they had just stepped out of it they still couldn't see it. It sat on a slant, with the opening obscuring itself unless one stood at just the right angle.

Nightingale flew down, fussing the whole way, and landed on Lark's shoulder. Keltree laughed at him, which made the bird hop around to face him, redirecting his displeasure. Lark stroked the feathered back, making soft, soothing sounds. She spoke to him in her own tongue, calming him. He piped a final squawk in Keltree's direction and flew off, sulking.

"Forgive him," she chuckled. "He... panicked."

"I can see that," Keltree said, still very much amused. He sobered quickly. "Now, we need a plan of action. Lark, see if he can spot a settlement or a building or an encampment of some kind.

We'll head in that direction, then set the dog to tracking if we find a trail. If nothing else, we can find where they landed the ship and start from there."

Lark nodded and stood there for a few minutes, staring off blankly as she communicated with the stubborn bird. She sighed, "He'll do but doesn't want to."

Ivaska began sniffing around, wandering rather aimlessly. While they waited, they readjusted their packs and readied their weapons in case of surprises. Lark made sure that her little bag of colored sand was within easy reach and that her scimitar was easily drawn.

Landros scouted the immediate area. There was nothing that remotely resembled a path or a trail, not even a deer run. He rejoined the others, shaking his head. Lark did not seem very upbeat herself. "No luck?" he asked.

She shook her head.

"You?" Keltree asked. There was something of a strain in his voice, just barely there.

"The only thing that's been through this tangle in the last season is me ...and maybe a rabbit or two."

"So now what?" Rog asked.

"We go up that way," Landros pointed, indicating the slope rising somewhat steeply behind the cave entrance. "We get to high ground, and we try to see the whole island. They have to have a fire going or something. We'll find them. If not, we'll pick a likely place and start there even if we have to find their dock and back-track them, as Keltree said."

They worked their way up the slope through rough woods and pathless wilderness. Landros led the way, followed closely by the dog. He stopped often, checking for tracks and perhaps a hint of a trail or a change in the lay of the land. After about half an hour of this, Keltree began to lag behind.

Landros stopped again and made a pretense of checking the ground and brush. He watched the human out of the corner of his eye. He was definitely in pain, but he was holding up, making a seriously determined effort to keep going and an equally determined effort to keep Lark from noticing that something was wrong. As long as he pulled his weight and did not jeopardize the mission, Landros decided not to say anything.

They pressed onward. It was not much farther on that Landros found traces of horsehair on the brambles and wide, obvious tracks cutting a path across the slope. There were bits of cloth as well, at about the level of a man on horseback. Ivaska began to growl. He stood staring north-west up the path of the horseman and gave a single low woof, looking over his shoulder at the group.

"Yeah, I see it," Landros said, giving the animal an affectionate thump on his side. He turned to the others. "At least four horses came through here, all four going fairly fast." He squatted in the middle of the trail and studied it for a few more minutes. "These are not too old, either. I'd say..." Several screams interrupted him from fairly nearby. "...Oh, maybe a few minutes at best," he finished, drawing his swords even as he stood.

Ivaska bolted up the path, and Landros was close on his heels. The others followed.

The ground ahead grew rockier, with large, jutting boulders breaking up the region. Ivaska outdistanced them all, and very soon, the shouts of men and the shrill neighs and grunts of horses echoed sharply all around, mingled with the barking and snarling of the wolfhound as he attacked.

Landros was the first to round the corner, with Lark just behind, and saw three scruffy horses and their scruffier riders dealing with the enraged dog while one of them dangled a screaming little girl in the air by the back of her nightshift.

"Lark...." Landros hissed, nocking an arrow and taking aim.

"Have her," she whispered, quickly summoning up a small poltergeist.

The arrow hissed through the air, striking the man just under the shoulder blade of the arm holding the child. The girl fell, screaming even harder, and disappeared amid the thrashing bodies of the horses. Above them, on a rock, they heard an adolescent voice scream, "Analie!!" just before the man who had been holding her was struck from the saddle by a ragged boy.

Lark lifted the little girl out of the combat, sailed her high up into the air, giggling now that she dared to look, and set her safely on the ground behind her.

"Get down!" Lark ordered her and then turned her mind to the rest of the combat. Her blinding spell was out of the question now that the boy had jumped in, and from the sound of things, he was giving his opponent a real what-for.

A second man sprouted arrows and fell beneath his horse's feet. Savaren, on the rock the boy had jumped from, reached into his quiver for another. Rog charged in, hammer swinging, a battle cry roaring from his throat. He was clipped in the forehead by a flailing hoof and wisely retreated, biding his time. Landros took aim and released. The third man staggered and reared his horse, blocking a further shot. Savaren drilled him from the other side, and the horse went over backward, screaming. One of the horses charged past them, fleeing the huge dog, joined quickly by the other two.

The boy was getting up off the still body of the man and looking around for the little girl. "Analie!" he shouted, then saw the elven ranger and the human woman standing there, watching him.

The little girl ran up to him from behind Lark and jumped into his arms, grinning. "I awight, Biwwy! Wady made me fwy!!" she giggled.

He checked her over quickly, making sure she was all right, and then looked up at the two strangers approaching. "Fank you," he said. "When 'e dropped 'er, I fought a' 'orses 'ad made 'er a gonnah!"

Behind him, Rog began to check the bodies, making certain they were dead and looking for anything that might identify them or who they were working with.

The boy was about ten or twelve, human. His clothes were thin and ragged, definite hand-me-downs and often patched. He, like Lark, was barefoot. She reached out and gingerly wiped away a bit of blood from the corner of his eye.

"Hell of shiner will wake up to," she smiled.

Landros saw the boy practically melt as he shrugged. "Won't be m'first, I'm 'fraid," the boy drawled.

'Is there no end to this girl's charms?' Landros asked himself. "Billy? Is that your name?" he asked. The boy nodded. "Where's the other one?" There had been four horses, of that he was certain, but there were only three here.

The kid's demeanor changed instantly. "Feldrin!" he whispered. He passed Analie into Lark's arms and ran out of the little canyon area full tilt.

Landros followed and nearly ran into him as the kid stopped just around the corner. Adrick and Keltree were engaged in a stand-off with the fourth man, who had a small, half-elven boy by the throat and waved them off with a short sword. Landros passed Billy slowly, coming up beside Adrick, swords drawn. Lark, slipping behind with little Analie clinging tightly to her neck, snagged Ivaska by the tail to keep him from charging in. He looked back at her and reluctantly obeyed her command to sit and stay out of it. He did not stop growling, however.

"Fewdwin!" Analie shrieked when she saw.

"Stay back," the man threatened. "Or I swear I'll open the brat like a midwinter goose!"

"Don' you buy it, sir!" Billy shouted, though he made no moves. "They needs us alive, they do. All o' us! I 'eard they boss say so 'imself!"

At that, the man snarled, threw the boy at them and attacked. Landros dropped his blades to catch him. Keltree lunged for the man. He was fast and very good with a blade, but he was very much slowed by his injury. As Landros set the child aside, Keltree locked swords with his foe and pressed close to him, ignoring the minor wound across his chest. A knife flashed between them as Landros snatched up his swords and charged. The man shoved Keltree back and kicked him full in the stomach, then turned to engage the maddened elf.

Landros laid into him with a vengeance, unaware of anything but his enemy until he was dead at his feet. He stood there for a long moment, concentrating on nothing but his breathing, trying to calm the rage, to get himself under enough control to trust his judgment. Lark's sudden shriek snapped him out of it.

He whirled, looking for another target, and saw her on the ground cradling Keltree's head as Adrick ripped open his shirt and began checking his wounds. The look on Lark's face sent his heart into his boots. He had seen that look before, a woman sitting with her lover's head in her lap while the man lay dying in her arms, and her hands touching his face so tenderly, so desperately, covered in his blood. The absolute despair in her eyes told him all he needed to know about her relationship with Keltree. It felt as if his heart had stopped beating.

There was blood coming from Keltree's mouth in a slow trickle. His eyes were shut tightly in pain, and his fist was nearly crushing Lark's hand. Adrick ignored the minor slice across his pectorals and concentrated on the slightly distended abdomen. Keltree flinched at the lightest touch. He began swearing almost immediately and grabbed his medallion, changing his curses to urgent prayers.

Savaren came over with Rog not far behind, leading the little girl by the hand. Billy picked her up and drew Feldrin out of the way, sat them on a nearby rock, and tried his best to soothe them. Savaren pulled a pair of biscuits from the pack Koss had given them to help keep the children quiet.

After a few minutes of prayerful ministrations, Keltree's grip on Lark's hand relaxed, and his breathing eased. He struggled to sit up and was stopped by another wave of pain. Adrick forced him to lay back down. "If you insist on keeping this up, Keltree Danhaven, even the Maiden's influence will not be enough to keep you from the Crone's Embrace!"

At the mention of the goddess of the dead, Lark gasped. "What is wrong?" she demanded of him. She turned to Keltree and shook the hand still locked in hers. "What is you not tell me! And no fib about 'little bang up in storm'! I am not *pashaska*!"

"I never said you were, girl," he sighed. "It's an old wound," he answered stiffly.

"Rue told him he was not well enough to travel yet," Adrick said.

"You promised me, priest!" he growled, and regretted the sudden move instantly.

"She's not pashacka, Keltree. Whatever the hells that is," he added in a mumble. "She'd figure it out quickly enough on her own!"

Lark's eyes darkened as she looked down at him, at the invisible wound. She turned his head to make him look at her. "Is vampire, is not?" she hissed. "Is where hurt you, and Rue and I closed wound. Are bleeding inside!"

"Yes," he grimaced.

Lark let go of his hand, almost throwing it away from her as she exploded. "Why you come then!?! *Sesket*?! Why, if Rue say you are not heal, do you come anyway!?" she screamed. Even Nightingale jumped at the sound.

"Why must you be so MAN about this?! Risk your life needless! Think you cannot be done without?!!!"

Landros did not understand a word she said. No one had, but lover or not, he knew the shouting could not continue. He crossed over to her and tried to pull her back, away from the injured man. "Lark, calm down and let Adrick do what he can."

She rounded on him. "You KNEW he was hurt!" she accused. Landros quickly and wisely let go of her.

"I cannot do anything else," Adrick said quietly. Lark looked at him, her eyes ablaze with rage and helplessness. "I am sorry, but the lout insisted on continuing. The small accident he had during the storm reopened the wounds inside, and he has aggravated them beyond my meager healing capabilities. I know little of surgery, mystic or otherwise. That is Rue's forte. I have exhausted my skills and my prayers."

"Lark, why don't you do what you did on th' bluff?" Rog suggested, trying to be helpful.

"Don't know what did on bluff!" she cried. She fell to her knees again and sank back on her heels, biting back tears of frustration. "I ...I don't know! WHY?" she demanded again, raising her fist but stopping herself from hitting him.

He reached out and took her hand in his. "I had no choice, Lark," he said tenderly, pressed a kiss to her stiff, bloody fingers. He sighed. "My niece... is one of the ones who were stolen."

Landros interrupted. "All right, that's it." He physically picked Lark up and set her aside. "Can you walk at all?" he asked Keltree.

"To save my niece, I would fly," he answered hoarsely.

"I'm not asking about flying. I'm asking if you can walk."

"Maybe," he grunted.

"I can give him something for the pain for the moment," Adrick said, "but it will not last, and I don't want him going far."

"Can you use a bow?"

Keltree shook his head. "But a crossbow...."

"We don't have a crossbow," Landros muttered.

"Yeah, we do," Rog replied and trotted back to the other three bodies and returned shortly with a crossbow with a slightly dented stock and a bundle of quarrels.

Adrick, meanwhile, pulled out his mug and crushed some herbs into it, adding a couple of ounces from his wineskin. He sat Keltree upright against a nearby tree and made him drink the brew. "This will dull the pain and maybe help stop the bleeding," he told him.

"What... a waste... of good wine," Keltree grimaced but drank.

Rog handed Landros the crossbow.

"All right," he said, squatting next to Keltree. "As soon as you feel you can travel, I want to take you and these three back to the cave. I want you to keep an eye on them and wait for us to get back."

"Right. Just give me a minute. Why don't you ask that boy what he knows about the stronghold and where the other kids are being kept while you wait?"

Landros put a hand on his shoulder. "Keltree, leave that sort of thing to me now, all right?"

He sighed and surrendered, albeit reluctantly. "All right."

Landros went over to where Billy sat with Lark, keeping the two smaller children quiet. She had given the little girl the doll she had found, and the child was holding onto it desperately, sucking her thumb. "All right, Billy, you said that they wanted you alive."

"Yessir," he answered respectfully.

"Do you know why by any chance?"

"Yessir, I do. ... But I'd raver not say in front 'o th' li'le ones, if you un'erstan' me, sir...."

He nodded and gestured for the boy to follow him off a little way. Billy handed Feldrin to Lark and followed. "So, tell me what happened?" he asked as soon as they were out of earshot of the others.

Savaren and Rog wandered over to them and sat listening on a nearby rock.

"Well, vis ol' man came into th' marketplace an' 'e 'ad 'ese dolls, which what 'e was givin' to th' li'le ones. I thoughts nuffin' of it at th' time. It was really nice of 'im, you know? I even went an' gots some uver li'le ones what I could find and brought 'em over, but 'e only 'ad twelve of 'em, see? Lucky enough, I was, or so I foughts, 'at some kid 'ad dropped 'is in an alley not far, so I broughts it to me li'l sister," he said.

"Go on," Landros said with a nod, though he half kept an eye on Lark playing with the children.

"Well, 'at night she was 'avin' trouble sleepin' so's I went over an' played wif 'er all quiet-like wif th' doll. All sudden-like I was inna woods an' 'ere was all 'ese uver youngun's wif they's dolls and in they's sleepin' clo'es and 'ese men was all 'round us. They's clap us all in chains an' drags us frough th' woods all day an' all night, which made th' li'le ones right miser'ble. F'ough you don' know 'ow glad I was to go, sir, knowin' it was me whats got caught an' not m' sis. Well, they puts us on 'is boat I don' know 'ow long, then theys puttin' us off 'ere."

"Where did they take you?"

"They's puts us all inna 'is wagon fing and carted us off inna th' jungle. They's an old fort stong'old up 'at way," he said and pointed up the mountain and around. "Is a good ways, sir, 'specially wif li'le ones. They's was keepin' us in a bas'ment room in 'ese cages. But I gots out, ya see," he winked proudly. "Gots th' locks open wif a bit a' twig, I did."

Landros crossed his arms sternly over his chest. "And two is all you let go?"

The boy became visibly uncomfortable. "Well, sir," he fidgeted, "theys two th' only ones in my cage and I didn't 'ave time ta spring th' rest. But I knows they'll be all right, see. 'Causa what I 'eard."

"What did you hear?" Landros asked, keeping his face an unreadable mask.

"I 'eard th' mage talkin' ta this tart, see, on'y she wasn' a tart a'tall. Not a 'uman one, any ways. She was differnt."

"Different?" Landros asked, cocking an eyebrow.

"Yeah, fough I can' say 'ow, quite. I suspeck she was one o' them succubitches me da's allus ravin' 'bout. She had dark skin, kinda reddish, wif jet black 'air and long red nails an' 'ardly anyfing on a'tall! Anyways, they's thinkin' we's all sleepin', fough I wasn't I lets 'em think it. She was sayin' 'ow proud she was a' they bein' able ta gets us, an' so clever-like, too. An' 'ow 'er master'd be very rewardin' ta this mage on account'a they gots all twelve whats was needed for th' ritual. 'Pparently they's plannin' ta use us ta summon 'is major demon character or use us fer a gift 'er summat. But can't do a fing wifout all twelve a'us."

Landros gave the boy an encouraging pat on his shoulder. "You did well enough to get those two out. Do you know how many men there are?"

The boy shook his head. "'At, sir, I don't know. We's seen quite a few, but more'n us. Maybe four fists full, not countin' th' succubitch an' th' mage."

Behind him, Adrick was getting Keltree to his feet with the help of Savaren. Landros turned to Adrick. "A succubus and a mage, plus maybe twenty men," he mused. "So much for leaving you to take care of Keltree."

Keltree put a hand on his shoulder. "Hey, you leave those three with me and a loaded crossbow and worry about the rest of them. Me? I'm only so much dead weight right now. Just get those kids out of there."

"You worry about getting better," Landros said. "Don't worry about your niece or the others. They're my concern now."

He gathered everyone and began to lead them carefully and slowly back down to the cave entrance.

The sun was high in the sky by the time they arrived, laying Keltree down just inside the hidden entrance and making him as comfortable as they could. He was already beginning to sweat with pain. Adrick took his wine skin and dumped the contents of the herb packet into it, shook it well.

"Here," he said, handing it to him. "Drink this as you need to, but go easy with it. It's all the painkiller I've got."

"No problem," Keltree croaked, and set himself up with his back to the wall, the crossbow ready in one hand and the quarrels close to the other. He took a deep pull from the wine skin, then set it aside. "Analie," he called to the little girl. "Come over here, sweetheart, and stay out of sight."

She shyly hung back, half afraid of him, until Lark bent next to her and whispered in her ear. "Is all right, Analie. Is hurt. Have to make him feel better. Go sit with him and do as tells you, *sesket*? Tell him story ...about doll?" she suggested.

"Awright," she whispered and slowly crept closer to the wounded man.

Feldrin plopped himself down next to her, "I'll tell the story," he said.

Lark went over to where Landros was talking with Billy.

"I want you to keep an eye out for anyone coming that is not us, all right?" he was saying. "If you don't see that bird over there first, or hear the whistle I showed you, get into the cave and keep the little ones quiet. If you have to retreat, go down the crevice. Take Keltree if you can... if not...," he gritted his teeth, "leave him there, do you hear?" Billy nodded. "There is a boat in the cave and a ship waiting outside of the ring of fog, but be very careful, all right?"

"What's wrong wif 'im?" he asked, nodding his head towards the cave.

"He was hurt in a storm last night, and the wound has opened up inside him. We don't know if he will survive or even if he will stay conscious. If he doesn't, you will have to take care of the others."

"Will leave Ivaska with you," Lark cut in. "Should warn if anyone come too close."

"Lark, we may need..." Landros began.

She shook her head. "Think children need more. Billy was giving good idea of layout of stronghold. Wait." She cleared a patch of ground to access the hard soil and began to draw out a rough diagram of the fort with her dagger. Billy made a few corrections here and there. "If stop at hill here, could take out with bows what in yard. I run 'round back, slip inside, get children out while you take out main force."

"Lark, if you think I am going to let you...." he began.

Billy was the one who interrupted. "'Scuse me, sir. It were my idear. Ya see, I slipped out frough 'is small space back 'ere. It's sort o' a chimbly, but wifout a stack, an' th' lady 'ere is th' only one o' yous what'll fit easy. She says she can move wifout bein' noticed, an' she'll need ta."

Landros glanced coldly at her. "Hard to imagine you doing anything wifout... without being noticed."

"Can be done," she grinned. She smiled, but she did not feel it. She had noticed a change in his attitude towards her from the moment Keltree fell in the battle. It confused her. "If make big attack there, will not look for little me back here."

"All right," he sighed, reluctant. "It makes sense. Rog? What do you think?" he asked the dwarf whom he had just noticed crouching between Billy and himself.

He shrugged. "Sounds good to me. She and the kids both'll be outta the main fight. We take out as many with a bow as we can, then go chargin' in full tilt. Lark, if you wait until you hear the battle cry to go in, the diversion'll be far more effective."

She nodded, "All right. Then will take little ones and bring straight back here. No wait for you. Get down to boat and loaded so if have fighting as you come, is less have to worry."

"But what if you get into trouble?" Landros asked.

She shrugged. "Will leave familiar. If go crazy, need help."

"Then we have a battle plan. We should get there towards evening, and hopefully, we'll take them out in the dark," Landros stood and went over to Keltree one last time. "Are you all set?" he asked as he bent down beside him.

"As set as I'll ever be. Look, I am terribly sorry it worked out like this. I wanted so badly to...."

"Save your strength," Landros told him. "We need you to take care of these three. You came this far, and that counts for something, though you should have had the wisdom to stay on board the ship."

Keltree grinned up at him. "Would you have stayed in my shoes?"

Landros stared at his feet for a minute. "No," he admitted, "probably not. But you just work on staying alive long enough to do that little girl some good. What is her name?"

"Navarie," he said. "It's not her name, but it's what she'll answer to in a flash because I'm the only one who calls her that." Landros nodded and started to rise, but Keltree held him back. "Wait. Be careful out there. Don't do anything foolish or stupid, or let Lark try any heroics. She will, you know. She's a brave girl, but sometimes.... She's like me; she does before she thinks."

"Don't worry," he said, with a reassuring squeeze to Keltree's arm. "I plan on carrying no bodies out of here today. And that includes yours. Your niece would be shattered if we brought you home in a box, not to mention how Lark would feel."

Oddly, Keltree sighed. "Ah, if only I could dare to hope. But I ramble, go! Go before they go without you!"

Landros was even more confused now. What sort of game was the girl playing? With a final admonition to Billy to keep an eye out, he led the small band back up the mountain through the woods and up toward the enemy encampment.

SEVEN

Lark followed silently as they shifted terrain from wooded to near jungle-like tangles. Landros kept to the front of the group, well away from her. When they stopped for short breaks, he did not even look at her. She was trying to figure out what had gone wrong and why she was so desperate to right it. What difference did it make? She couldn't keep him anyway. Why even try?

Landros watched her sinking into despair, wanted desperately to comfort her. But it only reinforced what he had already suspected. She was in love with Keltree. So, when she had put her arm around him in the woods just after that first encounter with the enemy patrol, was she just trying to make Keltree jealous? Was he being used? It made his head hurt to think about it, not to mention his heart. He decided to drive it all out of his mind and focus on the matter at hand: the children. And, if Keltree survived, then that would be dealt with ...by not dealing with it.

Their thoughts were interrupted as the jungle began to thin out rather sharply just ahead of them, unnaturally. Landros waved for the others to lie low and crept forward to investigate. He stopped just at the lip of the jungle and pulled his hood over his head to shadow his face, glad of the green paint that Savaren had given him.

The cleared area was a rather large kill zone, in which sat a nice little stronghold backed up against the rocky slope of the mountain. It was no wonder the bird had not seen it. There was a partial palisade and several men milling about within it, though only five appeared to be on guard duty. Every last one of them was armed and armored. There was a small corral in which several half-broken, feral horses were being kept. A few hundred yards away, he saw a series of protected outcroppings, which he thought might provide a decent vantage/attack point without being observed if they were careful. He crept back to where the others waited.

He gestured for them to cluster into a tight group so that he would not have to talk above a whisper. Damn it all to the nine hells if the girl did not have to stand so close! "There's a place over that way where I think we can get a good look at things. I want to back-track about fifty yards and loop over from the east. Move slowly and quietly."

They all nodded and prepared to follow his lead. Lark caught Landros's eye and smiled sadly. The expression disturbed him. His unwilling reaction to that look went all the way to his roots and back, and there was little doubt that was exactly what she had intended. Landros put a rein on his temper and led the way.

It was nearing early evening by the time they reached the outcrop. It was a perfect place for a sentry. Too bad the enemy had thought so, too. Savaren slipped a little ways past the outcrop to keep the guard from falling into the clearing and killed him without so much as a whisper. The body was quickly searched and disposed of.

"All right," Landros began. "Savaren, I want you to take up position on that outcrop. You will be our cover fire. Rog, you and I will take opposite sides of it and prepare, on the mark, to charge in or creep across the killing field as we need to. Adrick, you will be our backup. I don't want you getting in too close if you can help it, so follow at a reasonable distance, if you follow at all. If you intend on throwing something that might catch us, give us a heads up or an eyes shut or whatever. Lark," he sighed, "come with me."

He led her up onto the outcrop and crawled out on his belly to peer over the edge.

She watched him closely as he pointed out a small rise just on the other side of the palisade. He was acting very strangely, kept himself both physically and emotionally distant. She watched his eyes and face carefully as he spoke to her softly, trying to find the passionate, driven young elf she had spent the night with, had met in the marketplace not four days ago, and had traveled across the sea with. All that was left was the driven young elf, and she had to wonder about the young part.

"That's where Billy said he got out," he was saying. "I think if you work your way to it from the left here, it will be thick enough to hide you. You should be able to make it there before you have to have light. Nightingale should stay here and pipe us when you are in position. Once you give us that heads-up, we'll make our move. When you hear the commotion, go in, get the kids out, and head back. Have Nightingale signal us when you have them and are out of danger, then head straight for the cave... Why are you staring at me like that?" he asked. Her midnight eyes focused so intently on him made him uncomfortable.

"Because," she said sullenly, "are starting to sound like soldier." With that, she got up and headed back to the others.

He lay there a minute, cursing under his breath, before he followed.

As he approached, Nightingale landed on his shoulder and tapped him with his beak, gave a tiny chirrup that almost sounded like a cricket.

"Is signal for we are out and away, and you can retreat," Lark said, then turned and slipped into the jungle without another word. Nightingale made a low, sad whistle after her but obediently remained behind.

Slipping silently through the thick foliage, Lark tried not to think about Landros and his change in behavior. She knew her own attitude was not going to help. ...Perhaps it was not her at all, she thought. Perhaps it was the sudden weight of leadership that had been dropped on his shoulders. Perhaps he, too, was deeply worried about Keltree and was only trying to focus his thoughts. She was a distinct endangerment to that focus, even she realized that.

She stopped, froze in her tracks as something very large came near through the underbrush. Holding her breath, she waited, trying to make herself as invisible as she could. Something moved low in the bushes near her ankles. She stared hard at it, trying to make it out in the quickly fading light. A wild pig looked up from under a broad leaf, saw her, and bolted. She let her breath out all at once. Getting her nerves quiet again, she proceeded forward, trying to keep the lights from the encampment visible on her right as she went.

It was full dark by the time she found the unguarded back of the fort. Looking up at the thirty-foot palisade, it was easy to see why. What could get in?

She slipped silently across the narrow strip of ground between the mountain and the wall. It was shin deep in weeds and ferns and small feathery plants, as if trying to grow back into jungle. Suddenly, her foot met nothing, and she found herself face down in the weeds, with her leg hip deep in a hole and fervently thanking her skill as a dancer that she had not snapped the limb in half as she fell. "*Oh, pagan delights*," she swore and started to pick herself up when a bullseye lantern cast its disparaging eye down on the area. She lay as flat as she could, held perfectly still. She heard a voice high above her on the wall behind the light.

"What's the matter?"

"Don't know. I thought I heard...."

"What? What'd ye hear?"

"I don't know," the first voice insisted.

Lark decided to give them something to find other than herself. She cast an illusion of a large black wildcat stalking a small rabbit through the weeds. The lantern shifted to it as it pounced. She made it look up, eyes gleaming in the circle of light, and then tear off into the jungle. A crossbow bolt landed very near to her.

"Damn, missed!"

"That was a muckin' great cat!" the other whispered.

She waited a long moment as the light hesitated, then disappeared. She did not move until she was absolutely certain they had gone away. Then, giving Nightingale the heads up, she slipped her other leg down into the narrow hole and eased herself into the shaft.

Nightingale began to softly chirrup like a cricket.

"All right, that's it. Savaren," Landros whispered, "you start on the right, and I'll start on the left."

Landros and Rog crept along the sides of the broken, monolithic outcrop, concealing themselves at the edges of the jungle. Landros drew his bow and took careful aim. He and Savaren released at the same time, and the two outermost guards went down with arrows in their throats. As their comrades began to react, two more were shot down. They began to dodge, running for cover. The horses were screaming in terror of the unseen threat. As it began to take more than one arrow for each man, Landros dropped his bow, pulled his swords, and charged out across the open ground. Rog followed as fast as he could, letting loose a blood-curdling howl.

Adrick stood beside Savaren on the rock and began to cast. His first spell erected a barrier between the two of them and incoming arrows, which began to fly from the battlements as soon as he was seen glowing in the air at the edge of the jungle. Then he began chanting and gesturing, calling up the images of pirate ghosts rising up out of the ground and the surrounding trees. These he flew in, howling and moaning, causing those not in immediate combat to flee into Savaren's swift and deadly sights.

The elf and the dwarf fought like madmen, making as much noise as they possibly could as they fought their way to the quickly closing gate of the palisade.

Still maintaining the control of his 'ghosts', Adrick cast again, this time aiming his crossed fingers at the palisade gate. A bolt of eldritch lightning arched across the open ground and struck, shattering it. Splinters and large chunks of wood rained down on those inside the walls. Landros, Rog, and the ghostly army charged in.

Lark set her feet on uneven ground and discovered an opening no higher than her knees. She folded herself up and slipped out, found herself in a large, dim room whose dimensions were more hidden than revealed by the single lamp hanging in the center. There was a good bit of rubble between her and that light source, and the corner of the room which she was in was completely in shadow. The chimney from this side looked a lot smaller than it actually was. It was more likely a ventilation shaft of some sort rather than an actual smokestack. Across the room she could see, just within the edges of the light, four large cages suspended from the ceiling at the four cardinal points. One of them hung empty.

She crept closer and felt a heaviness in the air that pressed in on her. Something was off, but she could not place what. Entering the circle of light, she felt something sharp underfoot and looked down. A ringed pentagram had been chiseled into the floor and filled with a mixture of what looked to be ground glass and tar.

She stepped off of it and lifted her foot up to pick out tiny bits of glass. Her feet were tough, though, from running about barefoot most of her life. There was only a little blood and not much pain. She did not enter the pentagram but walked around it, in the shadows, towards the nearest cage. The children inside watched her with wide eyes and complete silence.

Lifting the lock on the small cage, she decided quickly that she had little hope of picking or forcing it. Summoning up her inner magic, she drew a small rune on the side of it, commanding it open. With a smile of triumph, it popped off.

Without warning, she was thrown up against the cage and pushed past it to the floor beyond it. The cage swung wildly, spinning. Inside, though they huddled against each other in terror, the children never uttered a sound.

A sharp pain embedded in her back, even as she landed hard on the tarred glass pentagram. It scrabbled and clawed and bit, pulling on her hair and making the most horrific noisome smells.

Lark resisted screaming. Instead, she half-rose, turned and slammed her back to the glass-encrusted floor. It only partially let go of her.

She quickly scrambled to her feet, the creature hanging on to her hair. She swung her head violently, finally sending the horrid little thing flying across the room, where it landed against one of the cages. A little boy kicked at it viciously but held his silence, watching Lark with hope sparkling in his eyes.

The creature crept across the pentagram towards her. It was a horrid little grotesque, a mockery of the children in the cages. It was no bigger than a toddler, with pointed, flappy ears, a twisted ribbon of a nose, and large eyes like black pits. Its belly was very round and protuberant. His stubby little limbs ended in vicious claws, and its gaping mouth was full of sharp teeth. It made faces as it stalked her.

Lark reached for her sand, threw it at the creature, and shouted her command word. The sand flew in a dazzling arch but failed to change into an array of blinding lights. No sound came from her mouth. The thing threw back its head, flapping its ears like a mad thing. Cackling, she supposed. It, too, was disturbingly silent. Then it charged her, leaping easily four feet from the ground.

She ducked, ignoring the pain in her soles and the thin trail of blood she was leaving. Darting out of the way, she drew her scimitar. The demonling made another jump at her. She swung, connected with its midsection, and threw it across the room. There was no blood on her blade, and the thing came right back for her. She hit it again, across the side of its face. And again, it was not fazed.

It came at her slowly this time, taunting like the demon it was, its arms spread wide as if daring her to kill it. Lark felt panic rising, choking her as she tried to back away. It lunged suddenly and landed on her, seizing her arms in its over-long claws, its hind claws digging into her belt.

Fear threatened to make her physically ill as it took her sword from her stiffened hand and threw it aside, silently cackling all the while. Still backing off, flailing, Lark bumped blindly into one of the cages and fell. The thing clawed at her chest, grinning sickeningly down at her face.

She was frozen in terror for what felt like minutes but had only been a matter of seconds. Her hand brushed against something hard at her thigh, and she remembered the dagger she had strapped there at Keltree's insistence. Convinced she could not hurt it, still, she thought she might surprise it enough to get it off of her and give her a chance to outwit it. She inched her skirt up with crawling fingers, reaching for the hilt.

The creature sat up in triumph, cackling in mad glee, and slapped its talons across her face, leaving three long trails of blood. The wounds numbed almost instantly. Lark tightened her fist around the dagger. In one swift move, she managed to free it from its hilt and embed it in the demonling's back. It loosed a silent scream and began to tremble. It still made no sound, but she could almost feel it.

She rolled it off of her, her dagger still in its back. It tried to scrabble away, clawing at the stone floor, desperate. Grabbing the hilt, she drove the blade deeper, pulled it out, and stabbed it again and again until the little fiend began to melt and sizzle. She jumped back as it burst into flames, screaming all the while. The tar that was used to cement the glass into the circle caught fire, and she suddenly found herself in the midst of a flaming pentagram.

She spun, trying to gauge the shortest path out. She took a deep breath and jumped, running heedless of scorched cotton and cut and burned feet. Safely out of the ring of fire, she fell to her hands and knees, finally acknowledging the pain she was in. She also noticed that her skirts were on fire. She rolled quickly, tucking the cloth under itself to smother it.

The air swiftly became stale and foul with the stench of burning tar and sulfur and other unknown, noxious things.

The creature's death must have ended the spell, that or the burning of the pentagram, as the children began to cry out. Lark looked up. In their silence, she had forgotten they were so close to the flames. She paused only long enough to pull the largest piece of glass from her foot and ran to the nearest cage. Tracing the rune, she opened the lock and the door, and the three imprisoned children scrambled out and into the safety of the shadows, away from the fire and the worst of the smoke. Lark opened the other cages and quickly ushered them to the chimney, carrying the youngest of them, which could have been no more than three.

At the shaft, she stopped long enough to count heads and issue some quick and unquestionable orders. "Are going to play game," she said. "Are going to play mice. Mice are going to climb up this chimney and out into darkness and are not going to make single noise that cat might hear. Understand?"

They nodded dumbly, one or two of the boys making gestures of sealing their lips shut. "Good. When tell you be rock, drop and make like rock, not move for nothing. Not even if someone walk right up and sit on you."

Someone giggled but was quickly hushed. Lark pointed to the three oldest of the children, roughly seven or eight years old. "You, each take two little ones. Are mama/papa mice. Help keep up and quiet and no get them lost, yes?"

They nodded.

She pointed to the eight-year-old, a strong-looking tomboyish human. "You, up first. Keep low down in grass. Help little ones climb. Walk up sides like little spider. Get all up and lay flat 'til I come up. No noise. Here," she handed her the long scarf holding back her hair. "Get to top and lower this. Help little ones up with."

The girl nodded, wrapped the scarf around her neck, and slipped into the hole, walking up the sides like a little monkey. The two other older children went up next to help. Lark ducked inside, beckoned the next child, squeezing herself as close against the wall as she could, and lifted him up onto her shoulders. She got him standing, and the scarf was passed down. In a flash, he was off her shoulders and sailing into the air up the short tunnel. The others followed quickly enough, and Lark climbed up with the baby clinging to her neck and holding on to her hair.

The cool night air was a relief after the choking cell below. Even though there was smoke on the air up here as well, it, at least, was clean smoke. "Heads up," she whispered, then counted the heads that popped up in the grass around her. All nine were here.

She did not like traveling through the dark woods with so many little ones and no weapon to speak of but a small magical dagger and an arsenal of illusions, but she had little choice. She arranged the children so that each little one had the hand of one of the three oldest children, with the last holding onto her own hand, and quietly led them into the jungle.

"Don't let go," she whispered. The hand attached to hers tightened in answer.

Once she was far enough that she could no longer see the glow of the fire and the sounds of the fighting, she told her familiar they were safely away.

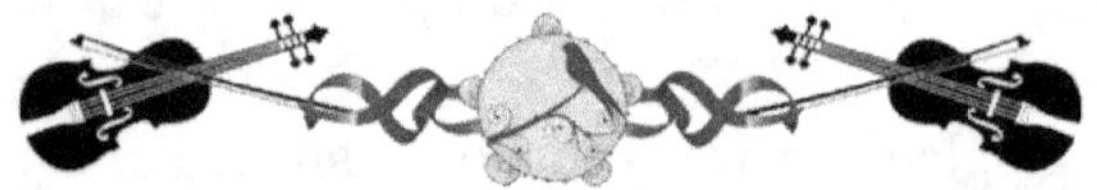

Nightingale flew over everyone's heads, darting in and out just beyond the reach of the firelight, crowing the retreat. Someone near the battlements took a swing at him as he sailed past, thinking him a bat and, therefore, an ill omen. Nightingale angrily flew at his face, screeching horribly. Trying to strike the bird away in terror, the man lost his balance and fell into a burning haystack below.

Landros did not acknowledge the bird's cry but began to circle around, back towards the gate. There were not many of the enemy left, and no sign had yet been seen of the mage or the succubus, but he wisely retreated. No sense in jeopardizing Lark and the children. He and Rog kept them busy another few minutes before they ran out of the gate and into the darkness beyond it. Landros let the horses loose and ran with them, using them to cover his retreat. Rog made a much less covert exit, but then, there was not much else the dwarf could do.

Adrick used a sling to hurl three small glass bottles into the fort as he saw Rog running out. Seeing the horses, he figured that Landros was among them. The bottles struck various places, each of them erupting into a ball of flames. The oil splattered and spread, and at least one of the enemy was seen running around madly, trying to put himself out. Adrick chuckled wickedly, knowing there was no mundane way to douse those flames. He turned and disappeared off the rock to join the retreat.

Savaren started to follow but looked back at the last moment and saw a robed figure stride out of a stone building at the rear of the compound as part of the wall fell. The figure began to gesture in rage. Savaren watched, noticed the beginning sparks of a spell forming, and drew his bow back. The arrow sailed almost true, striking the figure just below the breast. The sparks faded, and it fell, gestured impotently at its men to give chase, to do something. Savaren smiled and jumped off the rock to the jungle floor, picked up Landros's bow where he had dropped it, and ran off after his companions.

Adrick kept as close to Landros as he could, knowing that his sense of direction was questionable at best in a non-urban setting with no well-ordered streets or signs to guide him. Savaren and Rog ran apace but slightly off from them, sure of their direction and their purpose. They stayed close enough together to help one another if they had to but far enough apart to make pursuit harder.

Landros was actually enjoying himself. The run was exhilarating, no matter that he was the object of the chase so long as Lark was not among the pursued. He deliberately skewed the trail, not running straight for the cave to buy her some time and to throw off the pursuers if there were any. And there were. He could hear them in the distance. He almost laughed. He fully understood why sometimes the fox allows himself to be found and chased by arrogant nobles with their horses and their dogs. There was nothing like the feeling. Still, he kept his mind alert, doing what he could to keep the trail only as readable as he wanted it, despite the haste of his flight. Adrick and the dwarf would leave trails hard to conceal, even in darkness, but the two elves were like fish in water.

EIGHT

Lark heard a noise just ahead of them. It sounded like some large creature tearing heedlessly through the thick forest. She told the children to make like rocks, and they all huddled down in the underbrush, trying their best not to move. Lark pressed her back against a tree, using its width to hide her slim body, and drew her dagger. The sounds did not get any closer or any farther away. They paused, resumed, and paused again as if the creature making the noise were trying to catch its breath. It began to make other noises, low grunts, and half screams. It sounded... panicked.

After a long moment of this, Lark decided to get a closer look. She really did not have much choice. It was between her and the cave. And if it was free and dangerous, it was already too close to go around it. The wind shifted as she slipped silently closer, wafted towards her instead of across her as it had been. She caught the strong, musky odor of panicked horse. Confident that they were far enough away to risk it, she activated her pendant, bathing her and the animal in its soft glow.

It was indeed a horse, one of the ones that Ivaska had chased off earlier. It had gotten itself caught in a thicket, the reins tangled in the briers and the saddle hanging at an uncomfortable angle but far from falling off. He pulled his head back at the sudden light, the whites of his eyes obvious.

Lark began to whisper softly to him to calm him enough to let her approach. She reached out her hand, and, after a moment, he touched it with his nose and let her slide it down the reins to untangle them. She used her knife to cut the girth strap, letting the saddle fall. The horse kicked it. Carefully, she pulled the brambles away and guided the animal back to where she had left the children.

They jumped up when they saw her and the horse coming in the light. Their whispered cries were a mixture of relief and delight as she hefted the five youngest onto the beast's back. Lark's feet were killing her, but she could not complain, not if she wanted to keep them going. Perhaps now, with only the three oldest walking with her, they would travel faster. She lifted the three-year-old to her own shoulders and handed one of the reins to the oldest girl, had her form a chain of hands with the other two. She picked up the left rein and, turning out the light, led the children into the darkness towards the cave.

Savaren arrived first. He stopped just outside the clearing, uncomfortable with the stillness there. He kept a cursory watch for the others while scanning the area for the boy who should have been on guard. He saw Landros and stopped him before he could enter the clearing. "Where are they?" he whispered.

Landros gave the agreed-upon signal, and a shadow answered. Landros stepped out into the clearing, meeting the boy halfway as he emerged from his hiding place above the cave mouth. He stopped when he saw the crossbow over the boy's shoulder. He grabbed Billy by the arms before he could say anything and demanded, "Keltree! Is he...."

Billy shook his head. "No, sir. But ya'd be'er get 'at priest down to 'im 'm'dgitly, sir. 'E fell asleep 'bout an 'our 'go and I cain't wake 'im up."

Adrick heard what the boy said about Keltree, and headed immediately down. Billy shouted over his shoulder to him, "'E's down in th' boat! Fought it'd be faster fer gittin' out 'at way," he added to Landros. "The kids is down 'ere wif th' dog, keepin' an eye out."

Landros let him go, gave his shoulder a pat. "You did good, Billy. You did good."

"So, di'ja git 'em all out all right?"

He felt a sudden resurge of panic. "You mean they aren't here?" He pushed the anxiety back and looked over at the mockingbird settling himself down for a nap. He convinced himself that if Lark were in trouble, the bird would not be so calm.

"Relax, sir," Billy said quietly. "Gypsies is a rezourseful lot. An' some a' 'em kids is on'y two mebbe free years old. It's bound ta take 'er a bit longah."

Landros wanted to believe that. It was easier than what else he was imagining.

Rog came out of the woods, looked around, had a short word with Savaren, and then seated himself on a nearby rock and began to polish his hammer. Savaren continued his surveillance from the edge of the trees, listening for the inevitable sounds of children's footsteps. Landros paced. After a few minutes, he went down into the cave to check on Keltree and the others, mostly as something active to do to keep his mind off needless worrying.

Billy had made a torch, managed to light it, and wedged it upright with some rubble he found in a corner. The two children were huddled together on the wide ledge, with the dog keeping them warm, watching Adrick at his prayers over the body in the boat. Landros waited impatiently until Adrick sighed and looked up. Seeing Landros, he carefully pulled himself up onto the ledge as the tide had lowered its level some. He stood up, rubbed his eyes tiredly, and leaned back against the wall.

"Not much I can do for him now except watch him die," he whispered. Behind him, Feldrin deliberately began to sing softly to Analie.

Landros put his hand on the man's shoulder. He was uneasy with this new role of comforter and leader, but it had to be done. "You have done all that you could," he told him.

"If I could just get him to the temple, I might still be able to save him. But we are days, at the very least, from a temple of any sort. If he had listened to me and stayed on the Andromeda..." he ranted.

Landros held him still and softened his own voice as the echo rolled hard across the water. "He knew the risks," he said. "He chose to make that sacrifice. Any of us would have done the same."

He pulled away, glanced over at the two children, and lowered his voice. "I know you're right."

Landros was startled by that statement. In the twenty-odd years he had known the half-elf, he had never heard Adrick admit to anyone that he was ever wrong or that someone else was right.

"But damn it!" he went on, "if I had only not let him swear me to silence, we could have forced him to.... Or I could have drugged him and enabled us to leave without him...."

Landros grabbed him and silenced his friend's ranting. "Adrick, in the end it was his choice. Respect it," he said firmly. He thought for a moment, continued, "I think maybe we should honor his request of silence, though. The children do not need to know. His niece does not need to know. Lark is going to be heartbroken, and it would be best to get her on board the ship before we burden her with those facts."

Adrick nodded numbly. "You'd... you'd probably best get back up topside, keep an eye out for her and the others. You'll just be in the way down here."

Landros nodded and turned back to the crevice, stopping to ruffle Ivaska's ears first. The darkness wrapped itself around him, enveloped him, and allowed him a few moments of oblivion as he walked blindly up the winding tunnel. How was he going to tell Lark that her lover... No, *he* should not be the one to tell her. He...

The scent of brimstone in the air tickled his nose, and he saw a faint glow ahead. Then came the sounds of a scuffle and a Dwarven battle cry. He came as close to running as he possibly could up the narrow, twisting tunnel.

Scrambling clear of the hidden entrance, he was taken aback by what he saw. A demoness stood in the clearing, towered an easy fifteen or twenty feet tall. Her skin was a deep red which glistened in the light of the flames that were her long hair. Her four pendulous breasts hung bare to the world like the rest of her body. Huge leathern wings spread skyward, threatening the treetops with fire. Held tight in the talons of one of her four hands was Billy, kicking and fighting to get loose. All her concentration was on him and the questions and chastisements she bellowed at him. In her lower right hand was a long sword, wet with blood. In her lower left was a gleaming scimitar.

Landros saw nothing else, not the boy screaming back at the succubus in defiance, not Rog and Savaren attacking her legs uselessly. All he saw was the scimitar.

He was unaware when he drew his own blades, only of their sudden presence in his hands, the act of swinging them towards the demon's thigh, and the boiling hot spray of blood that arched from it on impact.

The succubus howled in pain and moved her leg in a reflex action that sent Landros reeling against the rocks. Even as he was regaining his wind and getting up to attack again, the demoness looked down and saw Savaren. Screaming in rage, she reached down and grabbed him, throwing him into the woods. She saw Landros coming at her with his swords and, grinning, parried neatly with the longsword. In the same sweep, she struck him across the shoulder with the scimitar. Neither combatant noticed the dwarf disappear into the fissure, running for the priest.

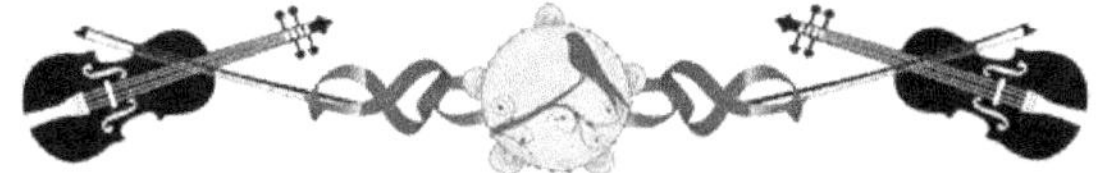

Nightingale was in a frazzle. She was not quite a mile away from him when he first began to be uncomfortable. She had hurried the pace but did not get half the distance when he went hysterical. He was completely unintelligible. There was trouble, and it was bad.

She stopped, set the baby down, and began getting the kids off the horse one at a time. They looked at her, confused, but did not say a word. They were terrified. Even the horse was getting itchy. Lark did not have to tell them to make like rocks as she seized a hand full of mane and vaulted onto the horse's back. She paused to cast an illusion of stones over them as further protection and moved the horse as quickly as possible through the underbrush.

It was not far, she knew. She could hear the battle from here. But her hurry and her fear made the journey seem miles. She saw the light of the flames through the trees, too high up to be a simple campfire. Smelling the foul stench of ozone and brimstone in the air, she knew the succubus had to have found them. She slowed the horse to a canter just before the edge of the trees and took stock of the situation.

She saw Landros, battered and bloody and in a battle frenzy, fighting off the three-armed attack of the demoness. The succubus was not exactly healthy, but in far better condition than her opponents. Adrick stood at the cave mouth, chanting.

Lark did not think. She drew her dagger and kicked the horse into a gallop straight for the succubus.

The demoness drew a deep breath, then unexpectedly screamed, spewing a cone of flames skyward that could have been seen for miles as Lark raked the dagger across the muscles of her back and rode past. Adrick cast a bolt of eldritch lighting, striking her full in the shoulder. She dropped the boy, shrieking in her agony and impotent fury. Out-maneuvered and severely injured, she vanished in a puff of sulfurous smoke and flames.

The horse kept on going, completely panicked, and Lark leaped off his back and landed in a roll to keep from hurting herself. She stood, balanced on the balls of her feet, dagger ready for anything.

The enemy was gone.

Rog reappeared, looked around and Billy, having landed badly, limped to the cave and hopped down the tunnel.

Landros turned on lark, still holding tightly to his sword. His relief at seeing her alive when he had believed her dead or captured was translated into anger at her foolish attack on a demon with only a knife in hand. "What the hells were you thinking?!" he demanded.

Lark stared into his eyes. The light was dim now that the succubus had fled. He could not see the condition she was in, nor could she tell how badly he had been hurt. But the starlight and slim moon were just enough to show her the pain and worry in his dark, golden eyes.

"Have you gone mad?" he practically roared.

"Yes," she said. "Must go get children now."

Landros's mind went completely blank. He watched the girl brush past him, a faint patch of ragged skirts moving lightly back into the woods.

Rog trotted after her, grinning.

Lark heard the dwarf behind her, jogging to catch up. She was more than happy to slow down for him. Her feet had reached a level of pain that she could, thankfully, no longer feel them at all, just a dull throbbing she actively ignored. Pretending there was nothing wrong went a long way to helping her keep going. She hoped desperately that the succubus had returned to her level of hell and not found the nine little rocks she had cleverly hidden in the woods a quarter of a mile away.

"Never seen that particular expression on an elf before," Rog mused cheerfully.

"Hmm? What expression?" Lark asked.

"Speechlessness. 'Are you mad?' 'Yes, can go now?'," he mimicked, doing a fair imitation of their voices and accents.

Lark suddenly giggled. She had been so fired up that she had not thought how silly Landros had looked, staring blankly at her as she admitted to insanity. Though, the insanity she had been referring to was not the same one he had meant. She had to be insane, she thought, to be even contemplating a relationship with the man. He was *gegenta*, yet fate kept thrusting the two of them at each other. Sooner or later, the storm had to break.

Lark suddenly realized that Rog had asked her a question. "Huh?" she asked.

He looked up at her, then shook his head and kept walking. "Never mind," he said. He stopped suddenly, staring at a pair of rocks.

Lark grinned. "What is?" she asked innocently, realizing where they were.

"It moved."

"No, must be shadow. Or imagination playing tricks. Too much excitement," she said.

"No, it moved!" he growled, hefting his war hammer.

Lark moved quickly between them as she saw the gleam of the metal head in the faint patches of moonlight filtering through the leaves. "No. Is all right," she said. She waved her hand and dispelled the illusion. "Is children, see? Hid them when left to help with demon fight."

Rog relaxed.

Lark got the children together, ignited her pendant, and, with Rog's help, led them quickly back to the cave.

Landros was physically relieved when they arrived. His face was pale and strained, and he felt cold inside and out. He gestured them into the crevice and followed, bringing up the rear so that he would not have to see Lark's face when she saw the contents of the boat. He deliberately avoided looking at her.

She stood on the ledge staring down at the pale figure wrapped in blankets just a few feet below her and did not acknowledge her familiar's gentle, nudging reassurances. She tried to think rationally. There was someone here to whom Keltree mattered far more. That was more important. She noticed the second bundle, more shrouded than wrapped in someone's cloak, tucked in with their belongings. She looked around and saw that Savaren was not among them. She did not say anything but began helping to lower the children. Gratefully, Ivaska did not press her for attention, and even Nightingale was quiet. That Keltree was not bundled up as the wild elf was reassured her that he was alive enough.

The niece, the oldest girl it turned out, thankfully did not shriek or scream or cry. She just stood there silently, allowing Landros to pass her down into the boat without noticing him. She sat huddled next to her uncle, between two other children, and gently touched his face. Her expression changed with that touch, opened like a sunflower kissed by the sun. "He's so hot!" she whispered. "That means...."

"He is not dead, yes," Adrick said flatly.

Lark was so absorbed with watching this that when Landros picked her up and set her down in the boat, it came as quite a surprise. She looked up at him through the screen of her hair.

"You going to take care of your hound?" he asked. There was a coldness in his voice, an attempt to keep emotions at bay, a refusal to meet her gaze.

She called up a small poltergeist and lowered the whimpering dog, made him crawl under a bench, and make himself as small as he could. The boat was crowded, barely large enough, and Lark had to put one of the children in her lap to make room for the rowers. She set a were-light in the prow, and Rog cut them loose, taking up one of the oars next to Landros.

Lark was wedged in between Adrick and Billy. She leaned into the boy and asked, "How is? Not hurt?"

He rubbed his ribs tenderly, smiled shyly back. "Not much, ma'am," he whispered. "Th' priest were quick ta mend m' leg and ribs. I'm still a bit tender. I've fallen farther 'afore," he shrugged.

No one made a whisper as they slid through the cavern, save for the dog, who whimpered occasionally, complaining about the boat and the tight quarters.

IV

The Long Way Home

ONE

Once they were safely out of the cave, Nightingale flew straight up into the air, above the murk, and flew to the ship still at anchor outside the ring. He perched on the rail, guiding his mistress and her companions to safety out of the blinding fog. The sailor on watch saw the bird staring into the haze and alerted his captain. By the time the light was seen skimming across the water, a small crowd had gathered at the rail, and a rope ladder was waiting for them. One of the sailors climbed down and hung there, guided them into place and took the mooring line back up onto the deck.

Lark handed the child in her lap to Adrick as they came alongside the Andromeda. "Let me go first. Can use poltergeist to catch if fall or cannot make climb."

He nodded, steadied her as she stood and reached for the ladder.

She climbed up the side of the ship slowly, mindful of her feet and beginning to feel a tiredness creeping over her that weighed heavy. Several pairs of hands grabbed hold of her and pulled her over the rail, helping her gently to the deck. She thanked them wordlessly, assured them she was all right. Then she turned and called up a poltergeist, gestured for the children to come up, one at a time.

It seemed to take forever. No one was entirely certain that pursuit would not be taken up or that they would not be found even out here. Only two of the children slipped, and only one of those did she have to catch. He giggled as he felt himself flying through the air up onto the deck. Billy tried to climb but without much success, the strain on his legs and chest was too much. Lark brought him up. Adrick followed the last child and sent them all, together with Billy and one of the sailors, to the galley.

"Are you still strong enough to help with Keltree?" he asked as he climbed over the rail beside her.

She nodded. "Is not like *I* am lifting. Though my strength does affect strength of my 'little winds'," she admitted and called up a second. Lark could feel the vigor seeping out of her summonings but willed them to last long enough to lift Keltree's still form from the boat and set him gently in the grasp of the waiting sailors who promptly disappeared below with Adrick. She turned to do the same for Savaren's body, but the captain, looking over, laid a hand on her shoulder, shaking his head.

"Do not waste your strength on this one," he said softly. "We have ways."

She saw them lowering a large net over the side and sighed. It seemed like such a waste to her, Savaren's loss. She brought Ivaska up and went below to the cabin. The dog walked close beside her and let her lean her slim weight on him.

Landros came over the side of the rail just as the body was being lowered to the deck. He motioned the sailors away from him and took him gently from the net. Koss, the pilot, came over, spoke quietly. "If you like, I think we have some extra sailcloth for a real shroud, and I might be able to find a place for him in the hold until we get to port."

Landros nodded numbly, picking up the light bundle carefully and followed the pilot silently into the hold.

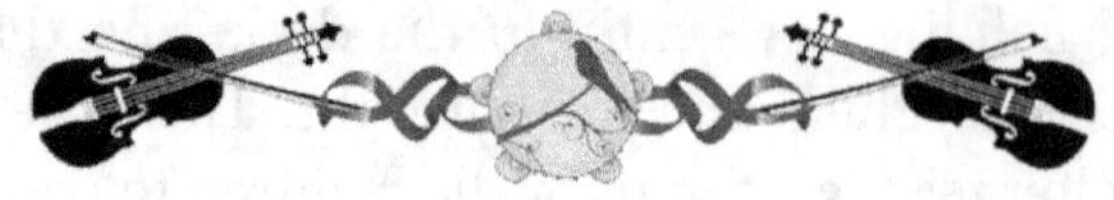

It was dim in the cabin, but Lark could see Adrick moving near the bed as she entered the room. Her pendant's light filled the space more brightly than the single, weak lamp. He looked up as her light reached him and finished his prayers. She limped over, gazed silently down on Keltree's still face. His breathing was labored, and his face pale and slick with sweat.

Nightingale tucked himself into his nook and buried his head under his wing. Ivaska threw himself down into a corner and began snoring almost immediately, but that could have been his stomach growling.

Adrick's voice came soft and blunt from beside her. "He's dying, girl," he said. Lark did not look up. "There is nothing more that I can do for him.

"I am sorry," he added when she did not respond.

She touched Keltree's cheek tenderly, brushed a lock of hair aside. She sighed and moved away. Finally, exhausted beyond measure, she sank into one of the chairs by the table. Sadness and misery caved in on her, threatening to crush her if she could not break free soon. "How," she began, afraid to ask the question. "How did Savaren..."

Adrick sat down and sank to rest his chin on his crossed arms. "Rog tells me the demon picked him up and threw him like a child throwing a rag doll in a tantrum. His body was broken ...in several places. I do not think he was aware of more than the sensation of flying through the air. ...It will be up to Landros how we take care of the body, though, because of whatever agreement he made with Savaren's tribe."

She nodded. She stared blindly around the room, not really seeing much until her eyes passed over the ribbons of her tambourine dangling from the shelf where she had put it. She made herself get up and take it down, ignoring pain and a growing stiffness. Removing the bag containing her rune stones, she pushed the rest aside. She stared at it for a long time, playing with the ribbons, debating. Finally, she loosened them and reached inside, pulled out a small handful of stones, and tossed them onto the bare table with a loud clatter.

Adrick watched without lifting his head but did not say anything.

She was somewhat confused by the results of her toss. Great deeds showed in his past, that she had more than expected. *Is*, the straight line, lay just beyond the first cluster, pointing away from her. *Is* was the standstill, the obstacle, a rune she expected to see and interpreted here as his dying. What confused her was seeing *Tyr*, the rune of the warrior, an upward aimed arrow, continuing the line of *Is* onward towards other confrontations, glory in battle before finally ending in a valiant death. It was obvious that *Is* was *now* from its placement, that the rest was yet to come, but it made no sense. How could he do these great things if he died here?

She could not take her eyes from the two center stones. *Is* and *Tyr*. She relaxed, focused on saving Keltree's life, making him live beyond this night. Again, she saw only the line and the arrow. She picked up *Is* and turned it in her fingers, without tearing her eyes from the other stone. "Can do nothing more?" she asked gently.

"Nothing," he grumbled, miserable in his failure. "My training in healing ended as a novice."

"But if get him to your temple, he will live?"

"More than likely," he muttered. "Why? What are you getting at?" His head rose a few inches, suddenly suspicious and hopeful all at the same time.

She rose. "Then is nothing to be lost, is there?" she asked of no one in particular.

Adrick followed her back to the bed. They just stood there for a moment: Lark watching Keltree and Adrick watching her.

"Will need wine," she said.

Adrick disappeared. A moment later, he pressed a cup into her hand. She took a deep draught of it and handed it back to him. "Hold," she said, swallowing. She reached over and opened Keltree's shirt, laying bare his pale, lean chest and swollen belly. She started to dip her fingers in the wine, then hesitated, decided this spell needed more power.

She drew the dagger Keltree had given her and, fully appreciating the irony involved, pricked her finger with it. She squeezed until the blood welled, then dipped it into the wine, ignoring the mild stinging from the weak alcohol. Chanting softly, she placed her wet finger just above his navel and drew it upwards to his breast, leaving the long line of *Is* in blood and wine upon his chest. It flared blue like her were-lights, then faded into his body, leaving no trace of itself behind. She touched her finger to the bridge of his nose and traced a line upward to his brow, capping it with an arrowhead. It, too, glowed and faded.

Adrick watched in surprise as Keltree's breathing suddenly seemed to cease. He touched his wrist, felt nothing, and looked up at Lark in shock at the tired serenity on her face. "You killed him?" he finally managed.

"No," she said.

He put his head to Keltree's chest to listen for a heartbeat and found one, though it was very faint.

"And yes. Is hard to explain. He is not get worse. But is not get better either. He is..." she paused, searching for the right words in Adrick's hard gray eyes. "Is hanging? Is in between life and death, touching neither. Is sleeping like death, but very much alive. Will go with to temple in Portswain. Take off spell so can heal. Pray to your goddess, though, voyage takes not much time. Too long in this sleep and I think not even your holy Maiden can keep him from Crone. She likes young handsome men, I hear."

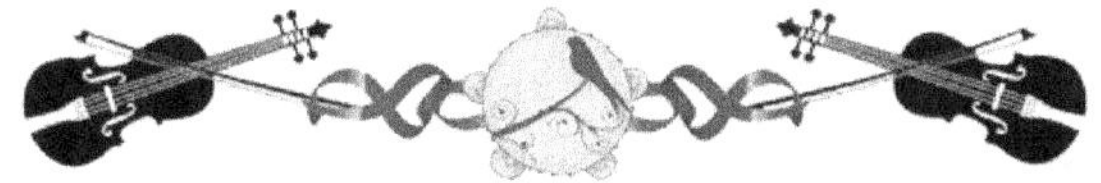

Landros came up onto the deck finally, momentary details taken care of. He had no idea how to proceed now, how he was going to get the body to the forest elves outside of Hallowell through enemy detachments. Not to mention how he was going to return to Portswain afterward. The sailors bustled about him, intent on their work, raising the anchor and setting the sails to get as far from this island as they could as fast as they could.

He saw one of the sailors scrubbing something from the deck, tossing a bucket of seawater over it. Stepping around the wet patch, he noticed what he was scrubbing away: blood. Footprints of blood, to be exact. They were not perfect prints by any stretch of the imagination, but to someone who had spent his life tracking obscure signs through a forest, these were an obvious, blazing trail. He followed them across the deck and down towards the cabins.

Adrick looked up as Landros came into the room but said nothing.

Lark did not even turn around. She pulled the sheets up to Keltree's chin, making sure that his body would be warm enough. As she started to move away from the bed, someone grabbed her ankle from behind, lifted her foot, and touched the sole of it. She grabbed onto Adrick for balance and gasped as the cold fingers slid across her injuries. She half-turned to see Landros holding his finger up to the light, seeing blood there, then glared at her.

The next thing she knew, he had swept her off her feet and set her on a chair. Of course, his arm around her back announced the presence of other injuries she had forgotten. Landros got on his knees at her feet, examined the bloody, blackened, oddly glinting soles carefully.

"What you....?" she hissed, gasped as his finger moved a long sliver of glass against her more tender insole.

Adrick echoed her response but stopped when he saw the condition of her feet. "My word, girl," he breathed. "How in the name of the Maiden have you been walking?"

"Rather stupidly, I'd say," Landros growled. "I come up from the hold, see bloody footprints running across the deck, and tracked them to her." He looked up. "Now, while he fixes this, you want to tell me what..." He saw a glint of red on the left side of her face, reached up, and moved her hair out of the way. Three long, deep, and bloody claw marks blazed along the length of her cheekbone. "What the hells happened to your face?"

He moved out of Adrick's way and let the priest get down to work on her feet. He stood to one side, arms folded across his chest. "Now, you want to tell me what in the name of the Abyss happened to you?"

Lark was tired and not in the mood to be bullied. She glared at his crossed arms, turned away from him. "Don't talk to me standing like that," she snapped, gesturing with a cock of her head to his folded arms. "Is rude."

He was taken aback by the outburst and sudden cold shoulder but dropped his arms, waiting impatiently. He glanced down at the crust of tar and blood and dirt that Adrick was peeling off.

"Is happen when…." she began. Landros held up his hand, stopping her, and disappeared out of the cabin before she could say anything else. She put her fists on her hips, giving a small squeak of frustration.

"Pain in the ass, isn't he?" Adrick smirked. He paused to examine the top of her feet and saw the marks of tar and glass there, too. Carefully, as if not certain whether or not he was going to get slapped for this, he grabbed the edge of her skirt and laid it across her knees. There were similar marks there and on her shins. He gently lifted her ankle, tilting her leg into the light, pulled free a small piece of glass and held it up. Landros came in with a pail of fresh water as Adrick looked up at Lark and asked, "Glass?"

"Glass?" Landros echoed, taking the bloody fragment from his friend. He stared at it, and then tossed it onto the table. He grabbed a chair, turned it around, and straddled it, folding his arms across the back of it. "Talk," he said sternly.

Lark was almost inclined not to tell him a damned thing. She did not like being spoken to like that. It was one of the reasons she had left the caravan. But Adrick was waiting for an answer himself as he put her foot into the water and carefully began to wash away the tar and dirt and the glass. She sighed. "Was when went in for children," she began. "Were kept in cages in room for summoning demon. Circle for spell was carved in floor in tar and glass, and sulphur to smell it burn. Little demon jumped me, like gremlin…."

"A homunculus?" Adrick nodded.

"Whatever," she said. "Is jumped on back, biting, clawing. Push to floor. Therefore, glass in foots and legs. Got off me, ouch!... used sword, but not magical, so did nothing. Demon knock blade away and push to floor again. Sat on chest. Claw face as gloating. OW! I grab magic dagger Keltree gave to me and stab demon. Was surprised even to hurt creature but more so to kill him. When dead, burst into flame, trapping me in circle of fire, because tar caught flames. Is why had no sword. No time to search for. Was probably in fiRE!" she yelped, flinching as Adrick moved to her shins.

Hesitant, Adrick asked, "These go any higher?"

She shook her head. Adrick seemed almost relieved and went back to work.

Landros understood now. The succubus must have come down into the room, found the children gone, her homunculus dead, and grabbed the weapon just lying there. "That does not explain why you continued to walk on your injuries, no doubt aggravating them further...."

"And what else was supposed to do?!" she snapped. "If I not go, they not go! Is long way for child. If grown-up cannot make it, think they will not sit down too, cry and complain is too far, is too tired?!"

"And what about that suicidal back-stab you tried?" he growled back. "Was that part of keeping the kids going?! Lark, you could have been killed!"

"You needed distraction!" she snarled, starting to stand up. Adrick forced her back down. "If not drew her attention, would have breathed fire on you, or you not notice?"

"Fine! Let her have breathed on me! Yeah, it would have hurt, but I wouldn't have been bleeding anymore! It would not have stopped me!"

Lark started to yell at him, slipping into Romeri without thinking, and tried to get up again.

Suddenly, Adrick's voice cut them both off. "ENOUGH! BOTH of you! Landros, if you do not stop baiting her, she will not stay still, and I cannot work! Lark, if you do not sit still, I will bind you to that chair until I am finished!"

Both of them sulked in silence. Lark crossed her arms over her chest and tried to maintain her composure while Adrick picked the glass out of her knees and spread a pungent salve on the cuts. He bandaged her swiftly from toe to knee and then got up to tend to her face.

"Hmm," he muttered. "That is a nasty one. Must hurt like hell."

She put her arms down. "No," she answered. "Cannot feel at all. Actually forgotten."

"Do you feel this?" he asked, touching the wound.

"Feel what?"

"That's what I was afraid of," he muttered. "Hold still." He tilted her head to the side and moved her hair off her shoulder to keep it out of the way. He noticed the bite and other claw marks just above her blouse. He laid his hand on her cheek and closed his eyes in prayer.

Lark felt nothing at all, not even his hand on her face, though she knew it was there.

Landros watched Adrick's hand begin to softly glow a reddish-blue, and a trickle of blood began to run down her face. Lark never flinched. When he withdrew his hand, the wounds were angry furrows just beginning to close over.

Lark looked up at him. "Is all?" she asked, surprised. She had expected to feel... something. Then the burning began. Her cheek began to throb painfully as the numbing poison faded and feeling began to return. She covered her cheek with her hand, eyes wide. "Is like knife opened face clean to bone!" she gasped.

Adrick chuckled. "Imagine that!" he mocked. "That is precisely what that little demon did. Now, take your vest off so I can tend to your back..."

She pulled away from him, still holding her hand to her cheek. "Think am let touch me after what do to face?" she exclaimed.

"Yes," Landros answered. She looked at him. His amber eyes were hard and unyielding. "You are," he said. Still, she did not move to take off the vest. "I do have a dagger," he said calmly.

She growled, began to rip the laces out of her vest angrily. It was obvious these two were going to force her to submit to this healing whether she wanted to or not. She tossed the vest onto the table and loosened the strings of her blouse, letting it fall open in the back, bared to her narrow waist.

Adrick moved her hair. Her back was a mess. Not quite as bad as her feet, but bad enough. There were deep bite marks up on the arch of her shoulder and long gouges where the creature had grabbed her and hung on. He sighed and began repeating his prayerful ministrations.

Lark stared balefully at Landros as she submitted to the healing. A lesser man would have folded under that gaze, but not him. Even her father would have turned away from her, not that he would have given in to her in the least. Landros met the stare with equal stubbornness. As she sat there, holding the front of her peasant blouse up to cover her modesty, stoically enduring the awakening pain, Landros found her to be even more beautiful than any elven woman he had ever met.

She finally closed her eyes, taking short, controlled breaths, as the pain began and steadily grew.

Adrick moved away from her, went to his pack in the corner, and rummaged through it. Lark did not move. She sat with her back stiff and straight, leaning slightly forward. She began to tremble ever so slightly.

"Is there anything you can do for the pain?" Landros asked. It almost physically hurt him to watch her like this, her dark lips pressed tightly together, a slight pallor spreading beneath her olive complexion. Still, he could not help but be impressed by her endurance. Well, she was a dancer after all, he thought, and endurance is the name of the game.

"I am getting to it now," Adrick mumbled. "I should have a numbing salve in here somewhere. Keltree had the last of my internal..."

Lark began to hear a noise in her ears, like a huge wave getting swiftly closer and closer. She felt a nausea rising up from her stomach, blackness closing in on her.

Landros jumped, pushing the chair forward onto the floor as he moved to catch her. His arm was killing him where she sank her nails in, vainly trying to hold her own weight. She gave up, rested forward in his embrace, heedless of the hard wooden floor pressing into her cut and bruised knees.

He stared in dismay at the condition of her back. It was no wonder that she had nearly fainted. He remembered how he had felt after tangling with a mountain lion some forty years ago. It had not been pretty, and he had not had the benefit of a healer on hand.

He softened a bit, his concern and sympathy getting the better of his cold, emotionless protection. He made certain that she was comfortable, cradled her head in the crook of one shoulder, and supported her weight with his arm diagonally across her chest.

With his free hand, he stroked her hair softly, lightly rubbed the back of her neck, anything to help her endure the agony.

"Ah, here it is!" Adrick came over and finished his ministrations with an odorless salve that he rubbed into her back and cheek. Lark's breathing eased somewhat with each bite and cut he covered.

No sooner had Adrick put his pot away, Landros shifted her, pulling the back of her blouse gently up to her shoulders with his free hand. Weakly, she pulled the strings herself, tying her blouse closed. He picked her up, as careful as he could of her wounds and his own, and laid her upon the nearest hammock. He had to get away from her and quickly. He felt awkward and self-conscious of how good and natural she felt in his arms, even with her dying lover in the bed just behind them. The smell of her was reeling his senses, and the feel of her soft breasts against his arm through the thin cloth of her blouse was inflaming his body. This... this was not right.

He made sure she was comfortable, lay her on her side. He put on the sternest expression he could manage at the moment and told her to stay put. "Your feet need time to heal," he said. Out of the corner of his eye, he saw Adrick shouldering his bag and opening the door. He followed, deciding that he needed a talk with the half-elf in private.

He caught up with him just as he reached the deck. "Hey, Adrick!"

The priest turned and waited for him. "I was just going down to check on the children, do a more thorough check for injuries. Would you like to come with me?"

"No," he said, shaking his head, partly to clear it of the woman's sensual influences. "What I want to talk to you about should not be said in front of them."

"Oh, I see." Adrick seated himself on a nearby box, one of several that had been brought out of the hold and stored here to make room for the children below. He set his bag down and folded his hands in his lap, waiting patiently.

Landros began pacing in a very small area, wondering where to begin. There was too much... "Keltree," he said. "How long does he have?"

"I believe the girl said a few days," he answered with surprising patience.

"The girl?" Landros asked. "You mean Lark?"

"And what other girl would I be referring to? The niece?"

"I am confused."

Adrick sighed, "What else is new?" He made himself comfortable. "The gi... Lark," he amended, "did something to him. She has a real magic in her," he mused with new-won admiration. "These runes of hers give her surprising power. She is wise to use it so rarely. That or she simply does not know much about it. If I could get her to study up at the temple...."

"Get to the point," Landros interrupted. "What did she do to him?"

The half-elf shrugged. "Beats the living hells out of me. He is ... sleeping," he said, using her words for it. "He's not getting any worse right now. But she said that it will only help if it does not take long to get back."

"Koss told me we're about two, three days at the most, depending on the winds," he said.

Adrick nodded, folded his arms over his chest. "Hmm, yes. It should be just enough. Once we get him to the temple, it will be up to Rue and Feldath and the other surgeons. I am not convinced he can be saved; the Crone has her hooks too deep in him. But she did something with those fortune stones she has and then got up and drew one of them in blood and wine upon his chest and another on his forehead. Then he changed. His breathing slowed; he seemed to be out of pain, or at least to not notice it. I thought he had died at first."

"So, you told her he was dying," he accused. "I thought we had agreed...."

"It was time to tell her, Landros," he said firmly. "If we had waited any longer, she would have been insulted and angry, and rightly so. As it is, if he survives, it'll be entirely because of her."

Landros sighed, leaned on the rail of the ship, staring out into the night, and tried to regain his composure in the salty wind. "What about her?" he asked.

"What about her?"

"Her injuries. ...Will she dance again?"

Adrick snorted, "That all you're worried about?" he huffed. "Don't worry, it will take some time, a few days at most. Hells, if you want, I can even take her to see Rue when we get in port, and she'll be dancing by nightfall. But I don't have that knowledge or skill. The Maiden gave me the gifts best suited me, but healing was not among them. I am little better than a walking bandage with a bit of hocus pocus, and you know it. My strengths lie very much elsewhere."

Landros did not answer, remained staring out across the water.

"Still, if she stays off them until port, she will be more than fine. Her back and face are healing even as she lies sleeping. Hells, there probably won't even be a scar by tomorrow night. Though if she had let those injuries go too much longer, if they had festered and turned black... she would have had black scars for the rest of her life. Not to mention what the poison in them would have done to her. Worse than a fever, that. It corrupts the mind as well as the tissues it poisons. You have to be careful with homunculi."

Silence.

"The girl has tough feet and a strong constitution. She walked the five or six miles from the fort to the cave without a complaint. She'll heal." Adrick gave up. It was like talking to a wall. He sighed, got up, and collected his bag. "I have to go check on the children and put them to bed. No telling what that bitch did to them."

Landros let him go. This voyage... had already proven costly and may prove to be more costly yet. And it could so easily have been worse. He seriously doubted the girl would have had the sense to ask the priest to look at her injuries, not until they were beyond helping. For the children, the helpless, innocent children, all their own deaths would have been worth it, but at the same time the cost seemed too high. He was not cut out to lead. He hated being responsible for other people's lives. Savaren's death weighed heavy on him. If Keltree had not been so stubborn, had been more careful with himself and let the more able-bodied deal with the bloody particulars, Savaren might still be alive.

He turned away from the water and went down into the hold from the opposite side that Adrick had. A small space had been set aside below, and Savaren's shrouded form rested across a pair of crates. On the other side of the wall of boxes, he could faintly hear the voices of the children and Adrick among them.

Any other time, and this might have brought a smile to his face, a joy to his heart to sit and listen to his friend suffering the innocent inquisition. But right now, he was in no mood to have his burden lightened. Not by laughter. That was a medicine he had not earned. Maybe his own wounds were a penance of sorts. No healing for him. He would live. At the cave, Adrick had stopped the bleeding on the worst of his wounds, but no more. There had been others more in need.

He set aside his cloak, which he had originally used to wrap the body. There had been little blood, so it was not stained, or wet or unwearable. But it still had upon it a pall of death. It had been a shroud, after all.

He sat on a smaller crate beside the body and gazed down at the still form. He felt lost for some reason, adrift. "*I always wondered what happened when an elf died in his prime,*" he said in Elvish. "*With a lifespan of four hundred years, one does not tend to think about death. I do not know what to do for you, what customs you follow. What happens to your spirit when the body cannot keep it safe anymore? Or what I need to do to help you go where it is elves go. I... I never had the luxury of having that explained to me. Never had the misfortune to need to know before there was no one left to tell me the answers. And I with a younger brother to explain it to.*"

He sighed, leaned back against the wall of crates, and listened to the quiet giggles of the children far on the other side. "*I am truly sorry, Savaren. You came with us in good faith, and I got you killed battling something you were not equipped or prepared to face for a cause that was not yours. I know, I know, you volunteered. But none of us truly knew what we were volunteering for; knew the price.*" He paused again, listened to the laughter that was fading out as the children drifted to sleep. *"Children are our most precious commodity, our most valuable treasure. Worth any price. I keep telling myself that. I think maybe if I tell myself long enough, I will start to believe that your death was worth something. My world has come crashing in on its ears, and there are no certainties anymore. I am sorry I pulled you into that."*

Emotionally spent, Landros got up, put on his cloak, and went up on the deck. Most of the lamps were out in the pre-morning blackness; only one or two hung in the breeze to aid the few sailors still minding the sails. Even the moon had already set or been obscured by clouds.

Ahead of him, he saw a shape sitting on a rain barrel near the rail by the quarter-deck. It fluttered and plumed in the breeze and spoke softly to something sitting on it. He stopped near the rearward mast, crossed his arms over his chest under the folds of his cloak, and listened, keeping his ire to a controlled irritation.

Lark sat with Keltree's niece in her lap, wrapped in her shawl. She brushed the rich brown locks from the girl's face even as the wind spread hers like a flag beside her. "Is all right to cry," she was saying, "Is good for you sometimes. If hold everything in, after time, you become like rock, like wooden maiden on front of ship. You feel nothing, and this not good."

"But men don't cry," the girl said. There were sniffles in her voice.

"Men are wrong. They think is not manly to weep. But man can weep for same reason as woman. Is not good to weep too easily, but when it hurts, have to let go somehow. Is not good to let whole world know you weep, but if you love, if you trust, *they* can see you cry. *They* can take hurts and make them joys."

"How can they make the hurt a joy when they are the hurt ...because they're not there anymore?"

Landros watched her pull the child against her breast, rocked her softly and tenderly. "Oh, child. Even when candle goes out, they are not gone. They are never gone. They watch over us still. But you need not worry for Uncle Keltree. Has strong will, that one. He will live, though will be weak for long time. I promise you this. Have seen his future, you see."

"In the stars?" she asked in awe.

Lark gave a soft chuckle. "No, in stones. I read marks made on them and learn from how they fall. Have seen many great things for him."

"A woman?" she asked excitedly.

"Oh, many women," Lark answered.

"No," the girl said, sat up. "I meant one woman. You know, the princess. His damsel-in-distress, like in the stories he always tells me, the girls that get rescued from the dragons and live happily ever after with their heroes."

Landros could hear the smile in her voice. "He tells too many stories." She paused. "No, is no one woman for this one. This I did not see. For him, no wedding ribbons. No ring."

"Why not? He's such a nice man, so prince charming," she complained. "Every woman wants him."

Lark did not say anything for a long moment. When she did, there was something in her voice that put Landros on edge, though he could not fathom why. "No. He wants what cannot have. I do not understand this, but I know. Your uncle... your uncle *will* die, Navarie. But not today," she added gently. "He will live while longer, do, see much. He will die as he lived, by his sword and his wit, with woman's name on his lips."

"But why? Why does he have to die at all?"

"Do not know, child. Why do any of us die? Why do we live? What does matter but that we do? Are too young to lose innocence. Can tell you this, and this is all I know. He will die protecting that he has always protected and always loved more than all things, more than life."

"What?" she whispered, as if afraid of the answer.

Lark touched the girl's nose lightly. "You. You are his damsel-in-distress. You are princess he fight dragon and demon for. You are reason he risk life and limb to cross sea even when surgeon told him is not ready to go be brave and heroic. He could do nothing else. You are his life, I think. Love him deeply, child. Enjoy him while you have him and make memories will hold to when he goes on. Is tough to carry, this burden. But is time began making lady of you. Is make you strong and beautiful."

"Like you?"

Lark blushed. "No," she said. "Like you."

"Oh, I'm not that pretty. But… when will Uncle Keltree die? Are you sure he is not going to die now? He looked so still."

She sighed heavily. "I do not know. Stones do not tell time of day and year. Only near and far. And that," she said, touching her finger to the girl's lips before she could ask, "is something did not look for."

There was such an unbelievable sadness in the child's eyes that Lark could not stand it. She knew how she would have felt if Gruma had told her the year before her mother had died that she was going to lose her. "Will tell you Romeri secret. When he goes away from you and think he might be in danger …will know in heart when… light candle and put in window. If flame goes out for no reason, no wind or breath or no wax left, then is gone. But is bedtime for you. Is almost dawn."

"But…"

"Shhh, do not worry. Here, I give you task. Quest. When he gets home, want you to stay with him, make sure that he does not go off gallywacking before doctor say is all right go gallywacking. Can you?"

"Yeah. I think I can. He listens to me, even when no one else does. And he never listens to my mother."

Lark giggled, sighed. "Men never do, dear. Men never do," she whispered as she set the girl on her feet and sent her scampering back to the hold where the other children had been bedded down.

Harden your heart, Landros, he told himself. He watched her for another minute as she just sat there, enjoying the night air and the sea. He deliberately thought back to the wounds he had seen on her, to his frustration and anger at her stubborn refusal to rest and heal, to do what was best for her. He stepped out of the shadows, finally good and angry enough to deal with her on an emotionless level. Anger, fury; these were emotions he was used to keeping at bay. These other, unnamed, unknown feelings and soft thoughts he had no experience with and no clue how to contain or control them.

Lark jumped when she heard a voice out of the darkness nearby, stern and cold, so much like her father's. "Why are you out here?"

She turned and saw Landros's cloaked form standing by the mast, hood drawn up to shield his face from the wind. She relaxed, looked back over the water. "Navarie woke me, crying over Keltree like he was dead." She shrugged. "Came out here with her, so not wake Rog. Is uncomfortable enough on water."

He felt an inexplicable pang of jealousy. If only someone had taken him on their knee eighty years ago and explained things to him, soothed him. ...He forced those thoughts and emotions from his mind, focused on why he was angry with her in the first place.

"*How* did you get out here?" he asked.

Lark found the absolute chill in his voice disturbing. It was unnatural, so unlike the man she had come to know. So calculated. She wrapped her shawl tighter around herself for warmth and stared out over the ocean. "How you think?" she snapped, sullen.

Landros snatched the hood off his head, untied and removed his cloak. He crossed the deck and wrapped it around her. "If it were not for your need to talk to the child, I would...." he grumbled.

"Would what?" she snapped, putting her fists on her hips, ready for the battle she knew was coming.

Landros was not up to this conversation, and he knew it. So, he avoided it altogether. "One of these days, child," he began and reached over to sweep her off the barrel.

He was startled when she suddenly pushed him away almost violently, striking at him. He gasped as her small fist landed against one of his many wounds. If he could have seen her eyes clearly, he would have seen that they had gone pitch black. She banged her heel against the barrel accidentally, but she rode the lance of pain on a wave of pure anger. "**Child**!?" she growled. "**I am not child**!" She lowered her voice suddenly. "I may not be as old you, but assure you, you arrogant, pointy-eared villain, that whatever else I be, am no longer child! *You* saw to that, remember!?" she hissed.

He was silent a moment, trying to get his now genuine anger under control. He most certainly remembered, but why had she flung the fact at him like that? Was there regret? Or was she just so mad she was not thinking? He took a deep breath. "Why," he began slowly, "will you not do as you were told and let yourself heal?"

Her head whipped around to look at him, her dark eyes reflecting a flash from the dim light from the lamp ten feet away. "And have you had Adrick yet heal you?" she countered. She had not been unaware of his reaction when she had hit him, realized that she had hit a sore spot, like now.

"That is irrelevant. We are not discussing my injuries. We are discussing yours. The whole reason Keltree lies on the brink of dying right now is because he did not listen to the doctors who told him he was not ready to fight. Is that what you want? To mess your feet up so far that you will never be able to dance again?"

"Look who's talking," she growled, looked away from him again.

"*I'm* talking," he snapped. "It does not make any difference that I am injured...."

"And what if she finds us, this demoness, sends her master to get children himself? How you fight injured? Less long is how you fight. Dead is how you fight, no match for demon bitch. Then how do children get home? Adrick and I fight to save? Sailors no match for..."

"Adrick cannot heal everyone of everything," he snapped defensively. "He has to rest; has only so many herbs. I will heal...."

"And so will I."

That silenced him for a moment. This was like arguing with his brother ...or with himself. "Are you finished out here?" he asked, not knowing really what else to say. Nothing else seemed to be getting through.

She looked away from him, out over the water. She was not getting anything through his thick head. He was so stubborn, so pig-headed, so concerned for her and the children. She had to think; he had a death on his hands already and likely a second if she had been wrong in her interpretations. He wanted everyone tended before himself, and in that way, he was as blind as Keltree to the obvious. But there was no use in telling him that. And it *was* getting colder out here. "Yes," she sighed.

Landros picked her up and instantly wished he did not have to. The smell of her was intoxicating; the feel of her slight body as he lifted her in his arms was arousing, and when she placed her arms around his neck and laid her head on his shoulder, the desire to hold onto her and never let go was overwhelming. But that was not possible. Just not possible. He carried her down to the cabin as quickly as he could without appearing in a hurry. He did not want to have to explain why he had to get away from her.

Rog was snoring loudly in his low-slung hammock, and Adrick was hanging half out of his when Landros quietly carried her into the cabin and set her gently into the nearest empty hammock. He drew a blanket over her as she handed him his cloak back. "Now stay put," he hissed and turned to walk away.

"Wait," she said softly.

Against his better judgment, he looked back. "Yes?"

She took off her rings, held them out to him. "If cannot get up, at least put these in rune-bag?"

He held out his hand, noticed as she placed the rings in his palm that she had left one on, a gold one with a black opal set into its smooth surface. It became her, he thought. He dumped the rings into the small bag which that was still on the table and put that in the larger, patchwork bag sitting in a corner with the other packs.

Lark watched him as he made a small bed for himself on the floor by their belongings, using his bag as a pillow and his cloak for a blanket. Ivaska got up, wandered over to him, and flopped down next to him. He looked up as the dog rested his head on his leg. He scratched the animal behind the ears and laid back down. Lark, exhausted, fell asleep watching them.

TWO

Landros heard something. He was not sure what it was, but it was nearby and definitely not the creaking of the ship about them. He silently wrapped his hand around the hilt of the sword next to him and glanced around the cabin. The light in the room was dim but enough for him to see that there was no one else here but the five of them. He looked over at Keltree, thinking perhaps the man had moaned in his sleep, but he was as still as death.

He heard it again.

In her hammock, Lark moved fitfully, whimpered. He watched her a few moments, forgetting why he had to keep his distance. He felt himself drawn to her inexplicably. She turned, her hand caught in the mesh of the netting. She struggled weakly, still sound asleep. She moaned softly.

Landros found himself getting up, walking over to her.

She was having another nightmare. She was aware of this. She was trapped in it and could not free herself. There was a desperation in the way the dream held onto her, as if it were running out of time. She could sense it, like the dream was a physical thing holding onto her. She was in a large room filled with swinging cages, and in them were the bones of children, hundreds of them. The mist swirled about her, ever-present, the core of everything, it seemed. She was trying to get out, to find a single child still alive and get out. But there was no door, no window, and, suddenly, no floor. She felt herself tumbling through the air and abruptly stopped.

Pain from her back woke her, and she was grateful for it. She opened her eyes and looked into the deep amber orbs she remembered from that night in the rain so long ago. Felt his arms around her, pressing into her wounds, but she didn't care. She breathed, put her hands on his shoulders.

"Are you all right?" he asked.

His voice was soft, tender. Perhaps his coldness had been part of the nightmare, and now everything was right again. "Am now," she answered, for some reason unable to speak above a whisper.

They just stood there for several minutes, staring into each other's eyes, almost afraid to breathe lest they break the moment. Landros had to put her down. She was not overly heavy, but his arms were sore, and his left was badly cut. And she was beginning to have that effect on him again. He could see Keltree still asleep just beyond them and did not want to have to explain why he was holding his girl if he should suddenly wake and see them. "Can... can I put you back in bed now?" he asked.

"No," she said too quickly. She did not want that at all, to be set away from him, where she could dream again. "No," she repeated, more softly, less urgently. She rested her forehead against his, whispered. "Please, just hold for while."

He sighed. Faced with such a plaintive request how could he refuse? How could he put her back down and walk away in her moment of need and still call himself gracious? Unable to continue holding her, he carried her over to where he had bedded down and set her on his cloak, wrapping it around her before settling down beside her. She curled up next to him almost immediately, resting her head in the crook of his shoulder. He found the position strangely comforting and unsettling for the very same reason. He felt her breathing slowly return to normal.

Ivaska resettled himself at their feet and went back to sleep.

"You want to tell me about it?" he asked softly.

Lark sighed, taking a deep breath of him, murmured softly, "No. Is nothing. Just bad dream. Come from fighting demons most like." Truthfully, ...thankfully... she found she could not remember any details.

He nodded in understanding. "You should try and get back to sleep."

"No," she said again. "Can... cannot sleep yet. Maybe later, but not now."

He sighed, decided not to try and push the subject. Now was not the time. He began to slowly, softly stroke her back under her dark mane of curls, hoping to soothe her enough to help her fall asleep in spite of herself. It was a trick he remembered his mother pulling on him in his youth. He felt a renewed pang of loss at the memory. Such a waste.

"So, tell me," he began, as much to drive such thoughts from his mind as out of genuine curiosity, "how much of that story you told Navarie is true?"

"What mean?" she asked, keeping her voice low. "All was true so far as know."

"You got all of that from your rune casting?"

"No. Only some. That will survive this, that I saw. That will live to do great things, that I saw. Rest... rest just knew. That little girl is center of his life, is his candle, could see that in his eyes."

"And the rest?"

She resettled herself so that she was looking up at the ceiling corner where Nightingale had made his nest, yet still close to Landros's warm body. "There are things... sometimes I say things... and not know why, but know they are true? Gruma does this all times. Says this is sign of *Ranie*, of coming into power."

"I am sorry," he chuckled softly, "you keep using these words that I am not familiar with. A gruma is...?"

"Is child's word," she laughed sheepishly. "Is grandmother. Like gegenta children say Granny, is Romeri to say Gruma."

"And *Ranie*?" he asked. He had never known a grandmother and did not want to dwell on the lack.

"Is caravan ruler, or clan ruler. Queen is closest gegenta word. Captain is mostly ruler, what he say goes. For Rushavska: is my father. Is not always *Ranie*'s husband, but often. *Ranie* is *real* ruler. Leaves mundane things to captain. But should she say he is not right, or something contrary, what *Ranie* says goes. There is no question. Is not like gegenta household, when man says everything. Do not know how can survive this way. Men do not have power, so how can they know for certain is right what they say?"

She stopped talking, sighed, and curled up closer to him.

He did not have to ask what she meant by power. "And one day, you will be this queen?" It seemed appropriate, then, that Keltree be her mate. He was by far the more worthy man, the kind of man meant to marry a princess. Wasn't that what the little girl had been talking about, that her uncle kept telling her? All of it made perfect sense, except this part, the part where he fit in ...or didn't.

"Maybe," she whispered. "If I want. Am not certain I want."

"Why on earth not?"

"Why should? Is make me boss, yes? So, am boss now. Can do as please. As Queen have whole clan to think about and am not old enough to want that burden yet. Maybe when I am twenty-five or so."

'Maybe when I am twenty-five or so,' she said, as if twenty-five were ancient and centuries away. He had to wonder how she thought of him at a *hundred* and twenty.

She sighed again, more heavily, and let her hands play idly with the strings on his shirt, not really in the mood to talk anymore. She was tired, in pain, exhausted. She could smell blood on him, sweat, salt, and a myriad of other things she could not name that smelled of comfort to her, comfort and strong arms and contentment.

Fate, that was what he was. And one of these days, she would admit that to herself.

Lark awoke, found herself back in her hammock. She sat up sleepily. The first thing she saw was Landros, sitting at the table eating smoked fish and an orange and bare to the waist. Adrick was sitting beside him, wrapping a clean bandage around his upper arm. There were numerous other cuts and marks on his lean chest, all showing signs of recent tending. She swung her legs over the side of the hammock, intent on getting up and joining them at the table.

"Don't even think about getting out of that thing," Landros threatened. "If you want breakfast, I'll bring it to you."

She was confused for a moment, then looked down at her legs. She saw the long white bandages and remembered. All of a sudden, she was none too keen on getting out of bed. She reclined forward, admiring the view.

Landros felt her stare on his body. It made him uncomfortable because he could feel the passion in that gaze. Maybe Adrick had been right about her? After all, what kind of woman looked at another man in that way when her lover lay dying not ten feet away? Perhaps it was just the Romer way. He had heard nothing of Romeri weddings, only Romer dealings and seductions and corruptions, and... and none of it seemed to fit her.

"That sword of yours leaves quite an impression. It's too bad you had to lose it," he said, flexing his arm after Adrick tied off the bandage, testing it for mobility. It was still sore with certain movements but much better than it had been. He was glad he let Adrick talk him into healing. That and he had not relished another argument with her.

"Better my sword than my head, yes?"

He glanced over. She was almost cat-like as she lay there, sinuous and sultry, and she was not even trying. 'The goddesses help her victim when she tried!' he thought. He decided he would be very glad when they arrived in Portswain. He did not know how much longer he could take being cooped up so closely with her.

He picked up the extra plate on the table and carried it over to her. She sat up and shook her head.

"No?" he asked, confused. "What do you mean no?"

"On deck. I wish to get air," she said pertly. "And since you will not permit to walk, shall have to carry me. Provided bandage will permit?"

He sighed. She was doing this deliberately. She *had* to be. He set the plate back on the table and lifted her out of the hammock. It was much easier with the bandage on, less strain on the wound. He noticed the marks on her face were all but gone, merely shadows that would vanish by the next dawn.

He carried her out onto the deck, set her down on the crates, and left again. He returned shortly with the food. He stood well away from her while she ate, leaning on the rail. "Captain said we should be nearing Evandair by tomorrow afternoon. We've got a good wind under our sails."

Lark shuddered at the mention of Evandair but kept eating, not wanting to show it. "Be in by tomorrow night, then?" she asked, feeding scraps of biscuit to Nightingale as he landed on her shoulder.

He shook his head. "No. He does not want to get anywhere near the bay until nightfall. He's going to slack us down long before then. That way, we will slip into the bay past the blockade and get behind the island hopefully unmolested."

Lark saw flashes of fire and shredded steel in the rind of her orange, shook off the images. "Hopefully," she echoed. "Warn him to be careful rounding island," she added. "Not long-ago discovered enemy were to send catapults to seal off bay. May or may not have arrived."

"Why don't you tell him?"

"Because will listen to you. *I* am only woman," she said snidely.

He looked over at her and simply nodded. The children came out on deck, swarmed over to her, and he quietly took his leave, glad for the opportunity to escape her.

The ship slid across the waters of the headland completely dark. Not a single flicker of light on board and the whole of the crew were on duty and silent as ghosts as they watched from their posts. Even the ships' bell had been muffled. An hour slipped by under the keel and no sign of other life on the water. Then tension had begun to wear on the nerves when they sighted the island rising out of the darkness ...and the ship in the distance. Nightingale flew towards the other vessel, as near as he could without being noticed. It was a fishing vessel running with few sheltered lights. Innocent enough, except the crew was far too interested in the Andromeda. Nightingale knew nothing about ships, but something about this one made him uncomfortable. He decided not to get close enough to be seen and followed his instincts back to his mistress.

Rog came up to where the captain stood at the rail squinting through a spyglass. "Just a fishing vessel," said the man, breathing his relief, "not part of the blockade,"

Rog tapped his arm, "Lemme see," he asked in a gruff but polite tone. He was handed the glass, and stared through it at the oncoming ship. "Hey, Lark," he said after a moment, holding the glass out to her. "Get a gander at this."

She limped over to them, took the glass and put it to her eye. It bore the marks of the Evandair fishing fleet, but the nets were up, and the sails set full in their direction. There were too many men on that ship, in her opinion.

"Look familiar?" Rog asked.

She handed the glass back to the captain without taking her eyes off the steadily closing vessel. "Too much. Is good cover, *sesket*?" she said, trying to keep her voice calm and steady.

"*Sesket*," Rog muttered. "Get the kids and the dog inta the cabin and barricade yerselves in. Cap'n, prepare fer attack."

"Why?" he asked, looking at the ship again. "It's just a fishing ship."

"Not anymore. It's part of the Evandair fishin' fleet ...that have been missing fer a month."

"Pirates," the captain finished. He turned and began bellowing orders.

"I will need saber," she told Rog. "In case..." she deliberately did not finish. He nodded and headed off to help prepare for the battle. Lark turned and called the children to her, began to lead them down to the cabin.

Landros came up from the hold, having heard the commotion, and crossed to investigate. He saw the sailors rushing about, preparing the ship for an attack, breaking out boxes of sabers and knives and crossbows. He strode over to Rog, who was getting a quick lesson in shipboard fighting from one of the sailors doling out weapons. "What in the name of the nine hells is going on?" he demanded.

Rog pointed to the ship getting steadily closer and popped another piece of root into his mouth. "Pirates," he said. "What, ya thought they'd let us just sail in unmolested, boy?" he laughed and turned, taking an extra saber from the pile. "Lark!!" he bellowed.

She turned, and he tossed the saber to her. She caught it neatly, tucked it into her belt, and returned to herding the children below to the cabin.

Landros stalked across the deck, his anger rising up again, more easily this time. Did the girl want to join her lover? he thought. She would at this rate. "You don't think I am going to let you fight, do you? When I won't even let you walk?" he demanded, taking the sword and sweeping her off her feet and over his shoulder.

"May not have choice," she snapped, struggling. She was beginning to tire of being treated like a complete invalid.

"Like hell I won't," he growled and began to haul her down to the hold.

"Pirates," she grunted as he shifted her so he could open the door, "may not let me not fight." He set her down on the nearest crate. "Will be in cabin, with children. Should be safe enough. But wish to be armed, ...in case," she said, held out her hand for the sword. "Give back and take me to cabin!"

"The children should remain here in the hold," he insisted. The children gathered wide-eyed around them, not certain what to make of all of this.

"Children," she corrected, "will be where can protect both them *and* Keltree. Cannot be in two places at once and no one is to spare for job."

"Keltree, for all intents and purposes," he hissed, lowering his voice, "is 'dead'. The pirates come in, they see the 'body' of an apparent noble laid out for burial. They won't give him a second thought until they have taken over the ship. ...Which they will not do!" he added insistently. "You are going to stay down here, where they are not likely to come until they have taken over, and where you have room to fight if necessary, and the children have places to hide."

She growled to herself, sullen as she realized he was right.

Landros turned to the children. "Billy, do you still have that crossbow?"

"Yessir! Right 'ere, sir!"

"Good. Use it if you have to."

"I've got two extra swords, sir," Villis said, stepping out of the shadows, one in each hand. Landros turned and looked at him in surprise. "Captain said fer me to come down and help here, sir. Ye need to go up. They's gettin' close. I've been drilled on pirate attacks, sir," he added. "Been through a few already. I know what to do."

"Landros, is nothing more to do here. Go up where are needed," she said gently, still holding her hand out for the sword. "Leave weak and wounded to me," she sighed. "Has always been my job, always will be."

There was no resentment in her statement. She had long ago realized that it was the most important job of all, and by far the most rewarding. She watched Landros's face go from one emotion to another until they vanished altogether, and nothing remained but a cold mask. She determined that, once Keltree and the children were out of danger, if that mask remained she would crack it one way or another.

Landros reluctantly handed her the sword and left. He could not take the calm, unaccusing gaze she was giving him. It made him want to take her into his arms and shake her until some sense rattled into place and then kiss the living hell out of her. The thought was unworthy of him, unworthy of her. So, he walked away rather than risk the temptation of another man's woman. ...A man in no condition to fight back.

Lark heard the door lock behind him. Villis dropped a bar on the door and got Billy and Navarie to help him move a few of the boxes in front of it. She gathered them around her, kept them close and quiet despite the strange noises from above. She entertained them by conjuring a tiny lady figure and animating the soldier doll to dance with her.

Ivaska curled up amid them, looking for comfort, his ears down and his tail tucked. The littlest children found it funny to see such a big dog shaking and scared, and soothed themselves by helping him feel less afraid. Nightingale was still outside, perched in the empty crow's nest, out of harm's way and safely keeping tabs on things for his mistress.

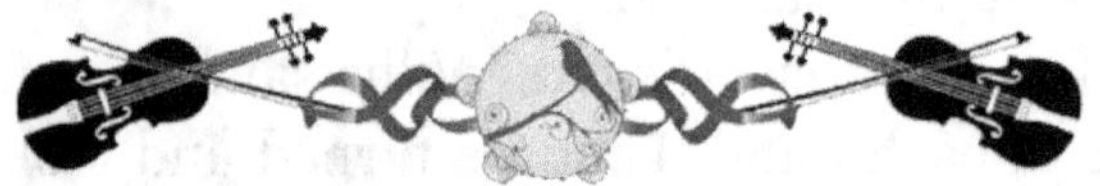

Landros grabbed his bow and swords from the cabin, paused to throw the sheet over Keltree's face, completing the image of death, before running out onto the deck. The enemy vessel was very near now, just in arrow range. He climbed onto the quarter deck and readied his bow.

As the ships closed and it became obvious that their disguise of innocence was not working, the pirates gave up all pretenses. No sooner the charade was dropped and the ship was well in range, Landros let fly with his arrows.

The pirates took moderate cover, hurled their grappling lines, and threw fishing nets with claws on the ends to secure the two ships together, forming a bridge between them. The sailors cut at the ropes as quickly as they could, pulling off the hooks as fast as they came, but by then the pirates were swinging over on other ropes, leaping from rigging to rigging, and the fight began in earnest.

Some of the children began to cry. Lark hushed them as quickly as she could, trying to soothe and calm them. "Remember our game in woods?" she asked. "We must play at mice. Cats all above us.

Make any noise and they will gobble you up!" They tried their best, muffling their sniffles in their sleeves and clinging to her and to each other as tightly as they could. They listened to the crash and clatter and shouting from above. It echoed all around them, pounding on the walls, threatening to cave in on them. More than once, the ship rocked as if the smaller pirate vessel were trying to ram them. Something large and heavy fell to the decks, and the children jumped.

Lark tried to get a report from Nightingale, but it was complete chaos above, and the bird's vocabulary left a lot to be desired.

"What was that?" Navarie whispered.

"Mast, maybe," Lark whispered, pressing the child closer to her. "Maybe nothing."

"Why are they doing this?" someone asked, on the verge of fresh tears.

"Do not know," she sighed. "For money, perhaps."

"But we don't have any!"

"They do not know this. May get this from someone else. I do not know, child. Be still. Why does one man attack another? Why is army sitting outside city gates? Why does one man have twelve children stolen to give them to demon? I do not know!" she hissed. She could not let her own fear show, would not. But when Ivaska lifted his head and suddenly began growling low in his throat, she jumped, had to force herself not to panic.

"What...?" Navarie whispered. No one moved as the dog got up and faced the barricaded door, showing his teeth.

"Someone's breakin' in," Billy whispered. He got to his feet, favoring his still aching leg, and helped Lark up.

"All right, run, hide like little mice and make no noise," Lark whispered. "If does not know are here, will not hunt you down to eat you!"

The children scattered, disappearing into the nooks and crannies of the cargo. Lark felt her heart skip as the crates blocking the door jumped, moved. There was no time for her to climb and hide. She drew her sword, wincing at the pain in her feet, but readied herself to protect her charges. Billy and Villis would not leave her in the open alone. They flanked her, ready to protect her as well, if need be. Ivaska stood between them and the splintering door, snarling. A few more blows, and it caved in.

No sooner a man was visible in the gap, Billy loosed the arrow from his crossbow into his shoulder, and Ivaska leapt for his throat, propelling him back through the opening.

The grubby man in the doorway was not alone. His companions left him fending off the massive hound, edged around the fight, and poured into the hold, looking for what he had to be guarding. They seemed surprised to see the Romeri girl and two young boys in a vee formation, bearing sabers and ready for them. One of them grinned, his mouth glinting with golden teeth, his bare chest glistening with sweat and blood. He laughed and said something to his companions in a clipped northern tongue. Four pirates tried to circle them, but they kept the wall of crates at their backs.

Lark did not understand the language, but knew a lewd suggestion when she heard one. Their body language left no doubts about what they wanted. The boys... the boys were pretty enough, might be made to pass. They were certainly no threat.

A hand reached out slowly. Villis lashed out, but the reaction was anticipated and parried, a far more deft grab made for him. Lark screamed and attacked. The more noise she made, the less she felt the pain in her feet as she kicked, connecting with hard muscle and bone. Billy fought like a wildcat, hurt or not. A lifetime on the streets had obviously taught him how to fight through pain, to deal with it later. Lark did not stop to think how this many of them had managed to slip down here unnoticed. She simply fought, swung, kicked, and clawed.

The three of them fought like hellions, protecting their precious charges, but two of them were heavily wounded, and the third was only a boy. None of them were a match. Lark felt her sword grow heavier and heavier. Beside her, Billy was knocked senseless by one of the pirates, who then turned to help his friend with her. Ivaska leapt in, out of nowhere, it seemed, landing on the man's back and seizing hold of the back of his neck. His screams were terrible to hear, but Lark had other worries.

One of the pirates managed to lay hands on her. She swung her sword upward. He caught her wrist neatly in one hand and punched her in the stomach with the other. Winded, she doubled over and was grabbed from behind by a second pirate. Still out of breath, she kicked out at the first with both feet, too desperate to acknowledge the agony. He grunted as she struck places she had hit before, wounds from earlier fights, but he still managed to catch hold of an ankle. He grinned, dodging her other foot while trying to snatch it, reeling her in.

He got a strange look on his face and suddenly sank forward to his knees, her ankle slipping from his grasp as he collapsed to the floor. Landros stood behind him, pulling his sword back for another blow. "Big mistake," he said. The expression on his face was cold and hard and angry. "Surrender now, and I might let them drown you."

The other pirate grabbed Villis and held him high, his sword close to his throat, snarled something unintelligible.

"Put them down," Landros ground.

Lark felt the pirate's grip tighten on her arms. In her weakened state, there was no way she could break that grip. So, she went limp, letting her body become a sudden dead weight. The pirate was thrown off balance, having been expecting struggle instead, and she slipped from his grasp and slumped to the floor. He scrambled to regain hold of his 'shield' while still parrying off the maddened elf, but she snatched up her dagger and stabbed it deep into his foot. He howled in pain, then fell silent. She looked up, saw his headless body falling towards her, and moved quickly. She was not quite fast enough, and the body landed across her lower legs, sending lances of pain shooting upwards. She did not cry out, though it took an extraordinary amount of willpower not to, and settled for slamming her palm on the deck instead.

The pirate holding Villis started edging towards the door, holding his saber at an upward angle against the boy's throat, making it unwise for him to try the same trick. Landros kept with him, waiting patiently for the slightest opening. Lark snagged Ivaska as he started past her. He almost bit her until he realized who had grabbed him. He continued to threaten the remaining pirate but did not attack.

Landros cut the man off from the door, forcing him to back up against the crates which, not too long before, had been serving as beds for the children. They found themselves at an impasse as neither party could understand the other. Suddenly, the pirate shouted, arching his back in pain, and everything happened in an instant, almost too fast to follow. The saber at Villis's throat scraped upwards, drawing blood from neck to cheek. The boy collapsed into a heap at the pirate's feet, covering his head to protect himself. The pirate turned, trying to pull something from his back, and revealed Navarie standing on the crate, backing away from him with blood on her hands and face. Landros lopped off one of the pirate's hands before its sword could reach the girl and killed him swiftly. The man collapsed over the small heap of the cabin boy and lay still on the deck, blood pooling around him and a dagger conspicuously sticking out of his back.

Landros picked Navarie up. "Are you all right?" he asked insistently, checking her for injury. She nodded numbly. He set her down quickly and pulled Villis out from under the pirate's body, checking him out thoroughly. The saber had made no serious cuts, just a thin scratch and a long scrape that might have taken off his ear if it had come an inch farther left. "A little young to start shaving, aren't you, boy?" he asked. "Even for a human."

He looked around the room, saw Lark dragging herself out from under the headless corpse and sitting there, nursing her wounds. He relaxed and turned his attention back to the children as Navarie looked over his shoulder at the cabin boy.

She gasped when she saw his wound. "Villis! I'm sorry!!" she cried, horrified. "I could not see that he had the... I didn't know! I could have...."

Landros took her by the arms, trying to be gentle. "He is all right, Navarie. You could not have known. What you did was a brave thing, and though it could have turned tragic, it did not. You are a very lucky young lady. Now, where are the other children, and are they all right?"

Ten faces popped up from amid the crates, each piping a sniffly response. Ivaska began sniffing at Billy's inert form, digging at him, woofing softly to try and wake him.

"The pirates did not get them," Villis said. Navarie began fussing over him, dabbing at the blood with a torn bit of cloth. "I'll live," he laughed, gently holding her off. There was a low moan from Billy's crumpled form, a resistance to Ivaska's licking. "But I'll bet Billy wishes he wouldn't," he added with a grin. He and Landros pushed the dog back and got Billy sitting up enough to check him out.

"Be aw'right, sir," he moaned. "Been in worse... fough not recently." He squinted up at Landros with admiration through his cut and puffy eye. "Gave 'em wot for, we did, 'fore theys took me out."

Lark sat there in the midst of the bodies, trying to regain her breath and to get her heart to slow to a regular pace. She looked around the cabin, counted heads as the children emerged. Everyone was well enough and accounted for, if a little scared. It was very likely that none of these young boys would be playing pirates for a very long time.

She felt a sudden jerk on her hair, which pulled her backward onto the body of the pirate who had knocked Billy out, the one she had thought Ivaska had killed. His mangled and bloody hand seized her throat before she could shout. She struggled, trying to claw the hand free, but it was beyond pain and stronger than she. She kicked wildly, hitting an upset crate with a shock of pain that ran from her heel all the way to her hip.

Landros heard the faint thumping behind him, turned, saw Lark in the death grip of one of the pirates, and lunged. He seized his sword, crossed the floor, and stabbed him through her hair. Leaving his sword embedded in the man's chest, he pried the fingers from her throat, breaking them where he had to.

She gasped for breath, replaced the dead hand with her own. He untangled her hair from the other fist, removed his sword once he was certain the man was dead, and helped her up.

Looking into his eyes, she clung to him weakly. She felt completely lost suddenly, as if she had been cut adrift without any warning or reason. She did not want to let go of him but did not have the strength to hold on.

He gave her a quick once over, glad for a reason to tear his eyes from hers. If he did not look, he could not see the need and pain and would not feel the desire to take her in his arms and comfort her, to kiss away the hurt. She was cut in a dozen places, but none serious. It was obvious they had wanted her mostly in one piece. He set her on one of the crates, made certain that she and the children were all right, and turned to leave.

'The fight, get back to the fight,' ran through his head over and over. 'Get away from her before you dishonor the both of you.' He felt a light tugging on his jerkin and looked down. Navarie was standing there with a very upset expression, beckoning him to bend to her. He leaned over, and she whispered in his ear. "You're supposed to kiss her, silly!"

He looked over his shoulder at Lark, sitting tiredly on the crate, children huddling around her, some of them crying, then down at the expectant girl. It became painfully obvious that some goddess somewhere was getting her jollies by making his life hell. He stalked back, stepping over the bodies, bent, gave her a quick peck on the cheek, and tried to leave again.

She was startled by the gesture, even more so by its chaste abruptness. Her surprise continued when Navarie put her hands on her hips and muttered, "That's *not* a kiss."

A loud crash from the other half of the hold cut off anything he had been about to say. There were shouts from above and below. He leaped past Lark and the children, disappearing swiftly up the partial wall of cargo and down the other side.

Five pirates had fallen through the hatch above and now lay in a heap with two of the Andromeda's sailors. Taking up a position halfway down the wall, Landros grinned madly, drawing his bow on them. The fight was over before it could resume.

THREE

Lark took the children up to the cabin and bedded them down there to keep them out of the way and sight of the massacre on the deck and in the hold. Even Villis stayed with them on captain's orders. Adrick only superficially tended to both of the older boys and Lark, bandaging what had not already stopped bleeding. Promising to be back soon for better care, he returned topside to treat the more seriously wounded sailors.

Landros kept away from the cabin completely, helped to toss the pirate bodies overboard and deliver the dead sailors to the hold where they were being taken care of. The captain split his remaining crew between the two ships, sending just enough able-bodied men to skeleton crew the fishing ship. He wanted to go with them, but Adrick convinced him to stay on board the Andromeda. He did not argue much, not wanting to explain why he wanted to go. He settled for climbing up into the crow's nest, alternating between keeping watch and napping with the man on duty there.

Nightfall came, but Lark did not sleep; she sat awake with her pain and the children, watching them. She went into her bag, looking for clean clothes, knowing she was not going to find any. In a corner, she noticed a small bundle of clothing draped over a chair and investigated. She found the clothes that Landros and Keltree had worn during the storm and had strung up on the hammocks to dry before leaving for the island.

Keltree's clothes were far too long for her, but Landros was just about her size, though narrower in some places than in others. Deciding that he would not mind the loan, she set them aside, folding Keltree's and putting them in his pack. Then strung up a blanket in a corner of the room to form a screen and went behind it. She washed her body and tended her injuries as best she could. The salt water stung a bit, but she knew it would help with inflammation. She even rinsed her hair in the basin before pouring the dark and bloody water into the slops bucket.

She began to sort through her clothes. Her vest she thought she might be able to repair, and put it back into her bag. Her skirt and blouse were beyond mending, both reduced to bloody, cotton rags after the fight in the hold. She tossed them into a corner, for bandages, perhaps, or scrub cloths, and fought her way into Landros's pants. As she had guessed, they were a little snug in the hips, but she laced them up loosely and made them do. She threw on the shirt, left it hanging out to cover the ill-fitting of the trousers, and belted it with two strips torn from her skirt and knotted together. She pulled her long, wet mane back and tied it into a ponytail to keep it out of her way.

Taking down the blanket, she limped to her hammock, sat next to the little girl dozing there and watched Keltree, lost in thought.

Rog entered the room, shuffled in quietly so as not to wake any of the children. He set aside his weapons and shucked himself out of his armor. He found the one hammock that was not occupied and crawled into it. Looking over at Lark, he grinned appreciatively at her attire. "Shoulda been on deck like that during the fight," he said quietly. "You look quite the pirate yerself. Would have put those Northern devils in a right fright." His grin deepened. "Or a right bloody distraction!"

She sighed, lay back in the hammock. "Works both ways, Rog. Could have distracted our side, too."

"Point taken," he shrugged. He was snoring away in short order, leaving Lark alone with her thoughts, her pain, and her fears.

When the two ships finally sailed proudly, if a bit raggedly, past the blockade and into the Portswain harbor, it was just after sunrise. They waited on deck, impatient to pull into the docks. Landros stayed away from Lark. The sight of her in those tight pants, *his* tight pants, and *his* shirt, looking very much the pirate wench, had him wishing he was still in the crow's nest. But he agreed with Adrick that they should disembark together.

He was still angry with her. Not about her borrowing his clothes, though he certainly would not be able to wear them again, not without remembering... He shook his head clear. No, she had insisted on walking down the gangplank on her own feet, however much they hurt. She would not be carried like an invalid, like Keltree, or a child. Damned stubborn pride. But, he had to admit to that fault himself and understood, even if he did not like it one bit. There had been doubts about her joining them on this mission, about her capabilities, and her walking away from this was symbolically important, and that was the only reason he had agreed, that and her promising to head immediately to the wagons for healing.

The dead and wounded were wrapped and ready, waiting just below the decks to be carried into the light of the city, and on to their respective temples. Ahead of them, on the wharf, it seemed that the whole city waited for them. The piers themselves seemed to have taken a severe beating. One of the warehouses had collapsed, and the few ships in the harbor were badly damaged. It seemed that the hurricane had journeyed here after throwing them from the Ride just off the island. It also explained why it had been so easy to slip past the blockade.

Nightingale landed on her shoulder, chirped gaily. Lark laughed and stroked his puffed-up chest. "*Sesha,* have done job well, my friend," she purred.

Adrick scanned the crowd eagerly with the spyglass, "Yes, he has!" he cheered, handing it back. "They've brought wagons and healers a plenty."

"'At's not all theys brought, sir!" Billy cried, hanging from the rigging and whooping like any other ten-year-old boy coming home a hero. "Look! Ain't 'at tha Magistrate's coach?"

"You've got sharp eyes, Billy," Landros said. He himself could barely make out the gold trimming on the black coach at the very back of the crowd.

Billy grinned, his puffy face making it more of a grimace. "Ya learn 'at sight right quick onna streets, sir! Ya gets a quick eye, or ya gets caught!"

"Caught at what?" Landros asked, folding his arms sternly over his chest. Lark cleared her throat. He glanced at her, but she was pointedly not looking at him. He noticed what he was doing, remembered her comment about it being rude, and put his hands down. By then, they were hoving to at the dockside, and all hands scrambled to secure her.

The Andromeda nudged herself into place, with the fishing boat tethered like a docile puppy at her side. The crowd held its collective breath. Few knew what to expect, but the rarity of a ship making it into port at all was cause enough for gawking, let alone having *two* ships successfully run the blockade. And every one of them wanted something to relieve their minds and raise their spirits from their trouble.

Lark walked slowly but determinedly to the head of the gangplank, holding her head high and swallowing her discomfort, forcing herself not to limp. The salve Adrick had rubbed on a few hours ago helped, but it was the difference between walking on knives and walking on nails. It still hurt.

Ivaska walked beside her on one side, Rog on the other, and the children all around. There was a mother's outcry as she recognized her son on the plank. Other shouts began to ring out until the docks were roiling with cheers. Adrick and Landros began their descent after the children, leading a far more grisly parade, one of wounded and dead. The crowd's mood shifted and became a meld of joy and grief, but the excitement remained.

Lark locked her eyes on the waiting wagons and the blue and purple robes waiting beside them. The crowd parted before them; she thought for the priests, but it was for a horseman. She was only barely aware of the crowd bowing as the bear-like form of the Lord Mayor dismounted.

Rog stopped and grabbed her arm as she would have walked on, intent on the wagons and getting off her feet. She paused, looked up in the face of the man who suddenly loomed before her. He clapped her arms, beaming. Tiny spots of light began dancing in her vision, and a strong vertigo overtook her. The circuit of pure will holding her up broke and she collapsed in the Mayor's arms, much to his surprise.

He held her up easily and looked over at Rog for an explanation. The dwarf merely pointed to the bandages on her feet. "Maid, Mother and Crone, girl!" he swore, swept her into his arms as if she were no more than one of the children she was leading.

As he carried her to the wagons, she dazedly tried to sit up, blinked, half-seeing, at him, muttered, semi-delusional, "Papa, I'm sorry. I... I tried...." and passed out again.

"It's all right, girl," he said, laying her in the wagon in the care of the priests. "You did good."

He turned to the others and began helping them load the children onto the wagons. "What has this cost us?" he asked.

Adrick nodded in Lark's direction, "Minor injuries, nothing that will not heal." He gestured to Keltree and the others, "One wounded who may not survive. Plus, four sailors dead ...and one of our own. We have a goodly amount of information, though, which we will report to you personally as soon as we have seen to the wounded and returned the children home."

He nodded silently. "Come directly to me," he said. "No matter the hour." He turned and mounted his horse. "Captain?" he asked of the one-eyed man supervising the care of the sailors. He nodded in response. "If you will join them when they come to report, we can settle on your reward in this and... perhaps the nature and price of your cargo?"

"Of course, Your Lordship," he said, giving a half bow.

"In the meantime, I hope you will forgive my assigning a small contingent of Watchmen to guard her, to protect you from the desperate?" The captain merely acknowledged the necessary evil and returned to see to his men. The Mayor then turned to the highest priest among them, "See to it that everyone here is healed. If there is a price to be paid, send the bill to me." With that, he threw himself into the saddle, turned his horse around, and trotted off.

In the background, the Magistrate scowled and began to give orders to have a small squad of watchmen police the docks to guard the two ships.

Lark came around to a warm, tingling sensation in her feet. She opened her eyes, sighed at the sudden absence of pain, and looked into the soft, friendly, smiling face of a blue-robed young priest. Beside her, she heard Adrick's voice talking to someone she could not see.

"Three days," he was saying. "I am quite certain he would be dead by now if not for her. I do not know what she did, but she said she could undo it when the time was right."

Lark turned her head, tried to see who it was, but the jostling of the wagon made it difficult. The young priest offered her his hand and helped her to sit up. She was surprised to see Rue kneeling over Keltree. The woman was puzzled, clutching her medallion tightly.

"She's going to have to. I cannot seem to do anything as long as that spell is up. By the maiden, I wish I knew what she used."

"You and me both," Adrick said. "I watched her do it and still have no clue."

Lark twisted, touched Rue on the shoulder. She turned and smiled. "Hello, dear. You mind lifting your spell?"

"Certainly." Lark crawled over, touched her fingers to Keltree's forehead, then his lips. He drew a single, ragged breath, then began to moan, moved restlessly.

Rue and Adrick both grabbed hold of him to steady him and went immediately to work. Thankfully, the wagon stopped shortly in front of the steps to the temple. Keltree was the first to be removed, and Lark was left sitting on the buckboard as priests, acolytes, and other assorted helpers ran about like ants to carry in the wounded. She noticed a small commotion going on over at the wagon carrying the dead. Adrick was arguing with Landros over something as the elf sorted out the body of Savaren and was trying to carry him off.

"They will take care of him," Adrick was complaining.

"He is *my* responsibility," Landros growled. "*I* was in charge when he died. *I* was given the responsibility of his welfare by his chief. I do not know what the burial customs of his people are, but..."

"The same as anyone's, I would guess," Adrick snapped.

"And what would *you* know about Elven customs?!" Landros snapped.

Adrick fell silent.

Landros shouldered his burden and started to walk off.

Adrick followed, "What about the reward?"

"Keep it, give it to the children's parents. I don't care what you do with it. I don't need it," he lied.

"What do I tell the Mayor? He will want to question you...."

"Tell him I have a debt to pay. If he still wants to talk to me, he can find me at the Golden Cygnet in about a week. If I am not there, I am probably dead."

He was leaving, going away without a word, back into the woods to find the elves, to take Savaren home. It was stupid, she thought. He did not know where to find them and had miles of enemy-infested terrain to cross in between. And he was not saying a word of good-bye to her. "Landros!" she shouted before she realized what she was doing. He did not stop. She got off the wagon, stumbled in surprise at the lack of feeling in her feet. She called after him again. "Landros!"

Finally, he turned. "Be careful," she said weakly.

He nodded and started to turn again. "Come see me when return," she added. "You know where to find."

He looked back, confused. "Why?"

She sighed, "Your clothes," she said, looking for some excuse. "Keep them."

"Promised you reading."

"It is not necessary," he began.

"You promised me picnic," she said finally.

He sighed. He had promised, and she had accepted. "When I get back," he said and left.

Lark allowed a young priestess to help her up the steps into the temple, mad at herself. It had been obvious that he wanted nothing from her. Why had she pushed it? If he had wanted to take her on that picnic, he would have reminded her himself. Whatever had happened between them to make him so cold to her was set in deep, but she had no idea what she could have done or said.

Landros hated the look in her eyes, the hurt. But he had to do it this way. Maybe one day she would be able to understand. Now, there was the matter of this picnic. Goddess, how was he going to get out of that one? 'No,' he thought, shaking his head, 'there are more important matters at hand. Get Savaren home and *then* worry about picnics and other men's women.'

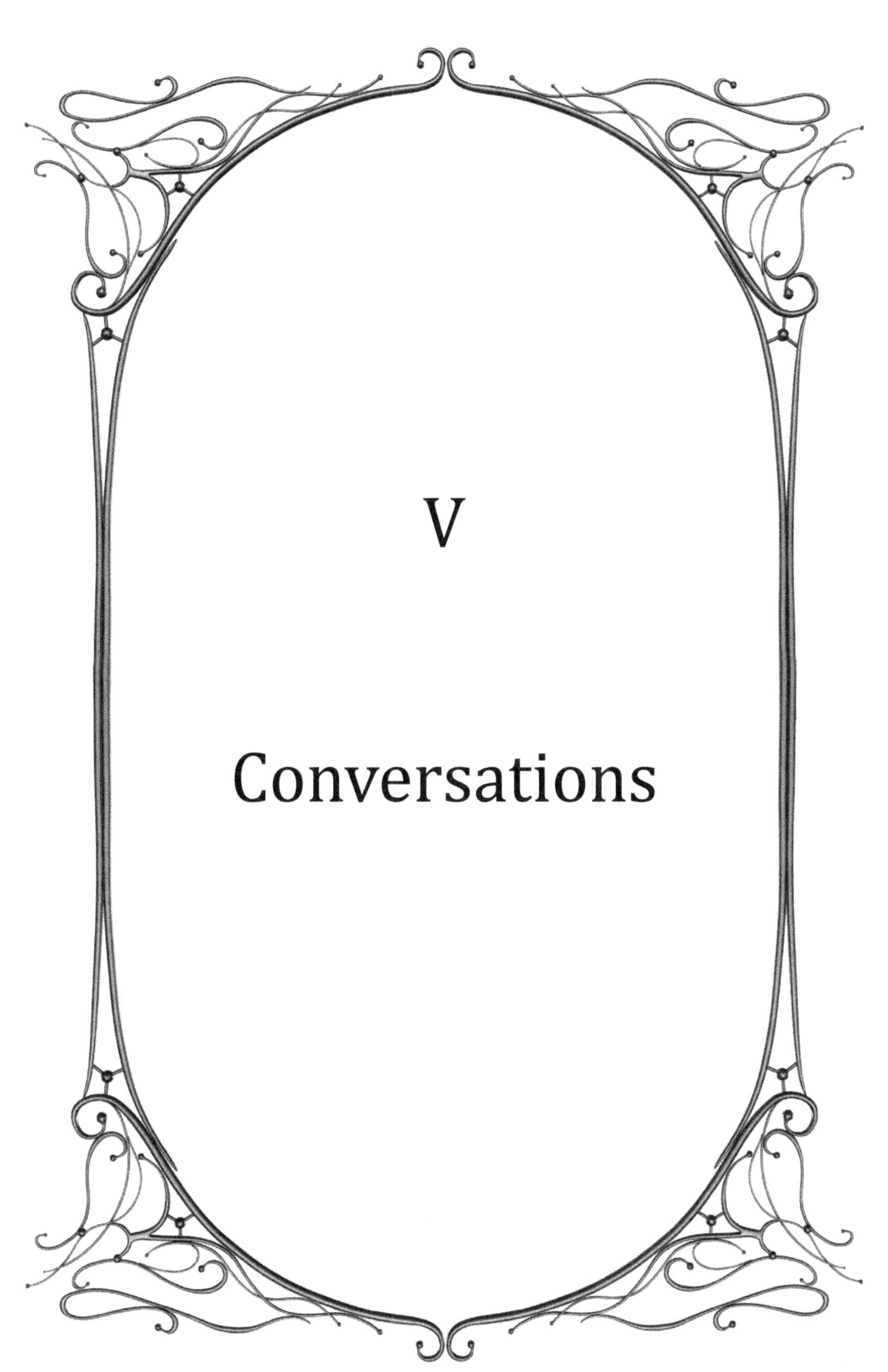

V

Conversations

ONE

Landros was in the process of borrowing a large backpack from a friend when Adrick came into the Red Griffin tavern. He sat down at the bar next to him without a word, ordered an ale, and drank silently. Something was bothering him besides the increasingly poor quality of the ale in town. Landros concluded his business quickly. "I should get this back to you in about a week or so."

"No problem," the man said and left them.

Landros then turned to the bar and finished his own drink.

Adrick pushed a package at him.

"What's this?" Landros asked, not opening it.

"Something from Lark. Your clothes, I think."

Landros pushed them back.

"Landros, don't be an ass. I don't know what is going on between you two..."

"Whatever it is, it's none of your business," Landros said quietly.

Adrick sighed and drank. "You're right, I suppose." They drank. "I still do not think this journey is necessary," he added after a few minutes.

"That is why you are not going."

Silence. Adrick half-glanced around the bar to ease the awkwardness. He didn't like the look of the few people in the tavern or the condition of the furnishings. They were shabbier than the last time they had been here.

"How is Keltree?" Landros asked, pushed his empty glass away from him and stood, getting his gear together.

Adrick watched him. "He'll live. Lark saved his life by mere hours, they tell me. He is on the road to recovery, but it will be a long one. She will be dancing again by tomorrow night. A friend of hers came by and took her home with her: a blond woman. I think she was that barmaid from the Cinnamon Tree, where we went the night we...."

"I did not ask about Lark," he snapped. He was angry now. Adrick's mention of the Cinnamon Tree had conjured up images of her dancing that night ...and what took place afterward. Things he had sworn not to think about again.

"So you did not." He sighed again. "Still, she said to remind you to go see her as soon as you return."

"I heard her the first time," he said, slinging the still-empty pack over his shoulder.

His friend pressed on, determined. "I want you to come see me the minute you get in. Keltree will no doubt want to talk to you. I still don't see why you would not allow us to heal you. You're going to need it."

"They've got their hands full already. Tell Keltree he is a lucky man."

Landros started toward the door, turned, and walked back. He just looked at Adrick for a second or two, and his features seemed to soften a bit. "I am sorry, and I know you are only concerned, but I have to do this my own way. I will see Keltree when I return and will deal with Lark as well. Thank you, my friend."

Adrick watched him walk out of the tavern, as headstrong as always. He crossed his fingers and made the sign of blessing at his back. "May the Maiden go with you and bring you home to us, my friend," he whispered.

Landros slipped over the wall under cover of darkness. It was easy enough for him to get past the guards, but he had to wonder if they were just not doing their jobs. It also made him question how they had not yet been overrun, but he would deal with that when he returned. ...*If* he returned.

Savaren was heavy but not more than he could handle, though the backpack holding him was somewhat cumbersome. He knew it would take him a great deal longer to make this journey out than it would to return, especially since he had to be extra careful if he wanted to get safely through. He would be lucky if he covered two miles in a night's travel.

He had no real idea how far he had to go or where exactly. The teleportation had thrown off his sense of direction. He had a mental picture of Rog's map in his head and tried to keep it in mind. If he went in the rough direction of Hallowell, he figured he might stumble across the elves or their hunting paths at least. If he was obvious enough, they would find him. And, if he was completely off track and made it all the way to Hallowell, back-tracking would be easy enough. It crossed his mind that, if he made it that far, it might be more helpful if he tried to find a ship to Ankreve, in case the Andromeda didn't make it out of the bay. Surely the pirates had regrouped by now after the hurricane.

The first half mile or so, he encountered nothing of the enemy. There seemed to be a zone encircling the city past which the enemy had yet to go in force. After that, he spent a great deal of time up trees and avoiding enemy patrols.

Three days out, and he was still not certain he was going in the right direction. It had taken them less time than this to get to Hallowell. He was fairly sure he should have recognized the terrain by now. He had been walking the last day and a half straight once patrols had thinned out some.

Sometime after noon, he found a huge old oak tree that would serve as a suitable resting place and climbed up. The branches all seemed to spread out from the center, providing a neat hollow. There was evidence that this had often been used as a nest by various small creatures and proved to be quite comfortable, even for one as large as him. He secured the backpack safely out of sight and settled back for a nap in the soft hollow.

He felt peculiar, uncomfortable, chilled. He shifted, tried to settle into a better position, but there was something strange in the air, something acrid. It smelled like no animal he knew. He opened his eyes, blinked in the darkness. He had not intended to sleep into the night and started to get up immediately, but was startled to find an old woman sitting on the branch across from him, watching him.

Landros drew his blade and stared at her. "Who are you, old woman, and how did you climb up here without my hearing?"

She ignored the drawn weapon and his question as if they were of no consequence. "Can I ask you a question?" she asked, in a tone that told him she would ask anyway. Her voice was soft and cracked, gentle, but weathered by many years. He nodded numbly. "What are you doing traipsing across the wilderness, through enemy-infested territory, I might add, carrying the body of a man you hardly knew?"

"Taking him home," he answered, somewhat miffed by her tone of voice. He lowered his weapon but did not put it away. "I have a debt to him and his people. I let him get killed, and I have to take the responsibility for..."

"That could have been any one of you, way I understand it," she interrupted. "He knew the price, knew what he was getting into, same as you. Was his choice."

Landros shook his head, his jaw tightening, but he managed to keep his temper from getting the best of him, barely. "I was in command at the time. Whatever happened, I was ultimately responsible. Besides, his chief placed him in my care. It is only right that I be the one who risks getting him home again."

She held her arms and watched him with her keen, dark eyes. "Admirable. Though stupid. Still doesn't explain why you didn't bury him in town."

'How does she know all this?' he thought.

"Because I do," she snapped. "Don't be rude. Now answer my question. Why not simply take him to the House of the Dead in Portswain?"

"Because that was not his home," he insisted.

"Was it?" she asked with an arched brow. There was a mild breeze through the branches, but her steely gray hair did not flutter in the slightest, though the leaves all around her sighed.

"I do not know. I am simply taking him back to his people, hoping they would know. I don't.... I don't know what else I'm supposed to do," he breathed. He felt oddly at ease in the woman's company, though at the same time slightly on edge. He did not understand it, or her, except to think that perhaps this was a dream.

"You don't know what to do, do you? You don't know what happens to elves, where they go when they die. Never had anyone to explain it, and now, faced with it yet again, you are very much feeling your mortality."

He stared at her. "How the hells do you know that?" He was beginning to feel fear. His grip on his sword tightened, but he did not lift it again.

"Ah, good. That means you are not ready for me yet. I thought you were giving up for a bit there. Thought you were out here looking for me. You keep this up, though, and you'll find my house soon enough."

"Who, how?" he stammered. "Enough of these games, old woman. Who are you?"

"Who I am is irrelevant. As for how? Savaren told me. You told me. Your mother told me. I can read it all in your face, on your heart."

The sword rose again as thoughts of his family came to mind, followed by the renewed sadness of losing them so violently.

It struck him, then. The Crone. That was who she had to be. He leaned back against the branch and letting the realization sink in. She smiled, set her hands on her knees. She did not seem the decrepit old hag that everyone in town made covert gestures to ward off and appease.

"I'm not so terrible. I have aspects other than death in this form. But few humans see them. Your people do, though. Your people know me in all my facets more intimately than any creature. Yes, I am that terrible one. But I am more than just a hag, more than death. I can be a grandmother, too, a keeper of wisdom, a caretaker. I am the first face you see and the last, the midwife and the death-bringer. I still want to know why you came all this way, why you sat up half the night with a bag of bones who can't hear you."

"How do I know he can't?" he said defensively. "How can I know that? For all I know, his spirit cannot rest until he is buried in his home soil. ...That is what I believed."

She nodded understandingly. "That's how the humans buried their dead, in that place where you buried your parents and your sisters.

"Let me tell you something. That bag of bones up there," she pointed, "is nothing more than that... *a bag of bones,* for elves or humans. Once I've come for you, you are mine. Everything else is merely respect. It does not matter what happens to the shell. What matters is what happens to the soul or the spirit. Savaren returned to the world moments after his body stopped breathing."

"Returned?"

"Oh, don't get the idea that elves're immortal, boy. You're not. Though the humans may think so, and you might like to think so. You're part of the world, like the rocks and the trees and the magic. You are like the dryads in a way, eternal in spirit, but very, very mortal in body."

"And humans...?"

"Ah, humans are different, and they resent that, some of them, because they think you are immortal. Humans have souls, which pass on, live on elsewhere. Depends on what they believe. Some of them simply vanish forever, as if they never were. But that's neither here nor there. You have to get back home."

"I still have a debt to pay. I have to...."

"Ah!" she exclaimed, waving her hand at him. "And getting yourself killed over a bag of bones is not the way to pay it!" she snapped. "Go home! Savaren is mine! Nothing you do can change that. Keep this foolishness up, and you will be, too. And then there'll be that damned Romeri to deal with.... A deal is a deal, after all," she muttered to herself. She stood, turned, and shuffled off, fading away completely before her feet ever left the branch.

"What Romeri? Lark? What of my promise to her? Wait!!" he cried. He leaned over the opposite branch, staring off into the woods where she just was, but found no trace of her.

He took a deep breath. He had seen many strange things, but that had to be the weirdest conversation he ever imagined having. Shaking his head, he pulled down the backpack and was surprised to discover its lightness. He opened it hastily, looked in, and found it empty! How could he have lost a whole corpse? He tossed the pack to the ground, dropped softly beside it, and shouldered it. He wandered through the woods in almost total darkness, lost and confused.

Less than an hour later, he found his progress abruptly halted by a twelve-foot stone wall. He could not remember any old settlements out this way that would have had a wall old enough to have ivy growing on it in such profusion. He did not think he was *that* thoroughly lost.

Confused, he was running his hands across the ancient surface when he heard something rustling in the brush behind him. He drew his sword, turned, and saw a hooded lantern flare to life just ten feet away. The bearer moved it to the side, allowing himself to be seen.

"This is most odd," the man said. He was a large human, not quite as large as Barak, but with a similar build. He had dark hair tied back in a queue and a thick, dark beard. Landros could not tell his station by his clothing, though it was in good condition. "To what do I owe this visit?" the man asked, polite but firm.

"Uh, I'm sorry, I was not aware there were habitations out this way," Landros answered cautiously, not certain yet that he was not in enemy hands and not willing to give much away.

The man laughed. "You are in a city; of course, there would be habitations."

"City?" he asked. His heart pounded. He looked back at the wall, "What the hells? That what I think it is?" he asked, pointing to it with his blade.

"If you think it a city wall, yes, though it is an inner wall, not one with parapets and guards. I take it, my friend, that you are lost?"

"Magically, I am afraid," he muttered.

"Is there any other way for men of our profession?" he smiled.

Landros was on edge again. "And what might that be?"

"Calm yourself, my friend. We are both men of the woods, though I gather you are probably a bit more attuned to it than I have been of late. Allow me to introduce myself. I am Lord Colwyn Abberwood."

"Landros," he answered, still cautiously. He frowned as he noticed a gilded rose embossed on the pommel of the sword at his hip.

"I know who you are," the man smiled, then followed the elf's gaze. "And yes, I am afraid I must claim affiliation with the knighthood of the Gilded Rose," he apologized.

"I feel I should warn you, I have little respect for your order," Landros said flatly.

"Ah, let me guess! You feel we are pompous, arrogant windbags full of meaningless ceremony with no true grasp of the meaning of chivalry and the protection of the public in general?" Landros nodded cautiously. "Then, my friend, we are in total agreement," he beamed.

Landros was taken by surprise.

The lord relaxed, resting his arm casually on the offending hilt. "I've actually been looking for you, but I've been told you were out of town. Fancy my coming out here to look for one of my horses and finding you standing quite literally in my backyard! Come, I have a proposal for you that might be to your liking.

"There is still supper available if you are inclined?" he offered when Landros did not move.

Landros sheathed his sword, though he did not take his hand from the hilt. Too many strange things had occurred already for him to relax quite yet.

The lord put up the hand not holding the lantern. "I understand your uneasiness, especially in the current times, but hopefully, before this night has ended, we will have a new understanding and respect for each other."

Finally, Landros allowed the man to lead him through the woods to a large, handsome house, which was still lit in a few lower windows.

TWO

The morning of the second day after his mysterious arrival, Landros left Lord Colwyn's house headed for the Red Griffin, to return the backpack to his friend. On the way, he passed by the Cinnamon Tree and remembered his promise to Lark with a groan.

He did not go in, doubting she would be there at this hour. Instead, he went on to the Griffin as he had planned. Once there, he ordered a meal and a drink, and sat trying to think of some way to honorably extricate himself from his dilemma with the Romeri girl. It was apparent that she wanted to go through with it from her comments just before he had left, but her reasons confused him. Perhaps Romers did not settle with one person but spread their affections with many. It would explain why he had never heard tell of a Romer wedding.

The ale soured in his mouth with the thought that Adrick might have been right about her. It might be perfectly acceptable for a Romeri princess to play at courting several men at once, but he did not wish to be a part of that. And it bothered him that he might have been. Perhaps if he got some of the others to go with them?

And why had the Crone brought her up? What could she have meant by having a deal with a Romeri? What kind of deal could Lark have made with Death? Or had she even meant Lark at all?

He sighed. These past few days had been more confusing than normal.

A shadow fell across his table. He looked up and saw a young man standing at his elbow. He held up his glass, indicating he would like a refill. The person shook his head. "Are you Landros the Pathfinder?"

"And if I am?" he asked, in a surly mood now and not inclined to come out of it.

"A priest up at the temple said I might find you here. He said to ask you to come to the temple at once. Something about a sick friend asking for you?"

Landros nodded, draining the dregs of his mug. 'Might as well get it over with,' he thought. He left the bag with the bartender with a coin to ensure it's proper return and followed the young man to the temple.

Adrick did not say much to him when he arrived, just guided him in to see Keltree. He was sitting up in the infirmary bed and looking much better, though still a little pale. There was a chair waiting beside the bed, and Keltree gestured for him to have a seat. He took Landros's hand and shook it heartily as he sat down.

"I see you are doing well," Landros said, trying to be cheerful. "How is your niece?"

"Holding up quite well under the circumstances. Though she is turning into a mother hen on me." He sighed, content, "but I expect that is Lark's doing."

He nodded, feeling suddenly uneasy bandying her name about so casually. "I expect Lark is quite relieved by this news?"

Keltree laughed, then quickly grabbed his stomach, "Oooh, that hurts," he grinned. "I expect she'll never be rid of that dagger at this rate," he sighed cheerfully. "But anyway, I understand you took an unpleasant journey just after our return?"

"Yes. I went to return Savaren's body."

"All went well, obviously?"

Landros hesitated. "Everything has been taken care of, yes," he hedged.

"Good. I want you to know how thankful I am for everything you did. I am sorry to have shouldered you with that responsibility without warning...."

"Don't worry about it. I take it you were filled in?" Keltree nodded. "I did what I could, and I take full responsibility for what happened."

"When you were out there, taking Savaren back, you didn't, by chance, gather any intelligence, did you?" he asked quietly, straightening the hem of his sheet meticulously as a visual focus, not looking directly at his guest.

"Already done," Landros answered just as softly. "That was the first thing I did. Not that what I discovered was much different from what we've already told them. Though I have to admit, getting out of the city was easier than it should have been."

Keltree made some indecisively agreeable noise, thoughtfully looking Landros over. It was obvious that he wanted to say something but had not yet figured out how. "Navarie asked about you," he said finally.

"Oh?" Landros was getting more uncomfortable but could not think of some polite way of extricating himself. No doubt Navarie had told her uncle all about the kiss in the hold in her romantic, girlish excitement.

"Yes. She seems to be of the opinion that you are a complete idiot," he said bluntly. He added quickly, "A handsome idiot, but an idiot nonetheless." He watched Landros closely. "From what I've been hearing, I think I quite agree."

Landros was trying to contain his anger at the moment. The look of amusement in Keltree's eye was not helping matters any. "Oh?" he asked tightly. "And why are the pair of you of that opinion? It was not I who went off on a dangerous mission when I was not physically up to the task." He started to get up, but Keltree held out his hand and asked him to stay.

"I have been wanting to talk to you about something for a while. Please, sit." Reluctantly, Landros sat stiffly, wary. "I understand you've stood Lark up? ...Well, not stood her up. You've promised her a picnic, I believe, and are having second thoughts?" He held up his hand for silence. "I do not know what happened between the two of you after I was left behind, but you need to work it out. She is deeply troubled by it, though she won't tell me anything. I saw the way the two of you looked at each other on the ship, in the woods, and some time after I fell, that changed. Now, you don't have to tell *me* if you don't want to, but I think you ought to tell Lark at the very least."

So, the truth comes out, he thought. He stood. "When I made that agreement, I had no knowledge that the two of you were together, and I am not an elf to interfere with another's romance. I may not know much about love, but she seems to have those kinds of feelings for you, and I will not interfere. As for standing her up... I am willing to carry that out if she remains insistent. I have been trying to fathom some honorable way of either fulfilling that promise or releasing it."

Keltree smiled ruefully, "Somehow, I had this feeling that was the case. Something Navarie said," he added, waving him to stay. "Sit back down, my elven friend, and let me enlighten you."

Curious, Landros sat and waited with surprising patience.

"First of all, I commend you on your integrity, willpower, and sense of honor. There are not many who feel as you do who would walk away from a woman they desire because she is another's girl if she is not already his wife. Second, she is most certainly not *my* lady. We met but a month ago on a mission to Evandair. The same mission where she earned the Magistrate's ire for being a woman and competent as well as beautiful. We are friends, and I owe that precious girl my life... I have lost count how many times. Yes, I have a lady love, but I assure you, it is not our lovely Lark. My love is more secret and far more forbidden."

Landros just sat there, stunned and speechless.

"Please, go to her. She is highly confused and hurt. She thinks she has offended you in some way but cannot fathom what she has done. Go on. And kiss her as you should have done back in that hold!" he said, shooing him off.

He settled back against his pillow as Landros left and sighed, pleased with himself.

Landros wandered out of the temple in a daze. It was late afternoon, and the sun shone brightly in a cloudless sky. He turned his face to its heat, feeling it suffusing his whole being with renewed energy and life. It was as if his entire life were suddenly falling into place. He walked out into the city, seeing none of the damage from either enemy bombardment or hurricane. He smelled only fresh air, saw only clean streets and people building new things rather than repairing old buildings.

He stepped into the nearest tavern, ordered up a lunch suitable for a picnic: cold fowl, bread, and cheeses, and added a bottle of wine. The price was unreasonable for the quality of food he received, but he paid without complaint, wrapped the food up, and stuck it into his pack.

He passed through the marketplace and saw the silk merchant glumly trying to hawk his wares. He stopped, seeing a bolt of sky-blue silk that reminded him of the clothes Lark had borrowed from him and why. "Have you anything made?" he asked, fingering the cloth. "Prepared clothes?"

"I have a few shirts and some trousers," he offered eagerly. "I have more than silk. I have linen and cotton, wool still, but not so much."

"No, these are for a lady," he corrected.

"What size lady?"

"Small. A narrow waist, about..." he held up his fingers, demonstrating a close approximation of the width of her waist, "about this size."

He nodded, "I have a few skirts, a blouse or two. My wife has gowns at the shop. What color does she prefer?"

"Red, I think," he said.

"Ah! I have red," the merchant answered, moving towards the back of his little booth.

"But I think she looks better in blue. She has blue eyes, you see."

"Blue! I have blue. Are her eyes pale or dark?"

"Dark."

"Sapphires?" he asked excitedly.

"Midnight," he answered, still not quite all there, still reeling from Keltree's revelations. "Dark like midnight."

"Ah, a raven-haired beauty, I shouldn't wonder." The man's voice was muffled somewhat as it came from deep in the back. There was the sound of huffing and puffing as he struggled with a chest. After a few moments, there was a shout of triumph, and he came forward, a dress displayed in his spread hands. It was a varied rainbow of blues ranging from sapphire to sky to powder and back, variegating across the vertical spread of the dress. The top was low cut, with an open neck and slightly off-the-shoulder sleeves of a sheerer silk. There was a simplicity to it that made him think it perfect.

"You like, ah?" he grinned. "I give you real good deal. Only three laurels. Normally, I would charge five or even eight for a dress of this magnitude, but food is rarer than silk nowadays, and business is scarce."

Landros laid five laurels into the man's eager hand and had him wrap the dress. He watched as the overly-eager merchant added a blue silk rose made of folded ribbons to the bundle, tying it all up neatly with a pale cord. "What is with the rose?"

"A gift, a bonus, a trifle really, but one the lady will no doubt enjoy for a lifetime after a real rose would fade. My wife makes them to keep herself busy now that the dressmaking business is slow. Nothing extra, just come again!" He handed the package to Landros as if he were handing over a crown instead of a bundle of silk.

Landros thought a moment. He remembered the outrageous price he had just paid for the food and realized that the price of this dress would not pay for a fraction of that meal. He reached into his pack, took out the bundle of food, and handed it to the merchant. "A gift," he said, thanked him again, and turned towards tent town, putting the package in his backpack. Behind him, he heard the exclamations of the merchant as he opened the bundle and smiled.

As he left the more structured part of town and entered the glorified campground which served as home to many of the city's residents, his mood sobered. Here, the damage from the storm was readily evident. Most of the structures, the tents and the ramshackle lean-tos made of salvaged debris, were gone. The people here looked worse than he remembered, most of them sleeping on the bare ground now, with not even a sheet of ragged cloth to cover their heads. They looked at him greedily as he passed but, sighting the sword and bow on his back, did not attack or approach. These people were getting desperate, worse than down Bayside way. He sincerely hoped he would not find Lark still here.

He was disappointed. The red paint on the roof was somewhat the worse for wear, and one of the shutters was broken and boarded over. The whole contraption leaned awkwardly on one side. The birdhouse on the corner was missing altogether, and the horses were nowhere to be seen. He came around the corner of the wagon, saw that the warning string had blown away, and the unusable bits were haphazardly playing wind-chimes in the tree, which was now missing quite a few limbs.

Lark was struggling with a broken wheel, trying to get the wagon up on blocks so that she could change it for the new one. Her neighbors watched her dumbly, as if this were merely another performance. No doubt they would pounce the moment the old wheel was cast off.

Lark sagged against the side of the wagon, felt splinters through her sleeve, and stood straight. In frustration, she kicked the broken wheel, snarling in rage and ranting in Romeri.

"Easy," came an all-too-familiar voice. "You just had those mended. Would not want to have to go and get them fixed again, would you?"

She turned and saw Landros striding up as if he had never been gone, had never snuck out of town to go gallivanting through enemy territory, never returned more than a day ago and not told her as he had promised. She sighed. "Yes, and wheel-wright said too busy to come fix. Can sell me new though!" she mocked. "And that *gosho pashaska* over there," she gestured at the man squatting outside his ragged tent watching, wrapped in one of her blankets, "is not man enough to offer help. Though is able enough to help himself to contents when all is broken," she added under her breath.

"Actually, I meant your feet, not the wheel."

She raked her hair from her face with her fingers, looked completely frustrated, and probably not just with the wagon wheel.

"Lark, I'm sorry I..." he began. He tossed his pack down and came over to help her. "Here, let me...." He put his shoulder to the side of the wagon and pushed. Lark, thankful for help at last, set her back to the underside and lifted.

"Not too far!" she cried, noticing the precariousness of the remaining wheels. "Hold there!" she said and, using a small poltergeist, placed the last block in place. "Down now!"

He slowly eased off and stood, spinning the broken wheel to make sure it moved freely. As he began to work off the pegged hub, he noticed the grass under the wagon was brown and the ground muddy, still covered in puddles. "Looks like it fared all right," he said, straining with the peg. "A broken wheel isn't too bad."

"No, but axle is. Had to bind under-joint with wet leather. Only hope holds until can get real repairs," she grumbled, helping him to remove the wheel and replace it.

She watched him carefully, trying to guess why he had come here and why now. She heard that he had been seen yesterday, but he had left no message with Lily or Adrick. Her assumption was that he was not really interested in her anymore and was not going to come. It had set her in a black mood, on top of her near despair at the condition of her precious wagon. She took the old wheel, half-rolled, half-threw it at the man in the next space. "You want this too?! Here! Is yours!!" she shouted, punctuating herself with a few choice Romeri swear words.

"That... is your blanket he has... isn't it?" he grunted, shoving the new wheel into place.

"Yes. Come back, find wagon on side, door open. Thieves take most everything, including mattress!" she fumed.

"How'd they get in?" he asked, calmly hammering the peg into place. "I thought you locked the door with that ward of yours?"

"When wagon fall over, door broke, broke ward. Thieves walk in as please."

"How much did you lose?" he asked, dusting his hands off. "There, all fixed."

"Thank you. Enough. Nothing not replaceable. But... is principle, *sesket*?"

"*Sesket*," he nodded. It felt good to be near her again, without having to worry about what anyone else thought about it or that he was offending a friend, without having to worry what her scent was doing to him.

"Did not get my good jewels, though," she said, moving her hair back to display a pair of opal and gold earrings. "My vas, or what else I keep in hideaway. That at least not break open."

"What happened to the horses?" he asked, half afraid to.

She sighed, perched on the side of the driver's box. "Lily sent stable boy to fetch, brought them to tree just after sent word would be gone. Wagon she could do nothing for. Ivaska is with her now, guarding hen-house. Have nothing here worth guarding. Now that is fixed, will bring horses back and move. Where, I do not know."

"Lily...?"

She shook her head. "Have no room. Is generous, but not so much."

"Come on," he said, holding out his hand to her. "You need a change of scenery, and I know just the place."

"Where is taking?" she asked suspiciously.

"I promised you a picnic, didn't I?" he asked, still holding out his hand.

She avoided it, jumped off the wagon, and went to inspect the traces. The glimpse he caught of her face as she went past was sullen. "Do not have to hold to this promise," she said. "If is not wanted."

"No. I promised you a picnic, and I think you need it," he insisted.

She did not look at him, examining the cross-tree. "Was not promise, was suggestion. Was idea to get Adrick to go away."

"It *was* a promise."

She shrugged, "I release you. Do not wish to force into something do not wish to do," she snapped. Why was he doing this to her? He had made it obvious before he left that he did not wish this picnic or anything else to do with her. Why....

"You are a damn stubborn woman," he said with a sudden growl of frustration. "I believe I owe you this at least. And according to Navarie, it's long overdue!"

He reached out, seized her by the waist, and pulled her to him. He then gave her a deep kiss that silenced her completely and startled her too much to think to resist. It felt as if her entire body was made of oiled paper and she had just been tossed on the fire. It was not until Landros finally released her mouth and looked into her dark blue eyes that she remembered to breathe again. "Does that feel like I'm being forced into this? I *want* to take you on this picnic. And I know just the place."

"Let me get shoes," she breathed weakly.

As she stumbled into the wagon, he wandered casually over to the man huddled under Lark's blanket. He picked up the broken wheel, made a show of examining it without really seeing it. "Might I make a suggestion, my good man?" he said quietly. "Several items have gone missing from the lady's wagon. It would be in your best interest to see that all of them are returned, probably by the time we return this evening. You would not want to find out what I am capable of when angered, and the lady is under my protection. I am not as forgiving as she is." He set the wheel rolling with enough force to break it completely on impact with the tree.

The man watched him with wide eyes but said nothing as Landros turned and met Lark at her door. He offered her his arm politely. "Shall we go?"

THREE

When he removed the blindfold he had asked her to wear for the last portion of the trip, Lark was amazed by the absolute wildness of where she stood. It was like any other forest she had ever been in, with emerald meadows filled with crocus and other budding wildflowers and a small, clean river rushing across it. The only difference was that this forest was in the middle of a city. It was peaceful and quiet, as if the war were a thousand miles away instead of five. If the hurricane had done any damage here, none of it was visible. Lark was startled to see a doe dart away at their approach. "Is beautiful!" she breathed. "How... how is this place not crawling with people?"

"This is not a public park," he explained, guiding her to where he thought was the perfect grove for the picnic. "It is a private residence."

A look of horror crossed her face. "Should we be here?"

He just smiled. "Yes. He is ...a friend of mine," he said. "I have permission."

A scowl crossed her face. "Is not right such pristinity not open to all. Land cannot be owned, should not."

"Because you cannot take it with you?"

She nodded. "Is whole principal of Romeri way. Is why have not attacked neighbors or called in Watch, not that they would do *gosho* thing, over things they have taken from me. I left wagon too long. Is my fault."

"It is not your fault," he insisted. "I have friends, I can...."

She held up her hand. "Like one who 'owns' this place? No," she shook her head. "Leave them be. When they need me most, I will not be there. Is simple as that."

He did not agree, but it was not his affair. He had to respect her ways if he expected her to respect his. "Actually," he said, "Colwyn does not think he so much owns the place as he protects it. Should the walls not be in place, or he not guard it so zealously, the people would destroy it quickly. He does not object to those who can appreciate it to enjoy his wood, which is why we are here."

He stepped aside with a flourish, letting her get a good look at the small, sun-speckled grove in the middle of the forest. She wandered in slowly, touching the leaves on the trees with loving hands. Leaned against one of them, he watched her appreciatively. She was like a child in her wonder. He himself was awed by the pristineness of the place. That eight acres of such wild beauty could be maintained within city walls filled him with greater respect for the man who could do it or who would care to try.

"Is not cultivated like other parks," she mused. "Grass is as long as grass wishes, not like neat carpet with all flower heads chopped off."

"That's the way Colwyn likes it," he said and set down his pack. He fished out his magic blanket and spread it on the grass. "Shall we dine?" he asked. She smiled, set her own bag down, and sauntered over. "I'll take that as a yes."

He said the command word, and a sumptuous feast appeared before them, the perfect picnic spread.

"You look surprised," she chuckled, picking a strawberry from its bowl and dipping it into the cream next to it.

"I am," he said. "I don't always get just what I want or what would be appropriate. I could not have picked a better spread. And look, there is just enough for two."

She sat down on a clear edge of the blanket and pulled out a scrap of paper and a stick of wrapped coal. Scrawling a quick note to Lily, she told her that the wagon was fixed and that Landros had taken her on a picnic. She added to the bottom: "Don't wait up." She folded it neatly and handed it to the mockingbird, who had perched on the lip of the strawberry bowl and was helping himself.

He complained when she held it out to him. He wanted to stay and enjoy the feast. She gave him a look that conveyed everything. Grudgingly, he took the note in his claw. "*Dasha*!" she said, jerking her thumb in the air, telling him to get lost. With a defiant chirp, he snagged a strawberry in his beak and flew off.

Landros laughed. "I think he's jealous."

"He like you. He just like food more," she laughed. She sat back, taking a glass of unwatered wine and helping herself to the cold roast fowl. "Feel guilty eating so well," she said.

"Don't," he answered. "I share this enough with those in desperate need to alleviate all guilt for one good meal," he added, thinking back to the silk merchant. "Besides, you don't eat enough," he said, digging in.

"Don't *you* start," she growled, playfully throwing a strawberry at him. "Get enough from Papa's woman, Rosita, about my weight!"

"Oh, I have no complaints about your weight or your figure, princess. Just that I've seen the way you eat, and you never seem to eat enough to keep your little friend alive, much less keep you dancing."

She shrugged. "I eat enough …when opportunity and timing are right. Though, yes, with siege and everything, have not been eating so well as used to. No one is. Except you."

She had not intended it as a barb, but it stung like one. "I hardly ever use this for myself, though I use it every day."

"Oh," she arched her brow, teasing. "And who do you feed?"

He shrugged. "The poor. The children. I go to the orphanage a lot."

She mused for a few minutes. "Can see why you were so intent on getting children back," she said. "Keltree is well," she added quietly.

He rolled over onto his back. "I know," he said, staring up at the treetops. "I went to see him just before coming to see you."

She grew moody again. Keltree, in his concern for her, probably talked him into the outing. Although Landros was in a surprisingly good mood. She was certain that if he had been forced to do this, he would not be. She studied him, trying to read him, but found no real answers there. He was relaxed, at ease, comfortable, and content, at least for the time being. It must have been her ill-timing that caused him to be so hostile on the steps of the temple.

He glanced over, saw her brow furrowed in thought, and sat up. "Lark, I'm sorry. I... I had some misguided ideas about your relationship with Keltree. I was trying to be gracious and back out, but ... I guess I hurt you without realizing it, and I'm sorry."

"Misguided ideas?" she asked, her whole expression changing. "Mean you thought Keltree and I...." She suddenly laughed. "Keltree is good man, but ... how you say... 'not my type'."

"I'm glad it was so obvious," he muttered, feeling somewhat needled by her blatant amusement with the idea.

"Besides, is very much in love with someone else."

"So he said."

"I think is brother's wife."

"Oh really?"

She nodded, leaned forward, whispered conspiratorially. "She came with Navarie to see him while was there. Saw how he looked at her. Is different than have seen him look at other women."

"That is very interesting," he mused.

Lark laughed again and popped a strawberry into his mouth.

She sat back, still thinking but on a happier note. He had thought her Keltree's girl. He had desired her still, but had changed after Keltree got hurt. It made sense. She found his intense sense of honor endearing.

They spent the rest of the afternoon in good cheer, catching up with each other's news. Her take at the Tree was thinner lately, and food prices had gone up considerably. Landros told her what he could of the enemy, what little he had seen that he had not been told to keep to himself.

Later, he took her to another clearing just off the river, and they sat side by side to watch the sunset. It was a spectacular sight, all red and gold over the treetops and the distant outlines of the temples and government buildings.

"Is strange," she mused aloud. "Is it not?"

"What?"

"Worse enemy does, more disasters they cause, more beautiful is sunrise and sunset."

"Probably has something to do with each day becoming more precious, more of a surprise to be still alive."

She looked at him, "You... think?"

Her face glowed almost golden in the fading light, the final flares of the dying sun. Her eyes sparkled as if stealing some of the sun's fire as it sank. "Yes, I think," he said finally. "Sometimes."

She laughed, got up as the colors began to fade, and turned a little pirouette. "Come," she said. "Have promised you reading. If still desire?"

"Oh, why not?" he said, rolled to his feet, and followed her back to the grove.

He sat down on the blanket, clearing it first with the command word. Lark summoned up a were-light, hanging it in the air above their heads. She pulled out her rune bag and spread it flat, gathering the runes in her hands. She rolled them between her palms for a moment, then dropped them onto the cloth and turned each stone face down, arranging them in a circle. When she looked up at him, the light cast a ghostly blue glow over her face, making her eyes unreadable. "Before begin, have to ask.... Is why hate reading for friends. Is required to cross palm with silver. It does not matter how little or what form, just that it be silver. I do not understand it, doubt any seer knows reason for any more. Is customary. Is useless otherwise."

"Is that why the money is usually given back if the fortune is for ill?" he asked, fishing in his belt pouch for a coin.

"Yes, is to hope that by returning money evil will not occur. But once silver is crossed...," she said, shaking her head. "How is you know this?" she smiled.

He shrugged and placed a silver coin in her open hand. "I've friends who've had their palms read or the Tarot cast. Once in a while, they get a bad one."

She smiled. "There are lot of fakes, so be careful. Not every Romeri woman can get Tarot or stones to speak true, though nearly any Romer can interpret what falls. And do not be fooled into allowing man to read your fortune. These *always* fakes. No man has that power. Is woman thing. Now, place in mind question. Do not have to tell, but think, and choose stone."

He thought a moment and placed a question in the fore of his mind, a general query about his future. In the back of his mind, though, as he watched her longingly, he was thinking about her. Without really looking, he reached out and touched a stone.

Lark flipped it over. "*Peorth*," she said. "Curious."

"What does *Peorth* mean?"

"Is initiation."

Landros did not smile. He had not put much credence to this whole business of reading fortunes, but this was like a slap in the face. Stunned, he ran a gloved hand through his hair, listened as she continued.

"Is rune of hidden happening and stresses importance of mystery, revelation of secrets and possibility of finding someone or something. Is rune of second chances." She looked up at him, smiled facetiously. "Have you need of second chance?" she teased.

"My whole life needs a second chance," he said evasively. 'And maybe *you* are my second chance?' he thought, surprising himself. "What happens now? How do I interpret this?"

Lark sat back on her heels. "That depends on question. This rune tells you to follow intuition. Solution to whatever is not in what you see, but in what you feel." She began to think, formulating an idea from the rune. It told her things, too. And she liked what it had to say.

Landros reached out for another stone. "All right. How about this one?" Lark grabbed his wrist before he could touch it. "What?"

"No. Is one question only. Tomorrow, if you wish, can give another. But not today."

"Why not?"

She let him go. "I do not know. Is bad, is all Gruma would tell me. 'Never cast twice in same day for same person. One coin, one question, no more'."

He shrugged. "All right. Would not wish to push the Fates," he said, remembering back on his own encounter just past.

Lark began to put her stones away. He noticed her take one, peek at it, then toss it into her bag followed by the rest in a swept handful and tying it off. There was a determined set to her face, though a smile on it. He sat up. "I'd better get you back," he said. "Lily's probably wondering what's keeping you."

She shook her head dreamily, still a mile away, "No. Note said am not working tonight. Will.... will be back," she said, got up and drifted into the darkness.

He watched her go, wondering as to the sudden change of her mood. He sighed and began packing up. 'Aren't women supposed to be like that?' he asked himself.

Lark wandered just a few yards away, looked back. She could barely see the were-light she had left behind. Satisfied she was unobserved, she untied her vest, noting as she did that it was in sore need of repairs. She hung it on a low tree branch and untied her blouse, hanging it beside the vest. Slipping out of her skirt, she hung it up, too. She was more than a bit nervous. She had never done anything like what she was planning before. There were no doubts in her mind that she *could* do it, but she was nervous nonetheless.

The were-light above Landros's head winked out suddenly. Looking up, he turned but could see nothing in the sudden dark. He grabbed his sword, wondering why Lark would have let the light die. He knew next to nothing about magic, and his first thought was that something was amiss. "Not now," he mumbled, tightening his grip on the hilt, waiting in a crouch for his eyes to adjust. "Please, don't let there be trouble now."

Suddenly, he heard the faint strains of a violin, and a thin, glowing mist began creeping in between the trees. The music was low and sultry, full of restrained passion and promise. He looked over, saw Lark's bag still sitting by the tree where she had left it. She had not brought her fiddle that he could tell, unless she had a new spell to allow her to summon it or carry it invisibly. It came to him then, that the music sounded just like that she had summoned on the ship, the ghostly violin.

Something was growing out of the mist in front of him, a faint, shimmering light. A cloth formed out of the mist, a pale blue, sparkling curtain, and from behind it, a soft glow. He saw a silhouette slowly twisting behind that curtain, the outline of a woman dancing naked in the moonlight.

He sat, his sword falling, forgotten, as he stared dumbfounded, watching her arch and turn sinuously to the music. Her body could have been the violin playing, so closely matched were her movements.

A tiny swarm of lights rose from her feet, spiraling around her but making her no more visible behind the cloth. The curtain shimmered, began to fold and collapse, wrapping itself around her until she was wearing a sheer skirt of starlight blue and a clinging, low-cut blouse that left her stomach bare. The were-lights settled into her hair, creating a soft aura around her.

The music shifted, became more passionate, more inflaming, faster, and her body moved to the new rhythm easily. Her eyes never seemed to leave him, which intensified his reaction. Her movements were subtly suggestive, wonderfully sensual without being overt or vulgar or leaving anything misunderstood.

Landros gazed, awestruck, at the woman dancing before him. He was not certain how to react and was unable to do anything but stare. Part of him wanted to reach out and touch her, to pull her into his arms and ravish her, yet he held back, afraid to touch her, or move, or make a sound lest he shatter the image and the mood that was beginning to swallow him. She was ghostly and gorgeous and utterly desirable.

He slowly became aware that the cloth around her body was melting away, breaking up into tiny pinpoints of light and drifting upward into the trees. Soon, she danced in all her natural glory beneath a starlight canopy. She was radiant, flushed, and completely infused with the heat of the moment. He knew this was no illusion. He could smell her, hot and musky, as aroused as he was.

She was moving forward, dropped to the ground at his feet, and crept forward slowly, one hand at a time. She straddled his body, stalking him like a jungle cat, her dark blue eyes holding his trapped. He fell over backward onto his elbows as she came closer, pushed him flat onto the blanket, and hovered over him. Her hair fell in a dark curtain to either side of his face.

She pounced, seizing him in a deep kiss. When she pulled back, she smiled sweet and sultry. She rolled one of his shirt strings between her fingers and tugged, began unlacing it.

He grabbed her hands, panicking. "Whoa, whoa," he began. "Listen..." She kissed him, slipping her hands free and tugging on his gauntlets. "We can't..." he continued, trying to ignore his awareness of her nakedness pressed against him, trying to protest between her ardent, insistent kisses, feeling his willpower weakening steadily. "...do this...."

"Why not?" she purred, kissing him again.

"Because... because...." He couldn't think of a reason. "Oh, the hells with it!" He pulled her closer, kissed her, and rolled over her. He pulled away long enough to throw his shirt off into the grass, then returned to her, tossing his gloves after it.

FOUR

Sometime later, they lay curled up together, gazing up at the night sky. The were-lights had faded, leaving the grove lit only by real starlight. Landros had thrown his cloak over their bodies to keep off the faint chill and was using his bedroll for a pillow. He wrapped his arms around her, pulled her close, feeling content and safe.

She let him hold her, basking in his warmth. Absently, she stroked his fingers, admiring his strong hands. She noticed a ring she did not remember him having worn before, a simple band of copper on his right ring finger. She played with it, turning it to see the faint etching of a falcon on its face.

"What is?" she asked curiously.

He lifted his head to see what she meant. She held up his hand and showed him the ring. The bottom suddenly fell out of his stomach. She glanced back, saw a look of complete horror on his face, and sat up. "What?" she asked. "What is matter?"

"You weren't supposed to see that," he muttered, cursing himself for his carelessness.

She grew angry, confused and hurt by his reaction. She sat up, put her fists on her naked hips and faced him. "What? Keeping secrets now? Thought were past keeping secrets?!"

He floundered. There was no way he could lie to her, tell her it meant nothing. "I... I can't tell you," he complained weakly.

She was genuinely angry now and started to get up. "Do not trust me? I give you real name," she hissed, pushing him away from her, "and do not trust me?"

He felt like a complete heel. He grabbed her and pulled her gently back. "It's not that," he pleaded. "Not that at all. ...Damn it!" he swore in frustration. Just when he was starting to feel comfortable...

She sat stiffly, looking imperiously down at him. "Then what?" she asked coldly.

He sat up, sighed, ran his hands through his hair, trying to think. "It... my own brother doesn't even know!" he exclaimed. She sat silent, waiting. If he wanted to redeem himself, now was the time. Without knowing why, he found himself explaining to her everything that had taken place between himself and Lord Colwyn only the day before. "It's ...it's a squire's ring," he blurted.

"Squire?" she asked suspiciously. "As in knight squire?"

He gave an ironic chuckle. "I can see you feel the same way about knights as I do. Used to," he corrected. "I've always believed in what knighthood stood for, what it was *supposed* to stand for, not as demonstrated by these Gilded Rose pansies," he explained. He wrapped his cloak around her shoulders to keep her warm and to keep her nakedness from distracting him. "I had all but lost faith in knights and chivalry. The Gilded Rose was an order instituted by the old king. He was very much like the Roses that we know: pretentious, arrogant, and genteel only to those of the nobility. They were full of pomp and meaningless ceremony, worth nothing in the long run.

"The new king, he, too, is of this order, but only because his father requested it of him. But King Feremon is a far different man than his father ever was, a better man. He believes in what knighthood is supposed to stand for, and so he created the Order Falconis."

"Is not what they call this young king?" she asked, remembering fragments of hear-say. Her people paid little attention to the affairs of sedentary kings. "Feremon the Falcon?"

He nodded. "Yes, that is why they named the order as they did. The Falcons are a secret order."

"Why secret?'

"King Feremon discovered that he could not rely on the Gilded Roses to accomplish the things that he wished them to because they were too public. They tend to stand out like bantam roosters, and that makes it impossible for them to gather accurate information. Information the king needed to effectively and fairly run his kingdom. He needed a network of individuals that he could trust implicitly for their tact, secrecy, and ability to discover things that no sane man would let a knight discover. These are his falcons, men who are content to ride his hand, hunt his prey, and rest, hooded, in the mews after their work is done."

She frowned, "Network of spies and secret police?"

He shook his head. "No. They are more problem finders and solvers: real knights. They are everything I believe a knight should be, everything I want to be associated with: humble, gracious, willing to do the deed that must be done and not caring who gains the credit for it or what the personal cost. I've never liked the boastful attitudes of the Roses. It turns my stomach to see one bragging about his exploits, his charities, being as gallant as you please to any beautiful, noble-born woman, yet treating the peasantry like vermin not worth his notice."

Lark watched him talk, watched him become impassioned by what he was saying, telling her about a cause he had decided to devote his life to, something he could respect. She found herself coming to respect these ideals, lofty and impractical though she thought they were, and even more so the man who could possibly have inspired such devotion.

"My liege lord is the man who owns this wood. He is also a Rose, but only for the public access it gives him. He is heart and soul a Falcon. He's been watching me, and was apparently impressed with my activities. It is believed there are people in the government who wish control of this city to fall to other hands. There are Falcons here trying to ferret out the truth of this, and why the king has not sent us word or aid, or why those who were sent to the Capitol months ago have not returned. My involvement with all this has to remain a secret or I simply will not be able to do what it is I have to do," he finished. "The ultimate irony is that I finally have a chance to become my ideal and I have to keep it hidden.

"This ring is a symbol of my rank. I am a squire to Lord Colwyn."

"Aren't squires boys? Children used as servant to knight while learning to be?"

He flashed a lopsided grin, "Normally, yes. But this is not an ordinary order, but a secret one. I am a squire in concept only. More journeyman than apprentice? I have to prove myself to be fully initiated." He paused. "No one knows this, no one but Lord Colwyn and you. Normally, the only person who knows someone is a squire is their inducting knight." He sank back and gave a rueful laugh. "I don't know what Lord Colwyn is going to say when he finds out you know. I get the ring, and the very next thing I do is tell you everything."

She smiled softly, took his hand in hers. He watched her gently kiss the copper band, then turned his palm and kissed that, too. He knew, or thought he knew, that Romers had little respect for laws not their own, or the ranks of anyone outside their clan. He prayed she would not think less of him because he desired this knighthood, held his breath as she stroked his hand tenderly, and smiled.

"Told you, I did," she laughed softly. "And now I understand."

"Understand what?"

"*Peorth*. No wonder you gave such look when told you was initiation. You did not come straight to me because had this to do. And yes, I know had to happen yesterday, or while were out of city, (though that makes little sense,) because did not have this ring on island." She smiled shyly. "I remember your cold hands after storm. They were bare, and there was no ring here. But can relax and trust me, as I trust you with my most precious secret."

He sighed, felt the warmth returning to his body as his fear receded. He reached out and touched her cheek tenderly.

She giggled, "Is cold still." She opened the cloak. "Come inside where is warm."

He went to her, laid back down beside her, and wrapped them both up tightly in the voluminous folds of wool.

"What made you think was sleeping with Keltree?" she asked suddenly. "Did not think I gave this impression."

"Well,..." he searched for a reason, some way to explain how he had come to the conclusion he had.

"Has been no one but you. Am not so much loose woman as most who see Romeri think." He looked at her in surprise. "Are free with our love, yes, but this does not make wanton."

"There has been no one?" he asked, uncertain how that made him feel.

"No. What makes think there has to be?"

"I don't know. You are so beautiful, so desirable...."

"I try not to associate with patrons, is lead to trouble, like Coolie. But surely you had other women more beautiful than I?"

"No," he sighed, now oddly content. "It is my confession that you are my first."

She looked at him. "How old are you?"

He hesitated, not sure how she would react. "A hundred-and-twenty-three."

Her eyebrows arched, "And you claim me your first? Surely there were elven women before me?"

"No, I... I have not spent much time in the company of elves. My parents... were not exactly accepted in Elven society," he evaded.

She sighed and settled back against his chest, thinking how interesting his admission had been. Again, fate seemed to be drawing the two of them together in spite of themselves.

He held her tighter. He was falling fast, and he knew it. Everything she said made him want to let go of her less and less. It would not be long before he would find it impossible. But she was Romeri, prone to wandering and not likely to settle down. Well, he had been known to be a bit of a wanderer himself and was no stranger to that life. 'For now', he thought, 'for now I shall take what she will give'.

She shivered under the blanket, beginning to feel the chill air. He whispered against her ear. "Perhaps I should get a fire going, if we plan on staying here all night?"

She nodded, sat up. Landros pulled his pants back on and went to collect some firewood. Still wrapped in the cloak, she went in the opposite direction to retrieve her clothes. She took them down, pulled on the blouse, tying it loosely, and stepped into the cotton skirt. She did not put the vest on but carried it back with her, tying it up with the laces.

When she got back, Landros was banking the unlit fire with rocks from the river. "Everything all right?" he asked as she slipped almost silently across the grass.

"Mmhm," she murmured contentedly, kneeling by her bag. She put her vest inside and began to take off her jewelry, putting it all in her rune bag and that into her patchwork.

"That is an interesting pack," he commented, working on getting the fire started.

She began brushing her hair languidly, watching him work. "Mama made this for me long time ago, from scraps of cloth, old clothes, leftovers from skirts she made for me. Has been mended many times, but serves me well. Suits me," she smiled.

"That it does," he said. He finally got the fire going and stepped back, stoked it until it was giving off enough heat. He folded up his pack for a pillow, unrolled the bedroll for ground cover, and spread the cloak for blanket. Lark lay down and folded back the covers for him to join her. He started to, thought better of it, and excused himself for a minute, slipping off into the bushes.

Lark sat up again, savoring the warmth of the fire. She could feel the chill in the air deepening. No doubt there would be fog come morning, this close to the river. The thought of fog brought to mind her nightmares. She did not wish to spoil this perfect night with ill dreams, knew the drug made her sleep soundly. But perhaps just a little...?

She quickly pulled the bottle out of her bag and opened it. Unfortunately, a little was all there was. Only a single drop rolled onto her tongue. It would have to be enough.

She heard Landros coming back and quickly slipped the bottle under the edge of the blanket, out of sight. She smiled at him, pulled back the cloak once again, and snuggled up close to him. It did not take long for the sounds of the wood, the crackle of the fire, and the kiss of laudanum to put them both to sleep.

FIVE

Lark heard a voice on the wind, calling to her. It was soft and silky, seductive. She sat up. It called again, whispered to her. She rose and followed obediently, caught in the grip of the drug and unable to question the summoning.

Landros rolled over in his sleep, reaching for the warm body next to him. His hand hit an empty blanket. He sat up, fully awake, in time to see a flutter of cloth disappearing into the foggy morning amid the trees. "Lark?" he called.

She did not answer. He lay back, thinking. Perhaps she just went to heed the inevitable call of nature? Still, she would have answered. "Lark, are you all right?"

Again no reply.

He decided that no answer was a negative answer and got up to follow her. He threw his cloak on against the chill. It could not have been long past midnight from the coolness of the embers. He snatched up a sword, not knowing what to expect and knowing that Lark would not fail to answer unless there was something wrong, out there or with her.

It was hard tracking her in the dark and mist. Shapes and shadows were everywhere, swirling in the fog. Her bare feet left few tracks to follow, only a faint, crushed dampness in the forming dew. After a moment, he heard her up ahead, a rustling of dead leaves and branches against fabric snapping in a sudden breeze.

He pressed on, saw her standing near a pair of great oak trees, confused, trying to get past them and failing for no reason he could see. She looked at them as if they were actively trying to block her path. Their branches had caught hold of her skirt and sleeves, and she stood there as if she were physically being held. "Lark?" he called softly. "Illyana?"

Slowly, she turned.

There were two men, small giants with rough hands who grabbed her and would not let her by. Suddenly, she heard the voice, clear and cold behind her. "Illyana," he called. She turned, saw the shock of long brown hair flowing from beneath the hood, the pale skin and gleaming eyes, red in the darkness. Her heart froze, and, for a moment, she was unable to breathe.

It was impossible. He was dead, scattered to ash by her own hands. He stepped closer, a smile upon his face of mock tenderness, his eyes filled with the promise of vengeance, pain for pain, and reached for her. She found her tongue.

*"No," she whispered, her voice refusing to cooperate still. "You cannot be! We killed you! **I** killed you!!" She began to panic as the giants gave her over to him, and he began to pull her close into his embrace, to fold his cloak about her.*

Landros, untangling her from the branches, was surprised by her sudden outburst. "Illyana, calm down. No one has killed me, least of all you. It is only a dream," he told himself as much as her. It had to be a dream that made her stare at him without seeing him, or to see him so wrongly. "Calm down, little one. Let us go back to our bed, and let me warm this cold morning from your bones."

His hands were everywhere, pulling her close. "No one has killed me. Least of all you, little one," he chuckled. "That was only a dream. Come, let me suck the warm blood from your bones...."

"I KILLED you!! Noooo!" she screamed, thrashing wildly. One fist struck him under his chin, the other somewhere in the gut. Her foot clipped his knee sharply as she kicked out, tearing herself from his grasp with a strength born of desperation. Freed, she fled.

It took him a few seconds to gather his wits. The girl was hysterical. Mistook him for someone else, someone she had killed. It was obvious that she believed herself in mortal danger. He took a quick assessment of the direction she had torn off into and realized that she was headed for the river. With the fog, she would not know the danger she was in until it was too late. He ran after her, his head still ringing from the unexpected blow she had landed, fervently praying that he would not catch up to her too late.

Lark ran blindly, leaving a trail easily followed, not caring that the branches and brambles and under-brush tore at her clothes as she went. She did not care that the briers tore at her tender flesh, leaving behind long streaks of blood; knew only that he was behind her, pursuing. She could hear him, hear the soft curses as his cloak caught on the thorns and stumbled against roots that she had sailed over. Her panic was complete.

She glanced behind her, turned back just in time to see the ivy-choked wall looming out of the fog ahead of her. She leapt, catching hold of the ivy tangle several feet from the ground, tried desperately to climb out of sight and reach. The ivy came alive in her hands, tangling about her wrists and legs, keeping her from reaching her goal. Some of the ancient stones came loose beneath her feet, and she fell. She held on to the vines for dear life, twisting her body to try and land without hurting herself. The scream that came from her throat against her will was cut short as the wall knocked the wind out of her.

She turned, looked to the forest, and knew that he was there, just beyond the mist, coming for her, hungry and angry. She tried to bolt, intending to flee along the wall and into the sheltering night, but the vines were still alive, and they refused to let her go. They changed to cold iron chains, pinning her to the face of the wall, holding her for him.

He emerged from the wood like a great winged demon rising out of the abyss, softly, seductively calling her name.

The wood opened up suddenly, where the wall stood just a few feet from the treeline. The fog was thicker here, so near the river, and obscured all but the lowest seven feet, but that was all that he needed. She was tangled in the vines growing up the face of the wall and fighting like a trapped animal. The more she struggled, the more tangled she became.

He decided to approach her slowly, as she did not appear to have seen him. "Illyana," he called softly. "Calm down. It's all right. There is no one here to hurt you. It's me, Landros. I am here to *help* you. It will be all right." He kept telling himself that, over and over in his mind, trying desperately to believe it.

"Illyaaanna," he whispered, tormenting her, approaching slowly because there was no need for speed. She was securely chained and at his mercy. "That's right. There is no one here to help you. Just me. Landros is not here to help you...."

She looked up at him, her eyes wild, "My blood is **mine**!" she growled and renewed her struggles. She fought her bonds like a hellcat, actually pulling herself off of the ground in her maddened efforts. There was blood on her hands, arms, and legs, but she did not seem to notice or care. She was too desperate to escape.

"Careful now." He approached slowly, steadily, making sure that when he grabbed her, he would be able to hold her. "Illyana, you are going to hurt yourself." He reached out towards her, attempting to be gentle but prepared for violence.

"Illyaanna," he purred, "You are going to hurt." His hand reached for her, towards her face, just like before, cold and dead. She stared at the withered claw as if it were a vile thing crawling out of some hole.

She screamed and lashed out at him as best she could, clawing and kicking. Tortured sounds that were barely human were torn from her throat. He pinned her easily with his monstrous strength, let her exhaust herself with struggling, waiting her out.

"I do not want to hurt you, little one," he said as she fought, flailing like a hawk caught in a fox's mouth. "But you must calm down. There is no one here but the two of us. It is all right." His voice was calm, steady, belying the panic that was rising in his own heart that she might be spelled or cursed or worse. He held her there, tight against the face of the wall, until she slowed and finally ceased her thrashing, exhausting her strength. He ignored the minor scratches and kicks he took from her limited range of movement, far more concerned with the blood-slicked arms he held above her head.

His bare chest pressed against her, cold and clammy, stealing her breath, draining her strength, her will. She could hear him laughing, the way he had laughed in the barn, deep and foreboding. It raised the hairs on her arms and the back of her neck.

"I do so want to hurt you, little one. To repay you. There is no one here but the two of us. And I have all night."

"Please," she whispered, finally hanging helpless in her cold iron chains, no strength left to physically resist. "Please, no."

He stood, no longer pinning her against the wall with his weight. She had whispered something he had not understood. Her head rested against one upraised and vine-wrapped arm, her hair falling across her eyes, tangled in ivy. He brushed aside her hair as tenderly as he could, away from her face, and tucked it behind her shoulder.

She turned away from him and shivered, her breathing ragged and irregular. "It's all right, Illyana," he said, trying to be gentle, to be soothing. "It's all over." He put his hand around behind her neck, burying his fingers in the tangle of her hair, and pulled her close to him, laid his cheek against hers, just holding her, placing a light, comforting kiss just below her ear. He breathed deeply of her rich, spicy fragrance, tainted now by raw terror; could feel the racing of her heart against his hand, hammering against his breast where he was pressed close to hers.

She shivered as he bared her throat and pulled her close. She could feel his hot breath just above her jugular, waited, stiff, as he caressed her, stroking her gently with the fingers laced in her hair to keep her from resisting, trying to relax her. "It's all over," he hissed, touching his lips to her throat, teasing.

"No," she breathed. "Please, ... please." *This last was little more than a whimper.*

This time, Landros understood her. He pulled back, surprised, moved his hand to tilt her chin up gently, looked into her face. She resisted, but weakly. There were tears on her cheeks, running freely. With his thumb, he gently brushed them away. She looked up into his eyes. They hovered for a moment, gazing up at him, pupils barely rimmed in midnight blue, then they rolled back, and her whole body went limp in a dead faint.

Landros seized his sword and cut her loose, holding her against him as he unwound the vines. With one arm still around her, he shifted his sword, swept her up, and carried her back to their camp. His mind was a tangled mess of confusion and worry. He had seen her ride bareback at a maddened demon with nothing but a dagger in her hand, yet she had crumpled completely before the vision of what he now thought to have been a vampire. She was a strong and fearless girl, full of life and happiness. What could have happened to her to wreak such a sudden and complete change?

He laid her carefully on the blanket that they had shared only half an hour before, covering her both with the picnic cloth and his cloak. Setting her down, his foot brushed something hard under the blanket, and, thinking it a stone, pulled it out.

It was a small brown bottle.

He sniffed it and turned away immediately. It smelled sickly sweet and made his head swim just a little. He wondered if it may have had something to do with her nightmare and resolved to question her about it when she was awake and clear-headed. He set the bottle with his things and began to gather more wood for the fire. Once it was again a merry blaze, he began rubbing her cold limbs carefully, trying to restore her heat.

When he was satisfied that she was warm enough, he ripped the sleeve off of his shirt and wet it from his water skin. Being as gentle as he could, he began to wash her wounds, getting a better idea of their severity and pulling any thorns he found there. And there were many. Her injuries were minor, mostly just scratches from her heedless run through the wood and more severe cuts and burns from the vines that she had battled. He noticed the opal ring on her hand as he cleaned her arm, flashing in the firelight. He tried to remove it, to clean the blood that had flowed beneath it, but the ring would not come off.

Curious, he poured water onto her fingers and worked the band until it turned easily, but it still refused to come off. He resolved not to panic. He would simply ask Colwyn in the morning or

Adrick at the temple if he needed to take her there. It bothered him, but he left it alone for the moment.

He finished washing her, laid her head in his lap, making her as comfortable as he could, and sat staring into the fire. His hands idly stroked her face and hair, as much for his own comfort as hers.

What was it with this girl? He seemed to have made many blunders tonight, starting with leaving that damned falcon ring on. She knew secrets even his own brother did not know, and for some reason, he trusted her with them in a way he did not trust Portholus. She stayed in his mind, ever in the back of it. Since that first rainy night, every jingling bell he heard made him look, hoping to see a flash of red and black calico and red velvet. He had taken no one to his bed since her but could not understand why. No one else interested him. Why?

'I am a pathfinder, I am Elven, and, except for Portholus, I am all alone in this world. I am neither a smart man nor a patient one,' he reasoned. 'Why, in the name of the Mother and the Maiden, does this human girl obsess me so? Why do I want to protect her? To shield her from the Coolies of this world?' He looked down at her, sleeping peacefully in his lap.

'She is so beautiful and full of life. Why did she choose me? Why not Lith? Why not one of her own kind, a human and a Romeri? I've seen her work her charms on other men. She could have any male in this city. Why me? What could I possibly have that she could want or need? And why do I desire to fill that need so desperately?'

She stirred.

He looked down, prepared to hold on to her should she try to take flight again. He brushed the hair back from her face tenderly. "Shh," he whispered. "It is all right, Princess. You are safe now. It was only a terrible nightmare."

She looked confused for a moment, as if not expecting to see him. She noticed the scratches that marked his bare chest and neck immediately. "What happened to you?" she asked, her voice raw and hoarse, lifted a finger to trace one long gouge.

He smiled, took her hand in his, caressing her slim, dusky fingers, and showed them to her. There were traces of blood still on her nails. "You happened. But it is all right now," he added as she moved suddenly, apologizing, horrified.

"It's all right," he said, for perhaps the hundredth time in the last few hours. "You had a bad dream. You walked in your sleep. You saw things... a vampire, I think. But all that has faded. Nothing will happen to you, I promise. There are still a few more hours of night left. You should rest. You can tell me what happened in the morning ...if you feel up to it."

"You," she began, gazing in complete adoration at him, "are too good to me."

"Nonsense," he murmured, pulling the pack closer where she could use it for a pillow. She laid down beside him, never taking her eyes off of his face. He moved to go stoke the fire, but she reached out, touched his arm, and held him back.

"No, please. Just hold me. Will keep each other warm. Just hold me for now," she pleaded.

Looking into her midnight eyes, how could he have said no? She lifted the corner of the blanket and cloak covering her to let him in, then lay with her head nestled in the crook of his shoulder, holding tightly to him as he rearranged the coverings over them both. It did not take her long to fall back asleep, exhausted, and he lay there, listening to the steady, finally peaceful rhythm of her breathing, watching the fire slowly dying beyond her. His thoughts wandered everywhere, finding no answers, only new questions. He softly stroked the curve and arch of her back where she lay sideways against him.

Towards dawn, he heard a soft chittering by the nearest tree. He looked over, saw a raccoon wandering over, stop and sit up, as if asking permission, if it was safe. With as small a motion as he could make so as not to wake her, he waved him away. Sullen, the animal dropped to all fours and meandered off, glancing back once or twice just to be sure.

SIX

When Lark woke the next morning, she felt very warm and secure. The arms that were wrapped around her were strong and comforting. She opened her eyes, saw a long scratch across his chest, and felt a sudden pang of remorse. She kissed it.

He felt her stirring, felt the feather-light touch of her lips, and looked down. "Good morning," he said. There was a touch of pain and regret in her dark eyes as she gazed up at him. "Not going to tear off into the woods again, are we?"

She did not answer. He allowed her to sit up and remained lying down with his head propped up on his fist, just watching her. She stretched first, folding herself in half and grabbing her feet. She let loose a long, groaned breath, hurting in so many little places. Straightening up, she looked down at the state of her clothes. There was little left but rags. Her arms were black and blue and red as if from severe rope burns, and there were similar marks on her legs amid thousands of scratches and scrapes. She combed her hair back out of her face with her fingers, tugging out twigs and leaves as she did. She tried to straighten out the tangled mess, but it was hopeless.

Landros pulled a flask of wine from his pack, filled a cup, and passed it silently to her. He could be patient when he desired to. That was another thing about this girl, he suddenly realized. She inspired patience in him. For her, he was willing to wait for just about anything, however long, or so it felt. Because time never seemed to move around her, or at least its passing went unnoticed. Unless they were arguing....

She took the wine, sipping quietly, gathering her thoughts before trying to speak them. What she had done last night was foremost on her mind. She knew *what* she had dreamed, but what had she actually *done*? She remembered she had broken, begged, and openly wept. Had Landros been witness to that, too? It was obvious that she had fought him physically; the marks on his half-naked body told her that.

He was waiting. He had been gentle with her, obviously trying to protect her from herself and the dreams that had been haunting her. He had not slept; had just held her closely the rest of the night. She was beginning to feel deeply for this man, and that feeling, she knew, would head her into trouble, especially when it was becoming obvious to even the casual eye that he was beginning to more than care.

"Had violent dream last night. But is not first time. They... started just after Evandair, nearly month ago." She shivered, remembering, and wrapped her arms around herself.

He sat up and draped the cloak about her, nestling her against him.

She merely nodded her acknowledgment and continued. "First time was on boat returning. I... fell out of hammock trying to escape. But still, this dream pursues me, night after night."

He put his arm around her, pulling her close to him. "But why this dream? Why do you keep having it? What... what is the dream about?"

"As you guessed: vampire. But not just any vampire. We were sent to Evandair, as told you, to help people there with 'plague'. Was vampire we fought, what was plague. I... looked into window, to try to find woman we thought was working with monster. Saw only his eyes. Was so handsome, so ... charming," she said wistfully, shuddered. He held her tighter.

"I went inside. Could hear and see nothing but him, and suddenly he reached for me. At first, I want nothing more in whole world than that touch; then, was as if blindfold was torn away and I saw what was so enamoured of. Jumped out of way, hid behind Keltree. By then I knew what he was. Threw bottle of holy water on him. Was furious, vanished. Knew he would hunt me down. Could feel it in my bones, like ice."

She just stared at her hands, trying not to think about what she was saying. "He lured me into barn, and when could not capture me, tried to burn me alive. Keltree was caught with me. We managed to break out through back, but... was close. Still he was laughing, luring me, in my mind. Could not get him out. Tracked him to cliff above town, fought him.

"Is where Keltree was hurt. Vampire broke wrist and put fist through stomach. Rue managed to hold him off long enough for me to soak net in holy water. Caught him in it and oh, how he screamed! Rog beheaded him. Then he just vanish. Poof! Nothing left but ash and sound of his raging scream in my ear and mind. Still cannot forget that sound. Raw hatred. Like nothing I have ever known. In that last moment, he stare into my eyes, full of fury and hate."

She sat there for a while. Landros did not break the silence, feeling somehow that there was more. He knew the difficulty of speaking of such deep-rooted terrors. He had a few of those himself, buried away. She drew a long, ragged breath, trying to control the need to sob again. "I see those eyes in my sleep. They haunt me. Last thought and emotion he had was hatred of me and desire for vengeance. Was like dark promise.

"Last night... I heard him calling me. Could not resist, felt so ...helpless."

Ah, he thought, at last, the root of it. He understood this feeling on the deepest levels, this helplessness.

"Harder I fought, worse it became. Should have known I could not run from him. Tried to climb wall to escape. Remember falling, vines coming to life, turn to chains, holding me prisoner to wait his pleasure. He kept promising me I would hurt, long and deep. I could not escape those eyes.... I knew he meant every word. Knew as he touched me so tenderly that I had only begun to know fear and pain. Cold iron and stone is death to Romer. I was wrapped in death, caressed by death. When he touched my neck, I could feel his breath as he hovered, about to sink those needle teeth.... I wept," she whispered, unwilling to admit it.

She stared down at her hands, picking unseen splinters out of her wrist. She did not look up at him; did not want him to see the tears that were falling again. She hated that he had seen her so weak, and was terribly afraid of what he must think of her now. He had heard her beg! "Feel so ashamed. I do not know why. He made me feel so... weak, so out of control of myself. When he forced me to look into his eyes again, I.... I do not remember what happened. I expected to die, to become his slave as he had done to Julian and rest of town. But instead, I woke to you."

She could not hide her tears any longer. He held her, stroked her soothingly, fighting tears of fury and compassion of his own, and not yet willing to let her see them. She needed his strength, not his weakness. It burned him to think that everything he had said to her had been somehow turned in her mind. Promises of love and protection turned to threats of agony and hate.

She buried herself in his embrace, openly sobbing now, filled with frustration and rage at her own helpless fear. "He's dead, damn it!" she screamed, the sound muffled against his chest and her own hair. "Why can't he just let me go!! Why won't he just **die**!?!"

She clung to him desperately. It was a long time before she could breathe normally again, before her tears had subsided and she felt once more in control. It left her weak.

She untangled herself from his grasp and tried to stand. He resisted, not wanting her to overtax herself or to leave again. But she was insistent. He relented, watched as she stood shakily, and took a deep, steadying breath of the crisp morning air. Drying her face on what remained of her sleeve, she walked to the edge of the small clearing in which they had camped. She paused, one hand on the trunk of a massive oak, and looked back at him. "Well, Kestrel, it seems that we give gift for gift. Secret for secret. *Lunasa,* but things always come equal between us!" she sighed.

It was a sign, and she knew it. But she was unwilling yet to face its consequence. She turned, walking into the forest. Before he could protest or ask her where she was going, he heard her laugh, a dry, cracked sound, but a genuine laugh nonetheless. "Do not panic, my heart. Will be back."

He sat there, thinking, trying to understand. He pulled out the small brown bottle, turning it in his fingers. It was empty, obviously some sort of drug. What exactly had happened to her on that island? What kind of hold could a vampire have over a victim even after its own demise? And where did this drug fit in?

He heard her return but did not look up. "Did he bite you?" he asked. Maybe, if he had, that would explain how he could haunt her, if that is what he was doing. When she did not respond, he looked up. She was staring at the bottle in his hand. "I found this last night, after I brought you back," he explained, holding it up. "I thought it was a rock," he added lamely.

She knelt, took it from him, and rolled it over in her hand. "No," she finally said. "He did not bite me. There was no time." She put the empty bottle in her bag, sat with her back to him.

"What was that?" he asked softly.

She did not move for a minute, then, "Laud'num," she said, pulling her brush out and trying to untangle her hair.

He watched her for a few minutes. Laudanum was a powerful drug, a useful painkiller, and a sleep aid, but there were side effects. "Were you taking this while we were...."

"Yes," she cut him off, ashamed enough without him rubbing it in, even if he did not intend to, "Is why slept so sound, could not wake that morning. I took very little and did not think would keep out so long."

"Lark, this stuff makes you almost comatose!"

"I stopped!" she snapped testily. "Besides, is no more.... And don't know where to get...." She drifted off and dropped the brush in frustration.

He came over, put his hands on her arms, and leaned his forehead against the back of her head. "Illyana, I'm sorry. ...I'm just concerned. You could have gotten yourself killed or captured or... or worse."

"I could have become slave girl Adrick presented me as?" she suggested.

"Easily," he replied. He took the brush from her, began dragging it gently through her hair, flinched every time it hit a tangle. And there were many.

"I needed it. You can't understand how I needed it," she whispered. "...Harder."

"Huh?"

"Can brush harder," she said. "Am not tender-headed little girl anymore. Won't hurt me, not with that."

"Oh." He firmed his strokes and felt the tangles finally starting to yield. "I do understand, wanting an escape from the nightmares." He did, had fought with nightmares of his own for many years after his parents died, the helplessness, the pain, without the benefit of being able to break down and cry because he had to be strong for Portholus.

"No, you don't," she insisted. "Was exhausted. Could not sleep but for these dreams which woke me all hours of night. What little sleep could get was wasted running through my dreams, trying to escape. These are not childhood nightmares. Not mere bad dreams plaguing a mind who has seen too much. There is something different about them. Something powerful.... Something primal," she said, drifting off again. "With drug he could not reach me. Was safe."

He put the brush into her bag, "That settles it."

"Settles what?" she asked, confused.

Landros got up, shook out the blankets, and folded them.

"Settles what?" she insisted, stopping him.

"I am taking you to the temple."

"Why?"

"Because you are in need of healing, and I think you need to speak to Rue about these goddess-damned nightmares."

Lark stood her ground. "Rue is busy enough."

"She'll make the time. This could be serious. What I witnessed last night was serious." He set the blankets aside, put his hands on her arms, trying to be tender and forceful at the same time, without being too much of either. "Lark, you saw me as something else, twisted every word I said. You were hallucinating and hysterical. If you had not gotten tangled in the ivy, I might not have been able to catch you before you got seriously hurt. You might even have fallen into the river and drowned, and one thing I am not is a strong swimmer." He tilted her chin to look up at him and smiled gently. "Besides, how do you expect to make any money looking like you've been tied into a sack with a pair of alley cats?"

She smiled in spite of herself, but she remained defiant. "All right," she said. "If you make me go for healing, you, too, have to sit for," she said, giving his ribs a poke.

He pulled away, not in the mood for tickling. "Now that is not part of the bargain. Hells, this isn't a bargain I'm making here...."

"Is now. You let priests heal you, and I tell Rue all about night-mares."

He sighed, "All right, if it will get you to go. But you have to promise me you'll tell her!"

"I promise," she said, her eyes not wavering from his. She moved away from him and began to help him clean up the camp.

He opened up his pack to put the blankets inside and saw the package sitting on the bottom of it, forgotten. He looked over at her, bustling about, deciding against putting her bracelets on. Her skirt had seen better days, but the blouse was hopeless. It was bloody and ripped, and he could see the cotton starting to give at the back seams. He pulled the package out and brought it over to her. "Here. It might be better than what you have on."

She looked up at him, saw the rose on the top of the package, and stood. "What is?" she asked, taking it.

He shrugged, "Just a little something I picked up in the market yesterday. I saw it and thought of you, and as a way to apologize for ...well, being such an ass the past couple of weeks."

She smiled coyly, brushing the rose against her cheek. She carefully unwrapped the dress, and her eyes grew big as it un-folded. She gasped. "Is lovely."

He shrugged, "A trifle. You might want to put it on now, though. Rue is liable to panic if she sees you in your present state. I... I hope it fits," he added and went back to packing up.

Lark held it to her chest for a moment, watching him. And so generous, she thought. She smiled. "Will certainly look better than your clothes on me," she laughed.

He held up a finger, contradicting her, "No. Different. It will look *different* on you than my clothes. Not better. There is something to be said for the sight of you wearing my shirt...." he mused.

Lark started to untie her blouse and change right there but changed her mind. 'Mamma always said never to change clothes in front of man,' she thought. 'Entrances make for better impact.' So she drifted off into the woods to change.

Landros looked after her, wondering why she had left. Had she suddenly turned shy on him? After her dance last night.... He shook his head and bent to remove all traces of the fire that he could.

A few minutes later, he heard her shriek. He grabbed his swords and ran after her, pulled up short when he saw her standing a few feet away, wearing the new dress with a most curious accessory: a raccoon.

"Scraps!" he growled, sheathed his swords, and stalked over, untangling the animal from her hair.

She laughed, still somewhat startled but delighted.

"I hope he didn't frighten you," Landros began.

"Well, that he certainly did!" she laughed. "Fell out of tree there and landed in arms. It was quite frightful, thank you," she said to the raccoon, who chittered in her direction.

"Jumping on her from out of a tree is no way to introduce yourself to a lady," he chastised.

Lark put her hands on her hips and leaned over to say hello, "I take is friend of yours?"

"Sort of," he apologized. "I caught him raiding my pack one night and well, ...he just followed me out of the woods. He hangs around," he shrugged. "When he isn't being lured away by beautiful women." He admired her as she took the raccoon from him, the creature going back to her eagerly. "It looks good on you," he said.

"Thank you," she said, giving a little turn, then began dancing off with the rodent. She returned after a moment, set the beast down. "But I think we had best be going," she said, collecting her discarded clothes. She paused in front of him, tucked the rose behind her ear, and said breathlessly, "Before we are here another few hours."

She sauntered back towards the camp. Scraps chattered something. Landros looked down at him, saw him sitting up, waving a paw in her direction. "Yeah, tell me about it," he said and followed her. The raccoon raced after him, climbed into the backpack, and curled up for a nap.

SEVEN

Rue brought the two of them into a cell, sat them down at the small table, and began working on their wounds. Scraps crawled out of the backpack and made himself right at home, but stayed out of the way of the foul-smelling concoctions the priestess was working with. She listened quietly as Lark related her nightmares and the problems she had been having since they sailed from Evandair. She put a salve on Lark's wrists and bandaged them snugly. "Just leave this on until tomorrow," she said. "There should not be any scarring."

"But what about these dreams?" Landros asked as she gestured for him to remove his shirt so that she might minister to his own wounds, a number of them older than the scratches of last night.

"I really wish you had let me take a look at these before you left," she chided looking one over in particular. "There will more than likely be scars now. Some of these could have been serious."

"Rue," he said, holding her still. "I know you. You do not avoid questions unless you are afraid of the answers. Now sit and talk."

She obeyed. She propped her chin on her fist and sighed. "I don't know. I have no explanation for it. To the best of my knowledge, the Evandair vampire is dead, gone, kaput. No longer the living dead but the dead dead. I saw Lark cast the ashes over the cliff myself."

Landros growled to himself in frustration. Lark sank back in her chair. "I told you, Landros, is nothing she can do."

Rue turned to her. "That is not true."

"You're not going to give her any more of this!" he said, holding up the bottle on the table.

"No, I am not. That is no more than a temporary solution. That will not make this... specter go away." Scraps, curious, climbed up Rue's robes and settled into her lap, playing with the medallion hanging around her neck. Rue scratched him idly.

"Specter? As in ghost?" Lark asked. "But my emerald protects me against ghost," she protested.

"Do you wear this emerald to bed?" Rue asked.

"No," she answered slowly. "Wear no jewelry to bed."

"Then it cannot protect you when you need it most, when you are most vulnerable."

"So, you believe she is being haunted?" Landros asked.

"It is quite possible. That vampire, ...you are certain it was *that* one, the same man?" she asked.

Lark nodded, sighed, "Yes, when... last night when I saw him, for first time, really, I saw Landros, but he looked like Eridinne's vampire, ...Asisath." She deliberately mispronounced the name, afraid to actually speak it if his specter were that close. "Trust me, Rue. I know what this man look like, and *was* him."

Landros could see the fear in her eyes as she spoke of him, reached out, and squeezed her hand reassuringly.

"Then he has somehow managed to latch his spirit onto you, and it seems he is slowly building power. For what, though, I do not know."

"But how? Why her?"

Rue made a generic 'who knows' gesture with her hand. "He was pretty pissed off at her. Lark, are you certain he did not bite you?"

"*Sesha,*" Lark growled, frustrated. "Have answered this before."

"Then he has to have a focus of some sort, something to cling to. I've checked her out thoroughly, and she is not currently possessed."

"You mean like an amulet or a talisman?" Landros suddenly asked.

"Yes, something like that."

"How about a ring?" he asked, holding up Lark's hand.

Rue took Lark's hand and examined the sparkling black opal. "Hmm, isn't this the ring from Evandair?" she asked.

"Evandair?" Landros asked, looking over at Lark.

Lark looked confused. "Yes. Keltree gave to me on boat, said was my share. Why? Is only ring."

"Is only ring?" Landros echoed. He held out his hand. "Give it to me."

Lark, even more confused, obliged. The ring did not come off. She looked down, startled. "Won't...."

Rue looked at Landros, a new worry in her eyes. "You've been able to take it off before?"

"*Sesha*. Always take off. I said I take all jewel off every night," Lark said, starting to panic as she tugged on the ring.

Landros took her hands and held them still. "On the ship, when you gave me your rings to put away, I noticed you left that one on."

"No," she insisted, shaking her dark head. "I took *all* off. I remember!"

"So do I, and you left that one on, just like last night," he softly insisted. 'Keep her calm,' he thought. 'Keep yourself calm. There is a reasonable explanation and a simple solution. There has to be.'

Rue got up. "You two wait here." Without another word, she left the room, closing the door quietly behind her.

They waited without a word passing between them. Landros sat next to her, holding her hands, gently stroking the bandages and minor scratches that were quickly fading under the glistening salves. He kept her quiet, touching her cheek, stroking her hair, keeping her calm. Panic was threatening to overwhelm her. About ten minutes later, Rue returned with a middle-aged woman in dark blue robes in tow.

The woman was elegant, had a regal bearing, and held herself tall and straight, but there was nothing imperious about her. She was gentle and somewhat sad of face; her long, straight black hair was wrapped into a braided cap, partially hiding her half-elven heritage. She took the seat Rue had vacated, and the younger priestess took up station behind her. "Mother," Rue said. "This is Lark, the Romeri I told you of. Lark, Landros, this is Mother Mylenai, the local Matron."

The woman looked Lark over carefully, with a stare that Lark was very familiar with. She was looking with an inner eye, as she had known her Gruma to do when checking a person for magic or supernatural influence. She had even seen her mother do it once or twice. It did not bode well. A chill ran through her body, leaving her completely washed out and devoid of strength.

The Matron held out her long, thin hand. "Give me your rings. All of them." Her voice was strong and firm, but tender in a motherly sort of way.

Lark obeyed without question, unable to shake this sinking feeling. She placed all five rings into the woman's hand.

"Is this all of them?" she asked.

"*Sesha*," Lark answered, confused. She followed the priestess's gaze down to her hand, saw the opal ring still on her finger, and thought for a moment that she might faint.

Landros saw her grow suddenly pale and put his hand out to steady her. She looked into his eyes, her own gone black and wide with fear. Without taking her eyes from his, she held her hand out to the priestess, unable to still its trembling. Landros took her other hand and kissed it reassuringly.

"Husband?" the priestess asked, startling both of them as she examined the ring closely.

"Lover," Lark said, looking at her at last.

"Mmmm," she murmured. She turned the hand over, twisted the ring on the finger. "As I thought," she said, letting Lark's hand go.

"What?" they asked simultaneously.

"This is an ancient item. I've only seen mention of this sort of thing in an old, obscure text once upon my youth. It is known as a Soul Trap, and it is a very unique necromantic item."

Lark felt her heart grow weak, her breathing quick and short. Her whole body stiffened as she listened.

"The ring, once placed upon the hand, cannot be removed until the body wearing it dies. It cannot be cut off, magically preventing the severance of the finger, hand, or limb bearing it. Once the wearer dies, their soul becomes trapped in the ring until such time as the body is restored or it is placed upon the hand of an empty body. It was created several thousands of years ago as a means of.... well, vengeful assassination, among other things. It was sent first as a gift to Sultan Theisodanus the Fiftieth, shortly after which he was assassinated, and the ring disappeared. The ring, now occupied by the soul of Theisodanus, was worn by his hated rival, who, knowing the secrets of the ring, used it to control the soul of the sultan, effectively enslaving him."

As if it were possible, Lark paled even farther, sinking into herself. Landros held her, pulling her to him. "There has to be something...." he began.

The Matron went on as if he had said nothing. "There are many uses for such things, as were discovered through the ages. The most benevolent of which was for the protection of the life of the wearer. It is speculated that no one still alive knows the secrets to the ring, preventing its use for the control and enslavement of souls."

"So, vampire is in ring," Lark surmised weakly.

Rue nodded, hesitant. "It was part of the treasure recovered from the vampire and the witch. It is probably safe to assume that Ebastion got that ring from the vampire's pile of ash," she said quietly.

"Then it should enable her to control the vampire," Landros said, "not allow him to haunt her."

"It should," the Matron nodded. "If she knew the secrets of the ring. Which she does not. There is little doubt in my mind that the vampire knew them and is now using them, along with his own unique abilities, to try and gain control of her or to get her hurt or killed in such a way that she can be healed easily, and he can take her body. But that is speculation.

"What is not speculation is that he is asserting himself to keep you from noticing the ring, to think you have already taken it off, clouding your mind to subjugate you. The laudanum you have been taking has kept him at bay and prevented him from growing in power by allowing you to rest. The dreams and lack of sleep were weakening you. The dreams are worse the more tired you are, am I right?"

Lark only nodded. "So, am trapped with this monster forever in my mind," she whispered, drew a sobbing breath, although she did not weep. She was beyond tears at the moment.

"No, you are not." The woman stood. "Rue, tend your patient. Young lady, you will come with me," she said, holding her hand out to Lark.

She hesitated, looked over at Landros. "But..."

"Do not be afraid, child. Where we are going, no man is allowed."

Lark took her hand, still looking back at Landros nervously. He half-rose, ready to insist, but she shook her head and gestured him to stay put. She put on a brave face and left with the priestess.

Landros looked at Rue as he removed his shirt and gloves, making certain that his falcon's ring remained covertly inside the gauntlet. "What is going to happen to her?" he asked tightly as she began to tend to him. "Where are they going?"

"The inner sanctum, and I do not know. I... I have never been there myself. Don't worry. Mother Mylenai will take care of her."

'She had better,' he thought vehemently as he finally submitted to the healing he knew he badly needed.

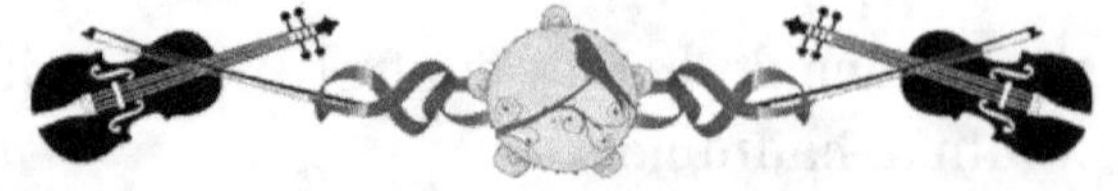

Lark was led through tangled, spiral hallways to a distant chamber deep in the heart of the temple complex. There were no windows in the room, but there seemed to be a natural light source from somewhere. There were three doors in the curved walls, each equidistant from the other. Between each door was a panel of a large mural, each depicting the goddess in one of her three aspects. In the center of the room was a carved stone altar, simple and ancient. It was nowhere near as ornate or beautiful as the one they had broken open a few months before to rescue the priestess within it, but it seemed to hold more power, more significance.

Mother Mylenai stopped just inside the doorway and held Lark in place in front of her, her hands firmly upon her shoulders. Lark was not entirely comfortable in here. There was a presence pressing in around her, at once familiar and alien. This was a holy of holy places, and she was far from devout.

"Perhaps I should not...." she whispered, trying to take a step back.

"Be here?" the Matron asked softly with a raised brow. She held her in place. Lark looked up at her. "Why not?"

"Because... do not worship...." she began sheepishly.

The Matron looked hard at her. Lark stopped fidgeting. "Respect without devotion? Is that not right, Romeri?" she said. "That is what you believe, is it not? Well, girl, you could not set foot in this room if you did not believe somewhere in your heart in what the Lady stands for. Every society that reveres its women and the power that only they can wield worships the Mother of All Things."

"Then... then why do feel I should not be here?" she whispered, strangely on the verge of tears.

"Have you yet run from the room?"

She looked up at the woman's face, so unlike her mother, yet so motherly. "No," she replied, feeling very much like a child again.

"Then you belong. It is the spirit in the ring which does not wish to be here, but he has no power here."

The door to the left of them opened, and a young woman, younger than Lark, stepped forward. She looked over at them, smiled, but waited just inside the door, even as the Matron did. She studied her: a pale slip of a girl, elven, with long, silky blond hair and flowing pale blue robes. On closer examination, the girl had to be much older; she certainly did not hold herself as the sixteen-year-old girl she appeared to be. Lark guessed her to be at least eighty or so in elven years.

Finally, the last door opened, and an old, human woman shuffled in. She was bent and weathered, with thin, flyaway hair of various shades of silver and gray, and walked with the aid of a gnarled stick. She, too, hesitated just inside the doorway. The two other women waited for her to catch her breath, then they began to intone a chanted prayer in a language that was ancient when the Rune tongue was young.

Lark realized suddenly that she was looking at the true power of the tri-temple, not the 'High Lord of the Mysteries' D'Meysen. That position was purely cosmetic. *This* was the heart of it all and the essence of everything her Gruma represented. She saw as well, in this strange triptych, the true place of the *Ranie* in the clans and the part she was expected, eventually, to play. The thought awed her, overwhelmed her to the point that she was not aware she was being led forward until she felt the altar against her hip.

Startled, she looked up at the Matron, who only gestured for her to lie upon it. It took Lark several minutes before she could push herself past her fear and obey. They waited patiently, as they had waited before for the old woman. She convinced herself that it was the spirit in the ring trying to keep her from this. She lay down on the warm stone and closed her eyes, trying to surrender herself to whatever needed to be done.

She felt three pairs of hands upon her, stroking her, arranging her hair and dress and hands carefully. She smelled the strong scent of attar of roses and felt the kiss of soft petals about her cheeks and eyes. The women continued to chant, lower, softer this time, and the steady rhythm, combined with the smells around her, began to lull Lark into a deep slumber, the sleep of the innocent.

Landros paced the cell like a rabid animal, ignoring Rue's protests that he needed to calm down. It was not until she threatened him with physical restraint that he sat in the chair, crossed legs and arms, and scowled. Scraps climbed out of Rue's lap and onto Landros's, tugging on his ear playfully, trying in his own way to cheer him. Nightingale appeared in the window, fluttered drunkenly to the table, and sat down, blinked up at Landros, then at Rue.

At the sight of the rather unwell familiar, Landros started to panic again. "Rue, what the hell are they doing to her?!" he demanded.

"I don't know!" she snapped, finally losing her patience. "Mother Mylenai did not say. They could be in there for days! Hours! I don't know! I may be a good surgeon and a high-ranking healer, but I am no more than that. I have not been initiated in the higher mysteries. The Triptych keeps certain things to themselves, and rightly so."

Scraps put his paws over his ears to block out the shouting.

Lark woke to silence in the chamber. There was an emptiness that bothered her. She opened her eyes, saw only a palely diffused, pink light. Her limbs felt like lead, and had not the strength to move. Something stirred near her; something silky brushed her cheek as the pink light was lifted away to reveal only a dim room and pink rose petals in the hands of the elven Maiden.

The girl smiled, kissed her cheek ever so softly, and vanished from her line of sight.

She felt older hands upon her, looked up to see the old woman smiling gently down on her and crossed her hands upon her breast as one does a corpse or a sleeping child. She paused to stroke her brow tenderly, kissed her other cheek, and then she, too, vanished. Lark found she could not even move her head to turn and see where they went, but she felt the change in the room as the stone doors silently closed behind them.

Finally, the Matron appeared, took Lark's hands in hers, and pulled her into a sitting position. She pressed a kiss to her forehead and helped her from the altar. Lark was surprised at how weak she felt, and allowed the woman to help her from the room back through the door they had come. Once out in the twisting hallways, she found the strength to speak.

"Mother," she began, calling her simply as Rue had called her.

"Yes, daughter?" she murmured, pressing her cheek tenderly to her head.

"Is he gone? Will nightmares come no more?"

"He is gone forever, Illyana," she said.

Lark stopped, looked up, startled. "I did not tell...."

"I am a Matron, a physical representation of the goddess in her middle aspect. It is a position not without certain powers. To free you, we needed a true name. It was not hard to find, and it is safe with us. Now come, your lover is waiting and no doubt losing his patience," she smiled, picked a rose petal out of her hair.

Lark sighed, sank back into the comforting support of the Matron, and allowed herself to be led back to the cell.

They heard the argument before the door was opened. "Sounds like we have taken too long," the woman sighed, and opened the chamber.

Scraps ran for the opening, pulled up short when he saw Lark and the priestess, sat up inquisitively. Landros left off his argument in mid-sentence, took in her weakened condition, and rushed to her. He picked her up. "Are you alright?"

"Will be fine," she sighed, oddly grateful to be off her feet, breathed deeply of him.

"Is she...?" Rue began, hesitated to finish.

The Matron nodded, and Rue sank thankfully into the nearest chair. "Take her home," she told Landros. "Let her rest. He had a strong hold, and the fight has taken a lot out of her." From the table, Nightingale peeped an emphatic 'me too!' agreement, which provoked a laugh from the priestess. "You are a very lucky young woman," she said. "Had you waited much longer, he may have been too strong."

Landros noticed the ring on her hand as she put her arms around his neck. "Why is she still wearing that damned ring?" he demanded.

"Because it is clean now and will do much to protect her life. With it, as I said before, all her body needs is repair and her soul will return to its shell."

"But what if body cannot be repaired?" Lark asked. "What then?"

"Or if the ring is stolen from her body?" Landros added.

The Matron nodded patiently. "If the body cannot be healed, then return the ring to the Hall of the Dead. The Crone will know how to release her spirit from the ring. As for it being stolen, as no one alive knows how to use its more malign powers, you should be able to assert yourself as our vampire opponent did and alert someone with knowledge of the problem.

"Fear not. The ring is far more a blessing than a curse, and, as I said, it will not come off until you have died. You are tuned to that ring now. It will guard your life and protect your soul. ...I... I must go now," she said with sudden weariness. "My reserves are exhausted, and I must rest, as must you. Farewell," she breathed and drifted from the room.

"Landros, please, put me down," Lark asked quietly. She touched her hand to his lips when he started to protest. "Will be fine," she smiled. "Am just... tired. Can walk. Is not my feet this time." He sighed, set her down. "Just help me home."

"You are not sleeping in that wagon, not in this condition," he said stubbornly.

She felt her ire rising and decided she was too tired for anger. "Have not slept in wagon since left for children. No mattress, remember?" she said firmly but gently. "Take me to Lily's. She will take care of me, as has been. Will deal with finding new place for wagon when am... up to it. Do not know why am so tired. Slept through whole thing."

Lark reached for her bag, but Landros picked it up first. He slung it over his shoulder with his own pack and put his arm around her to support her. "All right, I promise. Not another word or complaint until you've rested."

She nodded and clasped Rue's hand in gratitude. "Thank you for everything," she said.

"Next time, come to me sooner," she complained, "and bring him with you. Don't let him go traipsing around bleeding all over the place."

Lark smiled weakly.

Scraps climbed up Landros's shirt and disappeared into the pack.

"Hope that was your pack and not mine," Lark breathed, letting Landros finally lead her out.

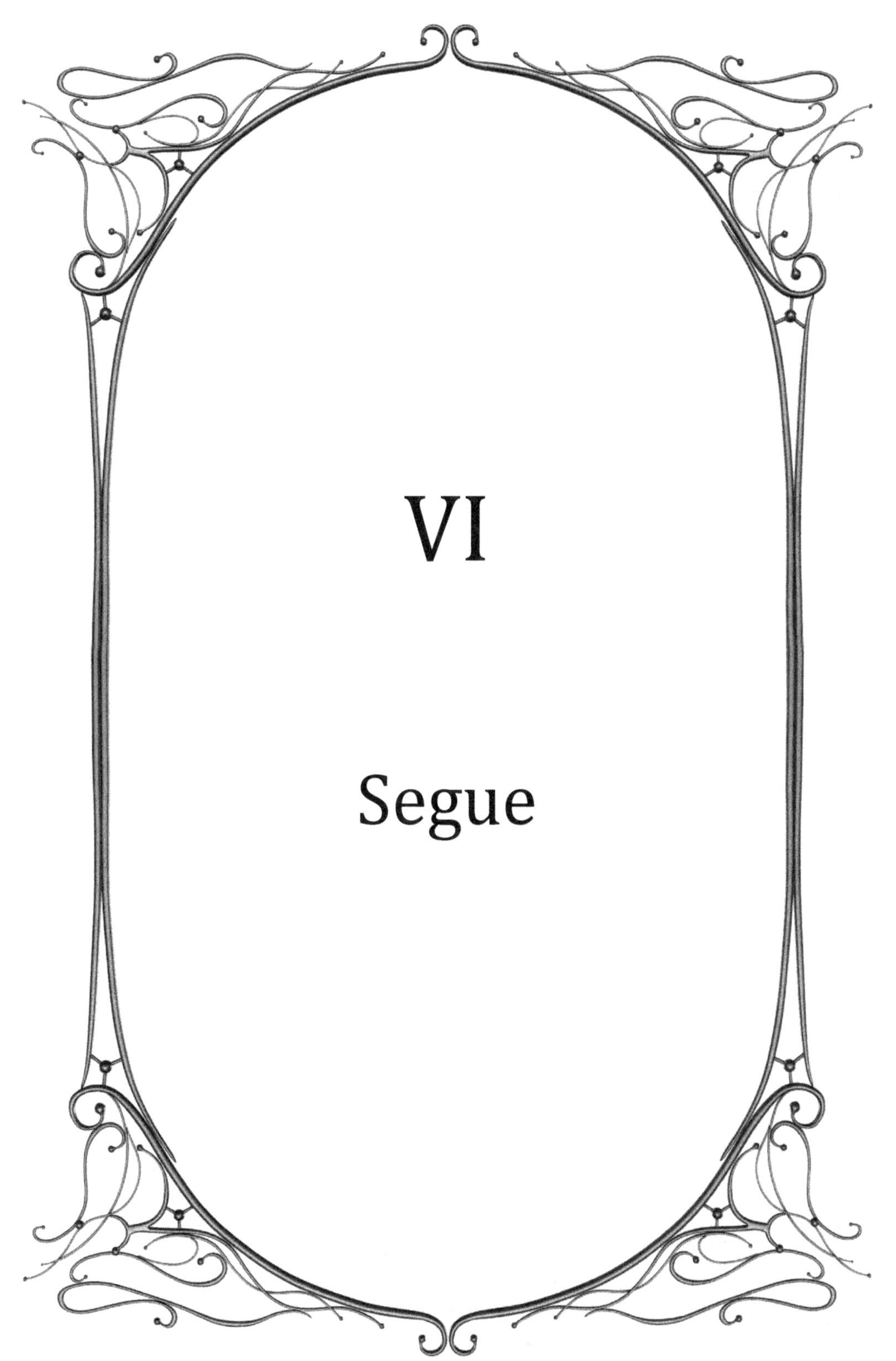

VI

Segue

ONE

Thankfully, the Cinnamon Tree was not that far. Lark only had to stop and rest twice the whole way. Landros still wanted to carry her, but she would not let him, insisted on walking on her own. She brought him in the back way, through the kitchen.

Lily was nowhere to be seen at the moment, for which she was grateful. The last thing she wanted was a panicked innkeeper on her hands. She looked up the tall, service staircase leading up to the second-floor rooms, and her resolve wavered. She leaned back against his chest. "All right, can carry me rest of way," she said.

Landros rolled his eyes, suppressed a grin, and obligingly swept her into his arms. Just inside the hallway on the second floor, she gestured to a small door immediately on the left.

He let her turn the knob, and kicked the door open the rest of the way. This was very much not the same room they had first shared together. And he was not impressed with the smallness of the room or its unfinished, almost attic-like appearance. Lark's violin and tambourine rest on the chest at the foot of the bed, evidence that she had been staying here the last few days. He placed her gently upon the narrow bed and put their bags on the floor beside the chest. Scraps crawled out almost immediately and began to investigate.

She handed the already sleeping mockingbird to Landros. "Put in nest, please," she asked, pointing at the joint of the ceiling beams.

He placed the bird carefully into the rough nest of scrap cloth and straw and turned back to her. She was still sitting on the edge of the bed, staring numbly in his direction, not really seeing anything.

"Are you going to sleep in your new dress?" he asked.

"Huh?" she mumbled, looking up at him befuddled.

He sighed, began to untie her sash, and helped her out of it. "Do you have anything you sleep in? A shift or something?" he asked, trying not to gaze longingly at her.

She wrapped her arms around herself, curling her feet up under her on the bed. "You're looking at," she smiled languidly. She rolled over, burying herself in the pillow.

He groaned, pulled the blankets from under her, tucking her in and covering her up. She was asleep almost before he left the room. Scraps crawled up onto the bed with her, looked from her to Landros and back again.

"Stay if you want to," he whispered. "You're going to anyway," he added under his breath. Taking up his backpack, he quietly slipped out.

He saw Lily coming out of one of the other rooms with linens over her arm as he softly closed the door behind him. She started when she noticed him but recovered quickly and came over. "Is she...?" she began.

He held his finger to his lips. "Shhh," he said and gestured for her to move away from the door with him. "She's sleeping."

"Sleeping? At this hour? What's wrong?" She put one fist on her hip and grinned slyly up at him. "What have you two been up to?" she growled playfully. "And how come you aren't in there with her?"

"The bed's too narrow," he said defensively, trying to control the blush threatening his dignity.

"Humph, that is no excuse," she retorted with a grin.

"She was ordered to get some rest by the Matron of the Temple. Is that a better reason?" he snapped sarcastically.

She just smiled, still waiting.

He sighed, embarrassed. "Can we… Can we talk?" he asked.

"Sure," she said, indicating the linens in her arms. "Let me get rid of these, and I'll meet you down in the kitchen," she said and bustled off into another room down the hall.

Landros went back downstairs and sat at the prep table to wait. She did not take long. She poured both of them a cup of coffee and sat across from him. "I'm sorry it's a bit weak, and I'm low on milk. You'll have to drink it without."

"Not a problem," he said, sipping the hot brew.

"Speaking of problems…?" she prompted.

He thought a moment, wondering how best to broach the subject. "Close to a month ago, she picked up an item that was possessed," he said in a low voice so as not to be clearly overheard by the large human woman bustling about behind them, cooking. "It was apparently fighting for control of her."

"Could that be the source of rather vivid nightmares?" she asked with equal caution.

"Yes," he said, relieved. At least Lark had confided in someone. "Well, they're gone now. The temple has gotten rid of the source, but it took a lot out of her. She'll probably sleep most of the day. I'd like for you to keep an eye on her for a while."

"Like you have to ask.," she laughed.

"Well, I do…." he said. "I don't want her thinking I've disappeared on her, but I've got some things I have to take care of." He leaned forward over his cup, toyed with it absently. "Do you think you could possibly convince her to stay here with you? I don't know, provide some incentive as an employer? I will gladly cover any cost…."

She held up her hand, shaking her head. "That will not be necessary. She pays her own way here. And what she cannot cover is gifted out of friendship."

He sighed, nodding, and continued. "I really don't want her staying in Tent Town. It's not safe anymore. Those people…."

"Are on an edge, I know," she nodded, sighed. "But I am afraid Lark is adamant about returning to her wagon as soon as she can find a place to park it. 'It's a Romer thing, I wouldn't understand it,' she said. And she's right. I don't. But what does it matter? I am not a carriage house. I have no room for a wagon in my yard. I'm working on getting her a new mattress for it..." she said, somewhat evasively, her eyes drifting towards her locked larder. "But it will take some time. Raw wool is kind of scarce since ships no longer run to Evandair, and the mountain flocks to the south are probably mutton by now."

Landros drank thoughtfully. "I have a friend with some property. I'll see what I can do about getting her a new location. Though it's a little farther than Tent Town from here, it's in a far better neighborhood. I have to ask first. As far as Lark goes, though, how much did she manage to recover?" he asked.

Lily thought for a few minutes. "Well, her stove had been damaged when they tried to take it too, but that's been fixed. The blacksmith was very helpful, she said. She has the important things, her instruments, and those few items of sentimental value. Most everything else but clothes she had with her. Thanks for bringing her back in one piece, by the way." He shrugged it off, and she went on. "Mostly clothes I think she's lacking. They took just about everything in that regard, and her dishes and pots as well."

Landros stopped a moment, thinking back on the generous silk merchant and his wife. "I think I know someone who might be able to help with the clothes, at least," he mumbled, drinking his coffee. "When she wakes up, get her some food and maybe a bath. Some of that stew I smell brewing over there would be good if there's any left by the time she gets up," he chuckled.

"She's going to be asleep awhile, I take it?" she smiled.

"Probably. It's more than likely the first undrugged, uninterrupted sleep she's had in weeks." He stood. "Thank you for the coffee, but I should go. I will be back later to check up on her." He drained the mug and slung his pack on his shoulder, which reminded him.... "Oh, and if you slip in to check on her, be careful. There's a raccoon in there with her," he warned.

"A raccoon?" she asked with disbelief.

He gave her a boyish grin, "Yeah, he's real friendly, though. He'll probably love you. And the boy will be loads of fun," he added as Dane felt his way into the room. "Just don't overfeed him." He tossed a small coin pouch onto the table. "This should cover what she and the beasts will eat. Farewell, madam," he said with a little salute and disappeared out the back door.

Behind him, he heard the boy ask his mother, "Who was that, mamma?"

"Lark's friend, honey."

"The elf man?"

"Yes, dear. Now don't go bothering her. She needs to rest."

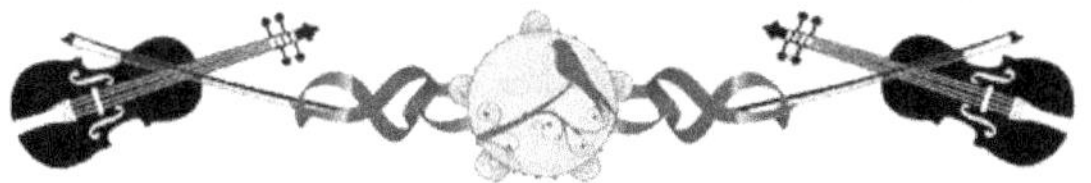

Landros made a quick 'blanket stop' at the orphanage before heading to Lord Colwyn's house. He arrived just in time for supper and found himself sitting at the dinner table in short order. It instilled a greater respect for his Liege Lord that the table was commonly set and the meal was frugal as became the times. As they ate, he noticed that Colwyn wore his gold knight's ring on an ungloved hand, which sheepishly reminded him of something else he had to discuss with him.

"So, tell me, young Landros," he began. "Did your lady friend enjoy my wood?" he grinned.

Landros coughed, not missing the subtle but polite implications that had been made. "Yes, my lord. She was... entranced, I'd say."

He laughed, a deep, hearty sound. "I'd say you were the one entranced," he said with a raised eyebrow as he refilled their wine glasses. "You were overnight, were you not?"

"I am sorry about the fire, but... it became necessary...."

"Oh, don't worry yourself about that. It's not like that particular grove has not served that purpose before, nor is a campfire foreign to it. I noticed you on the riverbank around sunset when I made my usual rounds. You looked so cozy I thought it best to leave the pair of you alone."

Landros concentrated on his food, not entirely comfortable at the moment with the subject of discussion.

"So, tell me, is she as beautiful as she appeared from the distance?"

"Oh, yes," he said enthusiastically. "Too beautiful, almost."

"That is always nice in pleasant company. She is Romeri, is she not?" he asked.

Landros looked up, uncertain of the motives behind the question. "Is that a problem?"

"Oh no!" he said quickly. "Merely an observation. I have met more than one in my travels, and some of the encounters were quite pleasant," he mused thoughtfully. "Some of the clans have an incredible appreciation for the wild. It was where I learned to erase a campsite," he chuckled.

"Which brings me to a request I have to make," Landros blurted before he could change his mind about asking. "She.... she came with us to rescue the children..."

Colwyn's eyebrows rose. "*She's* the one who wore the pirate garb coming off the boat? The one who promptly fainted in the Lord Mayor's arms?"

Landros was surprised. He had not known that Colwyn had been at the docks that day. "Yes. That was her."

"Magnificent woman," he mused. "I can see why Romeri women never wear pants," he added with some appreciation.

"So do I," Landros said under his breath.

"But you were saying....?"

"Yes," he nodded. "It seems that, while we were gone, her wagon took some damage from the hurricane, and... well, she was pretty much cleaned out. I think they even took her familiar's birdhouse," he growled.

"She has a familiar?" he asked with a slight frown. "She is a mage then?"

"Not really. She is a dancer," he said, cleaning his plate with the last of his bread. "She has some latent magic, I think. I've never seen her with spell or prayer books. But what I wanted to ask you is... well, I've come to.... I want her out of Tent Town," he said, finally getting it out. "It's getting too dangerous for a girl like her and... I was wondering if she could camp here, out in the woods."

Colwyn was quiet for a long time, drinking his weakened wine thoughtfully. He waited until his manservant had taken the plates and left the room before he answered. "The problem is... there are some matters of business that require privacy. As I have said, that grove has been used before as a campsite, a place of meetings where no ears can reach," he said pointedly.

Landros flushed and looked away. He slouched in his chair, not certain how what he had to say next was going to sit with his lord.

"What?" Colwyn prompted softly.

Sullen, he answered. "She knows about the falcons," he said quietly.

The man's face was unreadable. "Oh? She does?"

"...Yes."

"And how does she know?"

"I... I had to tell her last night." It came out all at once, then. "You see, I was getting ready to take her home, and she... came out of the woods, dancing... well, with very little on and... the next thing I know... we're rolling in the grass and... Well, damn it! When you're lying under the stars with a gorgeous, *naked* girl wrapped in your arms, you just don't wear gauntlets! I wasn't thinking about the ring at the time. Actually, I wasn't thinking about much of anything except ... well, her!"

He looked up as Colwyn began laughing quietly.

"What's so funny?" he sulked.

"Oh, nothing really. ...Only a Falcon for a matter of hours and... so quickly jessed by a woman," he chuckled.

Landros rankled at the comment but kept his peace. He felt terrible. "I'm not exactly happy about it myself."

Colwyn propped his chin in his fist. "So, she saw the ring," he said flatly.

"Yes."

"She asked about it?"

"Yes."

His voice was suddenly very serious. "So why did you tell her?"

"Let's just say that I wasn't going to lie to her."

"You have a problem with lying?"

Landros looked up. "Yes, I do. I can keep my silence. But speaking untruths is not a trait I find comely in knights," he said seriously. He watched his lord for any sign of what he was thinking. Perhaps there was something he had not been told, he thought, something he might find undesirable in all of this.

"Good," Colwyn said. "Because lies are not a knightly virtue. But keeping faith and maintaining secrecy are. You should have simply told her that it was a ring, which is a truth. And, if she pressed, that it was something she could not know."

"You don't know Lark," he muttered.

Colwyn did not say anything, merely arched an eyebrow.

"She... she has shared her secrets with me. More than that... she has given me that gift a woman only gives once...." Colwyn's other eyebrow came up. "And her name, to boot. She was highly offended that I might be keeping this from her. She... she means something to me. What, I do not know yet, but.... She is connected to me in some way that I do not understand. I do not believe she will breathe a word of this," he said, toying with his goblet, turning it in place. "Nor will I be taking my gloves off in the presence of others again," he added.

Colwyn relaxed and chuckled again. "That you needn't worry for. Your mistake was not in letting her see the ring but in telling her its meaning. That is the secret. The ring is meant to identify you to those of us who know what it represents. To do that, they have to be able to see it. Only those who know of the Falcons and are close to us know its significance. But from now on, if anyone asks you about it, if they do not flash a ring of their own... just give them a blank look," he chuckled. "It is just a ring, after all."

Landros breathed a sigh of relief.

"What, you thought you might lose your squire-hood over this?"

"Something like that," he mumbled, draining his wine glass.

Colwyn looked at him curiously. "Yet you told her anyway? Willingly risked it?" Landros did not give him an answer. He had none. "Hmm," he mused thoughtfully. "In light of her knowledge, yes. She may camp here. I know she will not damage or overuse the wood or its resources. The only condition is that, if I ask her to, she must agree to be scarce for an evening or more."

"I do not foresee that as a problem," he said.

"And if she does tell our secrets...." he asked.

Landros took a deep breath and gritted his teeth, "I will take care that it does not come to light. One way or another, my lord."

"Good. Take care that you do not betray her own trust, and it shouldn't come to that. If she gave you her true name, then she gave you a greater gift than merely her virginity."

Landros tipped his head.

Colwyn caught the look. "Did you never ask why her true name is a secret?"

He shrugged. "Some people are cautious about true names. Superstitious."

The knight nodded his head. "Yes, well, if you meet any who guard them for mystic reasons, best you beware their magic wielders," he warned. "But no. The Romer have two names, the one they give the world, and the one they share only with those they are closest to. So being privileged to both is a great honor, a sign of deepest trust. If you want to know why, you'll have to ask her yourself. It was something I was never brave enough to ask.

"Now," he said, getting up. "Shall we take a walk in that wood? I have something I need for you to do for me."

TWO

It was late the next morning by the time Landros had an opportunity to check in on her. Lily waved him to a back table as soon as she saw him come in. He meandered his way over and waited until she had a moment to talk to him.

"Hoo!" she exclaimed, taking a deep breath.

"Bit busy this morning," he commented.

"Word gets around quickly that I don't have rats on the menu yet. Lark's in the bath. Can I get you anything while you wait, or do you intend on sneaking in on her?" she grinned.

"Wine if you have any," he said, leaning back against the wall.

"Not at the moment," she replied. "Maybe tomorrow. There is some fresher beer that's not too watered down."

"That then," he ceded. She nodded and returned to work.

She came back a few minutes later with his drink and stole enough time to ask, "Oh, did you have any luck with the wagon?"

"Yes, I did."

She breathed a sigh of relief and bustled off again.

Landros watched the room, paying attention to the customers as he sipped. As he had commented, the place was busier than usual at this hour. He assumed it had a lot to do with the fact that her food, though simpler than before, was still of decent quality, and her prices had only doubled instead of tripled or quadrupled as had other places in town who were even still serving food. He was not certain she'd be able to keep this up for long.

He sighed, hoping the war would not last much longer. After all, there had been very little enemy activity since the hurricane, at least in the way of open attacks, though travel outside the city was still a dangerous proposition. Even the 'random monster attacks' that had been so prevalent before the children disappeared were almost non-existent beyond the occasional magically enlarged sewer rat or alley dog. And the beggars were actually taking care of those themselves, hunting them down and feasting afterward.

A flash of ankle, a tinkle of bells, and a swirl of blue silk on the stairs drew his attention from his brooding and darker thoughts. Scraps followed Lark, scrambling down the banister. Her hair hung damp down her back but was already starting to shrink into curls as it dried. She had tied her belled sash around her waist and sauntered barefoot into the taproom. Nightingale fluttered down after her. He flew to his usual perch on the mantle until he saw Landros, at which point he changed direction, settled on the rim of his mug, and called his mistress over.

Lark was radiant as she slid in next to him. She had a sultry smile on her lips, and her eyes were sparkling with life.

"I see you are feeling better," he said. He jumped as he suddenly felt something touch him under the table. He looked and saw Scraps climbing up his pant leg to sit up in his lap and stretched both paws for the beer mug. Landros pushed it out of his reach.

"Oh, yes," she purred. "Had most curious dream."

"Oh?" he asked, somewhat distracted by the raccoon and the bird teasing each other and trying to keep them apart. Lily drifted by on her way to the kitchen with a tray of dirty dishes, tossed a crust of hard bread onto the table. Nightingale pounced on it, taking it to the mantle and out of the raccoon's reach. Scraps sat sulking. "What was it about?" he asked idly.

"Well, was being chased through forest by handsome young elf and when finally caught me...." she leaned over and whispered into his ear what had transpired then.

It was all he could do to keep himself from throwing her over his shoulder and hauling her upstairs to bed. He purposefully picked up his mug and emptied it. "Lark," he began. "I... I have some things I have to do. Some things Colwyn has requested. I came by to see how you were doing and to bring you some good news."

"Oh?" she said, reaching into his lap and scratching the raccoon's furry stomach. Scraps promptly rolled over and splayed all four paws in ecstasy. She laughed.

"Yes. I would like for you to take the horses back to your wagon and hitch them up. You're moving."

She sat up, prompting a complaint from the raccoon. "Moving? Where?"

"You remember where we... spent the night last night?" She gave him a sideways look. "Right," he said, fidgeting. "Well, Lord Colwyn has given you permission to camp there. You will be safe within stone walls without the feeling of being trapped within stone walls, not really any different than Tent Town, but with better neighbors. You can move your wagon as often as you feel the need to and not worry for thieves or unwanted company. All he asks is that you... well, find another place to stay, or give him the distance he needs when he may ask it with no questions. Hell, he might even give you a bed in the house, I don't know. It should not be too often."

Lark was too stunned to say anything. "Thank you," she finally stammered. "Is... is... Am I to owe something? Rent, I believe, is called?"

Landros shrugged. "He did not say anything to me last night about rent. But you can ask him. He said to go over as soon as you are ready. I... have some things to do, as I said. Someone will be there to let you in." He gave her a quick kiss, afraid that if he gave her a longer one, he'd never leave. "That rose looks good in your hair. I'm glad the merchant gave it to me," he said, laid a silver piece on the table for Lily, and left.

She just sat there, still stunned, watching the raccoon shuffle out after him.

Lily stopped by, picked up the empty mug and pocketed the coin. "You heading out today?" she asked.

"Huh?" Lark looked up, startled. "*Sesha*. Be back tonight. Dane needs practice, and I need work. Have mattress to replace after all," she added, getting up. "Will see you. And thank you!" she called as she walked faster towards the stairs until she was running, skipping steps as she went. She suddenly paused halfway up, leaned over the rail, and called back, "You want I should leave Ivaska?!"

"No, take him with you!" she bellowed over the noise in the room. "Just bring him back tonight! No telling when that damned raccoon will take a shine to visiting again!" she said pointedly. Lark knew she was not referring to Scraps at all but more bipedal thieves who would steal whole chickens instead of just eggs. She nodded and ran upstairs to get her belongings together.

Lark was glad Lily had relented when she insisted upon this small back room instead of one of the larger ones. It was quiet and not too comfortable. It reminded her that she needed to move soon and kept her from getting too settled here. She threw her belongings into her bag and put all her jewelry on at once to save her from having to fit it all into her rune bag. She sighed. One of these days, she would find, buy, or make herself a bag for storing her jewels when she was away from the wagon. She tied her tambourine to the tails of her shawl and grabbed her violin case.

"Mom said to take the quilt with you."

She turned, saw Dane standing in the doorway with Nightingale cupped carefully in his hand. "Oh, I could not...."

"She said you're no good at dancing if you're feet are frostbitten."

She ran her hands through the boy's golden hair. "Your mother is too generous," she said.

The boy just grinned at her and sadly held the bird up.

She accepted, setting him on her shoulder. "All right. I'll take quilt," she sighed and turned back into the room. She took the old quilt from the foot of the bed, folded it over her arm, and slipped out. "Will be back for your lesson later, Dane," she said. "And perhaps, if are good, will let you play for me tonight," she added Dane went down the back stairs.

Ivaska was waiting by the door, got up as she came out of the kitchen, his tail wagging. Her two horses, Dolal and Kassie, were already tethered in the yard, waiting for her. The stable boy smiled and waved. She waved back. She tossed the folded quilt over the piebald's back, forming a makeshift blanket-saddle. Tying the strings of her mandolin case to the straps of her patchwork bag, she draped them across the horse's withers and vaulted onto his back. The stable boy handed her Kassie's tether and stood back to watch the odd little parade trot out of the yard, the mockingbird soaring overhead and the wolfhound happily tagging along, making sure that the mare kept up.

No one so much as crossed Lark's path as she trotted into Tent Town and returned to her wagon. There were bits of trash scattered all around it, some of it things that had been missing a few days ago: a dented pot, a broken plate, bent forks, and cloth remnants. Even the birdhouse had been returned, though it was badly damaged. Nightingale landed on the edge of it, looking down at it mournfully. Lark sighed and dismounted. She tethered the two horses to the tree and began to clean up. She made two piles: one on the tail of the wagon of things she could salvage, the other of things to be thrown out as useless.

It was a depressing sight, her caravan. Even the paint seemed to have dulled.

"The grass under your wagon is dead, Rushavska," ground an old voice in Romeri.

She turned, her temper flaring.

An ancient woman swathed in dark, worn greens and blacks and purples stood staring at her. She wore heavy gold rings on each of her fingers and two large hoops in one ear. Her thin, graying hair was pulled back and bound in an acid green kerchief embroidered with faded gold stars and moons and other astrological signs. Around her neck hung a single strand of heavy gold beads.

The woman just stared, waiting for her to say something.

Lark studied her for a moment, smelling the power she carried. This was not just some ordinary Romer charlatan. This was a woman who wielded real power, a clan *Ranie* more than likely. But which clan? She bided her time. The woman had known her clan by the red roof on her wagon, but Lark was at a disadvantage here, and it was obvious that the woman desired it to be so. There were signs of her clan all over her, in her choice of colors or fabrics, but she recognized none of them.

"*I know, grandmother,*" she answered politely, trying to perhaps place the woman's dialect. "*Am moving it now.*"

"*A little late, don't you think, girl?*"

She sighed, determined not to let this woman rankle her. It was bad luck for Romeri to allow the grass to die beneath the wagon, very bad. "*Yes. But I have been away.*"

"*Maybe should have stayed away?*" she suggested. There was a spark in her eye that reeked of malevolence. A crow flew in and settled on the woman's hunched shoulder.

"*Maybe. But I have not. And I will not. Please, if you will excuse me?*" Lark went to move past her to untether the horses.

The woman put her stick out to block her. It was as twisted as her gnarled hands. "*No, I would talk with you, Rushavska.*"

'At least she does not know my station,' Lark thought.

The old woman cackled, causing Lark to wonder if she knew how to read thoughts or, worse, *did* know her station. The crow cackled with her.

"*So talk.*"

"*Why are you still here?*" she snapped.

Lark just looked at her as if the answer to her question were not obvious. "*Am trapped here, same as everyone else.*"

The woman shook her head. "*You were outside of city. Days ago.*"

She nodded, "*And was honor-bound to bring children back.*"

"*Ah!*" she screeched. "*Gegenta brats! What care you?*" she demanded, poking her in the stomach with her stick. "*They were not Romeri children.*"

Lark shoved the stick away from her, beginning to get angry at this woman's audacity and callousness. "*They were* children," she snapped defensively. "*Innocent and frightened. What difference does it make whose child?*"

"*Why are you still here?*" the woman asked again, petulantly.

"*Wagon,*" she answered shortly. "*Cannot leave with caravan, so will not leave without.*"

The woman made a rather rude noise, interrupting her. "*Feeble excuses. That wreck of wood is not worth trapping yourself in warzone for! Besides, are always deals which can be struck to allow you passage out... with that firetrap if you really wish to.*"

"*What?*" Lark exclaimed, disgusted with the thought. "*Sell out to enemy?*"

"*Who's enemy?*" she asked pointedly. Her tone of voice left little doubt as to what she meant by the question.

"*Anyone who would sacrifice children...*" she began.

"*No.*" The woman cut her off yet again, turning a little away from her, watching the wolfhound pressing against Lark's legs, debating whether or not she was a threat and whether or not he was too afraid to deal with her. "*You are staying for another reason, admit it!*" she accused. She looked dead at Lark with her flat, coal-black eyes. "*Your virginity, perhaps?*"

Lark flushed with rage at the woman's knowledge and daring. "*You presume too much, old woman,*" she hissed. It irritated her that she still had no clue as to the woman's alliances or clan.

"*Watch your mouth, brat! If place any value on heritage or clan, leave him,*" she spat. "*Now. Go north, to warm lands, with rest of clan where you belong.*"

"*You are not my Ranie, crone,*" Lark ground, barely holding her temper. "*Do not presume to order me.... Or threaten me. I am not without power.*"

"*Gah!*" she sneered, waving a gnarled hand at her. "*Illusion, stage trickery, witch-lights,*" she spat. "*Weak magic. Simple locks and ghosts! Nothing!! A genti witch, that's what are becoming, and that is all will ever be if you keep your elven lover,*" she snarled, stepping closer to Lark, poking her with her gnarled finger. She moved away suddenly as Ivaska began to decide that she was indeed a threat. "*Ah! I waste my time with ungrateful brats!*" She shuffled away, her crow cawing and rattling his wings in Lark's direction. "*You've been warned, Petrovna!*" she sang over her shoulder, cackling as she went. "*You've been warned!!!*"

Lark buried her hand in Ivaska's fur, letting his strong back steady her. Nightingale came out of his birdhouse and hopped onto her shoulder, cheeped softly, timidly in her ear. She stroked his breast feathers softly, but she found no comfort there. Nightingale sighed. Ivaska sneezed.

"Agree," she said suddenly, reforming her resolve. "She was most loathsome old hag. And do think she has fouled air. Let's get out of here, *sesket*?"

Nightingale peeped a very emphatic agreement and flew to sit between Dolal's ears. Ivaska woofed and followed her to the driver's box, from which she pulled out the traces and began to hitch up the horses.

Half an hour later, and not a moment too soon, Lark was driving out of Tent Town towards Lord Colwyn's manor, with Ivaska sitting up proudly on the box next to her.

THREE

Before she had gone far into the better sections of town, Lark was stopped by a trio of Watchmen. They blocked her path, forcing her to halt the wagon. One of them foolishly tried to climb up onto the box to speak with her, but Ivaska quickly convinced him that it was not a good idea. Another grabbed Kassie's bridle, holding her head in case her driver took a fancy to fleeing.

"Good day," she said as politely as she could manage. She was still worked up over the incident with the unknown old woman, and this was not helping her mood. "Looking for song?" she asked.

"No, an explanation," the first one said. "What is your business here, gypsy?"

Lark took a deep breath, determined to control her temper. It would not take much provocation to get these men in the mind to arrest her, and she most certainly could not rely on the local justice to clear her ...*if* she saw a justice. "Have business."

"I didn't ask if you *had* business. I asked what it was."

"Am expected at house of Lord Colwyn. If insist to detain me further will make me late, and he will not be pleased. As for my business, why don't you come and ask for yourself?"

"Likely story," the third man mumbled as he began to walk around the wagon. "Ask her about the wagon," he called.

"What is in the wagon?" the first one demanded.

Lark took a slow breath to maintain her patience. "My home. What is in? Everything I own."

"Open it up!" the third man demanded, suddenly appearing on the other side of the box. He stepped quickly back as Ivaska snapped at him. "Control that beast, woman, or I'm going to kill him."

"And leave me without means of protecting myself?" she gasped in mock horror. "Have you reason for keeping me? If so, get on with. Am expected."

"Open the wagon," the first man said flatly, his hand on his sword.

"Is habit in this city for soldier to demand to be let into anyone's home? Have been robbed already; do not wish again. Have not much more to lose but temper."

"Are you threatening me?" he asked in a provoking tone of voice. Lark heard the hiss of steel sliding from leather. Kassie tossed her head fretfully.

"No, am stating facts. Let mare go," she warned. "Are spooking her. And you," she pointed to the first watchman. "I would not stand too close there, were I you. He kicks." The man sidled a few steps away from the back of the fidgeting Pinto.

"Set the reins down, woman, and get down off the wagon."

"Why? So can rough me up? What are you looking for? Money? Pleasure? Food? Will not find here!" she snapped.

Nightingale streaked across the man's path as he started to reach up and grab her. He jumped back and stared at the mockingbird perched on the horse's rump, fluffing himself up menacingly and screeching like a magpie at him. Ivaska growled, barked, and made another snap at the man on his side.

The few people on the streets eyed the group suspiciously and hurried past, not wishing to be caught near the fight that was clearly brewing.

"Hold!" called a voice. The watchmen looked up as a man rode up on a shaggy roan.

"Corporal!" the first man said with some surprise.

"What is the trouble?" he demanded.

"We saw this gypsy woman driving her wagon through here. We stopped to demand her business, and she has been giving us trouble," he said gruffly. "A woman of her kind has no business in this part of town, certainly not driving a ramshackle wagon!"

The corporal looked at the bird still fussing on the horse's rump, dodging a swinging tail, then over at the girl fuming on the box. "This woman has done more for this city than you have," he said grudgingly. "Let her pass."

"But sir!" he complained. He lowered his voice, "She says she's going to Lord Colwyn's," he added.

"Then she is. Believe her or not, the Lord Mayor himself placed enough trust in her to send her to rescue the children of this city. It is not for you or me to judge her," he said firmly but did not seem very happy about it.

Lark looked at him again, recognition slowly dawning on her. He was the corporal who had tried to keep her from entering the Magistrate's office the day they were sent to rescue the missing children. She gave him a slow, thankful smile, though it was somewhat forced. She was still angry about the whole incident. "Thank you," she said.

She made Ivaska sit down as she felt the watchman upfront release his hold on Kassie's head. Before she could drive away, the corporal gestured for her to hold for a moment more. "Yes?" she asked.

"Next time, I would suggest you get a letter from your patrons, even if you cannot read it. It would make stops like this go much more quickly."

"I can read," she snapped. "Which is probably more than can say for them," she added and slapped the reins, driving away before anything else could happen.

Lark was greatly relieved when she finally arrived at the gates of Colwyn's house near the Eastern edge of town. She was still nervous, uncertain of her reception, and not wishing to do anything to upset Landros's relationship with his lord. At the moment, all she wanted to do was melt into the woods and vanish.

A muscular, bearded man in plain workman's clothing opened the gate for her, let her into the carriage yard and closed them behind her. The carriage house and the stables were just yards inside the walls, and she could see the large but modest house set back some ways from both.

"You the Romer Lark?" he asked, cleaning his hands on a gray cloth.

"*Sesha*," she answered. "Am expected."

"Yes, you most certainly are. Though I must say, your loveliness was greatly under-exaggerated."

Lark gave a sudden, tired laugh and sank back against the wagon. "Do not know how relieved I am of friendly face," she sighed.

"Oh?" he asked, concerned. "You have some trouble getting here?"

She held up her hands, "Is over!" she said, shaking her head. "No discussion. Am mad enough without dwelling."

"All right then," he agreed amiably. "I won't ask. By the way, did you know your rear wheel is rattling?"

Lark swore in Romeri, something about last straws and broken backs, and jumped off the box before he could offer to help her. She bent down under the wagon, examining the axle shaft. The leather was holding, but the wood around it was not. She slammed her hand on the side of the wagon, swearing again.

"I take it you know," he said, tossing the rag onto a nearby bench. "Here, let me," he said, getting on his knees to look underneath. "That's not a bad patch job," he muttered. "You do that?" She nodded. "Too bad the roads in this burg need about as much in repairs. You weren't going to get much farther."

"Is wonderful," she growled, sitting down on the back ledge. Ivaska came over, put his head in her lap, and looked up at her with sad eyes. She scratched his ears.

"Well, you made it here, and that's the important thing. It can be fixed." He came out from under the wagon and saw the huge animal. "Nice dog," he said. "Wolfhound?"

She nodded, kept her hand on Ivaska's neck while he checked the man out. "Name is Ivaska. Was gift from one of my brothers. Is extra protection."

"And I'll bet he does his job very well," he mused, finally stroking his scruffy fur when the dog permitted it. He gave the animal a thump on his side. "Lucky you, I happen to have everything I'll need to fix it."

"You can fix!?" she exclaimed. "Ah, 'bout time something look upwards! Thank you! What is cost?" she asked.

He waved her off and headed for the barn for his tools. "Don't worry about that. It's that, or have you blocking the driveway," he laughed.

She waited patiently, petting the dog as she listened to the rattling and banging noises as he gathered what he would need. It took two trips, but he laid out all the tools necessary near at hand. With her help, he got the wagon up on blocks and went to work.

Lark plopped down out of the way to watch.

"So, how many brothers do you have?" he asked idly as he crawled under the wagon and began removing the axle casing.

"Five," she said. "And my father has two other sons."

"Big family," he commented.

"*Sesha*. Are sure this is all right? You fixing wagon? I feel should pay something, for wood at least."

"Don't worry about it. All of this is spare parts from fixing the carriage earlier last week," he grunted. "Damn it!" he swore suddenly as the pegging securing the axle broke off. "Oh, sorry," he apologized, reaching out for a crowbar.

"Don't be," she chuckled. "I've said worse."

"Still," he said. "It is a matter of courtesy."

Lark decided she liked this manservant of Colwyn's and smiled.

"Why don't you go ahead and unhook the horses. This is going to take a while."

"Oh," she said, disappointed. "I... I was hope to set up and go. Have little boy waiting for fiddle lesson."

He shrugged, "So, go. I should be finished by nightfall."

She smiled softly, shaking her head. "Working after. Have to earn living, you know. Even if employer is friend."

He thought a moment. "Tell you what. Where were you planning on setting up?"

"Was thinking about riverbank, near stand of white birch...."

"I know the place," he nodded. "Go ahead and unhitch the horses and let them go. When I'm done, I'll hitch up a pair, take it over by the river, and leave it there for you."

"Oh, is not necessary. I can do so when come back if this not in way?"

He looked at her, studying. "Do you always do that when someone offers to do something nice for you?" he asked.

Lark laughed suddenly, embarrassed. "*Sesha*," she admitted. "Fear I do. Is... is not in my experience for others to do favor for nothing, without expecting money ...or favors."

"Well, this really is no trouble, besides... guests are expected tonight, and it will be in the way if left here until you return."

"Very well," she relented, moving to unharness the horses. A few minutes later, she led them both to the back. "Where you say to put them?" she asked.

He looked out from under the wagon. "Beg pardon? Oh! Just let them go. They'll find their way to the pasture with the others. It's not like they're going to wander off," he chuckled.

"All right," she laughed. She led Kassie away from the outbuildings and gave her a slap on the rump to get her going. The mare looked over her shoulder at her and slowly wandered to the nearest patch of grass and began grazing contentedly.

"A bit lazy, isn't she?" he commented.

"Wee bit," she said, hooking Dolal's lead to both sides of his halter to make a crude bridle.

Something occurred to her. "Speaking of debts," she began, hesitant after his comments about imagining inconveniences and debts where none were.

"We weren't, but yes?" he asked.

"Do I... am expect to.... Did Lord Colwyn say anything about payment for staying? Money or service?" she managed finally.

He thought for a few minutes, an unexplained look of amusement lurking, barely hidden, on his face. "Just don't break my squire's heart," he said finally, completely serious, and disappeared under the wagon.

Lark just stood there, her hand covering her gaping mouth. "Lord C...." she whispered, in complete shock at the revelation.

"You are going to be late, girl!" he laughed.

Lark, still not quite certain what to make of all of this, picked up her violin case and tambourine, vaulted onto Dolal's back, and slowly rode out of the yard.

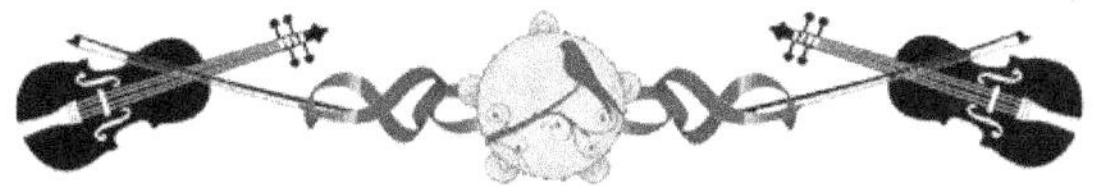

It was almost midnight when Lark finally came home. She was tired and cranky. Though her take had been somewhat higher tonight than the last few days, she had had a run-in with Coolie again, drunk as usual. He had actually followed her as far as the edges of the upper-class district but gave up after the night watchmen began giving him the odd eye. Lark, surprisingly, they did not harass, probably because she was riding in, her light pendant blazing, as if she belonged here. For which she was glad, as she had left Ivaska with Lily to guard the henhouse. She felt she would not have need of him where she was staying now.

There was no activity in the yard when she dismounted to get the gate. It opened easily enough, though it squealed, perhaps deliberately. A stable boy poked his sleepy head out, saw her, and came out to close the gate behind her.

Nightingale, eager for bed, flew on ahead.

Lark looked down at the tired child, put her hands on her hips as he locked the gate. "What, no questions as to who I am? Why am here?"

He shrugged sleepily and yawned. "Master said ta look for a big paint," he said, jerking his thumb to indicate Dolal. "Figgered I had the right Romer. I do, don't I?"

She sighed. "Yes, do, but is not good to assume. Until you meet face to face, should always question."

He shrugged again, "Whatever," and wandered off to his bed above the stable.

Lark swung up again, kicked the piebald into a gallop as soon as they were on the grass, and ran all the way to the riverbank. The wagon was waiting where she had said she wanted it, with its door thoughtfully facing the sunset. Smiling, she slid off the horse, untied the lead from his halter, and let him go.

She sat down on the tail of the wagon for a while, watched the moon rise up over the far wall and the towering roofs of distant buildings. It was a clear night, the first such that she could remember in a long time. It was like the war was over and gone, but she knew better. She would not be lured into the false sense of security the rest of the city was slipping into.

She watched Dolal wade out into the river, stopping to drink. It was a minor tributary, really, joining up somewhere under the center of the city with the main river that fed into the bay on the far side of the western walls. She suddenly decided that a cold dip in that moon-kissed stream would do her good. She jumped off the wagon, set her instruments just inside the door with her shoes, and headed for the water, slipping out of her clothes as she went.

She hung the dress and her belled sash on the branches of a birch tree leaning partly out over the bank and slipped, naked, into the river. The water was bracing and took her breath away the first few minutes, but as she moved towards the center, she warmed up, felt invigorated. She slipped under the surface and opened her eyes to stare up at the moon through the moving water. Shadows darted around her, glistening trout curious as to the invader, some trying to catch reflected stars as if they were insects popping about on the surface.

Landros slipped quietly through the wood, searching for the caravan. There were only so many places she could have parked it, so he did not figure it would take him very long. If Lark was still at the Cinnamon Tree, then he would slip in and wait for her. If not…, he grinned, then he'd just slip in and surprise her.

He saw the shadow of the wagon on the riverbank where they had watched the sunset just an evening ago and heard the faint tinkling of bells on the breeze. He should have known this was where she'd be, he thought. He slipped quietly up to the side of the wagon and saw the piebald climbing the far bank to graze. She was home then. He stopped as his hand reached for the door. What if Ivaska warned her of him? She might panic, feel less than safe here. He did not want that. And he was not even certain she would welcome his intrusion. She was more than likely tired.

He heard a splash in the river nearby that was too large for a trout and, hand on his sword, crept to investigate. He saw something fluttering from a tree, reached up, and caught the edge of it. It was silk. Lark's new blue dress, specifically. And her sash hung beside it, making soft music in the light wind. He looked out over the river and saw her come up for air, standing waist-deep in the water with her back to him. He crouched on the bank under the tree and watched as she tilted her head back in the water to smooth the hair from her face.

The moonlight washed over her damp curves like quick-silvered fingers. It was an arousing sight, to say the least, but it was more than that. He felt something more than just sexual desire, looking at her like this, so vulnerable. It was not a feeling he could honestly say he had ever experienced before. He found it disturbingly comforting. Comfort was also something he was not used to. He felt guilty watching her like this without her knowledge.

"I thought so," he said.

She jumped and spun as she sank to her chin in the water, relaxed when she saw him, standing back up. She cupped her hand and splashed an arch of water in his direction. He shielded himself but she was smiling, so he knew he was not in too much trouble.

"Thought so what?" she asked, pulling her hair over her shoulder and twisting the water out of it.

"That you're not human. You were all too alluring to be wholly human."

"Oh?" she asked, one delicate eyebrow arched. "And what is that I am?"

"A nereid. Come to lure me into your waters." She gave a deep, sultry laugh. "You know I cannot swim."

She beckoned facetiously. "Is not deep," she purred.

He shook his head, smiling. "Oh no. I can see how cold the water is from here," he said.

She began to walk towards him slowly. "Then shall have to come to you."

"Gods, you're beautiful," he breathed when she finally stood before him, the waters of the river lapping gently against her ankles.

She sighed. "Why is men always find wet woman so sexy?" she asked, lying on her side in the grass next to him.

"I don't know," he shrugged, tracing her wet curves with one finger. "You just are."

She closed her eyes, murmured softly. "Have you done what is need do?" she asked quietly.

He shook his head. "No. I am on to something, but it will take some time. I... thought I'd catch a bit of rest first."

She drew him down to her and kissed him.

"I'll be gone before dawn," he mumbled, feeling himself tumbling head over heels again, surrendering to the sensation of just being with her.

"Do not care," she said, wrapping her arms tightly around him, nestling her head against his neck. "Just hold me while you can."

He pulled back just enough to look at her. "What? Have a bad night?"

She sighed, sat up, wrapping her arms around herself. Now that she was out of the water, she was beginning to feel the cold. He took his cloak off, wrapped it around her, and took her into his arms, leaning back against the tree. "Now cloak is wet," she said.

"It'll dry," he said impatiently. "Now what happened?"

"Nothing," she protested. "Is... is nothing." She saw the stern, disbelieving look in his eye and knew he was not going to let her get away with not telling him.

"Who am I going to have to kill?" he asked.

"No one," she said quickly, not certain whether or not he was serious.

"All right, dismember."

She growled at him. "Is nothing that bad. Is only men being men. Was good night for money," she said, "when I danced. Singing was not... not what they wanted tonight." She rest her head back against his shoulder and stared up at the moon. "I received more proposals tonight... both creative and crude. ...City is waking up, starting to relax and move again, as if nothing is wrong."

"It's going to be a rude awakening," he mumbled.

"Is feel wrong. Something in air, waiting," she whispered.

"I know what you mean. I haven't found it yet."

"What *have* you found?" she asked softly.

It would not do any harm for her to know, he thought. Still, ...it reminded him of something else. "You must promise me something, Illyana," he said.

"Anything, my kestrel. What?"

"What I tell you, what you know that concerns the falcons, you cannot tell *any*one. Not your brother, not your grandmother. No one. The lives of Falcons may depend on it, ...your life," he added, more quietly. It hurt him, but if he could not trust her with this... he would have to kill her himself, here and now, and he was not certain he could do it. "I have to know without a doubt...."

Lark could hear the uncertainty in his voice, felt the tension in his arms. Her life, he had said. No doubt his Lord had stressed this to him, kind though he had appeared to be. This order of Falcon knights was bigger than she was, bigger than a few meager lives. And it was more important to him than she was. That hurt a little, but it was all right. For now, it would have to be enough. After all, she couldn't keep him anyway, so what mattered but the moment?

"You will not have to kill me, Kestrel," she said. Landros was startled and wondered for a moment whether or not she could read minds. "Will carry secret to grave and beyond. Mine and yours."

He sighed, relieved, wanting desperately to believe her, in her. To believe in something. He did not want to have to divide his heart, to have to choose between his desires. "Bodies," he said. "That is what we found. Twelve well-known adventurers, freelancers like Lithgorin, Barak, and myself, are missing. Three of them were found in the sewers two days ago by a group of watchmen chasing a prowler."

"Dead?" she asked.

"More than dead. They'd been mangled. Probably by rats, no doubt, but there was no way to determine how they'd been killed anymore. And they'd been completely stripped."

"How identify?" she asked.

"One of them was Ashanda. You've probably never met her. She was a tall, dark-skinned woman from the savannas to the north. When you find the corpse of an ebony woman that's six-foot-eight, there is no doubt as to who you've found no matter what's been done to the body."

He was not wrong. Lark had met the peoples of the savannas in the past; lean, obsidian-skinned giants all. They were a very fierce people but incredibly kind for all that. Aside from Barak, she had seen no one in town who could be of that tribe. They would have stood out.

The death of this woman disturbed him, she could tell. He remained tense, furtive. His body spoke volumes of unease. "You knew her?"

"No," he said, trying to relax. "I've met her... once. Never worked with her, but she had an impressive reputation. She was not an easy woman to kill and believe me, many have tried. That we don't know how she died disturbs me even more. There have been suspicions of magic, but... the body is too old, too decomposed to find any traces, if there ever were any."

"You think these other missing will turn up dead as well?"

He nodded minutely. Lark reached up and pulled him to her, kissed him, trying to melt away his distress.

There was a sudden booming sound from somewhere in the city, like thunder. They both tensed and looked around for the source of the sounds. In the distance, they heard the panicked squeal of horses, unnerved by the unnatural noise. In the sky above the north end of the city, they could see clouds of smoke beginning to obscure the stars.

Landros swore quietly in Elvish.

"Started bombardment again," she whispered. "I knew would not last."

She got up, let the cloak fall back into his lap, and took down her dress. She pulled it over her head, laced it up, and wrapped the sash twice around her waist. She looked down, saw Landros still sitting there, staring at the telltale clouds in the sky and the growing columns of smoke. "Go on," she said. He looked up at her blankly. "Go to him. I know will need you, or at least want to know where are."

He stood and took up her hands in his. "What about you?"

"Are not attacking here. Have yet to attack here. Now go!" she said, then turned away from him and ran to her wagon.

Landros watched her leave, uncertain why it hurt so much. Swearing to himself, he grabbed his damp cloak and began the short hike down to the now well-lit house just out of sight a couple of acres away. He stopped, turned, and ran back to her. He caught her by the arm as she started up the steps, pulled her to him, and kissed her. It was a deep, hungry, breathless kiss that left both of them weak and reluctant to let go. "I will be back for the rest of that," he promised.

Lark sat down on the step and watched him leave. He broke into a run before he reached the treeline, as if wanting to get as far away as fast as he could. She could understand that. Had he stayed a moment longer, he would not have left at all, and he had responsibilities. Trembling, she got up and went into the wagon.

When Lark opened the door, the smell of magic assaulted her. She hesitated, wary. But the smell was familiar and comforting. "Gruma!" she cried and rushed into the wagon. There was no one there. She sat on the edge of her bed shelf, hard in the absence of a mattress, feeling her disappointment and sorrow and fear more strongly now than before. Just when she thought she might actually break down and weep, there was a presence beside her, a hand rubbing her back softly.

"There there, child. No need for that."

She looked over in surprise. *"Gruma?"* she asked.

The ghostly image shook her ancient head. "*Am not here, child. Am only simulacrum. Are troubled, gramil. Are ready to come home then?*"

She looked out the open window in the direction Landros had disappeared, towards the big house. "*No,*" she sighed. "*Am not Ranie yet, Gruma. Not yet.*"

Old Ruby nodded her tarnished silver head and gazed at her granddaughter with her ghostly white eyes. "*But are woman now, aren't you?*" Lark looked up, not really surprised she knew. "*Your mother suspected as much. She says hello, by the by. You like this one too much, I think,*" she mumbled.

Lark gave her a rebellious glare, feeling fresh rage rising up from the other old woman she had met this morning.

"*Temper, 'Yani,*" Gruma warned. "*Mind your temper. It is senseless. All I ask is that you chose carefully. Be certain before you throw yourself away. Oh, I sent you some tea. If are going to be with man, you should take some precautions. Drink in mornings, after.... well.*" She chuckled for a second, then grew serious.

"*Be careful, 'Yani. Some evil is afoot about you. You are making enemies, and I can feel their weight on you. Trust your instincts. If someone bothers you, there is probably sound reason for it. That was always part of your problem. You never listened to yourself. If want to come home, to escape all of this... Just tell your mother, and I will send Ivan for you. Goodnight, Illyana Petrovna,*" she said, placing a kiss on her forehead. "*Oh, my! What hard bed you have! I swear ground would be softer, eh?*" She began to fade away, paused, and cocked her head as if listening to something Lark could not hear. "*You have visitor coming, child,*" she said, and vanished.

Lark felt a sudden wave of loneliness. She, too, had felt the evil beginning to close in on her but was not certain what or why. Of course, she had enemies. She was Romeri, a Gypsy. There would always be people who would hate her for what she was without first stopping to find out *who* she was. But Gruma had also said to trust her instincts; if someone struck her as off, they probably were. Who had she meant? There were quite a few people who 'bothered' her.

She sighed, took her jewelry off and put it away, then gathered up what few blankets she had managed to scrounge, including the quilt Lily had given her, for which she was far more grateful than she cared to admit.

Stepping out of the wagon into the chilly night air, she began to regret leaving Ivaska at the Tree. She crawled under the caravan, spread an old wool blanket on the grass, and wrapped herself up in the quilt, using her arm to pillow her head. She fell asleep to the peaceful rush of the river and the distant sounds of war.

It was not long before she heard a knocking on the caravan door. She sat bolt upright, almost knocking her head on the bottom of the wagon, and looked eagerly, hoping to see Landros there. But the feet were far too small.

"Hello?" she called.

After a moment's hesitation, a lantern, followed by a small head, appeared below the wagon, upside-down, with the straight, dark hair flipped ridiculously up. "Wot 'er you doin' unner there?" he asked sleepily. It was the stable boy.

"Sleeping," she said.

He got off the steps and squatted closer to her. "But I thought you slept inside?" he asked, pointing at the wagon above her.

"When have mattress," she said, propping her elbow up and resting her head in her hand. "What can do for you?"

"How come you don't got a mattress? I kin get you straw. All you gotta do is ask."

"Can't sleep on straw," she sighed. "Would rather sleep on ground under wagon. Had wool mattress, but was stolen, as my sleep is being now. Is some reason you come all this way in dark?" she asked.

"Oh!" he said. "Yes. My master wishes you to sleep up at th' house. Said would be safer fer tonight."

"Because of war?" she asked. She laid back down. "Is war going to end tonight?"

"No, milady, but..." He lowered his voice suddenly. "One a' th' neighbors... was attacked tonight already! Just up th' road. A great beast suddenly appeared in th' gardens and 'ttacked th' house! He ain't sure yet if this was singular or random, but he'd feel better if you was up at th' house. Besides," he added, "wouldn' a feather bed by a fireplace be more comf'terble than th' cold ground?"

She laughed and gave up. "Very well. But only for necessary. I came to stay on property, not in house. Could stay at Lily's and better for reputation," she grouched, crawling out from under the wagon. She went inside, tossed her blankets onto the absent bed, grabbed a shawl against the cold, and closed the windows. Stepping outside, she gently knocked on the birdhouse, sitting on the tail. She had not yet been able to fix it for hanging back up. A sleepy head popped out of the hole, gave her a disparaging squawk.

"Fine," she said. "Sleep here in cold wood box. Am going up to big house, to sleep in warm bed in room with nice warm fire."

He gave a questioning chirp. "*Sesha*, fire."

He was on her shoulder in a moment to the stable-boy's delight. "He a pet?" he asked as they walked towards the house.

"No," she laughed. "He is pest." Nightingale grabbed a lock of hair and yanked. "Ow!" she laughed. "Well, you are," she insisted petulantly.

"He understands you?" he asked in wonder.

"Unfortunately," she grinned.

"Wow!"

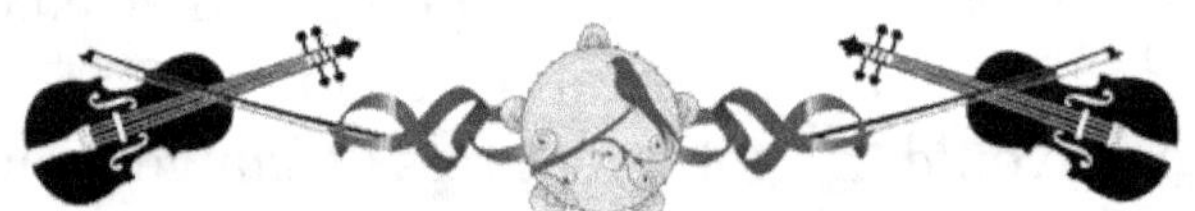

The room Lark was given was small but comfortable, more than enough to suit her needs. The bed was deep and soft, big enough almost for three of her, and the fire was already crackling merrily away when she arrived. The houseboy closed the door behind her and tiptoed off to his own bed. Nightingale went straight for the mantle and chirped his delight to her when he discovered a small basket filled with unspun wool waiting for him there.

"Yes, I see," she answered, turning to the bed. "*Sesha*, was very thoughtful of Lord Colwyn," she began. The bed had been turned down, and there was a white shirt laid out on it. She picked it up, smelled it. "Mmmm," she breathed. "But have feeling was not lord's doing."

She changed into the shirt, laying her dress carefully over the chair and curling up in the bed. Wrapped in the smell of a certain elf, she drifted to sleep, dreaming of warm nights by the riverside.

FOUR

Landros crept into the guest room somewhere after midnight. Lark was sound asleep, wearing the shirt he had left for her. She was curled up facing the wall, with her arms wrapped around the pillow. Nightingale made a sleepy noise from the makeshift nest on the mantle. He softly stroked the bird's back.

"Shhh. Yes, I'm glad you like the nest," he whispered, not really knowing what the bird had meant. "Go back to sleep. I don't want to wake her up." The bird flicked his wings in an avian shrug and tucked his head again.

Undressing, he slipped silently into the bed with her, curling up against her and wrapping her in his arms. She faintly stirred, snuggled back against him.

He slept for only a couple of hours and got up as the fire began to die sometime around dawn. He left as quietly as he had come.

Going down to the kitchen, he had a light breakfast tray prepared for her, then went out the back door into the small garden and picked a rose from the bush. He carried the covered tray back upstairs to her room and left it on the small reading table by the chair with a note.

Nightingale was stirring, peeped a sleepy good morning. He hushed the bird, not wanting Lark to wake just yet. If she woke while he was still here, he would never get out of here in time to meet with the men he needed to this morning. He gave the bird almost half of the slice of raisin bread he had taken for himself from the kitchen and left quietly.

Stepping into the street outside of his lord's home, he decided he had time to return to his rooms at the Golden Cygnet. He had not been back since the morning he had run into Lark in the marketplace and desperately needed a change of clothes. He had left his cleanest shirt with her last night. The apartment was paid up through the following Spring, so he was not overly worried about being gone from it for long periods of time. The Cygnet was well-known for its security, even in these times.

The apartments were not luxurious by noble means, but the Cygnet provided everything an inn provided on a fee-for-service basis, including laundry, while providing suites of rooms that felt more like a home than a hired chamber. It was the kind of place that the wealthy kept for when they were in town, and unless something big was happening in Portswain, it was never fully occupied. Every room was rented, however. He had been lucky to get this one. And just after a windfall which allowed him to afford it.

His was probably the humblest in the building. Well-cared for but appointed plainly. The small front room sported a fireplace with a fur rug, a long leather couch, and an over-stuffed chair for relaxing by the fire. There was a private bath off to the right in a large closet, complete with a large wooden tub and a wash stand with pitcher and basin. There was even a chamber stool in the corner, with a spare, covered jar, so the full one could be put outside the door for collection and not leave one without.

Going from the front room to the bedroom, he set his pack on the large feather bed and began to empty it. The bedroom was comfortable, with a heavy, braided rug on the wooden floor and a second, smaller fireplace. There was a rocking chair by the hearth, and he noticed that the stack of wood had been recently replenished.

The hairs on the back of his neck stood on end for a moment, then settled down. "Greetings, brother," he said, glancing over at the figure in black emerging from the shadows by the hearth. "I hope you have been staying out of trouble these past weeks."

"Nothing that I couldn't handle," he shrugged, plopping himself down on the edge of the bed. Portholus was a bit taller than his older brother and far more handsome, but that had never bothered Landros. He was every woman's dream: tall, lithe, fair of face and voice, with tigery-brown eyes and shoulder-length hair that rippled like molten gold in the sunlight. "Glad to see you have finally returned. Been gone a while. Mission for the city or something private?" he asked.

"City. Rescuing some stolen children," Landros replied, tossing his dirty clothes into a pile on the bed and going over to the dresser for clean ones.

Portholus picked through the pile of wrinkled clothes and noticed a shirt and a pair of pants that were neatly bundled together. He picked up the shirt, looked at it curiously, and sniffed it. An eyebrow arched, and a smile curved up one side of his mouth. "Was she part of the mission as well, or just a diversion?" he grinned.

"Who?" Landros looked over in the middle of changing and saw the shirt his brother was dangling accusingly at him. He remembered now. "Oh, Lark. Little of both, actually," he shrugged and tucked his shirt into his pants, trying not to make a big deal out of it. His brother would be merciless if he thought there was more to it. "She was the girl that I met a few months back. I ran into her a couple of weeks ago, and we ended up both being sent to retrieve the children."

"The ones that disappeared from their beds?"

"Yes."

"So, why was she wearing your shirt?" he grinned.

Landros snatched it from him. "Because hers got ripped up in a pirate attack. I couldn't just let her walk around…"

Portholus shook his head, thoroughly amused. "No, I suppose you couldn't." He twitched his nose. "Still seeing her?" he asked. "I'd say…" he bent closer to his brother, took a deep sniff, "oh, less than an hour since you left her."

Landros pushed him back onto the bed, snatched up his dirty clothes, and stuffed them into another bag to give to the laundress. Portholus propped his elbow up and rest his head on his hand, watching his brother put his leathers back on.

"Lark," he mused. "Isn't that the human Gypsy you told me about? The dancing girl?"

"Yes, she is the *Romeri* girl I spoke of," he corrected, sitting down to pull his boots on.

Portholus sat up and looked him over. "Be careful, brother," he warned. "Humans are a tricky lot, and their females even more so. ...As for her being a Gypsy... *Romeri*," he corrected when Landros glared at him.

Landros sneered, "My brother Portholus, the expert on women. You have been with how many now? I seem to lose count," he snarled, pulling his other boot on.

"I never take them seriously," he shrugged. "Only as a pleasant distraction. They seem to prefer elves. Especially the human women. It's... entertaining."

Landros got up, wiggled his feet in his boots to make sure they were snug, and crossed back to the bed to finish packing. "Someday, brother, you will find someone and settle down," he said with a shake of his head.

Portholus grabbed his wrist and looked at his with shock in his eyes. "What? You think that you have found 'her'? That one woman in a thousand? Be very careful, brother." Landros pulled away, and Portholus let him. He watched him, though. "Does she know...?"

"No," he answered, cutting him off. That was not something he wanted to think about right now. Not now. "And she will not know until I decide to tell her. That has been our secret and will remain so unless I decide to tell it, and that will be no time soon."

Portholus got up and crossed to the cold hearth, toying with a small, jointed animal figure on the mantle. "I will give you this: she smells nice," he mumbled. "Are you packing to go to her or on another quest?"

"More business. May see her later, though. Why?"

"Just curious, big brother. I actually *do* watch out for you ...and I am concerned. You should try to relax a bit more. This town will live on even without your aid. You behave almost as I would expect a knight sometimes."

"Would that be bad?" he asked, not looking at him, afraid his eyes would give too much away.

Portholus shrugged and set the doll down. "Not really, but I do not see either of us really following that path."

Landros finished packing. "I will be gone for a few days." He tossed Portholus a money pouch. "Here, you may need this."

Portholus looked at it and tossed it back. "You have a lady now. You may need it more than me. I am fine." He looked at his brother and smiled. "It has been over forty years, and still you try to take care of me."

"Old habits die hard. Just be careful, little brother. Stay here if you like," he said, hoisting his pack and heading for the door.

Portholus put a hand on his shoulder. "You are the one that should be careful ...with your journeys and the girl. I do not want to lose you as we lost our family."

"I will, little brother," he said. "And do not worry about me. Worrying is my job, not yours," he added, closing the door behind him.

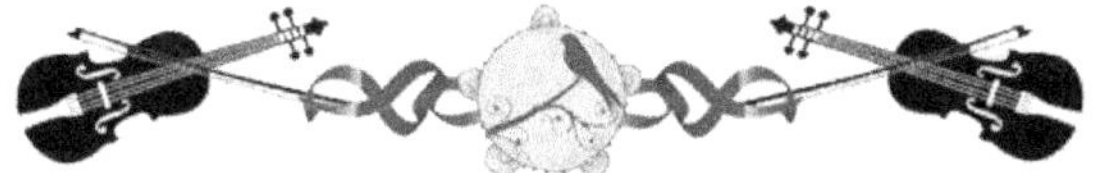

Landros's scent was stronger when she woke. She had been dreaming of him, and not all of it had been pleasant. Her dreams had been a fair mix of pleasure and tragedy, ending with his leaving to go off and do Gods only knew what. She turned, discovered that the place next to her was still faintly warm, and dented as if someone else had been sleeping there. She sat up and looked around the room, half expecting to see him stirring the fire. But the room was empty.

Nightingale was on the mantle, enjoying a hunk of what smelled like raisin bread. He looked up at her as she began moving and chirruped a cheerful 'good-morning, sleepy-head' to her.

"Good morning to you, too. I see you have stolen breakfast," she said grumpily.

He chirped back at her. "No?" she asked, getting out of bed. He said something as he went back to his breakfast, picking the raisins out and eating them first. She sat back down on the bed. "He was here? I didn't... he didn't wake me?" At Nightingale's insistence, she looked at the small table. On it was a tray containing a covered plate and a single rose.

She went over and lifted the cover. It was a meager breakfast at best but far better than she could have expected. There was even an egg. She sat down, picked up the napkin, and found a note underneath:

Lark,

I am sorry I could not stay longer, but duty is insistent, and I did not want to wake you. Hopefully, I will see you soon. Enjoy your breakfast, and please eat all of it! I will not have you starving yourself so long as there is food still available. We are not on starvation rations yet.

Landros

P.S. There is a dressmaker down on Delrouche who is waiting for you at her shop. I beg you not to fight me on this. It is something I want to do. Besides, I am running out of shirts, and I really don't think it wise for you to be running around in my clothes. Your sheerest skirt is less of a distraction.

Lark set the note down and looked over at the bird on the mantle. "You knew about this!" she accused. The bird chirruped innocently and began eyeing her breakfast now that his own was gone. "Why did not wake me!?!" she demanded.

He chirped nonchalantly. She put her fists on her hips and glared up at him. "He asked you not to, my *tushka!* Who's familiar are you?!"

Nightingale just flipped his feathers at her and flew out the window. Grumphing, she turned and began to eat.

VII

Skullduggery

ONE

Landros met up with Adrick in the back of a seedy tavern in Bayside that had no name. The priest curled his nose at the reek of the place but sat down without laying back his hood.

"Why," Adrick muttered, "did you insist upon this rat-infested dunghill?"

"You are dressed as I asked?" was all he said.

Adrick lifted aside a fold of his cloak to show Landros that he was indeed not wearing his priestly robes. "These were damned difficult to come by, I might add," he growled.

Barak came to the table with a fist full of drinks and pushed one in Adrick's direction.

Landros took his mug and leaned over it as if nursing the foul drink. And it was foul. Looking down, he was startled to see things of an unknown nature floating in it. He did not want to know what it had been watered down with. He made a minute gesture with his head towards a corner of the room, deliberately not looking in that direction. "You see the man in the dark gray cap?"

Adrick scanned the room as if looking for a barmaid, saw the man in question. "Yes."

"Vanishti," Barak whispered into his mug. "He's one of those who disappeared while you were gone. He used to pal around with Ashanda."

"Ashanda?" Adrick asked, wide-eyed. "Was he with her when..."

Landros shook his head shortly, warning Adrick to lower his voice. "He disappeared at about that time. He turned up again three days ago and has been acting suspiciously ever since. I have reason to believe he was and is still in the grip of the enemy. I've been talking to him, and he is of the opinion," he added with distaste, "that we can be bought."

Adrick gave Landros a long, calculating look, one which did not make him comfortable at all. "Can we?" he asked quietly.

Landros looked hard at him. "If the price is right," he said more loudly than he had been speaking. He leaned back to stare eye to eye with the gray-capped man, who grinned at him from behind the priest with a mouth missing quite a few teeth.

"You friends, yes?" he grinned. He was a dark man, with short, tight, curly hair, a Northman obviously not used to the colder clime from how he was bundled.

Landros shook his head and spoke as slowly and clearly as he could without being insulting. "No. Missing one," he said, holding up a finger.

"Not one?" he asked, grabbing Adrick's shoulder.

"Yes, one. Another one," Landros added. He ground his teeth. This man annoyed the hell out of him. He knew damned well that Vanishti played an elaborate charade at not understanding the Southern tongue. He did have trouble speaking Tembian but understood ten times more than he let on. He was a foul-smelling snake, and he knew it.

"Ah!" he exclaimed, making a great show of straightening Adrick's cloak. "So sorry, so sorry! Is waiting over soon? Must go. No patience these other men. No patience." There was a spark of genuine fear in his eyes at the mention of these 'others'.

As if on cue, Lithgorin lurched in like a drunken skunk with his arm around another young elf. He saw the group at their table, nudged his drinking partner, and pointed, slurring something in what Landros guessed was supposed to be Elvish.

'Great,' he thought. 'Either Lith is stinking drunk and absolutely useless, or he's putting on one hell of an act.' He held his breath as he got a whiff of the pair. 'I don't know who is going to be more surprised, me or the enemy,' he added to himself.

"Are you two sober enough to do business?" he growled.

The pair stood straight as arrows, puffed out their chests stiffly. It was then that Landros noticed the striking resemblance between the two men. "Yezir, bus'ness sir! Reporting for duty and all that!" Lith saluted. Then, the two suddenly bowled over with giggles, slapping at each other and calling for another round.

Landros saw a gleam flash across Vanishti's eye and vanish. That these two were soft and drunk pleased him. It did not please Landros. He stood. "Two more," he said, pointing at them. "Is all. We go now."

"We go? Yes? Good! Good! You keep friends quiet. Scare off our friends they make too much noise."

"I got it," Landros said, pushing the two elves ahead of him and following the Northman out the door.

"Landros," Lith hiccuped, grabbing the elf with him in a headlock and showing him to his friend. "Is my brother Lithandros... Lanithdros... -hic- What the hell is your name again?"

His brother laughed, belched, and pulled himself free. "Lithgorin, you dolt!" he growled, still laughing as he staggered down the street.

"No, I'M Lithgorin! ...ain't I? Landros!" he bellowed. "Which one am I again?" he asked.

Landros just walked on past them, trying to ignore the pair. He fell into step with Vanishti and growled just loud enough to be overheard. "I'd slit their throats myself if I thought I could get away with it. I told him to come alone."

Vanishti tried to be consoling. "Ah, is understanding, wanting family in on good fortune?"

"Food Gortune?" the brother piped, staggering up in-between the two. "Was in it? More wine? Women?" he leered.

"Lots, friend!" Vanishti said. "You will see. Lots more." The man staggered back to his brother, and Vanishti turned back to Landros. "Think not will be trouble. Big man in back can sit on two, yes?" he chuckled with a broad grin.

Lark entered the small shop, uncertain she had the right place. The dresses that hung on elaborate dummies all throughout the shop were of the finest materials and certainly far too rich for her. Not to mention not her style. Most of them had high collars that somehow left the necks open to the breast and tight, rigid waists with falls of cloth to the floor. None of them seemed practical in the least.

She was admiring the rich, dark wine-colored velvet of one of the dresses when the shop keeper appeared. She was a small, round woman with a ruddy face and plenty of laugh wrinkles, and seemed to be losing a lot of weight quickly, as her skin hung a little loosely over her collar and cuffs. She gasped with delight on seeing Lark come in.

"Oh, *please* tell me I can do something for you?" she chirped. "You like that one?"

"Am Lark," she said hesitantly, not sure quite what was expected. "Was told to come to you?"

"I'm Bianca Fitzwelm." The woman's face lit up suddenly. "Oh, *yes*!! Oh, my!" she breathed. "You *are* a lovely creature! He wasn't exaggerating. And such a tiny waist! Oh, how do you ever expect to carry a child in that tummy?"

"Will fatten up," she answered, not certain what to make of this woman. "Mother had no trouble."

"Oh, of course not! Silly me, listen to me chattering away like a magpie! Come in. Come *in*, dear girl! Oh, have I got just the thing for you! Your friend was most adamant," she began, taking her by the arm and leading her into the back of the shop.

Nightingale shyly followed, not willing yet to be seen. In the back, he perched himself quietly on the top of the elaborate mirror and watched.

Bianca had lain out several dresses and waded through piles of cloth and thread and half-made pieces to stand Lark on a small pedestal in front of a huge, expensive glass mirror.

"Is so crowded," Lark commented.

"Yes, yes, well. Not much business lately, you know. My last real commission was for Lady Ellenath's wedding dress at the Spring Festival." She shook her head sadly. "And then the war started. Such a shame. Very bad for business, ...and everything else."

"I know," Lark agreed.

"Now," she said, clapping her hands together. "I've spent all morning laying out some things that, from his description of you, would flatter you best. Your friend commissioned me for four dresses," she held up her hand as Lark started to protest. "Ahahah! He was most adamant about it. Very specific, except for the design, of course, which is up to you. Four, he said. Two nice ones for performing," she said, ticking them off on her thick fingers. "One for every day and one for... oh, yes, 'mucking about'!"

Lark laughed, "Mucking about?" Nightingale chirruped his merriment. "*Sesha*, do think our handsome elf has us quite pegged. Mucking about indeed!"

"Well, shall we get started then? Here," she held up a dress very similar to the ones on the dummies in the outer room. Lark shuddered at the thought of putting the stiff, glittering cloth next to her skin. Bianca held the dress up against her. "Hmmm, almost your color. But I think... I think you need a simpler gown. Your complexion just doesn't lend itself for anything too busy or complicated."

Lark let her breath out. Before the woman could reach for another of the stiff, uncomfortable dresses, she stepped off the pedestal and set a gentle hand on her shoulder. "Please, can we talk before you fit? Find something suitable after?"

"Why certainly, my dear! Why..." her face suddenly fell, "you don't like these, do you?"

"Is not that do not like them. Is beautiful. But is not me. Am Romeri, not court flower." Lark gestured down at her well-patched skirt and nearly threadbare blouse and vest, which badly needed mending. "These are kind of clothes for me." She made a broad gesture encompassing the beautiful gowns about her. "While all are beautiful, would look stolen on me, out of place. I need something is me. Short skirts," she said, drawing an invisible line with her finger across her shin, "and loose blouses with vests which cinch up soft but tight, or wide belts or sashes with tassel or bells."

"I see," she mused, began looking Lark over more carefully. "Stand up on the pedestal," she ordered, walking slowly around her, scrutinizing her closely. "What kind of work do you do? He said two were for entertaining. What kind of entertaining?"

"I dance and fiddle. Sometimes sing, not often."

"What kind of dance?"

Lark took a breath and mimed out a few examples.

"Alluring, subtle, passionate, enticing," she uttered. "Yes, I think we can work with this. How much of your leg do you tend to show?"

Lark blushed. "Sometimes skirts fly up to lower thighs if enough cloth. I like more to hint than display. More powerful." The woman seemed to be assessing her without passing judgment on her occupation as many higher-born ladies did.

Bianca nodded. "You like to tease, tempt without being tawdry. I think we can manage. Do you ever show off that taut little tummy of yours?"

Lark put her hand on the body part in question. "Never... thought about..."

"Well, you should," she said matter-of-factly. "Here, hop down," she said, picking up a well-worn book and stylus. She scratched out a quick sketch of a two-piece dress that was at once daring and modest. The waist was low across the hips, with a broad belt, and the blouse was a snug little thing that hugged the breast, ended high across the ribs, and had full, billowy sleeves. "How's that?"

"Is beautiful!" she gasped. It was strikingly similar to what she had conjured for her dance in the woods for Landros, something she had seen in rare storybooks in the North.

"Good. Now, let's find some material." She set the sketchbook down and began bustling about looking for fabrics. Lark glanced over her shoulder at Nightingale, who shared her growing excitement. "Here," the woman laid a drape of sapphire blue silk across Lark's shoulder and looked at it in the mirror.

"This will do for a nice start. Yes," she murmured, either ignoring or just not noticing the bird perched on the top of the heavy frame. "How about this for the bodice and the skirt? I'll have to line the bodice, or you'll show everything the goddess gave you right through it. And this," she added, lifting Lark's arm out to the side and draping a length of sheer, starlight cloth over it. Lark took the corner of it in hand and turned, marveling at how it flowed through the air and across her body. Lark loved it and found the color very striking against her skin. Bianca took in her expression of delight and smiled. "Yes, that's it, I think." She took the cloth and set it aside.

"Have any red?"

"Yes," she nodded, "he said you were partial to reds. I think some wines I have would go very well on you, though I would stay away from roses and pinks. You haven't the complexion for them. If you wear any shade of red, it has to be deep. But I agree with your elven friend, though. You look good in blue. I almost wish you had worn that blue dress today. I would have loved to see it worn."

"Blue dress?" Lark asked, looking up in surprise from the sketch. "You know about...."

The round dressmaker laughed. "Yes, I know about that dress. I made it. I always liked it, though it was too short for most of my usual clients. A real shame, though. I did wonders with what little of that cloth I had. Often thought about adding a contrast piece to the bottom to make it long enough, but I've always been glad that I hadn't. My husband told me he sold it to the same gentleman who commissioned these... I couldn't help but assume...." she shrugged with a grin and returned to digging for the right material.

"Is lovely," Lark smiled. "Looks good on me."

On the floor, in a pile beneath a chair, Lark spied a piece of golden yellow silk. She got off the pedestal and pulled it out. It was not very big, maybe a yard long and only four inches wide at its narrowest point and nine or so at the widest. With it, she found other scraps of bright cloth of all kinds, brocades, silks, and bright, printed calicoes. "Oh, these are nice," she said.

Bianca turned and saw Lark on the floor with her scraps all spread out in her lap and around her. "Oh my! Those are just my scraps, dear! Nothing there big enough to do anything with, but I never really have the heart to throw any of it out. I've been making quilts out of the stuff."

"Oh, are wrong. *Is* big enough," Lark smiled. "How about motley from this? Skirt?" she asked, fingering the gold silk longingly.

"A skirt?" she asked, blinking. "But none of that matches... Oh, a motley!" she exclaimed excitedly, getting the idea. She sat down on the edge of the pedestal and began laying certain pieces beside each other. "I must say, this would be a very striking skirt."

"*Sesha*, for every day, or ... 'mucking about'," Lark laughed.

"Yes. There, let's see... Find me another piece of this one," she said, holding up a floral brocade.

Lark found one and handed it to her.

"Hmm, yes," she mused. "Just out of curiosity (he didn't have much time to chat, he said, the poor dear), why are you in sudden need of so many clothes? Most just buy them one dress at a time, as they need them. Or is he just feeling sorry for my old man and me and courting you in the same measure?" she grinned.

Lark started to say something, but it got caught in her throat. Courting? she thought. Was that what this was?

"Oh, he is just bad luck for Romeri clothes," she managed, trying to laugh. "Was robbed after hurricane. Not being home, neighbors cleaned out anything not nailed in."

"Oh, that's too bad," she said, getting to her feet. "Here, I think I have just the cloth to make a vest to go with this."

Lark watched the woman disappear into yet another room and wondered how she could possibly have more fabric stashed anywhere. Nightingale landed in her lap, admiring a piece of black silk shot with gold, copper, and silver thread.

Courting, she thought again. For some reason, the thought evoked a mixed reaction. Part of her was absolutely thrilled, but another part felt a surge of fear: a fear of being caged, a fear of what the old woman had said to her about *genti* witches, and a fear that, not only was that what was happening, but that it was just what she *wanted* to happen. No matter what the consequences. These dark, confusing thoughts were quickly crowded from her mind as the dressmaker returned with an armload of measuring tape, pins, scissors, and a deep red velvet.

Landros just walked on, brooding. He hated this part of town. It smelled evil: of rotting vegetation and choking weeds, decomposing fish guts and alcohol, blood and every vice a man could dream up. It all could be found down here in the Bayside. Harlots hung their heavy, almost bare breasts out their second-story windows, calling down to the streets for paying company. Shadows lurked in places they shouldn't, and beggars could not be trusted to be just beggars.

Their guide suddenly led them down a narrow side street. They followed. The buildings seem to press down on them, closing them in. Even the drunken brothers fell strangely quiet, looking around them with glazed eyes.

Landros kept his on Vanishti, not trusting the man's suddenly more furtive behavior, the jumpiness he displayed. The alley ended abruptly in a high stone wall, and four well-armed men backing a tall individual wearing a hooded cloak which cast the face in shadow.

"Welcome," the hooded one intoned. The voice was silky, husky, androgynous.

"What the?!" exclaimed Lith's brother from behind them. Landros turned, saw four mounds of trash and rag rise up to become four husky men in leathers blocking them in.

Landros grabbed Vanishti by the shirt front. "What is the meaning of this?!" he snarled, drawing a sword.

"Patience, my friend," soothed the hooded one.

Landros turned, behaving like the rabid animal he had already established himself as being. "I am *not* your friend!"

"I would hope we are all friends here. Please restrain yourself and let us talk. My friends behind you are merely there to protect our conversation's privacy."

Landros waited a long moment before he let go of the North-man.

"There, good. Now we can do business, I hope?"

"What sort of business?" Adrick asked.

"We represent parties who are not pleased with the current government in control of the city."

'Ah,' thought Landros, 'here it is!'

"You mean the enemy??" Lithgorin asked in innocent, drunken shock.

The hooded figure laughed softly, almost feminine. "No. Not who you think. I am referring to the enemy *within* the city walls. Our leaders. Do you know that the leader of the 'enemy' forces first sent a warning ahead? Informed our precious Lord Mayor of their intentions and that a peaceful surrender was the only option aside from a massive and unnecessary slaughter. Were we, the citizens of this fair city, or even our ruling interests, the guilds of seamen and merchant and craftsmen, given the opportunity to voice our opinions? No. The Lord Mayor started this war, not the enemy at the gate. Out of some sick loyalty to a king who could care less."

The merchant's guild? Could the enemy be there? Landros asked himself. Possible. It made some sense. "Maybe the king does not know our situation, our desperation," he offered.

"Yeah!" Lith and his brother chorused. "Deprsation!"

The figure laughed again, deeper. "Tell me, how could he not know?"

Landros stifled a growl. The question bit deep.

"Oh, calm yourself. We mean the king no ill will. We just feel that we are too far away for him to properly protect us or rule us."

"Why us?" Barak asked slowly.

"Vanishti has been asked to find fine, helpful individuals such as yourselves, people with concern for this city and the people in it..."

Landros gave a snort at that.

"This city will fall. There is no question of that. You have no idea what the odds are against us, what lies outside those walls, or to what lengths they will go to capture the city. We are giving you an opportunity to have a hand in saving this city and line your pockets as well."

"What exactly do you want from us?" Adrick asked. "What will our 'cooperation' entail and ... how much is it worth?"

"We are not asking you to turn against the people in any way, only that... well, you not hinder the activities of those trying to save it from itself. The level of activity will, of course, dictate the level of the reward. If you are more the active than the inactive type, we can accommodate you easily enough. So, what do you say? Have we a deal?"

"I think," Landros began slowly, glancing at each of his companions, "that you can rot in hell!"

Before Landros could lunge, Vanishti grabbed his arm and pressed himself so close against him that Landros could smell his last meal. "You do not understand, my friend. Lives, Lives are at stake, yes?" He leaned closer, lowered his voice. "You see the man in back with double axe? Yes. He alone, by *himself*, I watch kill Ashanda. No help. Just Ashanda and he. You understand, yes? Take his money, take his promise. Keep your lives....."

Landros pushed him away in disgust. "You sold her out, you son of a bitch!" he yelled.

The man came at him again with a look of horror, "**No**! Not sold out! Sold *for*!! Loved her!! Was too late...."

Landros swung at him with his sword as he made another grab for him, the blade catching Vanishti across the face. Behind him, Lithgorin and his brother sprang to life, drawing their swords, no longer playing the ineffective drunks, and fell into place to cover the rear.

Landros wanted the cloaked figure badly but had the wisdom to remain where he was to protect Adrick.

The cloaked figure simply raised a hand, "Kill them. And this time, be more careful where you get rid of them." With that, they turned, stepped sideways, and simply vanished.

The defenders were surrounded, pressed themselves into a protective circle with Adrick in the center, where he might be most useful and best protected. The eight men closed in quickly.

The fight was a maddened tangle, two on two with the priest caught in the center. Lith took a glancing blow to his head, throwing off his own attack. His brother likewise danced just out of the way of an arm shot, parried a second and missing with his own.

The other four mercenaries closed, two on Landros, the big man with the axe and a smaller man going for Barak. Landros found his blows mostly parried, barely managing to counter incoming strikes. One swing clipped his ear uncomfortably close, striking him mostly with the flat but effectively blocking his companion's attack. Landros struck from below both arms, managing a nasty gash in the leg.

Barak ignored the little guy, concentrating on the giant with the axe. The double-headed blade swung downward towards his head, and he brought up his sword to block it, catching the handle just below the blade. He felt the impact of an ineffective strike across his mailed stomach. He threw off his opponent and caught him on the back stroke, inflicting only minimal damage through his armor.

Adrick, busily gathering his mystic energies, loosed an eldritch bolt of energy at the smaller man confronting Barak, throwing him back and out of the fight, stunned.

Lithgorin and his brother battled in tandem without much success, neither taking nor dealing damage. They landed several ineffective strikes, glancing off of armor. Landros held his own for the time being, and Barak and the axe-wielding fighter dodged each other's blows.

Landros was caught in the shoulder on the downswing by his second opponent as he parried the first. The blade bit through the leather, into the shoulder at his neck, and tore downward across his left arm. He turned, stabbing the second man through the gut, and used his speared weight as a balance point to kick the first man back, buying himself the time to free his blade.

There was a sudden crack-clatter as the axe broke Barak's sword and left his arm hanging numb at his side. he dodged the second incoming blow and, lowering his head, plowed him in the gut with a roar. Behind him, Lithgorin's brother took a slash to the head, opening him up for his other opponent, who dealt him a blow that opened him up from left hip to right shoulder. He fell back against Adrick, who turned, caught him with his left arm as he leveled his crossed fingers at the pair now confronting him and released a bolt of forked lightning that threw one of them off his feet and into the trash he had previously hidden in, and made the other stagger. Lithgorin saw his brother go down but was unable to do anything, having his hands full with a wounded leg and now four men to deal with.

Barak howled with pain as the axe struck him again in his right arm, just as the feeling was beginning to return in dirks and daggers. He struck out with his fist, the only weapon he had left, and made a solid connection with a cloth-covered breastplate.

Landros fought blindly on, lashing out in an almost berserker fury. He parried a blow, narrowly missing his unprotected thigh, and threw his entire weight and strength into the upswing. He caught the man just under the edge of his leather breastplate and tore clean through the rib cage. He did not even scream as he fell, showering Landros in hot blood. Landros turned to help Barak.

The man still standing from Adrick's lighting was not happy. Seeing the hand come up a second time, he charged, pressing in over the brother's body and striking the priest in his arm, forcing him to let go. A second swing cut into his leg, carrying through to hit Lithgorin full in the back.

Adrick went to his knees, eyes closed, praying for a miracle, for some intervention of Maiden or Matron to save their lives, and thus the lives of others who would follow their path and no doubt be killed by these unjust men. His medallion began to glow in response, and, clutching it in his bloodied hand, he prayed for a spell, any spell, opened himself to whatever was coming.

Landros felt a strange prickling and an unexplained wave of vertigo washed over him. His sword passed through the body of the man with the axe, not touching him. Landros saw the look of surprise on the man's face as his own weapon, which would have cleaved Barak's head like a melon, bit deeply into the ground instead. Before Landros could say or do anything else, solidity returned, and they were... elsewhere.

"What the hells?" he growled, looking around. They were in another alley, just as dirty and rat-infested as the first, but they were alone. Not far away, they could hear the surprised curses of their attackers. Landros looked down at Adrick, still sitting with Lithgorin's unconscious brother in his lap. The priest had a look of absolute shock on his face.

"Adrick," Landros said, nudging him with his knee, reluctant to lower either sword even for an instant. "Snap out of it! What happened?"

"I think..." he stammered. "I think I just entered a higher circle," he gasped.

Barak bent down and, grabbing the brother's hand with his good one, pulled him onto his right shoulder, ignoring the discomfort. "Let's get while the gettin's good," he said in a low voice. "Shouldn't take 'em long to start lookin', an' it don't sound like we went far."

Adrick snapped out of his shock and stood up. He dangled his medallion in front of his face, closing his eyes a moment as he mumbled a minor prayer. The medallion spun, pointing further down the alley behind them. He opened his eyes, pointed in that direction. "That way," he said. He then turned to face the opposite direction and erected the illusion of a dead end to stall their pursuers and followed his companions as quickly as he could with his wounded leg.

TWO

Lark stood still on the pedestal, listening to the dressmaker's constant chatter while she cut the bottom off of the skirt she was wearing. It was an ugly brown fabric, but it had been pinned and marked to fit, and the woman was cutting it to the length Lark wanted.

"There," Bianca said, struggling to her feet. "That should make a good pattern. Be careful taking it off; there are pins all over the place in there." She tossed the waste material into the pile under the chair, now much smaller for the absence of quite a few select pieces.

Lark carefully slipped out of the skirt and back into her own clothes, leaving her vest off and in the hands of the dressmaker. She could not remember the last time she had clothes that fit her just right.

The woman gathered the chosen fabrics, the marked skirt, and her sketches and took them carefully into the back room. She returned with a fist full of silk roses of varied colors and sizes. "What do you think of some of these to spruce things up, eh?" she asked, tucking one under Lark's scarf behind her ear. "Yes, yes, these will do nicely. Now you run along, dear," she said, shooing her out of the shop. "I have a ton of work to do now, thank you. Come back in a couple of days. I should have at least one of them done by then! Go on! See you later!! Bye!!"

Lark found herself very quickly out on the street, Nightingale on her shoulder and twittering confusedly. She laughed. "Never you mind," she cooed, stroking the bird's back to calm him. "Things are looking skyward."

No sooner had she spoken than someone across the street pointed to the sky and yelled. Lark looked up, saw the sun high above, but nothing out of the ordinary. Everyone stopped to stare, shielding their eyes against the glare of a sun that seemed to be coming closer. She took a breath, noticed something musty and acrid in the air. Magic. Slowly, as the 'sun' changed its course and began to fall, she realized that this was not the sun at all but a ball of fire, and it was not alone.

Several of them rained down upon the city. People fled every which way in terror. Lark ran for the nearest impact site, a couple of blocks beyond the shops. It was a house that was on fire; a nice, two-story building with a bakery on the lower floor and the roof of the living quarters in flames. There were already people lining up with buckets towards the nearest well, hauling water to douse the fire before it could spread. A watchman who happened to be on the site, trying to calm the panicked crowd, had his hands full with the baker's wife, who was screeching about her 'boodle' that was still inside.

Lark came over to her and took her off the grateful man's hands, leaving him to handle the rest of the crowd and coordinate the fire line. "What is inside? Nothing cannot replace," she said, trying to calm her. "Are alive, yes? What are things to Life?"

The woman grabbed Lark in her meaty hands. "My boodle can't be replaced!" she screamed.

From the upstairs window came a child's plaintive cry. Lark looked up as the woman screamed, "My **boodle**! Somebody save my boodle!"

Lark immediately began whipping up a poltergeist. Nightingale flew up to the level of the window, not too close, but near enough to try and see the child inside. He helped her to guide the poltergeist into the room to pick up the child screaming at the top of her lungs on the bed.

Feeling herself being lifted up by invisible hands, the child began to scream even louder, which convinced her mother that she was burning to death. It was all the watchman could do to keep her from running into the house. Lark ignored all of this and concentrated on getting the child safely out of the narrow opening. She was only half-out when the roof collapsed, was struck by part of the window frame as the entire wall fell inward. Lark set her down, checking her out quickly. The girl had only been scraped and bruised. The baker's wife ripped her out of her grasp, cooing and crying and hugging.

Lark then turned to helping those fighting the fire. She wove a minor spell, evaporating the water from the buckets and the well, ignoring the startled and despairing shouts from the men and women passing the pails. Within seconds, it began to rain in a very directed, wholly unnatural way.

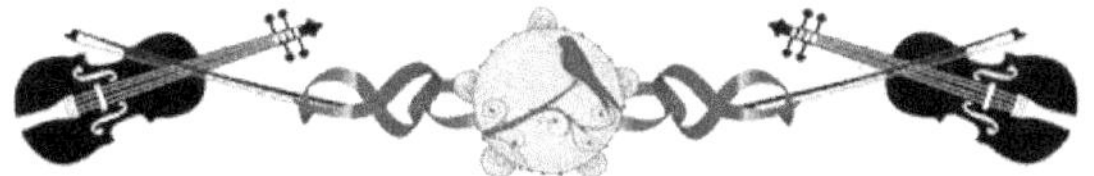

The temple was bustling, filled with the wounded and dying. Landros had known there had been an attempt on the north wall the night before, but he had not heard that it had been this bad. Lithgorin's brother was taken from them immediately, carried into the belly of the temple with Adrick limping after him. The others were shuffled out to the rear courtyard for triage. Acolytes bustled about carrying bandages and ointments, assessing the wounded for severity, healing those within their power, and passing off those with greater needs.

He, Lithgorin, and Barak were set down on the stone edge of a raised garden and asked to wait out of the way. Landros looked around, wrinkled his nose at the smell. The air was sick with the smell of burnt flesh.

"Looks like a fireball attack," Barak muttered, flexing his arm as the feeling started to return.

"Where've you been?" a woman snapped. She was sitting in the shade across from them with her back against another of the raised gardens. Her injuries had already been tended. The left side of her face glistened with ointment, and her hands were thickly bandaged. She was dressed in the worn, black robes of a lower priestess of the Crone, but as the cloth was not singed or burnt, Landros assumed they had been loaned to her in lieu of her own. She did not look like a crone, though she was older.

"What happened?" he asked, mostly to keep his mind off the searing pain in his shoulder and the ringing in his head.

"Fireballs. We lost count how many. They hit several different sections of town. Damned ingenious of them to attack close to noon so that the arch of fire would not be readily noticed. They seemed to come out of the sun. A lot of people were hit before they were really aware of what was happening." She shifted her position, shook her head. "You boys look like you've been in a fight. I'd offer to help, but..." she held up her white bandage mittens.

"It's all right," Barak said. "We'll live. I've had worse myself."

She closed her eyes a moment as if dozing in the sun. She gasped suddenly, opened her eyes, and stared at Lithgorin. "I'm sorry," she said.

At that moment, Adrick drifted out into the yard, limping still, his arm thick with dried blood, looking for them. "Lith...." he began, seeing them.

Lithgorin stood, looked from his friend's face to that of the woman across from him. Neither of them would meet his gaze. "No," he moaned, tore past Adrick, and ran into the temple, dodging startled acolytes as he ran.

Adrick hung his head as he came over. He saw the woman with them, nodded to her in deference as she rose and shuffled off. "There was nothing we could do," he managed.

"Ah, man!" Barak muttered. "Lith's gotta feel like hell."

"Who was that woman, and how did she know...." Landros demanded.

Adrick put his hand on Landros's good shoulder and sat him down. "She belongs to the Old One. That is one of her gifts, the comforting of the living."

"Comforting?" Barak asked. "I would not call that comforting."

The fire was out and the remains under control when Lark finally sat down on the curb of the street and took a breather. The fire had spread to the next house over before the rooftops were wet enough to prevent it, but thankfully, no one was seriously hurt.

The watchman crossed to her. "You the one who started the rain?" he asked.

She just nodded.

"Don't know how, and I'm not gonna ask. But thank you. Lives might have been lost if you hadn't," he said quickly and left, back to whatever duty called to him.

"Nice work," came a voice from behind her. Lark looked up and saw Ebastion Shadowfalk standing over her.

"Thank you," she smiled. "Have seat," she offered.

"Nah," he said, leaning back against a lamppost. "But thanks. Lark, this is my friend Lula."

The woman was a bit taller than her and very robust. She wore leather pants and a tight-fitting leather jerkin, high boots, and soft leather gloves. She was not particularly attractive, with tanned skin and autumn hair drawn back from a narrow face, but she was very striking.

"Ah, yes, you told me about her," she said, extending her hand to Lark. "And for the record, my name is Lulelani, not Lula."

Lark took the hand and allowed the woman to pull her to her feet. Lula gestured at the still-smoking building. "Your handiwork?" she asked.

"Rain, not fire."

"Oh, I wouldn't have suggested such a thing," she said rather charmingly. "Would you care to walk with us? I am sure you would like some fresher air than the smell of wet ash."

"Thank you." Lark walked with them, not caring where, just glad to be away from the burned zone.

"Are you alright?" Ebastion asked.

"*Sesha*," she sighed, smiling. "Just bit tired. Was long shower, hard to keep in place. Wind kept trying to blow elsewhere. Will be fine. So, tell me, what have been up to?"

"Oh, this and that," Ebastion shrugged. "Though I hear you've been busy. Saving Keltree's miserable hide again?"

Lula slapped his chest. The look that passed between the two told Lark that Lula more than likely had a sweet spot for Keltree Danhaven and that Ebastion just loved teasing her about it.

Lark laughed softly. "Yes. Word get around, *sesket*?"

Nightingale landed on her shoulder, peeped a brief hello to Ebastion, and began chittering at Lark.

"Oh, how lovely!" Lula exclaimed. "What's the matter?" she asked when Lark frowned as she listened to the bird.

"Is something ahead, wrong."

"Like what?" Ebastion asked. "Is he ever direct?"

"Like ...man in trouble. Blood, bad-winded... just...."

A man staggered around the corner ahead of them, grabbed at everyone who passed him closely enough, muttering almost unintelligibly. He was a dark-skinned Northman, and his clothes were bloody and torn. He had been in a fight, and recently. One where magic had been used. As he turned towards them, they saw a fresh, ugly slash congealing across his face, beginning from his right cheek and slicing across his nose and left eye.

"Never ends, does it Lula?" Ebastion sighed with a grin, drawing his blade.

The man staggered up to them. "Yes, yes," he hissed from the side of his torn, swollen mouth. "You have blades, you know trouble. You help poor Vanishti? Please, come quick, come fast! Kill them all they will!"

Ebastion took one arm as Lula hooked the other, turning him back the way he had come. "Who kill who and where? What happened to you?"

"Ambush," he hissed. "Yes, they not drunk. Were mad, snarling demons from frozen pits! Killed so many! Dying! Save them! You must have mercy! Help us! My brothers... they have my brothers...."

"Where?!" Lark growled, beginning to lose her patience with the man.

"I'll pay you!"

"To hell with money!" she snarled. "Where is trouble?!"

"Lark, you are worn out," Ebastion frowned. "You don't have to come."

"Have seen me heal," she said. "Maybe can do again if need to. Still have tricks up sleeves. Now where?!"

"This way! This way!" he mumbled, turned and started to shuffle off. He found his progress stopped by a burly man with a bare sword tucked in his belt.

"Trouble, ladies?" he asked. "Sir?"

"Yes, would you care to add your weapons to ours?" Lula asked.

He looked the shriveled, black man over, then the three of them, and nodded. "Looks like you could use it, judging from the looks of him."

"You come too? Rewards enough for all! Pay well if you help. Please come! This way!"

They followed him three blocks without another word passing between them. He led them down a short alley into a warehouse-like structure that had seen much better days. He opened a side door and gestured them to follow him in. "In here, quick quick!"

Lark made certain that her sand pouch was within easy reach and drew her dagger, instructing her familiar to remain outside, out of danger. Lula drew a fancy-hilted rapier and a small baton which she gripped tightly in her left hand. The two men charged in first.

The warehouse was dark, mostly empty, with only a few broken crates on the far wall, into the shadows of which their guide promptly disappeared. Lark activated her pendant, and light filled the immediate area but still left the majority of the room in deep shadows.

They started to follow Vanishti towards the crates, keeping their eyes on the shadows around them, when something ahead of them moved. The shadows began to shuffle and shift, and the small group found themselves shortly surrounded by a loose circle of battered and bloody fighters.

"We are here to help," Lula said cautiously. "Vanishti?" she called.

Lark backed up against the large man, secretly grabbing a handful of sand. She waited, waving her dagger ineffectively, like a helpless and frightened girl who had no idea how to use the thing.

A hooded figure appeared near the wall of crates. "Welcome, friends." The voice was neither clearly male nor female. The hands were gloved, to hide even that tell-tale sign.

"Where is Vanishti?!" Ebastion demanded. "He said there was help needed, people dying!"

"And there are," the figure said in a saddened voice. Lark could not tell if the sadness was sincere or not, being unable to see the face. "Everywhere. In the city about you. The enemy has no desire to burn this town to the ground, but the Lord Mayor would rather the town be destroyed utterly and the earth salted than surrender it. Greed, my friends, greed. If you would but side with us, aid us in our need, or simply not interfere, this siege would be quickly ended, and food would be brought in to feed the starving. No one else needs to die."

Silence.

"If patriotism does not stir your hearts, harder currencies can be arranged...."

'Treachery,' Lark thought. Perhaps this is what became of Ashanda and those others who had disappeared. 'Landros should know about this.' She sent Nightingale to find him, or Colwyn, ... someone, ...anyone.

Ebastion hefted his sword, "I may be for hire by anyone with enough money, but I am not a traitor," he snarled.

"Even when the currency is your life?" the figure asked.

"I have nothing if I have not my honor," he spat.

"Does this go for your friends as well?"

Ebastion looked at Lula. She gave only a minute shake of her head and tightened her grip on her sword. He looked at Lark, was met by her stony glare and fierce expression. He looked up at the new man, whose name they did not know. "Friend?" he asked.

The man did not look back at him, but kept his back against Lark's and his sword between them and the ring of enemies. "I stand with you," was all he said.

"How sad," the figure mused. "Kill them. And do it right this time."

Lark threw her handful of sand in an arc, catching the three men in front of her in the spray of dazzling light. Two of them went down, but the third lurched forward drunkenly, swinging his sword blindly, not caring what he hit, friend or foe. Lark easily ducked out of his way, and the other man with her turned and engaged him, finishing him in time to fend off another attacker from a different direction.

Lark darted in, burying her dagger deep in someone's thigh. Enraged, he struck her aside with his fist. She hung on to the dagger, ripping it out of his leg as she fell. She got up and darted for the shadows, forgetting for a moment that she was the source of light until the shadows retreated from her.

Thinking quickly, she broke the chain and threw the necklace into the fray, diving into the safety of the dark. She tried to think, to come up with some minor magic that could help them that she still had the strength to wield. She fervently wished she still had her scimitar. At least then, she would be able to stand in there and fight with the others.

Pulling together a poltergeist, she used it to gather up the bits of debris from the broken crates and add to the fray, trying to create ghostly images wielding the boards as a scare tactic. But the ghosts faded out before they had truly winked in, and the poltergeists were ripped out of her control. Suddenly, there was a gloved hand on her shoulder, jerking her back, and a sharp pain between her shoulder-blades. She turned, saw the hooded figure standing behind her. The pain stayed with her, making it hard to breathe.

Remembering the homunculus and the glassed floor, she panicked. She swung wildly with her dagger, but her arm would not obey her properly and the blow missed completely. The 'ghosts' she had tried to conjure returned, became more than illusion, battering her one way and then another, pushing her towards the wall.

She stumbled against things in the dark: crates, unidentified statues of plaster, a broken barrel. She fought the glowing shadows, slicing into them with her magic blade. Eventually, she began to make headway, to change her panic into usable rage. Behind her, she heard the sounds of her comrades fighting still.

Beyond the conjured phantoms, she could see the shadowed figure, feel the eyes upon her. The gloved hand raised, reached towards her, and pulled back. It was a gesture she knew well, a maneuver for controlling a poltergeist. A sudden, swift stinging erupted all over her back, followed by sounds not unlike that of knives being punched into the rind of a ripe melon. The pain blossomed and spread until it consumed her totally. The ghosts began to dim, though she could still feel them around her, pushing, clawing. And then nothing....

Nightingale had left the instant Lark had told him to go and get help. He knew *who* to look for but had no idea *where* to look. He flew towards the temple, remembering the priestess there, thinking maybe she might know or be able to help. He could feel Lark's panic and fear, flew as fast as he could. A distant pain made him stall momentarily, and he lost a few feet of altitude. He flew faster, spurred on by a near-complete panic that was not his own.

As he sailed down over the courtyard where lots of people were milling, he gave his distress call as loudly as he could. The wolf whistle cut off sharply as he felt something strike his mistress, something which caused her to fall and broke his conscious link with her. Stunned, he stopped flapping and fell.

THREE

Landros was finally submitting to healing, allowing his wounds to be bound, and the bleeding stopped, but only after Barak had been tended.

He heard something nearby, turned, saw nothing of interest, and looked back over at the large man. "It kills me that we have no way of identifying the mage," he growled.

"I'm sure he'll be around," Adrick sighed. "We have not seen the last of him, or her, or …whatever."

"Oh, look!" they heard just a few yards away. "The poor thing!"

Landros turned, saw a young woman reach into a flowerbed and carefully pull out a small, injured bird. The priestess tending to the woman leaned over to look, clucking her tongue at the creature. "That's a mockingbird, isn't it?" asked the priestess.

Landros felt a sudden surge of fear. Lark's familiar was a mockingbird. "Nightingale?" he called, pushing Adrick aside and muscled his way over.

"No, I'm pretty sure that's a mockingbird," the priestess answered.

Adrick growled at him to hold still, tried to keep up with him to tie off the bandage.

The bird, hearing a familiar voice calling his name, began to wake up and struggled in the grip of the woman. "Oh!" she exclaimed as he wriggled out of her grasp and flew awkwardly to the shirtless elf charging at her.

Landros caught the him with his open hands. He was in near hysterics, giving a wolf whistle over and over, maniacally. "Can you fly?" he asked. The bird jumped from his hand into the air, waited as Landros went back to his friends, picked up and unsheathed his swords, tossing the scabbards aside, and started to follow. The bandage on his arm still flapping behind him like a grisly pennant.

"Landros, where are you going?" Barak yelled.

"Lark's in trouble!" he shouted without stopping. "Grab your sword, and come on!"

"That man is going to get himself killed one of these days," Adrick snarled. "Come on, he's going to need help," he added to Barak, taking off after his friend, swearing in Elvish under his breath.

Landros practically ran the entire distance, slowing down only to dodge pedestrians in the streets. He tried not to think about what he was charging into. When he did, he found himself thinking all sorts of horrible things that he might find. Lark had to be alive, or her familiar would have reacted, possibly even died himself. He had heard of such things happening. Though, thinking about it, his falling out of the sky into the flowerbed....

He kept his eyes on the bird ahead of him and tried to focus on nothing else. When he darted down a side alley, he felt his heart jump with dread. They could not possibly have had time to proposition her and lure her into the same trap! It had taken him the better part of three days to solicit that invitation.

When the bird stopped outside a door, Landros did not pause or think; he just kicked it in. He found himself in a practically empty warehouse. There was a single circle of light, partially dimmed by the bodies surrounding it. There were only five people still standing: two burly mercenaries, one of which was holding up another unarmed man, and a pair of shadowed figures in the back. As he stepped into the room, the unarmed man spat at the one holding him up and was promptly run through. As the body fell onto the pile of corpses, the light fell on the killer's face, and Landros knew him. The man from the alley with the axe. The one who had killed Ashanda.

Landros gave a roar of rage and charged blindly into the room, unaware of Adrick and Barak backing him up. There was not much of a fight. The two mercenaries had been battered and wounded in two battles in less than three hours and did not have much fight left in them, though the axe man did manage to further wound him.

The two shadowed figures had disappeared.

Adrick's voice cut through his battle rage with three words he had not wanted to hear. "She's not here."

He looked down at the bodies, shoved them aside until he produced the light pendant laying on the floor. The chain was broken. Desperate, he began to toss aside the bodies of the mercenaries, checking each one for signs of life, looking for someone alive enough to find out where Lark was or had been taken. There were only the mercenaries they had encountered before and two men and a woman he did not know. All of them were dead. He looked down at the wrist in his hand whose pulse he had been seeking and saw a flash of gold on the third finger. He opened the palm to expose the band, saw the worn etching of a falcon, and his blood began to boil.

There came a squawk of feathered rage from the shadows. Barak drew his sword again and began to look around blindly. Landros picked his up from the floor as he saw a shadow moving in the darkness. He stalked over with the light dangling from his hand. Vanishti was there, hunched over a prone figure in ragged calico. Rusty nails crunched underfoot. The man looked up, his one good eye glaring whitely in his black face. He had a gold earring in his hand, tendrils of long black hair still clinging to it. Nightingale had hold of the earring and was fighting to get it back. Landros glared at him, said nothing, tried not to look at the still figure at his feet.

"Did not... did not wish this," Vanishti stammered, letting go of the bauble and backing away. "No, did not wish this!"

Landros tightened his grip on his sword. "Take it up with the Crone," he said and opened the man's throat with one swift stroke.

He dropped the weapon, unable to feel much of anything any-more except a cold emptiness inside as he fell to his knees beside Lark. The bird dropped the earring by her cheek and watched her sadly. Landros laid a hesitant hand on the back of her red shirt, re-alized as he did so that the fabric had been dyed in blood. He felt something hard and prickly under his hand, looked closer. Her en-tire back, from nape to calf, was studded with rusty iron nails! Numbness was replaced by rage, and he began to rip the nails out.

Barak caught his hand and stopped him.

"Let go of me," Landros growled in a low, choked voice.

"Didn't Adrick teach you anything?" the large man asked him. "Never pull the blade out! It's what keeps you from bleeding to death!"

"She's already dead, you simpleton!" he snarled, yanked his hand free and returned to his grisly chore.

"Adrick!" Barak yelled. "Stop him!"

The priest came over, having done all that could be done for the others. He ignored the two struggling men, bent, moved her hair, and touched two fingers to her neck. He looked up at him. "Her heart is still beating, though erratically. Landros, stop what you are doing and think."

The elf looked blankly at him. "She's alive?" Hope sprang like a light inside him.

"She's fluctuating in between. She's holding on but only just, like a candle sputtering in a draft." He closed his eyes and prayed, pouring what strength remained him into sustaining her for a little longer. Finally, he stood, exhausted. "Get her to the temple and quickly."

Landros immediately tried to turn her to lift her in his arms, and once again, Barak stopped him.

"Over your shoulder, simpleton," he said with a faint smile to show that he was not angry with him.

"Otherwise, you just drive the nails in farther," Adrick added.

Between the three of them, they got her draped over his shoul-ders in short order. "You sure you won't let me carry her?" Barak asked.

Landros did not answer him; just picked up his swords and walked out of the warehouse with the mockingbird in tow, daring anyone or anything to get in his way.

Adrick sighed and followed. "Barak, stay here and guard the bodies. In case our 'friends' decide to come back and get rid of them, or someone takes a fancy to strip them before we can find out who they were. I'll send the Servants of the Old One as soon as I get there."

Barak nodded and turned to try and sort out the bodies, laying each one out as neatly as he could.

Landros was not gentle as he stormed in the nearest door of the temple. Anyone who did not move out of his way quickly enough was roughed aside. Acolytes scattered as he tried to approach them, demanding a healer at once. A group of the older Acolytes tried to prevent him from proceeding further into the temple in search of one, as they all seemed to have disappeared. He turned in a circle, demanding one, then another to heal her, but none of them had the skill. He began to threaten.

He noticed blood on the floor and followed the trail in a circle until he realized it was dripping from her foot. He knelt, set her so that she was on her knees, leaning up against him. The acolytes just stared in horror, to his frustration and confusion.

"Will someone get me a healer!" he bellowed.

Adrick finally pushed his way through. He had been unable to keep up with his companion, having lost him in the crowd milling outside. He began giving orders immediately, not that anyone was really listening. A moment later, Rue arrived from deeper within the complex, led by the mockingbird.

She covered her mouth and crossed her fingers as she gasped at the sight of them. Both of them were soaked in blood. She recovered quickly, took a closer look at the severity and nature of Lark's wounds, and grabbed the nearest person. "Go get Mother," she said in a low voice. She pointed at two of the stronger-looking acolytes,

"You two, help me get her to surgery! You, take this man to one of the upper cells and get him some medical attention!"

Lark was taken from him and carried, face down, between the two men out of the room. Someone else gestured for him to follow him. Landros went reluctantly, all the while trying to maintain a glimpse of where they were taking her. He could not think of his own wounds, just Lark lying still in a pool of her own blood, long, wicked nails spiking her slim frame.

He sat down in the chair without thinking or realizing where he was. He was desperately trying to figure out what could have happened in that warehouse and who the man with the ring had been.

A pulling and sharp pain in his shoulder drew his attention. He looked up and saw the priest undoing the bandages covering his wound, pushed him away. "Leave me alone," he snarled.

He got up, began pacing the tiny cell. The priest tried again to tend to him, speaking to him in soothing tones. Landros grabbed a sword and held him at bay. "I said, leave me alone," he said slowly and deliberately.

"You are bleeding," the man said. "Rue said I was to give you medical attention. I am not your enemy. I am your friend."

Landros, still blinded with rage, grief, and worry, did not budge. "I will not be touched until I know that Lark is alive and well," he growled. "You should be in there helping her, not tending me!"

"Now you are just being stupid," the priest snapped, losing his patience.

Landros was not willing to hear him, and so he did not. He might as well have been speaking a foreign tongue. All Landros wanted right now was Lark alive and healed and answers to his questions, like: what happened to her, how Vanishti was connected in all this, and why the thought of her death made his heart stop and his breath fall short. What *did* she mean to him? More importantly, what did he mean to her? He was certain she was only still in the city because she could not get out with her wagon. What would happen when the siege ended? Would she leave without another passing thought? Or would he haunt her as she haunted him?

There were voices in the room with him. Voices he did not recognize. "He won't let me near him and…."

Landros turned and saw the little priest in the company of a young elven woman. She was beautiful and frail-seeming, with flowing golden hair and eyes like pale diamonds. She could not have been more than eighty. Before Landros could say anything, she spoke Elvish in a commanding tone he found no reason to disobey. *"Look at me."*

He looked into her eyes and found himself trapped by them, lost in a dream of unicorn meadows and fey groves. Distantly, he heard her voice again. "Now heal him," she said. But she was not talking to him.

There was someone else in the meadow with him, a gorgeous, dark woman dancing naked in the sunlight. He was entranced by her, by her laughter and ease with herself. She did not seem to notice him but continued to dance like a smoke genie conjured for the entertainment of small crowds. He knew her from somewhere but could not think clearly enough to place her. He felt himself growing sleepy and remembered a half-buried warning his mother had once given him about going to sleep in fey places.

The elven woman before him sighed, broke the contact, and left him blinking, docile, in the chair as the priest stepped back. For the first time, he noticed there was blood marring her creamy cheek, and her pale-blue gown was hopelessly stained. Her hair was heavy with sweat, hanging lank, and she looked tired. "Feel better?" she asked, not without some sarcasm.

Landros found he could only nod. Yes, he did feel better. And clean; he felt cleaner than he had.

She nodded to the priest. "You can leave him now. There are others who could use your attention if you have the strength remaining. I, myself, do not. Take care, elf," she said to Landros. "The next time someone offers you healing, take it. You will do your dark dancer no good if you are half-dead when she needs you most."

She left the room without a sound, not even the swish of her robes against her legs. Landros looked around him in confusion, realized he half-naked. There was a basin on the table beside him filled with bloody water and darker cloths. He had been washed, partly. He felt tired and calm. Whatever that woman had done to him had drained all the rage and fury out of him. His mind still in a cloud, he tried to put his sword away and found he had no scabbard. He remembered suddenly that he had left his things out in the courtyard. He got up, left the small cell, and found his way there.

The courtyard was not so thick with people now, and many, freshly bandaged and able to walk, were being let out of the back gate. Some pressed coins into the palms of the clergy seeing them off, some heartfelt thanks and promises of restitutions when times were better.

His things were where he had left them, along with Barak and Lith's packs. The woman with the bandaged hands was still about, talking quietly with people. He bent, pulled out a clean shirt, and struggled to don it with the heavy bandage on his arm. It was not easy. He did not remember his shoulder hurting so much when he had carried Lark all the way back to the temple.

He was strangely calm, thick, as if he were walking through a fog of sleep. Not quite sure what else to do, he sat down, uncertain whether or not he was waiting for something or someone. He looked up the woman with the bandaged hands sat down beside him.

"You saved a life," she said.

"I think I may have been the one to endanger it," he managed.

"Oh?" she asked, smoothing the wrinkles of her robe with her useless paws. "How so, do you figure?"

"I did not kill them when I had the chance. Didn't kill the black man with the gray hat. If I had, she would not have been ambushed, led into the same trap."

"Your head is still not clear from Maid Jeliana."

He looked at her blankly. "How..."

"I've been told," she said, shrugging off the question. "Besides, I've seen that look in the eyes before. The Temple's Maiden has the snake's gaze. She does not use it often. Why would you not permit yourself to be healed?"

"I don't know. I lose my head sometimes. In the heat of battle, I can't think; I lose control."

"Why?"

"I don't know," he said.

She sighed. "Lie to me if you want, but don't lie to yourself."

Landros felt a stirring inside but was still too fuzzy to feel real anger. "What is wrong with me?" he moaned, holding his head.

She put her arm around his shoulders. "You will come out of it soon. Maid Jeliana felt it the only way to get you healed. You are not the first to try to punish yourself for your perceived failures by refusing healing. It never does any good. Now, just keep your head about you; I think there is news for you."

He looked up and saw Rue crossing the small courtyard to him with Nightingale perched on her shoulder. He stood. "What news?"

"She is well. Come, I will take you to her." She took him gently by the arm and began to lead him back inside. She nodded her head towards the woman. "Thank you, Grandmother," she said.

"Don't worry it, Daughter," she said, getting up and wandering to another part of the garden.

"Grandmother?" Landros asked as they stepped into the cooler interior of the temple. "That was your...?"

Rue smiled, too tired to laugh. "No, she is a Servant of the Old One. All such servants are called Grandmother, Grandfather, as I am referred to as Daughter and Sister, or the Matron's women are called Mother. It is all relative, and we are all related in the scheme of things."

Landros's head was fuzzy indeed, not to have sussed that out for himself. He supposed it came from having encountered few of the Crone's priesthood, whilst the Mother and the Maid's clergy were in every walk of life.

Rue led him to a quiet room lined wall to wall with beds, and every one of them filled. Lark was on a cot on the far side of the room. She was lying on her stomach, her dark skin and black hair in stark contrast to the white of sheet and pillow. Her hair had been washed and braided, and she was dressed in the simple, sleeveless white shift of an acolyte.

Her dark eyes remained closed as he knelt beside the bed. He lightly touched her cheek and relaxed as she sighed softly, though she did not wake up. "Is it... is it all right if I stay here for a while?" he asked Rue. "I won't get in the way."

"No," she answered. "Neither of you can stay." He looked up at her. "We need the bed. There are others who are still waiting for healing and will have to wait until we have rested and restored ourselves. I've even sent Keltree to his brother's house. I need you to take her home and make sure she gets at least three days of rest before she tries to do anything strenuous. I want you to rest, too."

Landros nodded, understanding. Lark was healed, no longer needed a healer's specific attention, and he had no doubt that there would soon be others in greater need than she was now. He got up off the floor, pulled the sheet back, and started to pick her up. Pain lanced through his arm and shoulder, making him cry out in surprise. Rue just glared at him with her arms crossed.

"Are you quite through being the gallant hero?" she snapped.

"No," he growled back. Tried to figure out how he could carry her without causing either of them further pain.

"Do you remember why Keltree ended up back here, two inches from dead?"

He just growled, feeling helpless and weak and hating it.

Rue turned and called one of the other priests over. "Brother, are you busy?"

"No, Sister," he replied. "What do you need?"

"I need you to help this man get this young lady home. He is too injured to carry her, and I fear that if I do not get someone to tend to the matter personally, he will find a way to try and do himself more harm."

"Gladly, Sister," he said, lifting Lark easily from the bed. "I will welcome the chance for a little air."

"Thank you," she sighed. "Oh, and don't pay any mind to his rudeness. He's bound to be sulky." She reached under the bed and pulled out a small, locked box, which she opened with a tiny key from her belt and removed a pouch and a dagger. She closed the box and slid it back. She gave Landros the pouch and the blade. "Here, this is everything she had on her but the opal ring, which is still on her for obvious reasons. Her clothes had to be cut off, I'm afraid."

It hit him like a charging bull then, what he had been told about that ring and it keeping her body and soul together. Feeling thoroughly chagrined, he tucked the dagger in his belt and mumbled something in the way of thanks as he started past her. She caught him by the arm, held him back a moment.

"Landros," she said, hesitated, lowered her voice. "You saved her life, you know. Bringing her in when you did, about the ring, I mean. If you hadn't, she might have died, or he might have taken her over. Today might have gone very differently. Either way we would have lost her."

Landros nodded numbly, put the pouch in his bag, and tossed his pack over his good shoulder. Nightingale flew after them.

"So where are we going?" the priest asked kindly.

"The Golden Cygnet," he answered, sullen.

"Nice place. Didn't the owner used to be an adventurer of some sort?" he asked.

Landros was not in the mood for small talk. "I don't know. Never stopped to ask."

The priest began to get the picture and fell silent, much to his relief. He was in no mood for kindness.

Outside, the priest waved down a wagoner just coming around from the Old One's side of the temple. The man stopped. "Whacha need, Brother Ferin?" he asked.

"Just a ride, if you got the time?"

"Hop in," he shrugged. "I just made my delivery. I'm free for the time being."

Landros climbed into the wagon first, insisted on taking Lark into his own lap for the ride. The priest nodded after a moment, though he made certain that he held her in such a way that she did not put a further strain on his shoulder.

Landros held her close to him and stroked her cheek softly, tracing the invisible lines the homunculus had made weeks before. There was no sign of them now, but he could not help but wonder if all the trouble she seemed to keep getting into was somehow his fault. Everyone kept telling him that he had saved her life, that he should not feel guilt over her near-death, but he could not stop blaming himself.

It took the better part of an hour to get to the inn with the wagon. The priest, Ferin, jumped off first and tried to take Lark from him. He resisted.

The man sighed. "Don't make me have to carry you both in," he said quietly. "Sister Rue would not like that at all."

Landros reluctantly allowed him to take her, grabbed their things, and led him inside. Opening the door to his apartments on an upper floor, he instructed the priest to put her on the bed in the back room. One of the servants of the inn came running up and called to him before he could close the door. "What?" he demanded.

The young man was out of breath, panted, "The master wants to know if you need anything ...for you or the woman."

"No, but thank you," he said, turning.

"A bath drawn? Food, wine? Anything?"

"No. I'll send..." He glanced into the room and saw the bird flitting in through the window. "If a small bird shows up in the kitchen, send someone up to me at once."

"A bird, sir?" he asked.

"A mockingbird. He'll be quite friendly. Now I have to go," he said.

"Very good, sir," the man said and trotted back downstairs.

Landros closed the door and went immediately into the bedroom. Sometimes the staff here was far too eager to please, he thought. Lark was already tucked into the huge bed, lying on her stomach with the covers drawn up to her shoulders. The priest was busy building a fire. Landros grumbled, moved him aside, and began rearranging the logs.

"If you stack them this way," he said testily, "they burn longer and put off more steady heat. The other way, it puts off too much heat and burns too fast."

The man sat back on his heels. "I did not know that. Thank you," he said with genuine politeness. "Keep her warm and comfortable. When she wakes up, she may want something to drink." He got up, set a small bottle on the little reading table next to the bed. "If there is pain, for you or her, administer a small dose of this in some water or wine to keep it manageable. And keep her in bed for at least a couple of days. After that, she can start walking around in short intervals."

"You can be certain of that," he said, lighting the fire. Once it was fully ignited and he could feel the heat seeping into the room, he stood and shook the man's hand. "I am sorry I was short, I... I am deeply concerned for her."

"And for that reason alone, you are forgiven," he smiled, giving him a clap on his good arm. "I entered the priesthood to escape my temper, and so far, I have found a peace I never could have had. Well, you get some rest yourself, friend. I have to get back."

The priest left, and Landros went to the bed, made sure for himself that she was sleeping comfortably. He pulled her braid out from under her and laid it over her shoulder, fussing really just for the sake of doing something.

He could feel exhaustion creeping through him as the fire began to heat the room. Reaching back, he grabbed his collar, and pulled his shirt off over his head. His left arm felt stiff. The was not the first time he had taken a serious wound to that shoulder, nor the second even. Perhaps there was some flaw in his fighting skill that left that shoulder vulnerable. He would have to ask Colwyn later. He had a report to give after all, but later, after he had rested. He had put in a very long morning.

Peeling his pants off, he realized that they were covered in drying blood and decided it was time to wash the rest of him. The priest who had healed him had washed his chest out of necessity, but he was still bloody and dirty. He went into the watercloset, poured water from the pitcher into the basin, and looked at himself in the small steel mirror. The reflection shocked him. It was no wonder the servant had offered to draw a bath.

His hair was matted with dried blood, and his face was still dirty, except for a small area where he had received a minor cut. His legs were a rusty color, a blend of dirt and blood. He could only imagine what he had looked like before the priest had washed him. It was no wonder the acolytes had stared in horror at the two of them.

He made a mental note not to use that particular temple door again. It seemed, in retrospect, to have been some kind of dormitory.

He took a cloth from the edge of the tub and began to wash. Leaving the soap still lathered on his legs, he plunged his head into the basin, flinching at the chill of the water, and scrubbed the blood from his hair and face. Satisfied he was clean enough, he stepped into the tub and poured the rest of the water to wash away the suds, trying to keep his bandages from getting wet. He grabbed a towel and dried himself off.

With just the towel wrapped around his hips, he went back into the bedroom, fetching a nightshirt from his dresser and struggling into it. There came a chittering from the other room, a scratching on the bedroom door, which startled Nightingale. The bird hopped onto the bedpost, taking up a guarding position with his wings half-opened. Landros imagined that, to anything of similar or smaller size, it was quite a threatening gesture, but to him it was almost laughable.

He opened the door, looked down, and saw Scraps sitting up, nibbling on a piece of withered fruit, himself covered in soot. The raccoon looked up as the door opened, chattered at him, and offered him a bite.

"No, thank you," he said, opening the door wider. "Have you been hiding in the chimney again?" he asked as the raccoon trotted over to the hearth and shook himself, sat eating his prize. "One of these days, I'm going to light a fire under you," he warned. The raccoon just looked at him and licked his paws as the fruit disappeared. "You're right, you'd just shimmy up the flue and out onto the roof, find another way in, and give me what for," he sighed, tossed the towel over the back of the rocking chair to dry by the fire.

Scraps climbed up onto the little table, stuck his paws into the water pitcher and washed them and his face. Putting too much weight on the edge, it tipped over, spilling all over him, washing off the rest of the soot in the process. Landros laughed quietly, tossed his towel over the surprised little beast, and began to rub him dry.

Scraps put up with the rough buffing for only a few minutes, then wiggled free.

Landros let him go and bent to mop up the spilled water. Shaking himself, Scraps trotted towards the bed, intent on making himself at home. Landros saw him out of the corner of his eye and managed to snatch him out of the air just as he leaped for the mattress. He struggled, not exactly happy with the situation. Landros shushed him softly, took him to the bedside, and showed him why he had his leap arrested. "See?" he whispered. "I don't want you to wake her up. All right?"

He set him down gently on the bed next to her, watching as the raccoon sniffed her carefully before curling up beside her. Landros again laid the now soaked towel on the back of the rocker and, moving the raccoon over, carefully crawled into the bed next to her, trying not to disturb her. She sighed and shifted as she felt his approaching warmth. She reached over to him, traded the pillow for his body, and slipped deeper into sleep.

He was afraid to move. She had nestled her head in the crook of his good shoulder and draped her arm over his chest. He just lay there for a few minutes, needing to shift himself but not wanting to disturb her again. Little by little, he eased himself into a better position, pulled the pillow under his head, and made himself as comfortable as he could. He let his arm gently drape across her back, holding her close.

He drifted to sleep watching the firelight sparkling off the surface of her opal ring.

FOUR

Lark felt very warm and secure when she woke. There was a sense of comfort she was unaccustomed to, and she supposed that alien feeling was what woke her. Her whole back, from shoulders to thighs, was stiff and aching; every inch of muscle was tightly clenched. Her throat felt dry and sore, her head heavy. Something under her moved. She opened her eyes, realized why she felt so warm and comfortable and smiled.

"Good morning, Princess," he said.

She stretched, trying to relieve some of her stiffness. "Is morning?" she asked hoarsely.

"Probably not."

She directed a question at her familiar and rolled her eyes at his response. "Is always supper time!" she chuckled. "Says is evening."

"How are you feeling?" he asked, rubbing her back.

"Stiff. Sore. Thirsty."

"Would you like some water?" he asked, getting up.

"*Se'vah.*"

He got up and went into the front room for the pitcher that still had clean water. Lark felt something warm and furry brush against her feet and lifted the covers. Scraps grinned up at her, trotted over to say hello, and beg for some attention. Landros brought her a cup of water and helped her sit up to drink it. "I see someone has made himself comfortable," he commented dryly.

Outed, the raccoon wandered off the bed and disappeared. Landros set the cup aside when she finished and settled on the bed again, his back against the headboard, holding her. "*Ellinoia*," he began, burning to have his questions answered but not certain it was the right time to ask them.

"Yes?" she asked, snuggling up to him when he did not continue.

"Do you want something to eat?"

She shook her head minutely. "Not now."

He tenderly brushed loose strands from her face.

Lark realized something was very different about her hair; she did not feel its weight and warmth flowing over her shoulders and back. She ran her hand along the back of her head, feeling for the length of it, and found the braid, pulled it around so that she could see it.

"What is the matter?" he asked, noting her confusion.

"Never worn hair like this. Is... feel strange."

"I suppose it keeps it from getting tangled while they work," he muttered. "Lark," he began again.

She looked up into his troubled eyes. "What?" she asked softly. "What is wrong?"

"I hate to ask, but I have to." He stroked her cheek softly. "If you are up to it?"

"Up to what?"

"Telling me what happened."

She laid her head down on his chest and clung to him.

He rubbed her arm, held her tightly, "Hey, you don't have to tell me now if you can't, but I do eventually have to know."

She sighed and stared blindly into the fire, trying to put it into words somehow without running it visually through her mind, to be detached enough not to panic or anger him. "Went to dressmaker's today. Leaving there, fireball come. I stop to help with house on fire, made rain. Ran into old friend after and we walked. There was Northman, badly wounded and stinking of spent magic begging anyone who would listen for help, promising money, whatever we wanted if we would help his friends. He muttered on about ambush and men like maddened devils, that they had his brothers. No one would listen. We said we would go, and he led us down alley to warehouse. There was man there... I think. Could have been woman, hard to tell, wore hood and gloves. Even by voice was not certain of gender."

Landros stiffened, felt a chill in the room in spite of the fire. How could they have moved so quickly? Had this warehouse been a secondary site? Did they switch back and forth, or even to a third location, to keep from being observed, followed, or ambushed?

"Hood offered us opportunity to help him. When we refused, he ordered us killed, said something about 'get right this time.' That was when sent Nightingale to find you. I think this might be how Ashanda and other missing were killed," she added, looking up at him. "Is making sense."

He nodded. "I know that already. Go on."

She drew a deep breath, let it out slowly. "We were surrounded. Had only dagger and without sword am little good in fight. Was too close to cast effective, so slip into shadows. Threw pendant into fight, to give friends light and me shadows to hide in. No sooner I call up poltergeist, but I felt them ripped from my control. That was when felt dagger, I think, in back. I turn, saw hood behind me, controlling *my* poltergeists, attacking me with them. I could see fight going badly for others but could not help. Can only guess what they must think of me, fleeing fight, think I abandoned. I need to get away from fight, to have room to use magic and not hit friends." She choked back the tears threatening her, refusing to allow them voice. She could explain to them what happened, what she was trying to do, when she was well enough to see them. "I felt something, lot of somethings hit me from behind, and that was last thing I know."

Landros felt his heart tighten uncomfortably, did not want to have to tell her, but there was no way around it. She would not thank him for lying to her. "Lark, I need to know who those people with you were."

She thought about that before she said anything. Why would he have to ask her? Why wait until she was healed and awake if all he had to do was ask them? Unless he could not ask them. She sat up, not caring how much it hurt, and looked at him, trying to find the answers to her fears in his amber eyes. She found them. "I am... only... one?" she stammered, feeling her blood go cold.

Landros sat up, held her tightly as her arms began to tremble, unable or unwilling to hold her own weight. Lark was in complete shock, unable to breathe, to think. He knew survivor's guilt, knew that was what she had to be feeling. She drew a sudden, ragged breath. Nightingale hopped off the bedpost onto her knee and piped his concern. She breathed slow and deep, getting herself under control, stroked the bird's breast feathers softly. He rubbed his tiny head against her finger and made a sad little noise.

"Man was Ebastion Shadowfalk," she said without looking up at him. "Was with Keltree, Rue and I on Evandair. Killed vampire, ...well, body at least. Woman was named Lulelani. Was friend of Ebastion. Only met her few minutes before, was with him. ...Think Keltree knew her, or she knew Keltree. Might ask him."

"What about the other man?" he asked softly.

She looked up, "What other... oh! Him. Him I did not know. When Vashinti, or whatever name was, came to us and began leading us away, this man came up, thought perhaps black-skinned man was trouble for us. He looked fright. Asked if was trouble, Lulelani tell him yes, and would he like to help? So, he come with us to die. Never told us his name. There was not time."

"Damn it!" he swore, banging his head against the headboard in frustration.

"What is?" she asked, brushing his cheek with the back of her hand. "What is so important about this man's name?"

"He was a Falcon," he breathed, "a full knight. That is what is so important about his name. I have to report his death and I do not even know who to say has died."

Lark winced as she pulled her sore muscles, trying to sit up to comfort him. "Lot of people have died in last few days. Lot more will die and many nameless. We cannot save them all. *You* cannot save them all."

He took her hands from his face and held them in his own. "I am upsetting you," he moaned. "You need to rest. I... I have things I have to do."

He started to get out of the bed.

"What, now? Is nightfall," she protested, grabbing hold of his left shoulder to hold him back. She pulled back with a squeal when he flinched, giving a low shout.

He stood, turned to face her, holding his arm and trying to get his pain under control.

She grabbed his open shirt front and pulled it back far enough to see the bandage on his shoulder. "Are wounded," she gasped. "How... Rescuing me?" No, she thought, not more blood on my head!

"No," he groaned. "I.... Remember last night I told you I had some things to do? That I was close to finding out what was going on and why so many freelance adventurers had disappeared?"

"I remember conversation," she nodded.

"Well, I got into it this morning. The black-skinned man, that Northman with the torn-up face you met. That was Vanishti, a one-time companion of Ashanda, and that cut on his face was my doing. It turns out he betrayed Ashanda and sold her out for his own life. These men have been luring freelancers in and then petitioning them with promises of money, glory, whatever it takes to get them to turn coat. If they refuse, they die. There is no telling how many have taken the promises offered."

He began to pace. "Maybe I should have accepted," he muttered. "Gotten myself in and used that to discover who they had corrupted and how deep they have gone. Maybe found out just what the enemy is up to. We turned them down and they nearly killed us. If Adrick hadn't teleported us out...."

"Adrick teleport....?" she asked, incredulous. "Did not know Adrick could...."

"Apparently, neither did he," he mused. "He prayed for a miracle, and well... he got one. I took a shoulder hit. Adrick took some minor damage. Barak nearly lost his arm, and I don't think Lithgorin was too severely hurt. Which is more than I can say for his brother."

"Lith has brother?"

"Not anymore," he sighed, sitting down on the edge of the bed. He buried his head in his hands. "There has been so much blood lost already! If Adrick had not been so divinely inspired, there might have been no one to come to your rescue, princess. They outnumbered us two to one easily. How many men were there who attacked you?"

She rested her chin on his good shoulder and wrapped her arms around him from behind. "Five or six. Maybe more, I was little busy."

"Yeah," he snorted angrily. "Busy getting stabbed in the back." He covered her hands with his, relishing the feel of her so close, so caring. "Something has to give, Illyana. Somewhere the storm is going to break. I only hope that whatever is keeping the king does not keep him long. Or there may not be a city left to save."

"What do you suppose is keeping him?" she asked.

"The Goddess only knows. It would have to be serious, I am sure. Maybe another army? I don't know. With no news coming in.... The whole country could be at war for all that we know! All we have is what the Andromeda's captain told me, which isn't much."

Lark pulled him backward, laid him across her lap, and brushed his hair from his eyes. "Then what does any of this matter?" she asked. "All we have is now. What will be will be no matter what we do, and war, king, yes, even your precious Lord Colwyn can wait for sunrise. You need your rest, and I am not willing to let you go. At least not for few more hours."

Landros sighed, closed his eyes, and savored the soft stroking of her cool hands on his brow. It was so easy to just fall into her embrace and get lost there forever. "I really should head over to...." Lark bent forward and pressed a soft kiss to his lips, inadvertently pressing her breasts against his forehead, smothering him in her musky warmth. He gave a quiet moan. "Maybe I do hurt too much just now," he mumbled, reaching up to deepen the kiss.

She stiffened suddenly, held her breath. He let go and immediately slid out from under her. "What's wrong?"

She let the breath out slowly, took another deep one, and repeated the process. She shook her head. "Just... sore. Getting stiff," she said. It was more than that, but there was no sense in worrying him. It would pass. Even now, she could feel the spasm letting go, her muscles relaxing a little. "Am fine," she said, sitting up straight again, smiling intentionally.

"Do you think you could eat something now?" he asked her, kissing her fingers.

"Maybe little bit. Nothing heavy, would make sick," she groaned.

He kissed her fingers again. "I'll be right back," he said. He fetched the magic blanket from its cabinet and spread it on the floor in front of the fire. Scraps ran over and sat just off the edge, watching eagerly, rubbing his paws together as he waited. Landros concentrated on the kind of food he wanted and spoke the command word. A large bowl of a rich broth appeared, with a loaf of still-steaming bread and a large hunk of sharp cheese. There was a pitcher of mulled wine and a bowl of crawfish and apples. Landros was somewhat startled. When a pair of black paws snaked out and seized the nearest crawfish, he was even more so.

"What?" Lark giggled from the bed. "You look surprised."

"I did not ask for crawfish ...or apples," he answered, watching the raccoon run into a warm corner with his prize.

"You think maybe he did?" she laughed.

"I said before I do not understand the magic completely," he said, shaking his head. He got up and began carrying the food to the small table by the bed, dragging the chair over beside it. Lark sat on her knees with the sheet draped over her lap and accepted the mug of broth that he poured for her.

The two of them ate quietly and shared the meager bounty with the animals. Lark laughed softly as she watched the raccoon holding his apple up for the bird to pick the seeds out. She watched Landros watch the animals, lovingly memorizing his face, his expression. He seemed at peace right now. 'Ironic', she thought, 'that it takes nearly killing him to get him to unwind.'

She gasped as her back suddenly seized up, every muscle tightening.

Landros turned his head sharply to look at her and felt a pull from his shoulder as he did. "What? Princess, are you all right?!" he asked, tossing the heel of his bread on the table and grabbing hold of her to keep her from tumbling forward off the bed.

She let her breath out slowly, unfolded herself, and laid down. She pulled the pillow down to her instead of crawling up to it, digging her claws into it. "Hurts," she mumbled into the feather pillow. "So tight..." she gasped.

Next to him, on the table, he heard a dull clatter and turned to see the bird sitting with one claw on the over-turned bottle of medicine that Brother Ferin had left for them. He looked back at Lark and took her hand in his. "I think we both could use some of that," he admitted reluctantly. He picked up the bottle, made a face as he uncorked it. He hated this sort of thing, medicinal herbs, and drugs which fuddled the mind, but he could not stand to see her in so much pain, and the priest had left it here in the belief it would be needed.

He poured a few measured drops of it into half a mug of the wine and helped her to sit up enough to drink it. "Come on," he said. "It will help. Help you relax."

She drank it slowly. Laid back down. He set the cup back on the table. "It might take a few minutes to work," he said, hating, as well, this feeling of helplessness.

She barely nodded. "If like laud'num, will not take but moment," she wheezed.

For lack of anything else to do, he began to wrap the remains of the bread and the cheese in a cloth for later, put the empty bowl of broth back onto the blanket, and banished it. He shook it out and put it away.

He checked on her again. She was still tense, clenched almost into a complete ball, breathing spasticly. "You have to let go," he said. "If you want the muscles to relax..."

"Is not... me," she gasped. "Is muscle not relax."

He sighed and thought for a moment. Then, he remembered something, had an idea that might help her. He went into the watercloset, opening the small cabinet where the towels and soaps were kept, looking for a bottle he remembered having seen there, something his brother had left. He found it pushed towards the back, lying, forgotten, on its side. Grabbing it, he brought the bottle into the bedroom, setting it on the hearth to warm up. He then crossed to the bed, pulled back the covers, and laid a large towel down beside her. "Come on," he said, helping her over onto the towel, "On your belly."

"What, why...?" she moaned, not helping, but not resisting either. He began to pull her shift up, trying to get it off, over her head. "Lover, is not time for...." she protested. Her muscles were tightening up further, reacting to the pain, making it worse.

"Relax, my princess. It is not what you think." He stopped for a moment and looked into her dark eyes. "Trust me," he said softly, managed to get her on the towel, undressed, and returned to the hearth for the bottle. Pouring the warmed oil into his hand, he rubbed his hands together to further heat it, then climbed up onto the bed, straddling her hips. He then began to massage the oil into her shoulders in long, slow, deep strokes.

She gave a sudden, shuddering moan that had nothing to do with pain and slowly began to feel the tension let go. He worked his way down her back, trying to conserve his strength, to be gentle on her as well as himself. The oil made it much easier on both of them, letting his hands glide across her muscles without having to exert too much pressure, which might have done more damage than good.

She could feel the knots beginning to release as he rubbed, the muscles to stop complaining so loudly. The oil smelled strongly of juniper and wintergreen, and she began to feel a cool burn across her shoulders where the oil was drying. "What is...?" she moaned, surrendering completely to his ministrations.

"It's something my brother left here once. Something he swears by for getting a woman relaxed and... well..." he felt his face beginning to flush. "...ready," he finished. "I thought it would help the tightness, ease the pain. I'm not hurting you, am I?" he asked.

"No," she murmured.

He had his doubts, though. She was moaning an awful lot. He moved back as he rubbed, working his way slowly down to her thighs. There were small red spots all over her, evidence of where the nails had been, though the wounds had closed. By tomorrow, he knew the marks would be gone. In the middle of her back, just under her left shoulder blade, was a thin red line, no more than an inch or two long, a blade mark. Judging from its placement, the assassin knew the human body and where to place a blade to keep a victim from screaming. He should have hit her lung, but there was a chance that Lark had moved just in time, that the blade had slid in sideways, missing the intended target.

He finished the massage without being as thorough as he would have liked. His shoulder was beginning to ache again. He leaned forward and kissed her cheek softly. She was already asleep. He got off the bed, drew the covers up over her. He paused at mid-back, examining the small knife scar before covering her up completely.

He stood and mimed stabbing her there. From what he remembered, the hooded figure was a little bit taller than himself and, therefore, taller than Lark, so it had to be an upward stab. He tried it with both hands, imagining her standing in front of him. It felt awkward making a right-handed strike to her left blade, felt more natural, and therefore more likely, to go right with a right-handed attack. So, the hooded person was left-handed. That made things a little easier. Not many people were.

Well, it was a start, he thought. He checked on her again, made certain she was warm enough and sleeping soundly. He was restless himself, not ready to go back to bed. He figured she would probably sleep until morning, which meant he had time, if he felt up to it, to go to Colwyn's and make his report.

He only thought twice about it before he shrugged off his nightshirt and pulled clean clothes on. Scraps climbed up on the bed, sat up, and called attention to himself. Landros looked at him as he tucked his shirt in. "Yes, I am going out. Now, are you going to stay here tonight and keep an eye on her?" he asked in a low voice, indicating the sleeping girl, "Or do you want to come with me to Colwyn's and scruff around in the woods?"

The raccoon gave a soft chirr and crawled under the blankets. "Fine," he sighed. "Suit yourself. I swear you are as bad as Portholus about beautiful women." He put his cloak on and paused to have a word with the mockingbird. "I don't know how much you understand," he said softly, "but keep an eye on her. If anything happens, or she needs anything, go down to the kitchen, and someone will come up. If it is an emergency, I will be at Colwyn's, where the wagon is. You can find me there." He stroked the soft breast. "I just hope you understand enough," he said and left the room quietly.

FIVE

Landros slipped quietly past the watchmen in the streets, encountering no one the whole way to Colwyn's house. He snuck through the side gate and up to the manor, where he knocked on the kitchen door. The scullery let him in, greasy from head to toe from scrubbing the supper pots. It was not long before he was led up to the study, where his lord was pouring over maps and comparing them to reports.

Colwyn looked up. "Ah, come in, come in! Had you been an hour earlier, you could have had supper with me. Would you care for something to drink? Brandy? Wine?"

"No, thank you, my lord." He crossed to the desk, glanced over the papers spread on the surface, and then politely looked away.

"It is good to see you in one piece. I was beginning to wonder, what with all that happened today," he said, clapping him on his shoulder. Landros, of course, buckled almost instantly under the heavy hand. Colwyn grabbed for him immediately and set him down in the nearest chair. "What? You've been hurt? I'm sorry, man! I really... If I had known...."

"It's alright, my lord. It's alright. Just... let me get my breath," he gasped. "You have a hand that could damage a whole man, much less a wounded one," he chuckled. "Of course, it did not help that you picked the shoulder everyone seems to be favoring lately. Which is a matter I will take up with you later."

"Yes, you will," Colwyn said, pressing a glass of brandy into his hand whether he wanted it or not. "First, however, you are going to tell me what happened to you and what you found out this morning. I know *something* happened."

Landros did not even question how his lord had known. He just watched the man pour himself a glass and sit down across from him, waiting with infinite patience.

"We've got problems, my lord," he began. "Problems that might be more dangerous than the fireballs this past noon or the breach of the north wall last night."

"Do tell," he prompted.

Landros filled him in on the fruits of the last few days of skulking around Bayside. All the way up to everything he could remember about the fight in the alley and the people involved. Lord Colwyn was silent through the whole dialogue, studying the swirling brandy in his glass.

"And that is not the worst of it, sir," he added. He waited until the knight raised his eyes to meet his. "The worst of it is: how many people have survived this trap? Vanishti is probably the most obvious of the lot. The others will be difficult to find. And I fear the city has been seeded with traitors, beginning with who this damned mage is!"

"Any ideas?"

Landros shook his head, took a hard swallow of the brandy, and savored the smooth burn of it down the back of his throat. It had to have been the first unadulterated alcohol he'd tasted in a month that didn't come from his little white jug. "Not a clue. I don't even know whether it's male or female. All I do know is that they are about a head taller than I and left-handed."

Colwyn stopped in the midst of drinking and raised an eyebrow over the rim of his glass. "Left-handed? How are you sure?"

Landros rolled the glass between his gloved hands and studied the dark amber liquid, getting his emotions under control before trusting himself to speak. "Lark... was lured into a similar trap by

Vanishti, who is dead now, I will add, and encountered the survivors of this morning's battle."

Colwyn leaned forward, "When did this happen?" he asked.

"While we were at the Temple licking our wounds and mourning our dead. She was stabbed from behind by this hooded mage, and judging from the placement of the wound, this person not only had to be left-handed but also knew exactly what he or she was doing. I think the blade missed her lung only because she moved."

"She would never have even screamed," Colwyn finished with a nod. "This is a problem. I am sorry she had to get caught up in this mess. How is she?"

"Sleeping. Her familiar found me at the temple at about the time she was taken down. I barely got there in time. There... were three people with her," he added, hesitant. "One of them she knew, the second by association with the first, and the third... a man they met while being led into the trap who offered assistance. Lark said the man never gave his name."

"And these three are dead?" Colwyn assumed, leaning back.

Landros nodded. "The third man was a Falcon."

The lord's glass shattered in his hand. He got up quickly, began mopping at his pants and the spill with a handkerchief, tossing the largest pieces of glass into the ash bucket. "Are you certain?" he asked when he had regained his composure.

He nodded again, staring into his brandy. "He was wearing a gold knight's ring, fairly worn. ...Unless he stole it or it somehow ended up in his hands. But, from Lark's description of his behavior, I doubt that."

Colwyn rested his elbow on the mantle and scratching his chin with his thumb, thinking. "I'll go up to the House of the Old One tomorrow and see if I can identify the body. If he was local, I'll know him. I'll stop in and talk to Lark as well while I'm there. See what else she remembers. She is in the Maiden's House with the other wounded, I assume?"

"No," he answered, draining the glass and setting it aside. "She is at my apartments. They took her into surgery immediately. As I said, I barely got to her in time. Since she had been given healing, and they needed the beds for those who had not, they asked me to take her home. So, I did."

"So, what are you doing here?" he asked.

"Giving my report. As I said, she is sleeping. I gave her some of the medicine they gave me for her pain. She dropped right off."

"This could still have waited until morning." He moved to sit at the desk and ran his hands through his hair. "Go on home, take care of her. Rest yourself. You are no good to anyone if you can't take even a little jostling. We will need to find these other men, though, as soon as you are up to it. Before they kill or turn anyone else."

Landros got out of the chair and swept his cloak over his shoulders. "You can stop in and see them in the Hall of the Dead as well, my lord. Lark's friends and this unnamed Falcon all but finished what the five of us had not been able to this morning. Barak and I finished off the last two when we arrived."

Colwyn sighed, gave a tired smile. "Landros, you are going to have to learn to leave some of these men alive for questioning," he said, propping his head on his fist. "Now go home and get some rest. That's an order. The war can wait until morning. I'll send for you if I need you."

He nodded, gave a short bow as he left and wandered out to Lark's wagon, glad that she was now in the habit of not locking it. It meant she felt safe here. He sighed; it was just when she left the protection of these walls that she was in danger, but there was no way he could keep her here. To lock her up within these walls would destroy her, and he knew it. That was not worth her life. Even he had to admit that.

He lit the lantern on the hook outside, and went in, looked for a change of clothes. All that he could find was her new blue dress. He looked everywhere, but there was nothing. Not even a spare blouse. He began to wish he had commissioned more than just the four dresses. Taking down her pack, he checked inside it, but it was empty. He folded the dress up and put it into the bag. Then, he took her violin down in case she felt like playing to keep herself from going crazy. He did not think playing the fiddle would be too strenuous.

Stuffing everything into her bag, he slung it over his good shoulder and headed back to his rooms at the inn.

As he approached the front door of the Cygnet, he saw the figure of a young woman in a hooded cloak also headed for the door. He opened it and held it for her. She paused, laughed, and dropped her hood. "Fancy meeting you here," Rue smiled.

"Rue?!" he exclaimed, began looking around for the mockingbird who he thought had to have brought her. "Is there something wrong?"

"No, you paranoid goose. Come on, it's cold out here," she said and went inside. He followed, began to lead her up to his room. "I just got up, and, since things were relatively calm right now, I thought I would stop by and check up on the pair of you. Bring you something for pain if you need it. I see, however, that you are well enough to be out and about," she said, not without some sarcasm, which he chose to ignore.

"I had errands to run. I am home for the duration now," he said, reaching for his key.

She gestured to the patchwork bag on his shoulder, "Getting Lark some of her own things to wear? What, my hand-me-downs are not good enough for her?" she teased.

"Humph," he said. "That explains why the shift is a little long and a little narrow."

She chuckled. "It is good that I ran into you, though," she added. "I knew you had rooms here, but I did not know which. Brother Ferin could not remember, so I trusted the Maiden to lead me. I did not expect her to send me a guide." Her eyes twinkled as he unlocked the door and held it for her.

Rue admired the small apartments.

"It's not much, but it suits my needs more than adequately," he said, setting Lark's pack down on the couch.

"It's cozy," she murmured. "So, who's first? You or Lark?"

"Lark, if you don't mind waking her up," he said.

"Oh, I probably won't need to do that," she smiled, following him into the bedroom.

Scraps sat up as the door opened. Landros turned to tend the fire as Rue went to the bed, whispered a hello to the raccoon, and pulled the covers back from the patient.

"Oh, merciful Maiden," Landros heard her gasp behind him.

He turned. "What?"

She stepped aside. He crossed to the bed and looked down at Lark's still form. Her back was covered in dark red spots and tiny, yellowish striations. "What the hells...!" he began. "They were not this bad when I left her just over an hour ago."

"What was not this bad?" she demanded.

"The scars, the wounds. They were just small pink marks. She was having muscle cramps, or something. Said her back was tight. And it was. I gave her a back rub with this," he said, handing her the bottle of oil. "She fell asleep before I was finished."

"Muscle spasms?" she asked. There was no color in her face at all.

He put a hand on Lark's back, not comfortable with Rue's reaction. She was burning up.

"Landros, there were no marks on her body when she left surgery. We healed everything external."

Panic began rising again, followed by an anger with no focus. "Then what in the name of the Three is wrong with her?"

"Move," she said, snapping out of her shock, pushing him gently out of the way and laying her hands on Lark's back. Scraps watched, confused, as she closed her eyes and prayed, placed his paws on Lark, too. Rue's hands began to glow with a cold blue light.

Landros paced, worrying. He looked around the room, hunting for the familiar. He found him watching from the windowsill, pressed against the closed shutters where it was cooler. He did not look well. He picked him up and cradled him in his hands, using him as a focus for his attention to keep from venting his frustration physically.

Rue stood, moving frantically.

"What, what is it?" he demanded.

"She's been poisoned," she answered as she ripped the blankets from the bed, took her medallion off, and laid it on her back.

He grabbed her arm. "What do you mean she's been poisoned?" Nightingale protested as he inadvertently pressed too hard. He lightened his grip. "How? When?" he demanded.

"I don't know. The knife she was stabbed with was probably poisoned, or the nails. This looks like the nails."

"The knife? Nails? Then how the hells didn't you catch that when you were healing her?" he snarled.

Rue jerked her arm away and snarled back. "Healing is not a general art! You don't just lay hands on and pray, and the hurt goes away! There has to be skill and knowledge in the application! I have to know what is wrong with her before I can fix it, and we were not looking for poison! We were concerned with keeping her alive, getting the nails out cleanly, and preventing infections from the rust! Now, if you will let me alone long enough, I will get to work!" She turned from him and wet a rag in what little was left the water pitcher. She wrung it out, tossed Lark's braid out of the way, and laid the cloth on the back of her neck.

Landros stood watching from the foot of the bed, one hand clutching the bird to him, the other clinging, white-knuckled, to the bedpost.

"Landros," she said, laying her hands on either side of the medallion. "This is going to take some time. I would suggest you take the animals into the other room and do something constructive. Have a bath brought up."

Landros hesitated, not wanting to leave, but there was something in Rue's tone that told him she did not want him here. Rather than possibly distract her from her work, he coaxed the raccoon into his arms and carried both creatures into the other room.

He set the animals on the sofa, making sure that the bird was comfortable on a pillow, and went downstairs to order the bath water. The servants nodded and said that the water would be heated immediately. Landros got a bottle of wine from the taproom and headed back up. No one got in his way. He sat down in the chair by the unlit fireplace, poured a glass of the wine, and sat with it in his hands, not drinking.

He stared for a long time up at the Elven sword over the mantle, tried to take comfort in its history and heritage, tried to tell himself that she was only human, that her life was but a blink of his and her death, whether today, tomorrow, or fifty years from now, was inevitable and something he could not change. But he was not listening. Every reason he gave himself for not caring what was happening in the other room, he shot down with very little reason and pure, blind emotion. The answer was simple. If she left, the hole he felt inside him right now at the thought that he might be losing her would eventually swallow him whole.

She was a wanderer; he knew that. Not knowing how she felt about him exactly, he did not know if she would not be wandering off again no sooner the siege was over. He felt better now that she was staying at Colwyn's. At least then, even if he did not see her he would know that she had not just wandered off again like the last time. Still, even that uncertainty was far better than her dying. Too many had died already, too many trying to protect her, and she herself had saved so many more. Her death he would not permit.

He started to get up, to pace again and found himself dislodging the raccoon. He did not remember the critter climbing onto his lap. Scraps gave a surprised screech as he hit the floor, gave him a dirty look, and crawled into the fireplace and up the chimney. "I'm sorry," he called. Scraps did not respond. Landros sighed, resisting the temptation to go into the other room to check up on the women.

He sat at the desk instead and penned a short letter to Lily, telling her not to worry but that Lark had been seriously hurt and was in his care for a few days. He folded the note and carefully sealed it.

He looked towards the bedroom door.

Still no sound. He sighed, wrote a letter to Colwyn informing him of the recent revelations regarding the attack on Lark. Colwyn had told him how to word these letters, how to address them in such a way as to let a Falcon know that the contents were Order related without it being obvious to the uninitiated, as well as teaching him how to recognize when a letter was penned in full code. He was not to be taught the full code until he received his gold ring and jesses.

He heard a noise in the other room. He knocked his chair over in his haste and opened the door to see Rue sinking into the rocking chair. Scraps was on the bed, snooping at the unmoving form on the bed. "Rue? Everything...."

She looked up at him as if she had not just heard him charging in. "Fine. Everything is fine. I need something... to drink," she said weakly.

He went back into the other room, brought her the glass of wine.

She took it in trembling hands and sipped it slowly. "Thank you," she sighed.

Landros went to the window and closed the shutter. Apparently, that had been the noise he had heard: Scraps breaking in. The animal looked innocently up at him, chittered in his direction, and rolled over, begging for a tummy rub. He had no doubt learned that little trick from Landros's brother.

He covered Lark up with the blankets. There were no signs of her injuries on her dark, creamy skin now. He brushed the back of his hand across her cheek.

She stirred, felt the touch, and opened her eyes. She looked up at him and smiled softly. "Mmm, felt good," she sighed, stretching. "Thank you."

A knock on the front door called his attention before he could comment. He gave her a quick kiss and went to let the water bearers in.

Lark sat up, realized suddenly there was someone else in the room, and covered herself. "Rue?" she asked. "Did not hear you come in."

Rue smiled. "Quiet as a mouse, I am."

"Are alright?" she said. "Look exhausted."

"Oh, I am fine, my dear," she breathed. "Just a little tired. I will be myself again in a few minutes."

"Why are you here?" Lark wondered aloud, snatching up the shift on the floor by the bed and slipping into it.

"Oh, just checking up on you two."

There was something about the way she was smiling that gave the impression she was keeping something to herself which amused her. Lark got up, poured some wine for herself and, sat down on the hearth, stirred the fire.

"You really should not be out of bed, dear," Rue said gently.

She shrugged. "Why? Feel fine. You need rest. Cannot keep going without rest and expect to not fall over."

"I slept this afternoon," she protested mildly. "Just after Landros brought you here. I got up about an hour ago to check up on you."

Lark drank from her glass, thinking. "Do not look like just woke up."

She sighed, set the chair rocking. "You do not remember what happened after the back rub?" she asked.

There was something in her eyes that told Lark there was a point to the question. Something that reminded her of her Gruma, asking questions she already knew the answers to.

She shook her head. "Nothing happened. He rubbed back, and then you were here, though do not remember when you came in."

"You must have fallen asleep on him."

"Is possible," she shrugged, stretching, feeling the tension ease out of her. "Is felt so good."

"You were poisoned, Lark," Rue said bluntly.

She almost choked on the wine, coughed until she could breathe right again. "Poison? How?" Her eyes darted to the little bottle on the nightstand. "He gave some of that," she said, indicating the medicine. "Was this the...."

"No," Rue shook her head. "We just missed it. I think the dagger you were stabbed with was poisoned, or the nails. Something subtle."

"Rue," Landros said from the door. "I want this man... woman... whatever. I want this person in a real bad way."

"I can understand," she said. She got up, set her glass aside. "I should get back. There are others who will be needing my services. I just stopped by to check up on you two and to bring you this," she added, pulling a small, leather-bound book out of the medicinal bag at her hip. She handed it to Lark. "I thought you might need something to keep you from going back to work before you should. You can give it back to me whenever you finish it. It's not like I am going to have time to do much reading in the near future." She did not wait for a response and drifted out of the room.

Landros saw her to the door.

"I want you to rest as well, now," she warned, fastening her cloak around her shoulders.

"For a day or so," he agreed. "I won't promise any more than that."

"Go on," she said. "The bath is getting cold."

Landros closed the door behind her, went into the tiny chamber, lit several candles on the washstand, and then tested the water. It was not too hot. He went back into the bedroom for Lark.

She was sitting on the hearth still, idly scratching the raccoon's belly as she leafed through the pages. He walked over to her, gently took the book from her hands, and set it on the rocking chair. She looked up quizzically. Drawing her to her feet, he led her to the bath.

She took a deep breath of air and exhaled with anticipation. Steam curled enticingly off the surface of the water. She leaned back against his chest, tilted her head up at him. "You are joining, yes?" she purred.

"If you insist," he sighed with mock resignation. He perked up when she smiled and gave her a soft kiss. "That's what I want to see."

His hands began to lift her shift, intent on pulling it over her head. She gave him a sly look. "Thought Rue say no strenuous exercise?"

"Oh, there won't be," he answered, succeeding in divesting her of the garment.

She pouted.

He took a deep breath, feeling an ache inside at the expression. He gently touched a finger to her lips. "Princess, neither you nor I are up to that at the moment. Though later... later. I did make you a promise last night. Now, get into the water before I have to pick you up and hurt myself again."

End Book One

SNEAK PEEK AT BOOK TWO

SAGAVIS

ONE

Landros was sitting on the sofa in the front room, oiling his leather armor, salvaging the damaged shoulder, and trying to figure out a way to put more protection there without reducing his mobility.

Lark drifted in, slid her arms around him from behind, and kissed his cheek. She took a deep breath. "Mmm," she sighed. "Always loved smell of leather. Especially new leather."

He leaned back, kissed her, and noticed that she had put on the blue dress he had brought for her from her wagon, the one he had bought her less than a week ago. She had not worn more than the borrowed shift from the temple or one of his shirts for the three days she had been here. She had also put on her jewelry. "Going?" he asked, feeling an uncomfortable pull inside at the thought.

"Have things to be doing, life to lead," she said softly, letting go and coming around to stand in front of him. She set her pack down for a moment. "Is not like will not see me. Know where I live. ...And where I work."

"I know," he sighed. He had known that before. It still had not kept her from disappearing on him. But, to think about it, how much of that was his fault? She had not known where to find him, and he had known exactly where to find her. He pulled her down into his lap, his hands resting on the Romeri's ample hips. "Are you sure you are up to working again?"

She touched the tip of his nose with a playful finger, "Are you not also ready to *do* instead of sitting about?"

He had to admit that she was right; he had known this day was not long in coming and had not really expected to be able to hold her here. He reached down to the floor on the side of the sofa, felt for the sword belt he had lain there. Catching hold of it, he handed her the short sword and scabbard. "Here, I want you to take this. I noticed you have not replaced your scimitar yet, from the fight with the succubus, and this will.... What?" he asked as she gently pushed it back at him, shaking her head.

"This blade is useless to me. Do not know how to use. Thank you, but.... have looked for scimitar, even sabre would do, though not so well. But all swords are sold to army and blade-smiths have no time to forge special. I... I will have my brother get one for me when I see him next."

"And when will that be?"

She shrugged.

He took her hand. "No, that is not good enough. You said yourself that you might have stood a better chance in the warehouse if you had had a sword. I do agree that if you have never used a short sword, your knowledge of the scimitar will hurt you. But you cannot go about, especially not at night as you must, without something. There are monsters in the streets now. I've been hearing from the servants here that almost every night, something strange is reported, some mythical creature or well-known monster. It is more dangerous than ever out there."

"But is nothing to be done...." she protested.

"Not true," he said. He set the sword aside and wrapped his arms around her. "I know someone. He... collects things. The more unusual, the more he likes it. An exotic blade like a scimitar is something he just might have. Would you wait at least, until I can set up a meeting?"

She shook her head. "Have errands to run and boy to teach fiddle. Is daylight," she said consolingly. "Is not so dangerous now."

He thought for a moment and decided not to say anything about the fireballs or the warehouse incident that nearly killed her occurring in full daylight. She knew that fact as well as he did. "When will you be done with Dane?" he asked.

"Should start just after lunch is over and inn quiet. Maybe hour or so."

"I'll meet you there. Then, you and I will go to my friend's and find you a scimitar. Do you have anything unusual to trade for one? If you don't, I might."

She smiled, thanked him for the offer. "I think can find something." She slid off his lap. "Now, be good boy. Will see you then," she said, giving him a deep kiss.

Landros watched her gather her things and head out the door. Sighing, he went back to his armor and tried to rub her from his mind for the time being.

It felt good to finally be out and about. She took her time, strolling towards the temple mostly oblivious to her surroundings and the darker moods around her. Smiling at people, she hummed a soft little tune she had been tinkering with off and on for a year or more; did not even notice the strange looks she received for her cheerfulness.

The temple was her first stop. She went into the Maiden's House and asked the first person she saw where she might find Sister Rue. She was taken to a small cell, where she was asked to wait. Before the acolyte could close the door, she asked if it might be left open. The young man shrugged but did as she asked. Lark did not feel comfortable with the door closed. It was too much like a prison cell to her than the spartan waiting/meeting room that it was.

Rue was not too long in coming. She looked much more rested than she had the last time Lark had seen her. They hugged fondly. "How are you feeling, dear?" she asked, sat down beside her.

"Better, many thanks to you and Landros." She reached down into her pack. "Brought book back. Thank you. Is wonderful. Many of stories had not heard before."

Rue took the volume, smiling, caressed the leather cover fondly. "My mother gave this to me when I told her I planned to enter the priesthood."

Lark laughed, "Book of love stories is hardly gift for one taking vow of chastity."

Rue nodded wryly. "I think that was the point. My mother had 'plans' for me in the marriage department, I think. She was trying to talk me out of it."

"I see she failed," she commented.

"Good thing, too. The man she wanted me to marry has, well… the wife he did take has been here several times already for 'household' injuries. I somehow doubt that she is that clumsy," Rue said quietly. She took a deep breath, brushing all the gloom aside. "So much for true love, eh? No, I am quite happy here. This is where I belong. And if the Maiden *does* choose to send me a lover, then I will simply move next door. I hope you enjoyed the book?"

"Yes. Is well-read, I notice."

"That it is," she mused fondly.

"Was wondering," Lark began. "Is possible to see Keltree a moment?"

The priestess nodded. "Certainly, and I am sure he would love to see you, but he has gone to his brother's house. Tell you what, I am going to stop by tomorrow. I go every few days just to make sure he's not doing anything stupid and is *actually* resting. Why don't you meet me here after noon tomorrow, and I'll take you with me?"

"Oh, would love that! Have been wondering how had fared." She got up and shouldered her pack, now lighter for the lack of the book. "Oh, has been any luck discovering who was other man with Ebastion and Lulelani?"

Rue shook her head silently.

Lark sighed. "This bothers Landros. Which bothers me. Is obsessed with this; that, and hooded person." She snapped quickly back into her cheerful mode and again gave the half-elven woman a hug. "See you tomorrow noon!"

Rue sat back and watched the Romeri girl practically bounce out of the cell. "Too much energy in that girl," she sighed. "Could certainly use some of that vivaciousness around here," she added, getting up and moving back to her rounds of patients.

Landros heard the doorknob turn and looked up, hoping to see Lark breezing back in. The black-clad figure of his brother banished that hope, and he sullenly went back to work.

"I am surprised to see you actually here, brother," Portholus said. "I had expected you to be out and about on some secret mission again."

"Not this time." He set his armor aside and began putting his tools away. "Where have you been the last few days?"

"Oh, here and there," he mused evasively. "You know me." He slipped into the watercloset for a few minutes.

Landros went to the desk, grabbed a piece of paper, and jotted a quick note to his friend that he would be stopping by the shop that afternoon looking for a special item. He blew on the paper until the ink dried and folded it carefully. Tucking it into his pocket, he began gathering his things together, preparing to pay a visit to Colwyn to ask a few questions that had occurred to him.

He saw his brother leaning against the doorframe with his brush in one hand, pulling long black hairs from it with the other. He looked pointedly up at him, asking the question without saying a word.

Landros crossed over, took the tool from him, and put it back where it belonged. He wordlessly went back to packing.

Portholus continued to stand there, smirking in his irritating way. Landros did his best to ignore him.

"So, *why* is there long, silky, black hair in your brush?"

"Maybe because she borrowed it while she was here," he answered, trying to keep his temper in check. "I did not know you were so concerned about my grooming habits." He did not like being teased about Lark, especially by his little brother.

"She? No name, just 'she'?" he asked, moving to the fireplace where he tossed the hairs.

"I am not like you, little brother. I don't keep company with half the ladies in this town at once," he said curtly.

"This the Gypsy girl?" Scraps wandered in from the bedroom, saw Portholus, and ran over. "Hello to you too, little one," he said as the raccoon leaped into his arms, searching his vest for treats. "I am sorry, nothing for you today," he said. The raccoon sulked and jumped to the sofa. He noticed Landros pointedly ignoring his question, so he tried a different tack. "Tell me about this girl."

"There is nothing to tell about this *lady*," he answered shortly, folding the blanket up and putting it into his bag.

Portholus would not leave the subject there. "There has to be *something* to tell. She was here for several days, was she not?"

"She was hurt," he said. "I was hurt. We needed rest. She got it here. Again, there is nothing to tell."

Portholus smirked, amused by his brother's reluctance to discuss this woman. "Maybe I should ask her?"

Landros rounded on him, "No," he snapped. "You will not go anywhere near her! Do you understand me?!"

Portholus looked deep into his brother's eyes, realization flickering across his own. He grinned in disbelief. "You're afraid I'm going to take her from you!"

"No," he denied, growling, "You heard what I said. You are not to go anywhere near her!"

His face softened. "You really are afraid."

Landros looked away, unable to look into his brother's face and lie to him, lie to himself. "Just stay away from her," he said quietly.

Portholus just stared at his brother, incredulous. "You really think that I would take her from you?"

Landros did not even look up. "Yes." He paused for a moment, staring at the shirt in his hands before shoving it into his bag. "You have never had a problem with the ladies. Most of them fall over themselves and each other to get to know you. Yes, I have noticed it and have envied it. For some reason, this one has chosen me, and I do not want that ruined in any way. Just... Just leave this one be."

Portholus stopped him, made him look at him so that he could see the truth in his eyes. "I would never do that to you. She obviously means something to you. What I don't know, and I don't think you know either. But you have nothing to worry about, not from me. Why would I want to destroy what little I have left?"

He sighed, moved away. "Just leave her be. For me," he said weakly. He picked up his pack and hefted it to his right shoulder, as his left was still sore. "I have to go; I've got people to meet and things to do. Try and stay out of trouble, will you? Scraps, you coming?"

The raccoon hopped off the sofa and ran across the floor, scrambling up his leg and into the pack on his shoulder.

"Landros," Portholus called. His brother looked back. "Just be careful with these humans."

"Don't forget to lock the door," he said as he left.

Landros had mixed feelings about his brother and Lark, and needed time to sort them out. His feelings for her had to be strong to pit him against his brother. He did not want to have to choose between them and did not know if he could.

Lark entered the dressmaker's shop with Nightingale on her shoulder. Bianca came out of the back and fairly lit up when she saw her. "I was beginning to wonder! Oh!! Turn about for me, girl!" Lark laughed, spinning obediently. "I am *so* glad I never lengthened that dress! It is absolutely ravishing on you! Come on, I've got most of your others ready. And I need for you to try on the fourth for me. I was wondering what was keeping you! I thought, oh horror of horrors, what if you had gotten hurt out there when them fireballs came hurtling down? We're just so lucky it didn't hit us!"

Chattering away, she led her into the back room and took her bag. There was a young girl there Lark had not met before, who handed her a red dress. She was fairly pretty, with a round face and dark red hair.

"Oh! Where are my manners!?" Bianca exclaimed. "This is my niece, Sara. She helps me out when I get orders in. Wouldn't be as far along as I am without her help," she said, giving the girl a pat on the shoulder. The girl smiled demurely and began helping Lark change without a word.

Lark was almost overwhelmed by all of the attention but allowed the two seamstresses to pin her into the dress and tuck her up, put up with the poking and shifting of her body. When she turned to look in the mirror, she almost did not recognize herself. The dress was breathtaking. The bodice was daringly cut, showing a good bit of cleavage as well as giving her a bit of a boost. It was in a rich velvet of deep red with a latticework in gold thread embroidered all across it. The sleeves were long and billowy, of a nearly sheer red fabric akin to silk. She held out her arms for Sara to gather and tie the sleeves at her wrist, leaving a wide ruffle. The bottom half was in layers of subtly varying shades of red, the same material as the sleeves, but the panels curved from the waist, creating a spiral effect when she turned.

"Yes," Bianca sighed. "You were very right, dear," she said to Sara. "I *do* like the gold threading. I think some sort of trim at the hem, though. Something subtle. Maybe a spiral wrap of gold thread over a strip of velvet? Sort of like a unicorn's horn. What do you think?" she asked Lark.

She could not think of anything to say. "At this point," she said, "anything you think will look good will be gorgeous. Could not have imagined something so beautiful!"

"You'll probably need to get some red slippers to go with it, but that should not be too hard. It's not like there's a demand right now for dancing shoes."

Bianca and her niece made their adjustments and eased her out of the garment. She fitted herself into the two-piece blue one and was thrilled at how it looked and the way it moved with her. Tonight was as good a night as any to try it out, she thought with a smile.

"Beautiful work," she said. "Looks better than drawing."

"They always do, my dear. If they don't, I scrap 'em!" She made a tiny adjustment at the waistband of the blouse. "Bend back a bit, dear," she asked. "Hold that." She pinched the fabric together. "How's that feel?"

"Tight." She loosened it a tiny bit. "Better. Snug, but not cutting in half."

"All right, can you get it off without my letting go?"

In answer, Lark unfastened the front clasps and shrugged out of it. Bianca took the bodice over to a chair and began to sew the adjustment immediately.

She looked back at herself in the mirror and turned, moving in a slow, sinuous dance. She smiled. Just once, she wished she could have seen that dance in the woods through Landros' eyes. Perhaps the opportunity would avail itself for her to repeat the performance?

She felt a tug at her hips and looked to see Sara, who had yet to say a single word, unfastening the side clasp of the broad belt and sliding the skirt to the floor. She handed her a second skirt and a blouse, took the blue one, and folded it carefully. Lark dressed herself.

This skirt was the bright motley they had laid out together. It was beautiful. She missed her black and red calico skirt, the one that had been torn to near shreds by the pirates and the homunculus and his fiery mistress. This just about made up for it. The new vest fit better than her old one, especially after Bianca had her put it on inside out and pinned her into it. While she tried on the last outfit, Bianca stitched the front seams of the vest, making it tighter.

The last outfit was for everyday wear: a plain but vivid green skirt with no trim or markings or fancies, a simple white blouse, and a striking vest of a tapestried cloth in dark burgundies, browns, and golds with green accents. It was almost plain, but Lark liked it, especially with the vest not being designed to be so shaped, though it flattered her silhouette nicely.

Bianca bit off the last thread and gestured for her to put the red vest back on. She puffed and lifted and adjusted the blouse line and bust in a rather familiar but disinterested manner. When she finally stepped away and let Lark see, the vest did absolute wonders for her figure. Her breasts arched in soft mounds over the edges of the blouse, seemingly on the verge of self-exposure, but were actually far from it. Not to mention looking fuller than they really were.

Lark bent forward and looked up to check how much she showed. There was nothing to see. Nothing was revealed that could not already be seen when she stood straight. But, oh, would it encourage men to try! She wondered for a moment what Landros would think of it, whether or not he would be jealous of her taunting of other men. She brushed that aside. He knew what she did for a living. If he was not comfortable with it, then she could not be comfortable with him, as she would never be able to give it up. It was part of her.

Bianca was pulling the rose-colored suede laces loose, drawing Lark from her reverie. "That just about does it. I'll have the red dress finished by tomorrow, so you can stop back in and pick it up late in the afternoon."

Lark slipped out of the red vest, put the tapestried one back on, and buttoned it. The girl, Sara, handed her the rest of her new clothes, including the blue dress she had worn in, all wrapped neatly up in a black silk scarf shot with copper, silver, and gold threads. "There you go, dear," Bianca said. "Now, come back tomorrow for your last dress, and any time after that you need new clothes, hear?"

Lark thanked her profusely. "Are certain Landros paid enough? Surely...."

The woman began to shoo her out of the shop. "Now, none of that. I've already been paid, and he was most adamant about you not addin' one copper royal to my fee. It's all taken care of. Now, if'n you want something else, then we can talk laurels. If not, mosey on!"

Nightingale flew out the door, leaving Lark little choice but to follow. She thanked the woman again and turned down the street towards Colwyn's with her bundle clutched to her chest.

Landros was, at that moment, in Lord Colwyn's office. Neither man was very happy with the news he had just called attention to. "You can see why I have to ask the question, my lord?" Landros asked. "I know the source was dodgy, but it was so casually thrown out...."

The knight nodded and waved him to silence while he paced the room. Landros remained seated, staring into the fire, absently turning the copper ring on his finger. He did not know whether or not to believe what the hooded mage had said about the King and the Lord Mayor's responsibility in the siege. There was a great deal about recent events which bothered him. They had yet to identify the dead Falcon; not even Colwyn had known him, and there was nothing on his person that might identify either him or his purpose. People had already been sent out to try and discover his identity without much success so far. Efforts were also being made to keep the luring of hapless adventurers to their deaths to a minimum, with similar results. Four others had already disappeared without a trace. No one he had personally known, but still....

Colwyn's voice snapped him out of his musings. "This is something that definitely bears looking into. There is far more going on here than meets the eye, and, as you have mentioned, I have long known that there is a traitor in the government, but not whom. There are spies everywhere, but what kind is the question? We already know they have magical aid... If only we had enough of a force to leave the city and make an outright assault, we might be able to break the siege or, at the very least, get someone out far enough to reach the king's ear."

"We do have the forces," Landros said. "We just have to convince them to give up their time and greed and safe little lives to go out there and do it."

Colwyn looked over at him. "And who might that be?"

"Think about it. The enemy has already seen it," he said, making noise of exasperation. "Twenty of those vital resources have already vanished or been killed. Others have been convinced to be less than helpful, if not outright part of the problem. There are still plenty more hiding about in places like Bayside."

"The trouble is convincing them," he mused as he realized of whom the elf spoke.

"You convince the mayor to make a speech in the square and put forth a call to arms. You encourage those who can to gather and outfit a unit, register them as irregulars, and get them out there on the field with the regulars, and we *can* make a difference. These are people with skills at fighting and skulking and strategies with the odds out of kilter. Better yet, they have the magic to help. Magic swords, small rings, minor spells, wands, little things that the army does not have access to and would never be able to get handed over to them, not without an out-and-out revolt. Some of those items are heirlooms, but useful nonetheless."

The Lord mused a moment, "Makes perfect sense. And no harm can be done in trying. This might also help us in other ways as well." He stopped pacing and stood straighter. "This was your idea, so I think you should be the one to present it to the mayor. You convince him. I will bring this to the Knight's Council. And between the two of us, we might just pull this off."

Landros hesitantly interrupted. "I... I don't think that's a good idea, my lord. I have this... difficulty in dealing with bureaucrats. I simply have not the patience for them."

Colwyn shook his head. "The Lord Mayor is not exactly a politician," he grinned. You put the plan to him as you put it to me, and he will give you a fair hearing. Just leave a letter with his secretary up at the hall, or even better, at his home," he amended, thinking on his feet as he paced, "and an appointment will be set up for you. I think it best if this sort of idea comes from one of those you are talking about recruiting. Oh, and while you are in his office, any information you can gather, covertly or otherwise...."

"I understand," he sighed, standing as he realized there would be no arguing this. Accusations had been made. They had to be investigated. "Though I must confess I feel downright shifty investigating a man like the mayor for treason without harder evidence."

Colwyn gave him a clap on his right shoulder, even though he had to reach across him to do it. "How else does one gain hard evidence? And very often, it is just such a person. Saintlier men than he have assassinated kings. By the way, how is your shoulder? I remember you said something the other night about my picking the wing everyone seems to favor?"

"Oh, yes," he winced, rubbing his left shoulder self-consciously. "It is fine now, if a little stiff. Lately, every time I've been wounded, it's been to that left shoulder. I am beginning to wonder if it is not some flaw in my defense or attack strategies. I thought maybe, when you had some time, we could spar a bit. Help me figure out if that is the case, and if so, what can I do to correct it? A real fight is no time to be studying your moves to see if you are leaving an opening."

"Certainly. One of a knight's responsibilities to his squire is to teach him to fight. That you came to me a seasoned fighter has perhaps made me a little lax in that. I would be glad to help. When you are ready, let me know. Your shoulder probably needs a bit more rest and a little loosening up first. Now, out with you. You have things to discover and a traitor to root out."

"Yes, my lord," he said with a bow. He gathered his things and left.

Romeri Glossary

Droshvi	Hello
Gegenta	Outsider
Genti	Romer who does not roam
Goshaksa	Outcast
Gramen	Grandson
Gramil	Granddaughter
Gruma	Granny
Ilyen	Light
Lunasa	Oh heavens
Magruma	Grandmother
Maharen	Blood Brother
Mahren	Mother
Mahril	Maid
Pashaska	Idiot
Sagavis	In the blood or irresistable
Se'vah	Please
Sesha	Yes
Sesket	I want you to agree with me, yes?
Tushka	Ass
Vas	Life-Belt

Elvish Glossary

Ellinoia	Songbird
Simoya	Mine

Other Books By
S.L. Thorne

Love In Ruins

The Speaker

Mercy's Ransom

Fang and Bone

The Gryphon's Rest Series:

Lady of the Mist

The Gloaming

SHIFT Books 1 & 2

Stag's Heart

Dragon's Bride

All Available in hardback, paperback and ebook

at:

Thornewoodstudios.com/books

or

Amazon.com